THE RIVER LIME

A Gathering of Friends

Irwin L. Hinds

Order this book online at www.trafford.com
or email orders@trafford.com

Most Trafford titles are also available at major online book retailers.

This is a work of fiction. The characters in this book do not actually exist. They are creations
of the author's imagination. Any likeness to any person or persons, dead or alive, is purely
coincidental. With the exception of well known historical events and/or places, all incidents are
imagined and dramatized.

Printed in the United States of America.

ISBN: 978-1-4269-3573-2 (sc)
ISBN: 978-1-4269-3574-9 (hc)
ISBN: 978-1-4269-3575-6 (e)

Library of Congress Control Number: 2010909040

Trafford rev. 11/07/2011

www.trafford.com

North America & international
toll-free: 1 888 232 4444 (USA & Canada)
phone: 250 383 6864 ♦ fax: 812 355 4082

This book is dedicated to John H. Bailey, aka T-Boy.

ONE

It was a sunny Sunday morning in May and young men from Pierre Ville and Mafeking had assembled on opposite banks of the Ortoire River. They were there to swim or learn to swim. Why was the river and not Mayaro Bay chosen for that activity? No one could say with certainty. The fathers of many of the young men had done the same thing years before and so did their fathers before them. The river was by no means an exclusive venue for swimming but it was by far the most convenient place for friends of the neighboring villages to meet. Everyone felt safe there. Hostilities among individuals or groups of individuals were nonexistent or extremely rare, even though the gathering consisted mostly of young men between the ages of twelve and twenty-two. Occasionally there might have been someone older or younger. Most were there without their parents' knowledge or permission. That perhaps was the reason there were never any young women or girls there. Clearly, that was a double standard but it was an acceptable standard then.

The water was crystal clear and the current moderate that morning, a welcome change from what was experienced during the rainy season when the river was muddy brown with silt, and flowed in one direction as it meandered its way to the Atlantic Ocean. The old Spring Bridge that spanned the river was so unstable that buses with passengers were not allowed to cross. Passengers were asked to disembark and walk across the bridge. Only then would the bus drivers risk their own lives and drive the buses across. There were no female bus driver then but no one gave it much thought. Some things seemed to have been accepted without question.

Heavy equipment destined for the oil fields in Guayaguayare could not be taken across the rickety old bridge. As a result, the petroleum mining company constructed a cable operated ferry to the left of the bridge on the approach to Spring Flat. Since no equipment was ever transported on a Sunday, the ferry served as an ideal platform from which the youngsters could dive into the pristine water. Of course there was the occasional sighting of a caiman but no one was ever deterred by it. In fact, the sheer numbers of young men, a dozen or more, in the water at any given time, probably would have scared even the caiman away.

About two miles up the river in Mafeking, another group of young men of the same average age, all of whom were friends, gathered on the riverbank in the vicinity of the saw-mill. Their make-shift diving platform was a raft constructed of steel drums and hard wood planks. The raft was used primarily by the logging industry to move timber down river to the saw-mill. Moored nearby was a light weight paddle boat made from the dugout trunk of a large sandbox tree. It was owned by a lumberjack known only as The River Keeper or Keeper Jack.

Occasionally both groups of youngsters would converge in Grande Basé, an area where the Ortoire River meandered greatly along the Mafeking Branch Road, also known as Inner Mafeking. There, a widening of about eighty yards or more was created. Many believed that was also the deepest area of the river. Only the most accomplished swimmers and divers ever ventured there, although no one was ever forbidden from swimming or diving. Whether or not an individual participated in the Grande Basé *lime* was self-determined. It is reasonable to say that most exercised good judgment, in that, of the many generations that have participated, there was only one drowning on record. That though, was still one too many.

All of the participants were from the same socio-economic group. In fact, with the exception of the cocoa and coconut estate owners, shopkeepers, and two other families, everyone else in Mayaro had a similar socio-economic background. Children of the estate owners, shop keepers, and those of the other two perceived wealthy families, did not participate in *the river lime*. It wasn't that they had access to private swimming pools. No one in Mayaro had a swimming pool. There were no public swimming pools either, and it was rare that parents ever took their children to the beach to picnic or just to swim. As a result, the children of the wealthy or perceived wealthy in Mayaro just never learnt how to swim. So the commonly heard statement, *everyone in Mayaro is a swimmer*, was a misnomer. Only the disadvantaged men were swimmers. They were good at it too. With proper coaching, some could have reached Olympic caliber. Strangely enough, those youngsters were also the best cricketers, soccer players, and track and field athletes. They were never coached in those sporting endeavors either.

Interestingly also, the academic achievers of the community emerged from the ranks of the river limers. Strict parental and community discipline rather than athletic prowess may have been the dominant contributing factor. In Mayaro every adult acted as the parent of every child. Raising a child was a community effort. As a result, crime as we know it today did not exist. Of course there was praedial larceny but never for economic gain. Children helped themselves to mangoes, oranges, Tonka beans, cocoa pods, golden apples, and other fruits, only because they were plentiful and delicious when in season. Often, as was the case with the Tonka beans and cocoa pods, estate owners did not object but instead, pleaded with the youngsters to return the seeds when the pulp had been sucked clean. Some even provided appropriately labeled receptacles in the field for the purpose of receiving the seeds.

Joshua Jacob, aka JJ and Sydney Canton were regulars at *the river lime* in Mafeking. They were related and were also close friends. So too were their single parents. In fact, both youngsters were being raised by their mothers. In JJ's case, his grandmother was as much a contributor to his upbringing as his mother. One major drawback was, they neglected to send him to school. Neither of the mothers nor JJ's grandmother was gainfully employed. Like most other people in the community, they lived an agrarian subsistence type of life. No one was ever hungry or malnourished though. Eggs, chicken, pork, fish, chip-chip (a mollusk harvested from Mayaro Bay), and other seafood were plentiful and available to all. In many instances families sold the livestock they raised or the crops they grew in order to acquire other necessities such as school uniforms, or the necessary materials to make the uniforms for their children. Resourceful parents such as Sydney's mother sewed the uniforms themselves. Most homes were of a modest nature but no one paid rent. As modest as the homes were, parents in that tropical paradise owned them.

Joshua and Sydney were related because their mothers were first cousins. Their maternal grandmothers were sisters. Both lived next door to each other, and the boys played together often, though not always. Although no one in the family was gainfully employed, neither family accepted government assistance. Their pride, genuine or false, would not allow them to. Since both families, like most others in the community, owned their homes, rent was not an issue. The boys did some indoor chores and all of the daily outdoor chores, one of which was tending their goats and other livestock. In the course of taking care of the animals which they tethered in fields close to their homes, the boys took their chances at joining *the river lime*. They joined the gathering at the river bank on those beautiful sunny Sunday mornings without their parents' permission.

It was not unusual for Joshua and Sydney to tie their animals in fields that were not owned by their parents. To some it may seem strange that land owners would allow other people's goats to graze freely on their property. However, it was never frowned upon. On the contrary, the land owners, especially those who owned coconut estates, preferred to have the grazing animals in the fields. It saved them the expense of having to pay to clear the thickets very often.

On Sunday morning, May 6, 1956, a group of friends gathered on the oil company's ferry at the foot of the old Spring Bridge. At about the same time, there was a gathering on a raft near the saw-mill two miles away up river in Mafeking. Both groups consisted of accomplished swimmers and novices. The two groups of swimmers were identified by villagers as Group A and Group B. The names had no bearing on the accomplishments of individuals within the groups. The gathering at the bridge became known as Group A boys while the group that gathered at the saw-mill was called Group B boys.

There were no coaches responsible for the young men who gathered on the river bank to have fun every Sunday morning in the dry season which ran from January to June. No membership was required, so individuals were never limited to Group A or to Group B. They were free to move from one group to the other on a whim, or because of the convenience to them at any given time.

On that Sunday morning the cousins, Joshua and Sydney decided to join the lime at the Spring Bridge. They sat at the foot of the bridge towers to relax and converse before jumping into the water. Soon they were joined by other young limers. Although the bridge was determined by the Public Works Department to be in an advanced state of deterioration, meaning, the masonry at the anchorage was spalling, and over the years, the weather had adversely affected other structural components, the youngsters sat under it, or walked on the tension cables, and jumped from them into the river below with no fear whatsoever.

The depth of the river in the area of the bridge was said to be fifty meters. That, however, was inconclusive. According to a widespread rumor, Keeper Jack once measured it years earlier. It is believed that he used bamboo rods of different lengths to determine the depth of the river at different locations. None of that mattered to the men who were there to have fun. One idea of fun was the interjection of ridicule of others during conversation.

It was referred to as *fatigue* and often drew laughter from members, including the member who was being bantered.

One of the older members of the group, a young man whom the others called Sub (that was short for submarine), said to Sydney, "Ah eh see you last Sunday, boy. What happened?"

"I had too much homework assignment to complete for the next day."

"Yeah man! Sydney never misses a day of school," said another young man known as Dolphin. "No wonder he is always at the top of his class."

"My mother wouldn't have it any other way," said Sydney. "She thinks that education is the way out."

"The way out of what?" Submarine asked.

"I don't know. She never said."

"She never told you why education is important but she expects you to pursue it?"

"Yeah, that's my mom."

Sydney fully understood what his mother said and what she meant. He, however, didn't want any of the other young men to look at him differently. He was comfortable with himself and felt at ease in the group. He was accepted. He enjoyed *the river lime* and wanted things to stay the way they were. His second cousin, Joshua, saw it differently. His mother and grandmother, in their private conversations made it a habit of criticizing Sydney's mother in JJ's presence. At every opportunity they got, they derided her for her efforts in ensuring that Sydney received an education. Somehow, that made JJ feel confident enough to say, "Aunt Curley thinks she knows everything. In the meantime, her son here is eating paper to go to school." That statement drew an uproar of laughter from the group. Sydney was laughing too but more out of chagrin rather than the humor Joshua intended.

Sydney's mother was Joshua's cousin, his older cousin, but he called her Aunt Curley out of respect. On that day though, by any standard of the time, he disrespected her badly. Sydney did not try to counter JJ's remark and none of the others followed up on it.

There was no bantering as JJ might have expected. They simply let it rest, or so it seemed to JJ. He felt dejected and was determined to strike again at the first opportunity he got. Meanwhile, Sub, whose legal name was unknown to anyone in the gathering that Sunday, got up, walked to the roadway and climbed onto the tension wire of the bridge. Suddenly everyone's attention was on him. Within seconds of being on the tension wire, he dove into the river below. He barely caused a splash, although he was six feet three inches tall and weighed 260 pounds. Several individuals checked their watches to see how long Sub would remain submerged. It was his ability to hold his breath under water longer than anyone else in the gathering that earned him the nickname Submarine.

After three minutes under water, he surfaced. The crowd applauded. That seemed to have been a signal for the other young men to enter the water. On that day, there were no novices among the swimmers. The chap known as Dolphin was the first to get out of the water. He was perhaps the best swimmer in the group. Hence the nickname, Dolphin. When he wasn't swimming long distances up and down the river, he preferred to sit on the deck of the ferry and observe the others. He was doing just that when he noticed that one of the young swimmers, Kendal O'Connor was struggling in the water. Without hesitation, Dolphin dove in and nudged the young man toward the ferry until he was able to grasp the deck. Another of the limers, Arjune Bidalloo, grabbed Kendal's right arm and assisted him onto the deck. He was never submerged and he did not get water into his lungs. He was shaken up though, so after he composed himself, Arjune asked him, "What just happened out there?"

"My legs cramped up," said Kendal. "I was unable to swim. Thank you." He was clutching his right thigh as he spoke.

Keep moving," said Arjune. "That would increase the circulation in your leg." The others in the water never realized that Kendal was ever in difficulty. He, however, continued to thank Dolphin and Arjune, both of whom were on the deck of the ferry with him by then.

"You are welcome, Kendal. That's enough already," Dolphin said.

The cramps in his leg eased. He felt a lot better and was contemplating getting back into the water. As he moved toward the edge of the deck, Dolphin said, "Eh! Eh! Don't you even think about it." Kendal heeded the advice, retreated, and sat down on the deck with his legs hanging over the water. Although at age 25, Dolphin was only three years older than Kendal, he valued his opinion.

Dolphin and Arjune jumped back into the water. Only then did Kendal focus his thoughts on his loved ones, his mother, Dorothy O'Connor, and his girlfriend, Henrietta Riggs. One month earlier he graduated from the Police Academy. That marked the beginning of improvements in the quality of life for his mother and himself. It also heightened his desire to do the best he could for his girlfriend, Henrietta who was then twenty, a mere two years younger than he was. Nevertheless, every little progressive move he made in life was with her in mind. That was until Dolphin and Arjune rescued him from drowning. Thereafter, his thoughts of love and caring for Henrietta and planning a future with her became more focused and intensified. *Had I drowned this morning Henrietta may have been able to move on without me but Mom would have been devastated*, he thought.

Kendal was an only child. His mother was single and his father, though well known in the community, was not involved in his life. His mother struggled to raise him as a well disciplined child and to provide for him the best way she could have. In his pre-teens and early teens he often challenged her attempts at strict discipline. Fortunately for both of them, the fifties were times when people in Mafeking Village, particular the women, took a keen interest in the behavior of every child. Children in turn, were cognizant of the fact that they had to be respectful to everyone, especially their elders. That sort of community interaction in Mayaro kept Kendal and others like him out of the legal system. Juvenile delinquency, somehow, was limited to *the river lime.*

It was the one thing youngsters became involved in without their parents knowledge or permission. That was as delinquent a behavior as it got.

To many, Dorothy O'Connor seemed overly concerned and protective of her son. Based on her own experience, however, she did not want him to do anything so silly that it could compromise the promising future she envisioned for him. When she was only eighteen, she became pregnant and was forced to forgo her dreams of becoming a nurse. Overly strict moral codes of the day forced her to withdraw from the nurses training program at the General Hospital in San Fernando. She did not reveal that fact to her mother immediately. A week after she returned home her mother asked, "Dorothy, when you goin' back to San'ando, guul (girl)?"

Dorothy was afraid to say that she was expelled and said instead, "I don't know, Ma." What she didn't know really, was that the gossip mongers had already spread the news of her expulsion from the nursing program, and her mother had gotten wind of it.

"Weh you mean you don't know? Ah done hear that you in the family way. Everybody 'round here talking 'bout it."

In 1937 Dorothy was eighteen years old. Back then in Mayaro, people did not use the word pregnant in conversations. Even those in the medical profession shunned the word. In her anger Kate Lynn O'Connor kept repeating to her daughter, "You eighteen years old and you're in the family way."

Among angry parents of that period, it was common practice to use so-called *comfort phrases* or *easy sentences* when they spoke. It was not uncommon also for angry parents of a pregnant unwed teenager to confront the father of the unborn child. There is no evidence that the practice was ever fruitful but parents, especially mothers, continued with it. Mrs. Kate Lynn O'Connor did just that. It turned out to be an exercise in futility which made her even more annoyed and distressed than before.

"You have shamed me," she said to Dorothy a day later. "You better think 'bout weh you go live because you kah (can't) live here."

In her confused state of mind, Dorothy packed a few of her belongings into a pillowcase and left. She was uncertain as to where she would go or what she could do. Fortunately, she was rescued by her aunt, her mother's only sister who was also her godmother.

By the time Kendal was born, Kate Lynn O'Connor became seriously ill. There was no one to care for her. Dorothy did the only thing she thought she could have done. That was, return home to care for her ailing mother. Those events gave her the impetus and determination she needed to make sure that her only child, Kendal, would persevere and ultimately achieve all that he could.

When Kendal returned home that Sunday, he made no mention of what occurred when he was at *the river lime*. He was a relatively good swimmer and conditions were perfect for the activities he and others had engaged in, yet he almost drowned. He had no idea why he suffered muscle cramps. He had heard of swimmers having that experience after swimming long distances but he was in the water for only a short while. When the gathering of young men started to disperse and he was leaving the river bank, his only thought was, *I do not wish to give my mother this disturbing news, so I will not tell her.* She, However, had already heard of it.

At lunch that Sunday, Dorothy asked her son, "How was *the river lime* this morning?"

"Okay," he said.

"Just okay, Is that it?"

"Yes, Mom. That's it" said Kendal. "It was just okay."

"Kendal! You have always been honest with me. What is different today?"

"Nothing is different, Mom."

"Okay! Since you wouldn't be straight up with me, let me tell you that I heard about it."

"What have you heard about?"

"I heard that you almost drowned in the Ortoire River this morning."

"Then why are you so calm about it?"

"What should I do? I have already thanked the good Lord for saving your life."

"Well, it was Dolphin who actually saved me."

"I heard that both Dolphin and Arjune contributed to your rescue. Thank God for them." Kendal did not respond so his mother continued by saying, "They could not have done that without some divine intervention."

"Whatever you say, Mom."

"I haven't said it yet, so don't you get fresh. Now! You and I would visit both Dolphin and Arjune this evening."

"What for, Mom?"

"So we can thank them personally."

"I already did that."

"Now we would do it together."

Kendal took a deep breath and exhaled loudly. He didn't want to be reminded of what happened earlier that morning. Although he knew that it was something he couldn't really forget. He also didn't want to go against his mother's wishes, so he said, "Okay, Mom."

Joshua and Sydney had arrived at their respective homes about the same time Kendal reached his. They too had their lunch, although in a much less formal manner than Kendal. They were served and they ate wherever they chose to. Sitting at a dining table with adults to have lunch was a luxury not afforded to them. There was an unwritten rule that said children were to have their meals with other children or have them alone. Neither Sydney nor Joshua was ever bothered by that. They knew that most other children in the community experienced the same thing. It had become the norm. Dorothy O'Connor, on the contrary, wanted something different for her son. She thought that when they sat together to have their meals, that gave him a sense of family unity. In her case though, it was not an extended family. She also found that when they ate together she and Kendal seemed more relaxed and open to discussions. She was right. They discussed just about everything at breakfast, lunch, and dinner, especially on weekends.

The situation was quite different in the Jacob's and Canton's households. With the Jacob's in particular, Velma seldom spoke with her son, Joshua, except to give him directives. Most of the conversations in that household were between his mother and his grandmother, and it focused mostly on the criticism of other people. Close relatives were no exceptions. Philbertha Jacob-Canton and her son, Sydney, took the brunt of their criticism. Although young Joshua was never included in the discussions, he was never out of hearing range because the dwelling was so small. He knew that he couldn't contribute anything to their conversation, even when his mother and grandmother spoke about things with which he was quite familiar. He had been told often enough that when adults were having a conversation he was allowed to speak only when he was spoken to directly. How that affected his confidence and or self-esteem is still inconclusive. Coupled with his lack of schooling though, it undoubtedly would have had a profound effect on his quality of life later on.

One form of ridicule that was repeated often and leveled against Philbertha whom everyone, except JJ, referred to as Bertha, was that she was trying to be something she was not. Early on Sunday, May 6, 1956. JJ heard his mother say to his grandmother, "She is always forcing that child to go to school." He knew the reference was to his cousin, Sydney.

"Yeah! She sends him to school hungry," Velma said.

"What can a child learn when he is hungry and always wondering about what there is for him to eat?"

"He just might end up eating the paper he is supposed to write on."

"Ma you too much, oui," Velma said while laughing. The French word for yes was commonly, though unnecessarily used at the end of sentences, perhaps as a remnant from the influence of French rule of the twin islands. In fact, many of the older residents spoke a form of broken French known as patois. Joshua smiled. He knew that he should not be heard laughing at the joke his grandmother made. Velma, however, noticed the smile on his face and asked, "What are you grinning at, boy?"

"Nothing, Aunt Velma," he said, and the smile vanished instantly.

No one ever instructed young Joshua to call his mother, Aunt Velma. He decided early on that because both he and his mother called his grandmother, Ma, it was appropriate to make a distinction between the parent and grandparent. Consequently, he started calling his mother, Aunt Velma.

As was the case at the Jacob's household, at the Canton's, Philbertha and her son, Sydney had a simple lunch that Sunday at noon. They listened to the radio and discussed the events that occurred earlier that day, including the near drowning of twenty-two year old Kendal O'Connor. Philbertha felt a great deal of empathy for Dorothy O'Connor and decided that she would visit her that evening. In the mean time, she grasped the opportunity to emphasize to her son the importance of parental consent in all juvenile undertakings outside of the home.

"Mamie! That would not have prevented what happened this morning."

"Mamie nothing! I need to know where you are at all times," said Philbertha. "I do not want any surprises, good nor bad. Do you understand?"

"Yes, Mamie," said Sydney. Then he asked, "Does that mean you are okay with me joining *the river lime*?"

"Do you participate now?"

Sydney paused, took a deep breath, exhaled and said, "Yes, Mamie."

"All I am asking is that you inform me whenever you plan to go swimming in the river."

Philbertha knew that her son could swim. She was, however, unaware that *the river lime* was more than just a swimming outing or event. It was like a brotherhood, an assembly the participants looked forward to every Sunday morning in the dry season. It was a gathering where the comedian among them found a ready, patient and appreciative audience. It served as a venue for intellectual exchanges for those with such persuasions. Consequently, it served as a place of learning for those who, for reasons that were no fault of their own, did not attend school, or did so sporadically.

Joshua Jacob was one of the truants who looked forward to the gathering on the bank of the Ortoire River on Sunday mornings. He was eager to learn all he could, and he was a quick study. He did not fault his mother or grandmother for his lack of schooling but he often exhibited jealousy and hostility toward his cousin, Sydney, for being able to attend school regularly. Nevertheless, they remained good friends. Sydney never allowed his academic achievements to get in the way of their friendship. His mother, Philbertha, made sure that the family remained close by staying in continued and constant interaction with her aunt, Umilta and her cousin, Velma. She was aware of how they truly felt about her. Nevertheless, on that day she walked over to her aunt's place to ask Velma to accompany her on a planned visit to Dorothy that evening. Velma agreed and by 5:30 p.m. they were at Dorothy's.

"Hello!" Bertha called out as she and Velma entered Dorothy's living room. Dorothy was in the kitchen and didn't hear them come in. As they reached the kitchen, Velma called out, "Hey, Dorothy!"

"Oh! What a pleasant surprise," Dorothy said.

"Yeah, after we heard what happened this morning, we agreed that we will drop in," Bertha said.

"We couldn't stay away," said Velma. "It is a sure reminder of how blessed we are."

"It certainly is," Bertha confirmed.

"That is so sweet of you," said Dorothy. "I have been trying to think of it as something that nearly happened this morning."

"You are so right," Bertha said.

The two cousins with one of their best friends didn't want to celebrate or rejoice. They wanted only to give thanks. All three were single mothers, each with an only child, a son. They were all proud of their sons. Dorothy and Philbertha took pride in the academic achievements of their boys. Velma's pride was rooted in the athletic prowess of her son, Joshua. There was never any emphasis on education when she was growing up. As long as the chores were done and the crops grew well in the field, her mother, Umilta Jacob, felt comfortable. She was loved and respected and that meant the world to her. Velma in turn, with her mother's influence in the house, passed those values on to her son, Joshua. Hard work, dedication, and respect were the buzz words around the Jacob's home. Education was never emphasized.

After a quiet Sunday evening with Dorothy during which time they expressed their best wishes, Philbertha and Velma said good bye at 10:00 p.m. Dorothy was grateful and made that known before the cousins returned to their respective homes.

TWO

On Monday, May 7, 1956 Sydney returned home from school. He was in a talkative mood and his mother, Philbertha, was willing to listen. She always listened patiently to whatever Sydney had to say. On that occasion he was elated that he had been one of three students selected to write the GCE (general Certificate of Education) examination early. Students in high school normally took that examination in their senior year at age sixteen or seventeen. Sydney was fourteen and not yet a senior. His teachers believed that he could be ready by his fifteenth birthday. His mother was also confident that he was capable but she wasn't as excited as he was about it and said, "I know you can do it and be successful, but please do not put too much pressure on yourself. You are not quite fifteen. There are at least three more opportunities for you to take the exam while you are still in high school."

"I know that, Mom. I know that. Thanks."

Sydney would have liked to share the good news with his cousin and best friend, Joshua. However, he realized that for Joshua that would have been bitter-sweet. While Joshua was capable of appreciating the achievement, he was known to exhibit fits of jealousy over the academic successes of his peers. His mother and grandmother would have downplayed the achievement. They always did. Based on that knowledge, Sydney decided to say nothing about it. He didn't want to appear as a showoff.

Philbertha Jacob-Canton grasped the opportunity to reiterate what she had said to her son many times before. "You are on the right path, son. Education is the way out."

"You always say that, Mom. Yet, you have never indicated what it is that education provides a way out of."

"I know."

"Don't you think that I should know, Mom?"

"I believe that you already know, son"

"I do not."

Bertha wondered, *how could a bright kid like Sydney, my son, not know this?* But she said, "Just look around you." Sydney did not respond. He was bewildered, so his mother continued, "Let's start with us."

"What is wrong with us, Mom?"

"You see nothing wrong with the way we live?"

"No. We are no different from anyone else in the neighborhood," said Sydney. "I still don't understand what it is that education is supposed to do for me that it hasn't done for anyone else."

Suddenly Bertha realized that her son, as smart as he was, saw life through the eyes of a child, a very happy child. He did what he was supposed to do and did not focus much on anything beyond the next day. She realized that she was faced with a dilemma. *How can I enlighten him without shock and awe, or completely and adversely change his perspective?* She wondered. Obviously, Sydney was not only a happy child but also a contended child. He was friendly and well liked by all those who knew him. He studied hard, played hard, and achieved his goals which were not always the goals his mother had in mind for him. *Could an attempt at changing his perspective hurt or help him?* She wondered. Then she said, "Son, education is a way out of the cycle of poverty that grips this society. It is not the only way out but is a sure way out."

Sydney appeared to be confused by his mother's remark. He went to school every day as she always demanded. Truancy never crossed his mind, although he knew of other children who frequently stayed away from school even when their parents thought they were in attendance. He had performed well and was always at or near the top of his class. So he couldn't quite understand what more his mother wanted or expected of him. He decided that one way to find out was to ask her, and that he did.

"What more can I do, Mom?"

The question took Bertha by surprise. Suddenly, she realized that Sydney might have been receiving mixed messages from her, even though that was not at all her intent. On the one hand, she asked him not to put too much pressure on himself because he was already quite advanced for his age. On the other, she was constantly harping on the fact that education was the way out of the cycle of poverty. *How does that resonate in the mind of a child?* She wondered. Then she said, "The educated among us are the ones who are regularly employed. If you look at the cabinet maker, you would see that his job is seasonal. He is busiest around Christmas time. The tailors and seamstresses are busiest around holiday times such as Christmas, Carnival, and Easter. The fisherman's earnings are also seasonal, so too are the earnings of those who work in the agricultural sector. At the other end of the spectrum are those in law enforcement; the police, the court clerks and other court officials, the lawyers and judges. The people who work in the Health Care industry are also regularly employed. So too are teachers, civil servants, and those in the banking industry."

Sydney listened attentively to his mother's diatribe. When she paused, he asked, "What have I done to deserve your stern criticism, Mom?"

"Is that how you see it, son?"

"What else could it be, Mom?"

Oh! That is how it resonates with him, she thought but said, "I was only trying to point out to you how education determines the quality of life one enjoys for the rest of one's life."

"Suppose I decided that I want to be an entrepreneur when I grow up? Is anything wrong with that?"

"What?"

"An entrepreneur, a businessman who takes financial risk."

"You will still need an education, and a very good one I would imagine."

"Well, suppose I wanted to work in the petroleum industry when I grow up, is something wrong with that?"

"No. However, you must keep in mind that even in the petroleum industry, there is a hierarchy, so you must decide at what level you would want to enter. To be a chemical engineer does require a great deal of education and training. The same is true for the mechanical and electrical engineers in the industry. You decide. Do you want to be the grounds-man or one of the engineers? Whichever one you choose, the quality of life issue would still be valid."

"What kind of life would JJ have? He does not go to school."

"I don't know, Sydney."

"But you said earlier that.............."

"I know what I said earlier. My concern is for you, not Joshua."

"Mom, JJ is family. Why aren't you concerned about him?"

"If I show that kind of concern, I might be usurping the responsibility of his parents,"

"Can't you ask Aunt Velma to send him to school?"

"No, Sydney."

"Why not?"

"If I do, I would be out of place," said Bertha. "As parents we make choices for our children. I chose for you to attend school every day if you are not seriously ill. I have my reason for that choice which I think you understand clearly."

"I do understand that. What I do not understand, is why Aunt Velma chooses to keep JJ home from school every day."

"All I can say is that as parents, we have responsibilities to our children. One of those responsibilities is making important choices for them, or on their behalf. When we carry out those responsibilities, we do so in good faith and in the best interest of the child."

"Is Aunt Velma acting in JJ's best interest when she keeps him home from school?"

"I don't know, son," said Bertha. "Perhaps he is home schooled."

"If that is the case, how is it he is unable to read the headline in the Sunday paper when we are at *the river lime*?" Bertha did not offer an explanation to Sydney's latest query. Instead she asked, "Who takes the newspaper to the river bank on Sundays?"

"Kendal always buys the paper before we get there and everyone reads it either before or after swimming."

"Everyone reads it?"

"Well, almost everyone."

"Who are the exceptions?"

"Everyone reads the paper except JJ and Arjune."

"What is Arjune's problem?"

"When he is not in the water, he actually spends his time doing mathematical problems under the bridge. Sometimes he challenges us to solve problems."

"How old is he anyway?"

"I don't know for certain. My guess would be eighteen or nineteen."

"Isn't he a clerk at the Warden's Office?"

"Yes."

"Then why is he so into mathematics?"

"He said he wants to study in the United States."

"I wasn't aware that mathematics is a pre-requisite for study abroad."

Sydney laughed, and Bertha asked, "Why are you making fun of me, boy?"

"I am not. What you said is funny."

"What is so funny about that?"

"Arjune wants to be an actuary. Mathematics is a pre-requisite for that."

"How was I supposed to know what he plans to study? You never did say."

Sydney was laughing again. He suspected that his mother did not know what an actuary is or what an actuary does. She in turn tried not to let her ignorance be known when she asked, "What?"

Sydney was still giggling and trying to speak at the same time. "You really don't know what an actuary does, do you?" he asked.

Bertha did not answer. Instead, she pumped her fist in the air as if to fake a punch at him. Then she said, "I think you better get ready for bed."

"Okay. Good night, Mom." Sydney said as he left the room snickering.

A few minutes later, Bertha got up, went to her bedroom, took a dictionary from among the books she kept on a shelf and looked up the word *actuary*. She smiled and closed the dictionary. As she sat on the bed smiling, she looked at a family portrait on the dresser and thought, *Your father would have been so proud of you, son. You are on your way to accomplishing what he hoped that I would have accomplished.*

Adolphos Canton passed on at a critical juncture in the lives of Bertha and young Sydney. He had been ailing for a long time before he succumbed to a rare debilitating illness. For many years he was unable to sleep and relied on both herbal and conventional medicine for relief. None was effective. Sadly enough, his condition was not diagnosed for years. It was not until a young physician who had been trained in the United States examined him at the clinic, that the condition known as *fatal familial insomnia* was diagnosed. By then, the inability to sleep had debilitated his body, and although Bertha struggled to care for him, he died when Sydney was only three years old.

If only you were here to see him now, I know that you would have been proud, Bertha thought again and started to cry. She loved her husband. Her love was unconditional in spite of the difficulties she faced and the uncertainty of a future without the husband she depended upon totally. She regretted dropping out of high school to get married simply because she was pregnant. As she sat in her lonely room and reminisced about the past, she felt an overwhelming amount of anger which she didn't quite understand. She was still struggling with the thought of what could have been and what she could have become. The shock of Adolphos' death and the void she felt in her life forced her into celibacy. She just could not bear the thought of ever becoming so dependent on a man again, and although she has had many proposals since her husband's death, she managed to refrain from getting involved with anyone.

Her major concern was for her young son, Sydney. She wanted to raise him the best way she could have or knew how to, without the influence of some stranger who may or may not have been genuinely concerned about the best interest of the child. She tried her very best not to be judgmental and was aware that one or more of those showing interests in her may have been decent, hard working, and caring individuals. She, nevertheless, felt that none could have filled the void left by the father of her child. She believed also that any involvement on her part would not have been in the best interest of her son. In her continued dismay over Adolphos' death, she turned the radio on and lay back in her bed. She dozed off quickly but was just as quickly awakened by a knock at the front door. She got up, pulled on a robe and answered the door. Her cousin, Velma Jacob was standing there, tears streaming down her cheeks.

"Come in, girl," said Bertha. "Oh my, God! You are crying. What is the matter?" Bertha was alarmed. She had seen Velma cry only twice before; at her wedding and when Kirk Vance, Joshua's father died.

"It's JJ! It's JJ," Velma said excitedly in response to Bertha's question.

"What is wrong with JJ?"

"He was rushed to the hospital."

"Why?"

"He....he....he was attacked by two fellas (men) with cutlasses." Velma was sobbing so her speech was slurred. Bertha's first objective was to get her to calm down so the full story could be heard.

"Sit down," she said. "Let me get you something to drink."

Velma sat in a loveseat that was close to the door while Bertha went to the kitchen to heat some water for making tea. Once she got the fire started, she placed some bay leaves and sour-sop leaves in a kettle with water, placed it on the fire, and returned to the living room.

"Where did this attack on JJ take place?" she asked.

"He was attacked by the Community Center."

"Was it by the Community Center or at the Community Center?"

"He was in the Community Center playing cards with them fellas."

Bertha thought, *that is one of the things they always criticized me for not allowing Sydney to do*, but she asked, "Were they playing for money?"

"Me eh think so."

"You don't think the men were gambling, or you do not believe JJ was gambling?"

Velma did not answer Bertha's last question. Instead, she started sobbing again. She knew that she and her mother had openly criticized Bertha as being too strict with Sydney by imposing curfews on him and restricting, or attempting to restrict the activities he engaged in, while Joshua was free to do just about whatever he wanted to do. She knew also that in Bertha's absence, they said a lot of dreadful things about how she was raising her son. They did not live exemplary life styles themselves and made no effort to improve their lot but instead, they looked at every progressive move Bertha made with regard to her son's education and conduct, as terribly wrong.

"Dry your eyes, girl," Bertha said as she handed Velma a napkin and left the room. She quickly returned with a teapot of hot water on a tray with milk and sugar, and two teacups and saucers for serving a herbal beverage.

"Try some of this. It would soothe your nerves," she said.

"Thank you," Velma said, although her body language indicated something different. She was uncomfortable. She never served herself or anyone else like that, and it was only at Bertha's or Dorothy's that she received that kind of hospitality. Those were the very things she and her mother, Umilta always gossiped about when they would accuse Bertha of pretending to be something she was not.

Bertha finished her beverage and said to Velma, "You need to drink that tea while it is still warm. In the meantime, I will get dressed."

Oh! I am sorry. I didn't know that you were going out," Velma said.

"We are going out," replied Bertha.

Velma appeared puzzled so Bertha asked, "Who went to the hospital with Joshua?"

"Ah doh know. I heard they took him there by ambulance."

"Who are they?" Velma didn't answer because she didn't know so Bertha asked, "Which hospital did they rush him to?" There was still no response from Velma.

The things you ought to know you don't, Bertha thought but said, "First, we are going to the Community Center and try to get some detail about what happened. We will find out which hospital Joshua was taken to and we are going to try and get there fast." She then left the room to get dressed. She was angry. Velma remained seated. She felt remorseful when she thought, *the very person to whom I was most unkind is about to do the kindest thing for my son and me.*

Bertha got dressed quickly and rejoined Velma in the living room. "Let's go," she said. Velma got up and they walked outside, stood at the curb and hailed a taxi. Fifteen minutes later they arrived at the Mayaro District Hospital. They did not stop at the Mafeking Community Center.

"We are here to see Joshua Jacob," said Velma to the nurse who approached them. "Is he here?"

"Yes. Mr. Jacob is still in the treatment room. He lost a lot of blood and is very weak but he is stable. He might be kept overnight though."

"Can we see him?" Velma asked.

"Are you related?"

"I am his mother."

"Who are you, madam?" The question was directed to Bertha who replied, "I am his aunt." The two cousins so closely resembled, the nurse saw no reason to question Bertha's statement. Joshua, at times called her Aunt Curly or Aunt Bertha anyway. Because she was his older cousin, he called her aunt out of respect. However, no one seemed to recall how the name Curly came about.

"He will be receiving intensive care because he lost a lot of blood. Otherwise, his wounds are not life threatening," the nurse said.

"Can we see him?" Velma asked again anxiously.

"I will let you visit with him but you must not try to engage him in conversation."

"Are you saying that we shouldn't speak to him?" Velma asked.

"Not unless it's absolutely necessary."

Philbertha rolled her eyes but said nothing. She was thinking of all the criticism and ridicule she had been subjected to by her aunt, Umilta and her daughter, Velma, simply because she disciplined her son. They laughed at the fact that she imposed strict curfew on Sydney and demanded continued good performance in his school work. He never let her down and that may have been the basis for the jealousy of her relatives. Bertha, however, did all she could to prevent their actions from becoming key notes in any form of discord.

After about five minutes, the nurse said to Velma and Bertha, "You may visit him now." Both women looked at the nurse puzzled and although they did not ask, where is he? The nurse realized their concern and said, "He is in room 6A down the hall. It is the third door on the left."

They walked to the doorway and stopped there momentarily before entering the room which was occupied by Joshua and another patient. Both were on stretchers and waiting to be transported to the intensive care unit. There was a nursing assistant looking after them, but when Velma saw the IV (intra-venous) tubes, the bandages, and the blood transfusion tubes, she fainted. That created quite a commotion as the nursing assistant called for help and security responded quickly. Shortly thereafter, two young doctors and a nurse, the same nurse who directed them to the treatment room, rushed in. Suddenly, the focus of attention was on Velma. A security officer brought in another stretcher and three officers lifted her onto it. The nurse took her vitals and found that her blood pressure was elevated. It was 200/110. The doctors worked frantically to revive her. The senior of the two declared, "We must start treatment right away to lower that blood pressure."

"Agreed," said the other physician.

Through it all Bertha remained calm but she was frightened. *What could have caused that?* She wondered. Then she overheard one of the doctors say to the nurse, "Her BP might have been elevated before but was pushed up further by the anxiety. In addition, she is….. " He whispered whatever else he had to say, so Bertha didn't hear.

"We would have to keep her overnight," the nurse said to Bertha.

"Why?" Bertha asked.

"It is necessary for us to monitor her blood pressure. Both her diastolic and systolic are too high."

What does all that mean? Bertha wondered but she did not ask, so the nurse continued, "The doctors may want to speak with you. Can you please stick around for a little while?"

"I certainly can."

"Okay. I will call you if or when you are needed."

"Thank you."

As Bertha walked off to take a seat in the lounge, an attendant wheeled Velma out of the treatment room and into the ward where she was to spend the night. Bertha sat bewildered. She was thinking of her son whom she left at home alone. She did not wake him up to let him know where she was going, so naturally, she was concerned for his safety, even though crime was not typically an issue. Her main concern was about the kerosene lamp lighting system and the possibility of an accidental fire.

As she sat pondering what should be her next move, one of the doctors came to speak with her. "We may have to keep your sister longer than one night," he said. He took it for granted that they were sisters based on what the nurse told him. Philbertha said nothing that would have indicated something different. Her concern, however, was heightened and it showed in her facial expression even before she asked, "What else is wrong with her, Doc.?"

"After we examined her, it was determined that she may have suffered an acute ischemic stroke." the doctor said. Bertha was unsure about what the term *acute ischemic stroke* meant, although she understood what a *stroke* was and she was very concerned.

"We will give her some medicine intravenously to bring her blood pressure back to normal. We would have to do this slowly and monitor the process continually."

"How long will she have to stay in the hospital, Doc.?"

"If she responds well to the treatment, she should be home in two days. Most people do respond well when treated with this medication."

The doctor did not tell Philbertha what medication he was considering to administer to Velma but earlier she did hear him and his associate discussing the merits and downside to treating stroke victims with nitroglycerin[50]. She assumed that was the treatment her cousin would have received. They recognized Bertha's concern and said, "Don't you worry too much. Your sister would be fine in a couple of days."

"Is there anything I can do for her right now?" Bertha asked.

"No," said the doctor. "It is late. You should go home and get some rest."

"What about her son, Doc.?"

"Oh! He is resting comfortably."

"Thank you," said Bertha as she got up and left the hospital to get a taxi that would take her home.

THREE

Tuesday morning Kendal woke up early as usual and got dressed to travel to Matura where he was to report for duty. He had been assigned there as a rookie police officer. He was unable to report the previous day, and although he had gotten a note from the District Medical Officer (DMO) indicating that he would be unfit to work for at least one week, he was determined to show up, so he did. His plan was to return home every evening after his assignments.

He was an ambitious young man who planned to attend law school at one of London's famous inns or at the prestigious University of the West Indies, School of Law. The impetus for his determination as he strove to achieve his goals was deeply rooted in his love for Henrietta Riggs, his childhood sweetheart. He envisioned a bright future with her, not because she was smart and successful, or rich and famous, but because he loved her. Consequently, every little step he took to achieving his goal was with her in mind. Every examination he prepared for and passed, was with her in mind. Every college application he completed, and every scholarship he sought was for her future benefit. In spite of small town gossip, rumors, and innuendos that hinted at her promiscuity and unfaithfulness, he persevered as if with blinders on.

That morning he arrived in Pierre Ville by way of a Rio Claro taxi that brought him from Mafeking. As he waited at the Sangre Grande taxi stand for transportation that would eventually take him to Matura, Henrietta arrived from Lagon Doux apparently on her way to San Fernando. He was delighted to see her and walked over to the cab in which she sat. To his surprise, she was not as enthusiastic to see him. On the contrary, she appeared uneasy, nervous, and unsure of herself. She did not, or could not exhibit the sort of exuberance for which she was well known. *Perhaps she heard of my mishap at the river lime on Sunday*, he thought.

"Hey! Henrietta. What a pleasant surprise it is to see you this early in the morning," he said.

"I am going to San Fernando," she replied gruffly.

"That's good," he said, not knowing what else to say. He didn't ask her why she was going to San Fernando. He considered it none of his business. Instead, he said, "I am going to Matura to report for duty. Yesterday was supposed to be my first day but I was unable to go." Henrietta was indifferent. That puzzled him but he didn't dwell on it.

While he stood there in amazement at her sudden indifference toward him, a Sangre Grande taxi arrived on the stand. There were three other people waiting for transportation and Kendal was eager to get in line. He did not want to miss that ride, so he said to her, "I will see you when I get back this evening. Love you."

"That's fine," she said coldly. She never inquired about what happened to Kendal on Sunday morning. *Perhaps she hasn't heard*, he thought. *I will bring her up to date this evening*. He reached in through the left front passenger window and gently touched her cheek. The taxi driver turned and looked at them but he said nothing. Kendal, however, said, "Goodbye," and left with a smile. Henrietta was not smiling.

The drive along the Manzanilla/Mayaro Road was fast. The cabby was driving at between 60 and 70 miles per hour for the duration of the trip. Kendal was not comfortable with that but he did not object. He was, however, hoping and praying that he would have no more mishaps or near mishaps in the same week. To his surprise, two of the passengers stopped off in Ortoire Village. The third was dropped off in Manzanilla.

"I wasn't aware that your other passengers were not going all the way to Sangre Grande," he said.

"Yeah, man! I take people to their destination instead of waiting only for those who are going to mine. At the end of the day, I make as much money as anyone else and I do not use any more gasoline."

"That is a good way of looking at it"

"Yeah, man! Life is too short to sweat the small stuff. Today we are here but we can be snuffed out in a flash."

"Tell me about it." Kendal said. He was thinking of his own near life ending experience of two days prior.

"You are a good fella (guy), Kendal; quiet, level-headed, and bright. You have a nice guul (girl) too; very pretty, gentle, and friendly. You are a smart fella, so you know that beauty is only in the eyes of the beholder. I can't tell you what to do. The guul is nice but you have to give it time. Doh (don't) rush in to anything, man."

Kendal found that the cabby was intrusive and rambling. Nevertheless, he got the message and said, "I can't. Today I am starting my first job."

"Yeah, man. I can see that you have a bright future ahead of you, so take your time. If you rush the brush you are going to get daubed."

That last statement from the cab driver was a proverb Kendal heard repeatedly while growing up in Mayaro. He knew exactly what it meant but chose not to discuss it with the taxi driver. He simply dismissed it, paid the cabby, who by then had arrived at the taxi stand and parked.

"Thank you so much," Kendal said when he received his change.

"You are welcome, man. Don't you forget what I told you, take your time."

"I will always remember that," Kendal said as he thought, *Too many people get into too many other people's business too often.*

To him all that mattered was his love for Henrietta. He was a devoted, caring, concerned individual, planning for what he hoped would have been a bright and happy future with her. There were notable differences between them that neither paid much attention to early in their relationship. They were in elementary school when they first realized their attraction to each other. Gradually, they grew closer and closer. Soon they were constantly in each other's company. In their early teenage years, they partied together, and traveled together. As they grew older, however, their differences became more and more pronounced, but neither saw those differences as damaging to their relationship.

Unlike Kendal's strict, disciplined upbringing as an only child of a single mother, Henrietta was the first of nine children; eight girls and one boy. She was fortunate to have both parents in the home. Unlike most parents of the day, hers could have been considered liberal, in the sense that they were not strict disciplinarians. As a result, she was adept to interacting socially, and interact she did. Many people referred to her as, Etta, the social butterfly.

How much of her social activity was exaggerated or imagined cannot be determined precisely but it generated a great deal of gossip about her. None of it was flattering. Much of it was brought to Kendal's attention, either causally or maliciously. Some folks were very direct and told it to him exactly as they saw it. Others were subtle and used well known adages to describe what they thought they witnessed. The connection both Kendal and Henrietta had with the Mayaro public could only be described as strange. Both were admired greatly, although for different reasons; Henrietta for her stunning beauty and pleasing personal manner; Kendal for his keen acumen, determination, and drive. As a couple, people generally wished them well. Their parents were extremely proud of them, both as individuals and as a couple.

Their first disagreement came when Henrietta decided to enter the Ms. Mayaro beauty contest. Kendal objected. He wasn't sure why and Henrietta didn't care why. She was like that at times. When her mind was set on doing something she couldn't be dissuaded, so the argument was short lived. She contested and was placed second, the first runner-up, that is. Kendal did not attend. In fact, that Saturday of the contest, two days prior to T & T carnival, he traveled to Port of Spain for the week-end with the intention of staying there for carnival Monday and Tuesday. It was a spur of the moment decision. Prior to that, he and Henrietta had always spent carnival together in Mayaro.

Several months after carnival rumors abound that Henrietta was in a romantic association with Rudolf Vargas. Kendal heard them and tried desperately to ignore them. He was confident that their love for each other was such that it could endure and withstand any threat or distraction. He decided that one sure way to stem the tide of intrusion from what he termed, amateur actors and pretenders vying for his lover's attention, was for them to spend more time together. He suggested it to his mother, Dorothy, and she agreed. She adored Henrietta. As the situation was then, when he wasn't in school or at work, he was with her. How much more time could they have spent together, was anybody's guess.

Kendal took notice that whenever Henrietta had to travel, even for short distance commutes, she waited for a specific taxi; the one driven by Rudolf Vargas for his stepfather. Mr. Vargas was much older than they. He was a personable man though tone deaf, unable to read, and totally out of touch with any of the youthful, social activities Henrietta liked to indulge in. She gravitated to him only because of the convenience and accessibility to transportation with his stepfather's car.

It appeared as if Mr. Vargas never charged Henrietta for trips she took in his cab, something that concerned Kendal greatly and caused him to say to her on several occasions, "In this town, nobody gives you anything for nothing."

Her response was always the same. She laughed and said, "Kendal, you are so silly." It mattered little to her that Rudolf Vargas didn't go dancing with her, that he didn't picnic with her, or take her to the movies. The only thing he did for her was not charge her the fare whenever she traveled with him. That of course became something she did often. One thing was certain. Mr. Vargas knew how to count and he no doubt calculated that whenever Henrietta traveled with him, it was necessary for him to overload his cab. That was, for him to take one more than the full complement of passengers to compensate for the one lost fare that he never took from Henrietta. Overloading one's cab was an illegal act but Mr. Vargas did it anyway.

On Wednesday, May 9, 1956, after his second full day as a police officer in Matura, Kendal O'Connor returned home to Mafeking. He relaxed for a while then had dinner with his mother, Dorothy. They discussed the job and whether or not he was satisfied with his choice of a vocation.

"I am not sure that my satisfaction or dissatisfaction matters, Mom," Kendal said.

"Of course it matters whether or not you are satisfied," said his mother. "If you are happy on the job, you are more likely to be productive."

"Productivity is not an issue in law enforcement, Mom, at least not in Matura. Moreover, for me this is something temporary."

"Why would you say that?"

"Mom, are you forgetting that I plan to further my studies abroad?"

"No. I haven't forgotten. Very often we make plans not knowing whether they can be implemented, so we must be prepared to adjust our plans as the need to do so becomes apparent and or necessary."

"I know that. You have told me time and time again that it would take a while before I can accrue sufficient funds to study abroad."

"That was true the first day I said it and it is true today."

"You are forgetting something though."

"What?"

"You are forgetting that I have applied for several scholarships."

"That is like counting eggs the hen hasn't laid yet."

"You are never that pessimistic. Did something happen today that you haven't told me about?"

"No." Dorothy said. In reality though, the rumors about Henrietta's flirtatious ways were taking their toll on her. She adored the young woman and somehow couldn't see what other people of Mayaro were seeing.

"So what accounts for this change; your sudden lack of confidence and optimism?"

"Huh!" Dorothy murmured. She was concerned that if Kendal left Trinidad and Tobago, eventually both she and Henrietta would lose him. What she didn't know and couldn't foresee, was that Kendal may have walked away eventually from what he felt would lead to a life of unhappiness and regrets.

"Is that your response?" he asked.

She was silent with a sullen expression on her face. Suddenly Dorothy O'Connor, the strong, confident woman she was known to be, was concerned that she might be alone. She realized that her only child had grown up and she was cognizant of the fact that one day, sooner rather than later, he would leave home. That thought frightened her.

"What is that look about?" Kendal asked.

"It's nothing."

"That can't be. I know you well, Mom."

"It's nothing, really!"

"Okay. That being the case, you wouldn't mind if I visit Henrietta this evening?"

"Dorothy smiled and said, "Not at all."

"Not at all, meaning I shouldn't go? Or not at all, meaning you wouldn't mind if I go?"

Dorothy laughed a hearty, joyous laugh and said, "Do whatever you want, son."

Kendal looked at the time. It was 7:20 p.m. He wondered whether he should ride his bicycle to Lagon Doux to visit his girlfriend or whether he should go by taxi. He realized that getting there by taxi would not be a problem but getting back at 9:30 or 10:00 p.m. could be very difficult. He decided, therefore, to ride the six or seven miles from Mafeking to Lagon Doux. He made the journey by bicycle several times before and knew that it would have taken him about an hour to get there. Neither he nor Henrietta had access to a telephone. Only two households in Mayaro had telephones. Kendal, therefore, had no way of notifying her of his planned visit. He never thought that anything was wrong with that. No one would have thought so. That's just the way things were. If one wanted to see a friend or relative, one dropped in. If that person had been out, one was out of luck and had to try again at some other time.

"I will leave here at 7:30," he told his mother.

"Okay," she said.

"I will probably be back by ten o'clock."

"That's fine with me. However, remember that you have to leave here early in the morning to go to work."

"I know," said Kendal. He kissed his mother and left.

Dorothy sat for a moment. Then she decided to visit Philbertha who wasn't far away. When she arrived, Bertha was about to visit her aunt Umilta who was at home alone since her daughter and grandson were hospitalized. "I am sorry. I came at a bad time it seems," Dorothy said.

"No! No. You can come with me if you don't mind."

"I would love to. I haven't seen Ms. Umilta in quite some time."

"Okay then. Let's go."

Philbertha put out the kerosene lamp and together she and Dorothy walked over to Umilta Jacob's place. As they entered the open front door, they saw Bertha's aunt sitting in a rocking chair with a hymnal and a lighted candle in her hands. Her bible was on a table close by.

"Aunt Umilta, good night" Philbertha said.

"Good night, meh dear," said Ms. Umilta. "Who is that with you?"

"This is Dorothy. Do you remember her?"

"Oh yes. Isn't she Kendal's mother?"

"You do remember," Dorothy said as she walked over to where Ms. Umilta was sitting and rested her right hand on the old lady's shoulder. "How are you holding up?" she asked.

"Not bad, you know."

Bertha then asked, "Have you had something for dinner, Auntie?"

"Yeah, guul. Ah had some dasheen and corned fish; salted cavallies."

Dorothy and Philbertha looked at each other as if to say, *no wonder Velma's blood pressure was so high*, but instead of vocalizing those thoughts, Bertha asked, "Is there anything else you would like to have, Auntie?"

"No, my dear. I am alright, oui."

"Have you been outside at all?" Bertha asked her aunt.

"Not since Velma has been in the hospital. Ah just sit and worry about them. Ah eh have no way of knowing anything." Ms. Umilta said. Apparently she had forgotten everything Philbertha told her the day before about the progress of her daughter and grandson.

"The doctor assured me that both Velma and Joshua would be fine and should be home in a couple of days."

"When you go see them again?"

"I am going to the hospital tomorrow."

"Huh!" Her aunt murmured as she looked around the room.

"Are you lonely?" Dorothy asked.

"Yeah, guul! Ah deh here for the past two days like a pooh-me-one."

"Then we will have to come and take you out tomorrow."

"Yes. You need to get out, Auntie." Bertha confirmed.

"Ah ha," replied Ms. Umilta.

"Is that a yes?" Dorothy asked.

"Ah ha."

"Then Bertha and I will come and take you out tomorrow. You need a little sunshine. The vitamin D would do you good."

"Me eh know 'bout that noh, guul."

"Yes, Auntie. We can sit by the savannah for a little while," Bertha said. She then gathered all of the dirty clothes her aunt had in the house and placed them at the front door to be taken away with her.

"I will see you in the morning, Auntie."

"If God spares our lives, my dear."

"Okay, Auntie. If God spares our lives, I will see you in the morning."

Bertha kissed her aunt who then said, "It is a blessing to have you as family, dear."

"Thanks, Auntie," said Bertha. "I have to leave you now. Sleep well."

"You too."

Dorothy walked over to where the old lady sat, stroked her back and said, "I will be here with Bertha tomorrow."

"God willing," said Ms. Umilta.

"God willing," said Dorothy as she and Bertha headed for the door. Bertha collected the dirty clothes she left on the floor there and as Dorothy walked down the step, she closed the door behind her. The two friends then started walking in the direction of Bertha's home. When they got to the entrance, Dorothy said, "It is already late so I would not come in. I shall see you at about ten in the morning."

"God willing," Bertha said. They both laughed and parted ways. Bertha entered her home, threw herself across the bed and quickly fell asleep.

FOUR

Kendal arrived at the home of Mr. and Mrs. Fitzgerald Riggs at 8:10 p.m. He entered the yard, walked up the short flight of stairs and knocked at the door. Mrs. Claudia Riggs said, "Come in." She did not ask who it was, nor did she get up to see who it was. She and two of the younger children sat in the dimly lit living room conversing and listening to the radio. Kendal entered and greeted them.

"Oh! What a surprise to see you here this late, Kendal," Mrs. Riggs said.

"It is not that late." He looked at his watch and said, "It is not even 8:15 yet."

"Oh, is that so? Perhaps I am fooled by the moonlight. Yesterday there was a full moon, so tonight the moon shines at its brightest," said Mrs. Riggs. Cognizant of the fact that Kendal was there to see Henrietta she said, "Henrietta is downstairs."

Where downstairs? He wondered. *This house is barely four feet off the ground,* he thought, but went down the steps anyway. Henrietta did not see him come down the steps and was startled when he ducked under the house. To his surprise, there she was, the woman he loved so dearly, sitting in a hammock in the dark with a male companion. In the glimmer of moonlight that reached the hammock, he recognized the man as Karish Sagaloo, someone he knew from the neighborhood. As soon as the young man realized it was Kendal, he got out of the hammock, and fled, leaving Henrietta alone with Kendal who by then was livid.

"What the hell were you doing here in the dark, in this hammock with him?" he asked.

"We were just sitting and talking."

"You were sitting and talking in a hammock in the dark?"

"Yes."

"Do you really think that I am stupid?"

"No."

"So how do you explain what I just saw?"

"There is nothing for me to explain. You only saw me sitting and talking with a friend."

"Is that so? Then let me ask you this."

Kendal paused so Henrietta asked, "What?"

"Would you say that I am a friend of yours?"

Henrietta thought about Kendal's question for a moment, then said, "Yes."

"So how is it you never sat with me in this hammock to talk?"

"You never asked me to."

"Did Karish ask you?"

"Yes."

"So why didn't you suggest that you sit with the rest of your family upstairs as I always do?"

Henrietta did not or could not answer that question. She started to realize the folly of her ways but was unsure what she could say because she had never before seen him so angry. He too didn't like what he was experiencing, so he said good night, jumped on his bicycle and left. He had never before left the Riggs family home without saying goodbye to Mr. and Mrs. Riggs.

He arrived home at 10:30 p.m. that night and sat in an easy chair near the door. There, he contemplated what he should do next. His first impulse was to walk away, end the relationship. *Perhaps Karish or Rudolf might be better for her than I am*, he thought. As he reclined in the chair, the words of the cab driver who took him to Sangre Grande on his first trip to Matura to begin his new assignment kept ringing in his ears, *doh rush in to anything, man.* The more he thought of what the cab driver said, the more inclined he was to believe that what was happening was in his best interest because he was only twenty-two and had not invested too much time in the relationship. After that thought he fell asleep.

He slept soundly through the night. It was 5:30 a.m. when his mother, Dorothy came out and saw him. She wasn't alarmed because he had slept in that chair before, though not for the same reason. Although at the time she was unaware of the reason for his action. Dorothy O'Connor had to shake her son several times before he woke up. She was concerned that he might be late for work and she made that known to him. He sprang to his feet and nothing else was said until he was ready to leave.

Philbertha meanwhile, was up early and started washing her aunt's clothes. She was happy to do it in spite of all the horrible things Ms. Umilta and her daughter had put her through. When she was finished, she prepared breakfast for herself and Sydney and saw him off to school. Only then she decided to go over to her aunt Umilta's and take her something for breakfast. While there, Dorothy arrived.

"I knocked at your door and got no response so I figured you might be here," she said.

"Yeah, I am here. It wasn't too long that I arrived. Sydney should have answered the door though."

"Oh, he had already left for school. I saw him while on my way over here."

"That boy is probably the one who opens the school every morning. He just hates to be late."

"Why should he be late?"

"Yeah, you are right."

"So how is your aunt this morning?"

"She is resting. After breakfast she complained about not feeling well. I think she doesn't want to go out." Bertha whispered.

"You know something Bertha, when people reach that age they are entitled to do whatever they want."

"Auntie is not that old."

"How old is she anyway?"

"She will be seventy-three next month."

"While seventy-three may not seem that old to you, Ms. Umilta had a tough life."

"Maybe you are right."

"I am right."

" Perhaps I should go in there and ask her whether she still wants to go out?"

Both Philbertha and Dorothy seemed to forget that it was never Ms. Umilta's wish to go out in the first place. They proposed the idea but she never really agreed to it. They assumed that because they were much younger and made what they thought was a reasonable suggestion, that seventy-three year old Umilta Jacob would have no recourse but to follow blindly. There was a common misconception in the 1950's, that older folks were obligated to conform to whatever rules, standards, or suggestions that were put forward to them by their younger, more vibrant offspring, siblings, or relatives.

Philbertha returned to the living room and said, "I don't think she wants to go."

"How is she?" Dorothy asked.

"She is resting comfortably."

"Then we can go to the hospital, and check on her when we get back."

"That's a good idea. There is only one drawback though."

"What is that?"

"The visiting hours are actually from three o'clock to eight o'clock."

"Oh, don't worry about that. That rule is never enforced in Mayaro."

"Okay. Then let's go."

Philbertha stepped back inside to check on her aunt once more before leaving. When she came out, she looked at Dorothy and shook her head indicating that it was okay for them to leave.

When they stepped outside, Bertha pulled the door closed behind her. She did not lock it.

They waited at the curb in front of Umilta Jacob's house for about 20 minutes before they were able to get a taxi to take them to the Mayaro District Hospital. Upon their arrival, Velma was sitting outside of her room and conversing with other patients. She seemed relaxed but as sedentary as she had been at better times. When she realized that Bertha and Dorothy were there, she sprang to her feet, rushed over to where they were standing, and hugged them both.

"I am so glad you are here," she said.

"We had to come," said Bertha. "Auntie couldn't come but she misses you a lot."

"I miss her too."

"How do you feel?" Dorothy asked.

"I feel good. The doctor said that I can go home today."

"That's good news," said Bertha. "How is Joshua though?"

Velma's eyes became filled with tears when she heard the question. She choked up a bit. Then she wiped her eyes, regained her composure and said, "He is doing much better. They took out the tubes and he is able to talk to me now." At that point she couldn't hold back the tears. Dorothy handed her a napkin. She dried her eyes, blew her nose, and said, Thank you. I want to thank both of you for all you have done."

"You are welcome," Dorothy said.

"Girl, we haven't done anything for you that you would not have done for us."

"I am so grateful to you, and I thank God for having you in my life."

"Can we see Joshua?" Bertha asked.

"I think so. I can't go with you though."

"Why not, aren't you his mother?" asked Dorothy."You should grasp the opportunity to be with him."

"I agree, but only two visitors are allowed at any given time."

"Only two of us are visiting. You are still a patient here."

"I know but I don't want to upset the staff. You can go. He is down the hall; the second to last door on the left." Philbertha and Dorothy walked down the hall and entered the room where Joshua lay with his face toward the wall.

"Joshua." Philbertha called out softly.

He turned around slowly, smiled, and said, "Aunt Bertha, you came."

"Yes JJ. I am here."

"Ah so glad to see you. Oh, ouch!" Joshua cried out.

"Are you still in a lot of pain?" Philbertha asked.

"Yes. It's mostly my back and shoulder." he said. He didn't say which shoulder but he didn't have to. Bertha and Dorothy saw clearly that his left shoulder was bandaged. They looked at each other as if to say, *this could have been avoided if only he was disciplined, educated, and not allowed to be so wayward.* Their thoughts were interrupted when he asked, "Aunt Bertha, how is Sydney?"

"Sydney is okay. He said he would drop in to see you this evening."

"Did he go to school today?"

"Yes, JJ. He did."

"Is he going to come after school?"

Bertha hesitated. Then she said, "I think so."

Bertha chose her words carefully. She always did whenever she spoke with Joshua. He was sensitive about certain topics. Foremost among them was his schooling or lack thereof. While he enjoyed being able to run around town and do whatever others like him did, he also had a yearning desire to be like his cousin, Sydney. He wished he could read a newspaper, a sports magazine, or even his name on a roster of athletes. To him, his athletic prowess paled when compared to Sydney's ability to read and write, or Arjune's aptitude for mathematics.

"Do you think I could ever go to school, Aunt Bertha?"

"Of course you can, JJ."

"They will put me in ABC (kindergarten), wouldn't they?"

"Not necessarily," said Bertha. "You can attend extramural classes with young people your own age."

"Will they teach me from ABC just like they teach the little children?"

Joshua was sixteen years old but his last recollection of school was when he was about six or seven. Bertha found herself having to tread delicately between giving advice in response to Joshua's questions and not offending him nor his mother and grandmother in the process so she said, "You might be tested and placed in an appropriate group based on your ability."

"Test? Ah doh like that."

"It's not that bad, JJ. In fact, it is not bad at all."

"No! No, no, Aunt Bertha. That eh for me."

"The only reason you will be tested is for the counselors to be able to give you the proper instruction."

Joshua turned to face the wall. He was crying. That made Bertha nervous and uneasy. She looked at Dorothy as if to ask, *what now?*

"I'll suggest that you stay here and try to comfort him," Dorothy said, as if she read Philbertha's thoughts.

Dorothy walked out of the room. Bertha pulled up a chair and sat down at Joshua's bedside. She either didn't know what to say or she wasn't sure what she should say. She didn't want to say anything that would have further aggravated the problem she faced of trying to comfort her nephew without making him feel deprived, worthless, and inferior. She decided, therefore, to say nothing further about schooling unless Joshua asked her something specific. She patted him on the back of his head and said, "Everything would be okay, JJ, once you are better and regained your strength." Joshua did not respond so she continued patting him on the head.

Dorothy went out to the lounge area and sat with Velma who immediately asked her, "Did they catch the fellas who hurt my son?"

"Yes. The police arrested the two young men yesterday. They are now being held in jail awaiting bail."

"Why they couldn't keep them there without bail?"

"I don't know. Perhaps the law requires that they are offered bail," said Dorothy. "However, I understand that bail was set at one hundred thousand dollars each and neither was able to raise the money."

"Good! I hope them idiots rot in there."

Dorothy wrestled with mixed feelings of sympathy and anger toward Velma. *You are not without blame woman*, she thought. *You allowed that child to roam the streets and do whatever pleased him without parental supervision since he was six or seven. Like many of us, you are struggling to raise him as a single parent but unlike many of us, your mother has been there to lend a hand. There is no justifiable reason why you couldn't see to it that he stayed off the streets, away from the other wayward boys, go to school and attain a good elementary education, which is free, for Christ sake.*

Even before that thought, she sensed the anger in Velma's voice and immediately became concerned about her health issues. "You need to calm down, Velma. According to the doctors, Joshua would make a complete recovery. He would need you around when he gets out of the hospital, so please don't stress yourself out. Let law enforcement handle it. So far they have done a good job."

"You are right. My doctor said that I have made remarkable progress. He also suggested that I should follow the recommended diet and avoid stress."

"Your doctor?"

"Yeah, he told me his name but I do not remember."

"You don't remember your doctor's name?"

"Ah really doh remember."

It is the first time you have seen a doctor in your adult life and already he is your doctor, Dorothy thought but said, "That's funny."

"What is so funny?"

"The fact that you saw the doctor once and you are referring to him as, *my doctor.*"

"Actually, he saw me three times."

You are just so silly, Dorothy thought. She was known to be a very compassionate person. However, she did not always entertain the best thoughts of some people with whom she made frequent contacts. There was a brief period when Dorothy and Velma were not conversing. They were observing the antics of another patient who appeared to have been berserk about not being able to get a prescription filled within the hospital's pharmacy system. Security was trying desperately to calm him down when Philbertha arrived in the lounge where Velma and Dorothy sat and asked, "What's going on with him?"

"Apparently he is being discharged and the pharmacy does not have the medication the doctor prescribed for him?"

"I hope they have mine in stock," Velma said.

"Did you get a prescription?" Bertha asked.

"Yes. He gave it to me this morning."

"Who gave it to you?"

"My doctor. Who else?"

"Well, it could have been the head nurse."

"The head nurse?" Velma asked.

"Never mind what I said, Velma. You have gotten the prescription." said Dorothy. "When will they discharge you?"

"The nurse said at 3:00 p.m."

Dorothy looked at the time. It was 12:00 noon and she wasn't comfortable with the thought of having to sit around the hospital for three hours until Velma was discharged. At the same time, she didn't want to appear too controlling by suggesting that Velma ask to leave earlier. After all, she was only there to accompany Philbertha who herself was uneasy with having to wait around for three hours.

"Velma, could you ask the nurse to allow you to leave now?"

Velma shook her head indicating the negative. Then she said, "I am afraid."

"What are you afraid of?" asked Bertha. "She can only tell you yes or no."

What you should have been afraid of you were not, Dorothy thought. *You allowed your child to grow up with virtually no parental supervision and you weren't afraid of what could happen to him.*

"I will ask her." Bertha said as she walked away to look for the nurse. She felt disgusted with her cousin. At the same time Dorothy turned to Velma and asked, "Why don't you pay your son a visit?"

"I eh know 'bout that noh."

"What do you mean? There is no one in there right now and he needs you more than ever."

Velma didn't budge so Dorothy hissed her teeth and walked away in disgust. She was about to walk out of the building and sit on one of the benches under the spreading almond tree in the front of the hospital when Bertha approached smiling.

"The nurse gave me the discharge papers and a prescription for Velma."

"She gave you another prescription? Does that mean she can leave now?"

"Yes."

"So tell her."

"Come on. Let's get her."

"Sorry, Bertha. I am not going back in there. I will wait for you here." She pointed to the benches under the almond tree.

Bertha went to give her cousin the news. When she got to the lounge where Velma was sitting and told her that she didn't have to wait until 3:00 p.m. to leave the hospital, Velma wasn't pleased.

"Big deal," she said.

"Is that all you could say, big deal? You seem to forget that we have other things to do besides sitting here waiting for you."

"Other things like what?"

Velma's question angered Bertha and she feared that if she stayed there she might have disrespected the other patients and their families in the lounge. In the process also, she might have disrespected Velma and herself, so she walked away to join Dorothy outside. "Let's go," she said to Dorothy.

"Where is Velma?"

"She is an ass. I can't be bothered. I am tired with her stupidity."

"That's not what I asked you though." Dorothy herself was tired of Velma's antics but she didn't think that they should leave her there.

"I heard what you asked."

"So, where is she?"

"She is in there, still in the lounge I guess."

"I will be right back," Dorothy said, as she got up and started walking toward to front door of the hospital. When she reached the lounge area, she noticed that Velma was still sitting there looking at the TV monitor. At the same time one of the nurses walked by and said, "Velma, it looks as if you don't want to leave."

Velma smiled broadly but said nothing. She remained fixated on the television show she was looking at. She did not even acknowledge Dorothy's presence.

"Did you go in to see Joshua?" Dorothy asked.

"No."

"Aren't you going to visit your son before we leave?"

"No"

"Then get dressed. We are ready to leave."

Velma looked at Dorothy. It was a look of disdain but she said nothing. She got up and walked to the room she shared with another patient. There, she changed into her own clothes and placed the hospital garb in a hamper in the room. She walked back out without saying a word to the other patient who looked at her but said nothing either, but she smiled at Dorothy who waved at her upon leaving the room. Velma, meanwhile, was wondering why both Bertha and Dorothy were so eager to get her out of the hospital and back home when she was enjoying every minute she was there since the doctor assured her that she would be fine if she took the medicine as prescribed and took good care of herself. What she was experiencing, was a welcome change from the sedentary lifestyle she had become accustomed to since the death of Joshua's father some twelve years earlier. It was not something Dorothy, Bertha, or anyone else could ever have understood. She herself didn't quite understand it. She just loved it. By the time all three women were together and considering getting a taxi to take them to Mafeking, it was already 2:05 p.m.

"Wait a few minutes," said Bertha. "I want to say goodbye to JJ."

"Make it quick," Dorothy said. Velma rolled her eyes and sighed.

What a Fool, Dorothy thought but said nothing. While she and Velma waited for Bertha to return they did not speak.

"JJ." Bertha called out softly as she entered the room where Joshua lay in bed. He was on his right side and he faced the door.

"Aunt Curley, you are back."

"I came to say goodbye. I will try and see you tomorrow. Sydney should be here soon because it is already after two o'clock."

"What time is he leaving school?"

"School is dismissed at three."

"Okay," said Joshua. Then he asked, "Where is Aunt Velma?"

"She is outside."

"Is she coming to see me?"

"I don't know, JJ. I hope she would."

Bertha kissed Joshua, reassured him that Sydney would be there and that she would see him again the next day. She then walked out and rejoined Dorothy and Velma in their quest for a taxi to take them home. It wasn't long before an empty taxi showed up on the stand. Bertha approached it and asked the driver if he would take them to Mafeking.

"How many?" he asked.

"Three of us."

"Ah doh generally make short runs but ah go take you." The taxi driver was no other than Mr. Rudolf Vargas, who, was also from Mafeking. He figured that he could take them to their destination, stop off at his home and be back on the taxi stand in the same time that he would have waited for a full complement of passengers for a trip to Rio Claro. He was right. When he got back to the Mayaro taxi stand, the other plying taxis he left there were still on the scene and none had a full complement of passengers.

When Bertha and Dorothy walked into the house with Velma, Ms. Umilta said, "Praise the Lord!" It was a cold sounding praise of joy. She was like that. She never got excited about anything at all. Velma behaved similarly. *Is that a learnt behavior, or is it inherited?* Dorothy wondered. *Perhaps it is learnt because Bertha does not behave like that and they are closely related,* she thought. She did not consider the possibility that Bertha may not have inherited the specific gene.

"Now that you are safely home, Velma, I must say goodbye until tomorrow," Dorothy said.

"Yes. I have to leave also. I must fix dinner before Sydney gets home," Bertha said.

"Where is he?" asked Ms. Umilta.

"He went to school."

"School, huh!" Ms. Umilta said. Velma giggled.

What the hell do they have against schooling? Dorothy wondered but she said, "I have to go now, bye."

"I too must leave you now," Philbertha said and left.

As Dorothy approached the entrance to her home, she noticed a taxi stopped at the gate. It was the same taxi, the one driven by Rodulf Vargas, that less than an hour earlier, brought her, Bertha, and Velma to Mafeking. *Why is he stopping.........?* She started thinking when she noticed a young lady stepping out of the car. It was Henrietta. She smiled as they spotted each other.

"What a surprise!" exclaimed Dorothy. "I have never before seen you here in the middle of the week."

"I know. However, I felt I should come and speak with you."

"Well, that's nice. Come on in." Henrietta followed Dorothy into the house and stood in the living room uncertain as to what she should say or do next.

"Sit down, girl. Make yourself comfortable. You are no stranger."

Henrietta sat in the easy chair near the door. It was the same chair in which Kendal slept two nights earlier. She, however, did not know that. She knew that when he left her that night he was very angry. She assumed that his mother, Dorothy knew all about it. She was wrong. Kendal did not discuss their disagreement with his mother. Henrietta was in somewhat of a quandary. She came not to apologize but rather to give her version of what happened. She didn't know how or where to begin if Dorothy hadn't heard about it. She decided, therefore, that small talk was in order until Dorothy touched on the subject. To Dorothy the evening was going to be chatty and pleasant. She knew nothing about their dispute, and even if she did she would not have gotten involved. She was that kind of person. She loved them both and wanted the best for them.

"Why are you staying all the way out there?" Dorothy came in and asked. "Come. Join me in the kitchen," she said.

"I will be happy to," said Henrietta. "Are you about to fix dinner?"

"Yes, girl. I am a little late today because I went to the hospital with Philbertha."

"Is she ill?"

"No. Her cousin, Velma, and her son were both hospitalized."

"I am sorry to hear that."

"They are both feeling better now although the son is still in the hospital," Dorothy said. She then went on to explain how the events unfolded. Henrietta was genuinely sad to hear it and promised that she would visit with Velma before returning to Lagon Doux.

"Why don't you stay the night?" Dorothy asked.

"I could, except that I did not bring anything with me."

"What do you mean?"

"I did not bring a change of clothing."

"Hey, we are about the same size. I am sure I can find something for you to wear now, and I have lots of night clothes you can choose from."

"Then I will stay for the night."

"Your mother knows where you are, doesn't she?"

"Of course she does. I never leave home without letting her know where I am going."

"Never?"

"Well, almost never."

"Good. Then let's work on getting some food on the table in the next hour. Kendal should be here shortly thereafter."

Bertha had already prepared dinner and eaten. She was about to place Sydney's meal on the stove and go out to the bakery to get a loaf of bread for breakfast the next day when Velma walked in.

"I came to say I am sorry," she said.

"Sorry about what?"

"Sorry for the way I acted earlier."

"You weren't acting, Velma. That's just the way you are. I am accustomed to it by now. Don't you think so?"

"You can say whatever you want. I am saying that I am sorry."

"Okay! An apology is good. However, the person you should really be apologizing to is Dorothy."

"I will when I see her again."

"That's not good enough. You know where she lives. Just how you found your way here to say to me that you are sorry, you can go over to Dorothy's and tell her the same thing."

"I can do that tomorrow."

"Why tomorrow? You are not doing anything right now, so why put it off? I was on my way to the bakery. You can walk with me and stop off at Dorothy's."

FIVE

It was 6:10 p.m. when Kendal arrived home. That was a little later than usual so he was famished. He walked into the living room and shouted, "Hey, Mom! I am home." He went to the kitchen to greet his mother and was taken aback when he saw Henrietta there. Had she been in the living room, he would not have entered at all. However, since he was already there, he looked at her, smiled and said, "Hi."

The O'Connor's home like most in Mayaro, had a relatively large kitchen so most activities involving small gatherings took place there. That day was no exception. Kendal kissed his mother and inquired as to what kind of day she had. She sighed deeply and said, "That is a long story, son."

"I would love to hear it, Mom, but I have to run a few errands, so please hold the thought until I get back."

"The events of the day are indelible in my memory, son."

"That's good because I could be out for quite a while," he said as he left to change from his police uniform. He changed quickly, returned to the kitchen and said, "I might be out for the night, Mom."

"What! Where are you going?" Dorothy asked as he was walking away.

"I am going to Pierre Ville," he said, and before she could ask him anything further he was out the door. She found it strange that from the time he arrived home to the time he changed and left again, he said nothing more than *hi* to Henrietta. That was so out of character for her son, so she turned to Henrietta and asked, "Did you two have a quarrel?"

"He is upset with me."

"It must be serious because he is never like that."

"He thinks it is."

"Don't you think it is serious?"

"No."

"Huh!" Dorothy murmured. She didn't know what else to say and she was unwilling to ask Henrietta for details of whatever the discord might have been about. Henrietta volunteered no information. Instead, she said, "I think I should go home."

Something had to have happened and whatever it was had to be serious, Dorothy thought but ask, "Do you think you would get transportation from Pierre Ville to Lagon Doux at this time? I know that you would have no problem getting a taxi from here to Pierre Ville."

"Whatever taxi I get here I will ask the driver to take me home."

"I still think you should stay the night."

"I can't, Miss Dorothy."

"Okay then. I will go out with you to wait for a taxi."

Dorothy kicked off her slippers and slipped her feet into a pair of flat-soled shoes while Henrietta gathered her purse and a couple of magazines she brought with her. The two women then walked out of the front door leaving it ajar.

"Wouldn't it be nice if we had an efficient telephone system and we could just sit inside and call a taxi?" Dorothy asked.

"I guess so," replied Henrietta in a detached sort of way.

As they stood at the curb waiting, several taxis that were filled to capacity went by. At other times a taxi with a full complement of passengers may have stopped for one more. It is possible that on that occasion, none stopped because drivers assumed that both Henrietta and Dorothy were traveling together.

"I really think you should stay the night," Dorothy said again out of frustration.

"I really can't, Miss Dorothy."

"Only you and Kendal know why," Dorothy said hoping that Henrietta would reveal something. She didn't. Suddenly it started to rain. It was a heavy downpour and it came without warning, something that generally happened during the day when the sun was very hot and evaporation and condensation occurred in rapid succession. Dorothy found it strange that it rained when it did and said, "This is weird."

"What is so weird, Miss Dorothy?"

"That it would rain so heavily this late in the evening," said Dorothy. "Don't you think that's weird?"

"No. This happens all the time in Lagon Doux."

"Perhaps it is because you are so close to so much water," said Dorothy. "Let's get back inside."

They ran back into the house to seek shelter. Within minutes after they entered, the rain stopped as quickly and as suddenly as it came.

"Huh!" Dorothy murmured.

"Now, that is weird," said Henrietta.

Dorothy did not respond directly but took two umbrellas from a rack at the door and handed one to Henrietta. "You may need this when you leave the cab," she said as they walked back out to the curb to await a taxi.

"I doubt it," said Henrietta. "The drivers usually drop me off directly in front of the house." Nevertheless, she took the umbrella.

Shortly after they came out of the house and stood at the curb again, a car came to a screeching halt. It stopped a few yards away and the driver reversed to where Henrietta and Dorothy stood. It was the same taxi that brought Philbertha, Velma, and Dorothy home earlier that day. It was driven by no other than Mr. Rudolf Vargas. "You are in luck," Dorothy said

"Yeah. Thanks. I will try and see you on Sunday," said Henrietta as she left Dorothy's side to enter the cab. They waved to each other as the taxi drove off.

Dorothy walked back into the house somewhat dejected. She pulled the door closed behind her but did not lock it. There was no door bell and Kendal did not have a key. There was only one key to the front door. Cell phones were not yet invented and only two households in town had land lines. It was customary, therefore, that in most households, the last person who arrived home at night would lock the door. That night Dorothy unknowingly slept with the door unlocked all night because her son never came home. He somehow reasoned that Henrietta might be spending the night at his mother's and he did not want a confrontation with her. He also did not want his mother to try and influence him one way or the other. If there were to be a reconciliation, he thought, it must be voluntary between Henrietta and himself without influence or persuasion from his mother.

Henrietta also did not go home that night. Her parents assumed that she spent the night at the O'Connor's. Although they were comfortable in that thought, they were wrong. After three other passengers who traveled with Mr. Vargas from Rio Claro stopped off in Pierre Ville, He invited Henrietta to join him for a drink.

"I am not going to any of those rum shop bars," she said.

"We can go to *The Junction.*"

"Not me. No!"

"Do you have to get home in a hurry?"

"No. I was going to spend the night in Mafeking but I changed my mind."

"So what is the problem?"

"I don't have a problem. Do you?"

"I eh think so," said Mr. Vargas. There was a brief pause, a period in which he thought, *so she is not expected to be home tonight.* Then he said, "There is a cozy bar and lounge at The Beach Front Hotel.

"So?"

"We can go there if you wish," he said. There was no response from Henrietta. She was thinking; *as it is, I may have already lost Kendal, so why not.*

"Do you want to go?" Mr. Vargas asked.

"Do I want to what?"

"Spend a little time with me."

"We have been together since you picked me up."

"Ah doh mean like this."

"Then what do you mean?"

"Ah mean alone."

"We are alone. Haven't you noticed?" Henrietta asked.

"Come on," said Mr. Vargas. He placed his hand on Henrietta's thigh and asked, "What do you say?"

She paused for a moment, took a deep breath and said, "Alright."

Mr. Vargas was already on the Guayaguayare/Mayaro Road heading toward Lagon Doux when Henrietta said alright. He was approaching St. Ann's Road at the time, so without asking anything further, he turned left up St. Ann's Road and pulled up at The Beach Front Hotel.

"Give me a second," he said. Henrietta did not respond. Instead, she reclined in the front seat as he left the vehicle and entered the lobby of the hotel. He approached the front desk and said, "Good night."

"Good evening," the concierge said and asked, "What can we do for you this evening, sir?"

"Ah want to get a room for the night," Mr. Vargas said.

"We have several vacancies but reservation must be made for two nights."

"Why? I only want to stay one night."

"It is company policy, sir."

"How much is the room?"

"It is a hundred and fifty dollars per."

"Per?"

"Yes. The cost is $150.00 per night."

"Wow!"

"We can upgrade you to one of our luxury suites for the second night at no extra cost, sir."

"Ah doh want ah luxury suite. Ah just want one room for one night."

"I am sorry, sir. That is the best I am allowed to offer you."

Mr. Vargas had never traveled outside of Mayaro. He, therefore, had never stayed in a hotel before so he was unable to determine whether or not he was offered a good deal. His major concern was that $300.00 for two nights at The Beach Front Hotel represented much more than his share of what he earned all week from his many trips to and from Rio Claro.

"Leh me think about it," he said to the concierge.

"Take your time, sir."

"Thanks."

Mr. Vargas walked away from the counter and sat in the lobby. *This is comfortable*, he thought of the seat. Then his thoughts shifted to Henrietta. *Why ah doing this?* He wondered. *This could make Pa very angry. If ah tell 'im it was a slow day he eh go believe once he check the mileage.*

On average, Mr. Vargas made between ten and fifteen trips from Mayaro to Rio Claro and back every day except Sunday. On the busiest days, Friday and Saturday, he consistently made fifteen trips. On the slower days, Monday to Thursday, the trips varied between ten and twelve per day. His stepfather checked the mileage on the odometer at the end of each business day. He consistently took $180.00 from the receipts each week without even counting the total. It was up to Mr. Vargas, therefore, to be responsible for his own earnings, petrol (gasoline), and the maintenance of the vehicle. The strategy worked well until that day.

He still wasn't sure why he wanted to spent the night with Henrietta. He didn't love her. Love was an emotion he had never really experienced. The opportunity for erotic pleasures presented itself and he wanted to take advantage of it. He thought of the consequences and acknowledged it was risky but decided to take the chance. He got up walked back to the counter and told the concierge, "Ah want to pay for the two nights."

"Okay! Would you want a single or double for the first night?"

"A Single or a double?" Mr. Vargas repeated the concierge's question.

"Yes. For the first night you can have two single beds in the room, or you may have one double bed. It's up to you."

"Mr. Vargas thought about it and said, "Double." He was still uncertain though, as to whether he made the right choice.

"For your second night you can either have our luxury bridal suit or our superb presidential suite." Mr. Vargas did not answer. Once again he was unsure of what choice he should make.

"What will it be, sir?"

"Either one. It doesn't matter."

"I will suggest the presidential suite for you, sir."

"Okay."

"Then if you step down to your left, Pauline will get your paper work started. Enjoy your stay with us."

"Thanks."

Mr. Vargas did as the concierge asked. Pauline had everything ready except for his identification. She smiled and asked, "What is your name, sir?"

"Rudolf Vargas."

"I would need one piece of identification and three hundred dollars from you for a two-night stay."

I eh staying no two nights, Mr. Vargas thought but he handed the clerk the three hundred dollars and his newly issued party affiliation ID card."

She looked at the photo ID card, looked at the patron and said, "That's good." She then entered the relevant information on an index card and placed the card in a rolodex. She handed Mr. Vargas his ID card together with a receipt and two keys. "Thanks for choosing The Beach Front Hotel. These keys are for your first night with us. After 11:00 a.m. tomorrow you may return these and we will issue the keys to your luxury presidential suite. For tonight's stay, your room is on the second floor. The room number is on each key. Please enjoy your stay."

"Thank you." Mr. Vargas said. He took the items and left.

When he returned to the parked car, Henrietta was still reclined in the front seat with her eyes closed. As he opened the door on the driver's side, she sat up. "What took you so damn long?" she asked.

"Ah was talking to someone."

"You stood in there talking and left me sitting here?" she asked. Then immediately she thought, *Kendal would never have done that.*

"I am sorry about that."

"What are we doing?"

"We go have that drink."

"I am hungry. I cannot have a drink on an empty stomach."

"Ah sure you could get something to eat in there."

"Then what are we waiting for?"

"Nothing."

"Let's go."

They walked into the lobby of the hotel and stood at the door of the lounge momentarily before they were ushered in by a waitress who asked, "Do you want to sit at the bar? Or would you prefer a table?"

"We would prefer a table, please," Henrietta said. She knew the waitress but there was no personal conversation between them.

"Please come with me."

Henrietta and Mr. Vargas followed the waitress who seated them at a table for two at a window overlooking the ocean. Then she handed each a menu and said, "I would be back shortly."

At the same time in Mafeking, Philbertha had been trying desperately to get her son, Sydney to eat his dinner. He had visited his cousin and close friend, Joshua, in the hospital and was traumatized by what he saw and heard. Throughout their lives they played together, did their outdoor chores, including tending the goats in the fields together, and more recently, they participated in *the river lime* together. They were close, very close, not just as relatives but as friends.

In spite of all his pain, Joshua had two major concerns, one of which he kept repeating to Sydney, "I don't want to miss the *lime* this Sunday," he said.

"You will not be able to swim with your arm in a sling," said Sydney. Joshua did not respond to Sydney's comment so he continued. "Once your arm is healed, you would be able to go swimming again."

"I wouldn't be able to swim as fast, would I?"

"I don't know for certain but I think with proper exercise your arm would be as good as it ever was."

"I hope so."

"Just try and get better," Sydney said. His eyes were red but the tear drops were not exuded. He paused and Joshua remained silent for a brief period. Then he asked, "Why doesn't Aunt Velma let me go to school?"

"I don't know, Joshua."

"Aunt Bertha lets you go to school and you are able to read and write and everything."

"That is true."

"Why?

"I can't really explain. She constantly says to me, *it is the way out.*"

"What is it the way out of?"

"I am not sure. I think it is the way out of a lot of things."

"What sort of things?"

Sydney hesitated. He was extremely cautious about what he said to Joshua. He didn't want to hurt his cousin's emotional and fragile state of mind but he also didn't want to give him any false hope. Eventually he said, "I think Mom meant that education is a way out of abject poverty and all that is associated with it."

"Abject poverty? What is that?"

"It is a miserable state of life."

"Are we poor, Sydney?"

"We are the abject poor, Joshua. We don't know it or don't realize it because everyone around us is also poor."

"How do you know these things? Do they teach you that in school?"

"No. I did not learn any of that in school. Mom taught me a lot of things that are not taught in school."

"How do you know that she is right?"

"She is right. Mom is very smart."

"Does that mean that Aunt Velma isn't very smart?"

"No. In fact, I heard that she was smarter than Mom when they were in school."

"So why doesn't she want me to go to school?"

"I don't know, JJ." It was the first time in their conversation that Sydney referred to Joshua by his pet name.

"Will I ever learn to read, write, and do mathematics like you and Arjune?"

"I can teach you to read and write when you get out of the hospital."

"Can you teach me to do mathematics too?"

"I can but Arjune might be better at that."

"Do you think that he would be willing to teach me?"

"I can ask him."

"Will you, Sydney?" JJ asked with a sound of elation in his voice.

"I certainly will and I will let you know what he says tomorrow."

"Will you be back tomorrow?"

"You bet," said Sydney. JJ smiled, and Sydney said, "You take care and I will see you after school tomorrow." He walked out of the door smiling and waved to JJ as he left.

At home that evening Sydney was trying to explain to his mother that seeing JJ injured and in the hospital had given him a new perspective on life. He tried to assure her that he still wanted to achieve all the things she said were good for his quality of life for the rest of his life, but he was more determined than ever to become more involved in some sporting activities other than swimming. In some respects he wanted to be more like JJ. At the same time, he was determined to help JJ to become more like him.

Philbertha listened to her son with pride and emotion. *You are wise beyond your years*, she thought. Most of all, she was impressed by his caring and compassion. She was tempted several times to say, *son, do not lose sight of your goal. You are on track, ahead of many your own age in your school, please don't let me down.* As difficult as that was she managed to refrain from doing so. Instead, she said, "Your plan is excellent. If there is anything I can do to help you to achieve your goal, please let me know."

"There is something I can think of already."

"What is that?"

"Huh! Sydney murmured. Then he laughed.

"Seriously, What is it Sydney?"

"JJ wants to learn how to do math and I told him that I would ask Arjune to help him."

"So?"

"Can you?"

"What do you want me to do, Sydney?"

"Can you ask Arjune if he would be willing to help JJ with math?"

"That would be difficult for me to do."

"Why, Mom?"

"First of all, I am not JJ's mother. I am not even his aunt, I am just a cousin. Secondly, I do not know Arjune well enough to approach him about something like that."

"Are you saying that you would not do it, Mom?"

"I am not saying that."

"Then what are you saying?"

"There are two people who are well suited for that task and I am not one of them." Sydney appeared puzzled by his mother's statement so she continued, "Those two people are your Aunt Velma, JJ's mother, and you."

"Why is that so?"

"In the first place, you are the one who offered to speak with Arjune on JJ's behalf. You could not now renege. Secondly, you are very familiar with Arjune. You may even be friends for all I know. Thirdly, If I were to approach Arjune about this matter, I would be usurping your Aunt Velma's responsibility."

"She does not take her responsibility seriously anyway. So what difference would it make?"

"That is enough now, Sydney! You are getting beside yourself and overstepping your bounds."

"I am sorry, Mom."

"You better be. You are fully aware of how I feel about that. I have told you repeatedly that you are not allowed to make derogatory remarks about adults, let alone your aunt, your older cousin that is."

"It wouldn't happen again, Mom."

"Okay. Now sit down and have your dinner." Philbertha was stern though not angry.

The situation made Sydney even more uneasy than before. Not simply because of the trauma he was experiencing from seeing JJ in the hospital, and knowing the circumstances that landed him there. His uneasiness had become complicated because of the way his mother spoke to him. He tasted the food and immediately vomited. Philbertha knew right away what was wrong with her son. Since infancy he was unable to eat whenever he was upset. The situation was no different that evening.

Back at The Beach Front Hotel the waitress returned to the table where Henrietta and Mr. Vargas sat trying to have a conversation above the noise of the music and the voices of other patrons trying to do the same thing. "What would you have?" she asked.

Henrietta pointed to items numbers 6 and 14 respectfully on the menu and said, I will have this and he would have that." They were both seafood dishes but it was easier for her to point them out instead of trying to speak above the loud sounds.

"Would you like something to drink?" The waitress asked complementing the question with a hand motion which, though it was not authentic sign language, everyone understood.

"I would have some wine," Henrietta said.

"And you, sir?"

"Geh me the same thing," Mr. Vargas said. For a while it seemed as if he was unable to think for himself. He simply agreed with whatever Henrietta suggested.

"Is there something in particular you would like?" the waitress asked.

"What would you suggest? Henrietta asked.

"We have a chardonnay from New Zealand that is very good. If you prefer something sweet, we have a sherry from England and one from Spain. Both are excellent."

"I think we will try the sherry."

"Which one?"

"It shouldn't matter. Either one would be fine."

The waitress left with the orders and Henrietta and Mr. Vargas resumed their conversation. He wanted to know whether Kendal or his mother, Dorothy, suspected that they were having an affair. Henrietta, however, objected to the connotation.

"We are not having an affair," she stated emphatically.

"So what is this?"

"I don't know. It certainly is not an affair."

"Is this just a date then?"

"We are out together so you can call it a date, I guess."

The waitress returned with a bottle of the sherry from Spain. She looked at Henrietta with a great big smile. For some reason she was trying to avoid looking at Mr. Vargas but she was trying desperately to read something into the expression on Henrietta's face. Nothing showed. *It would be an interesting thing to see Kendal walk in here right now,* she thought but said, "Your dinner will be ready soon."

"Thank you." Henrietta said. Mr. Vargas fiddled with his car keys that were on the table in front of him but he said nothing to the waitress. He was content to let Henrietta do all of the talking. In fact, on that occasion it appeared as if she was making all the decisions.

She poured herself a glass of sherry and sipped it. All the while she was thinking that could mark the end of whatever good thing she and Kendal may have had. She was looking directly at Mr. Vargas when she took a second sip of the wine and wondered, *what do you have to offer me?* At the same time the waitress returned with their meal. She looked at Henrietta and she thought, *what a mismatch. He has nothing to offer her.* In a most professional manner, however, she said, "Enjoy you dinner, and if there is anything else I can help you with, don't hesitate to ask."

"Thank you," Henrietta said. Mr. Vargas just stared at them but said nothing. Henrietta gulped down the rest of the wine in her glass.

"Ah thought you didn't want to drink on an empty stomach?"

"I didn't, but the food is here now. Can't you see?" Again Mr. Vargas acted as if he didn't hear what Henrietta said. He did not respond and acted as if he had been deaf, or dumb, or perhaps both. Her hostility toward him was obvious although she went to The Beach Front Hotel with him on her own volition.

Kendal was at *The Junction*. He had gone there not to punish Henrietta but to cloud his mind to what he witnessed, or thought he witnessed the night before with her and Karish Sagaloo. His friends Arjune and Dolphin, the guys who actually rescued him from drowning the Sunday before while on *the river lime,* were there. Other regulars from *the river lime* were also at *The Junction* that evening. Together they took the opportunity to celebrate Kendal's good fortune. Every time someone bought a round of drinks the same refrain resonated throughout the lounge, *a toast to Officer Kendal O'Connor.* Kendal was delighted but true to form, he limited the amount of alcohol he consumed that evening. After being there for four hours he still had not finished the glass of scotch and ginger-ale he received upon arrival.

It was 10:00 p.m., when Henrietta and Mr. Vargas finished their dinner. He accepted the check, paid the waitress, included a gratuity, and they left the lounge. Henrietta was heading toward the front door when he noticed and said, "This way."

"Where are we going?"

"It's this way. Come with me."

"Come with you, where? Can't you say where we are going?"

"It's a surprise."

"Surprise my ass. You aren't fooling me."

"Ah doh intend to."

"That's good because I don't like being fooled."

"I know. You prefer fooling around."

"Now you are acting like a smart ass. That is not going to help you tonight" Before he could respond, Mr. Vargas realized that they had reached their assigned room."

"This is it," he said as he unlocked the door and stepped inside. Henrietta followed him and pulled the door in behind her.

"Do you know that you have no manners?"

"What did I do now?"

"You walked right in here and left me standing in the hallway."

"Woh ah was supposed to do? Lift you up?"

"No. You were supposed to be a gentleman and let a lady in first."

"First or last, you are in the room, right? So what's the big deal?"

"Right," Henrietta said while thinking, *what a rude and crude fool. Kendal never would have done that.*

"It's nice," Mr. Vargas said.

"What is so nice?"

"This room is nice."

"What is so nice about it? To me it is just a single room with a double bed in it."

Mr. Vargas wondered whether he might have been gypped. He wondered also whether he should tell Henrietta that he paid for a luxury room for the next night. He was concerned about the total cost of it all, more than his entire net earnings for the three days prior. He had never been an adventurous or groovy individual, so the mere thought of what the night was about to cost him placed a damper on any semblance of what could have been a romantic evening. Henrietta sat on the bed in deep thought. The alcohol she consumed had taken effect, so her thoughts were random and racing. She thought mostly of Kendal, with whom she might have had a promising future. She thought of Mr. Vargas whom she began to view as a spendthrift who appeared willing to blow a great deal of money on her at any given time. She was wrong about that. For Mr. Vargas, that evening was tuning out to be an enormous sacrifice, one he might eventually regret, and he was wondering about its worth.

SIX

Kendal and two of his friends left *The Junction* at 4:17 a.m. Since he didn't have a car, he had no way of getting home that late at night, or rather, that early in the morning, unless he walked the one and one half mile journey. He was prepared to do so when Arjune decided to leave with him. They both lived in Mafeking and Arjune would have driven there irrespective of when he left *The Junction*, so it made sense for him to leave together with his friend. They arrived at Kendal's home at 4:30 a.m., and after a brief chat with a promise to meet again on Sunday at *the river lime*, they parted ways. Kendal went inside, showered quickly, and went directly to bed. He had hoped to get at least one hour of sleep. His mother, Dorothy was asleep so he had no way of knowing whether or not Henrietta was still there. Based on a pattern that emerged from her prior visits, he assumed she wasn't.

It wasn't long before he fell asleep and slept soundly. He woke up early at about 6.55 a.m. He needed no prompting from his mother. Strangely enough, he wasn't thinking of Henrietta who was also awake at the time. In fact, she woke up an hour earlier and was thinking about him and the situation she had gotten herself into. Mr. Vargas was still asleep naked in the double bed they shared that night. Although it was Friday morning, the dawn of one of the busiest days in the plying taxi business, Mr. Vargas showed no sign that he would have gotten up anytime soon. Henrietta thought of shaking him in an effort to awaken him but then ruled against it. Instead, she looked at the small refrigerator which had a coffee percolator on it and thought of brewing some coffee, but she quickly decided against doing that.

After lying awake in the nude and with wandering thoughts, she decided to get up and take a shower. *I have made a complete ass of myself,* she thought as she turned the shower on and adjusted the hot and cold water to a temperature that was tolerable for her. *None of this is making any sense,* she thought again. *There was no love, no caring, no tenderness, no passion, not even an interesting conversation all night long.* "What the hell have I done?" she asked herself quietly. Then she started crying in the shower. She sobbed loudly but Mr. Vargas never stirred. Finally, she comforted herself in the thought that Kendal may not know about her night out with Rudolf Vargas if she didn't revealed it. What she realized, though a little late, was that Vargas didn't care enough about her as a person to mention their night out (she couldn't call it a date) to anyone.

After showering, she found it difficult to get dressed. She had never before showered and gotten dressed in the same soiled clothing she wore before. On that occasion, she had no other choice, so she did what was necessary. Mr. Vargas was still asleep and she was determined not to wake him up. She took her purse, magazines, and the umbrella Dorothy gave her and left the room. She approached the courtesy counter downstairs, said good morning, and asked the clerk if it were possible for her to get a taxi from there.

"You certainly can. They come around every ten to fifteen minutes. I do hope that you had a good night's rest," the clerk said.

"Not really."

"I am so sorry about that. Hopefully, tonight would be better in our luxury presidential suite."

"Thank you," Henrietta said and left the counter to take a seat in the lobby. *What presidential suite?* She wondered. She wasn't sitting for more than five minutes when Mr. Vargas came rushing down the stairs. He looked sleepy and disheveled. He didn't shower, didn't comb his hair or brushed his teeth. He didn't say good morning to Henrietta, or asked how she was doing. The first thing he asked her was, "Why you eh wake me?"

"I didn't know that I was supposed to."

"Today is Friday and you know ah ha to work."

"Didn't you know that? You are a grown man."

Mr. Vargas did not respond specifically to Henrietta's last words. Instead, he said, "Come on. Leh meh take you home."

She got up, although her first impulse was to say, *no thank you*. She simply glanced at the clerk sitting at the counter. It was an existential glance.

"Enjoy your day, Miss," he said.

"Woh he mean by that?" Mr. Vargas asked softly.

"It seemed self-explicit to me. He is wishing that I have a good day."

"Why?"

"Perhaps he is just a gentleman, or perhaps he is assuming that my night wasn't so good, and since he knows that you reserved a room for tonight, which may not be any better, he is wishing me a good day."

"That is shit!"

"Call it what you want. One thing is certain. I am not coming back here tonight."

"Ah doh care."

"I thought so. Anyhow, now I know that your interest in me was only physical. You care very little about my existence."

Mr. Vargas chuckled and said, "You are okay, Etta."

Henrietta was furious. By then they reached the Guayaguayare/ Mayaro Road and Mr. Vargas stopped at the stop sign with his left indicator signal blinking. Henrietta opened the car door, stepped out of the vehicle and said, "You can go to hell."

"What is that about?" Mr. Vargas asked with a silly grin on his face, but before waiting for a reply or getting one, he changed his turn signal to indicate a right turn. As soon as the traffic cleared, he made the turn and headed toward Pierre Ville, leaving Henrietta standing at the intersection to try and get home however she could. She was livid. *Kendal would never have done that*, she thought again. She did not consider the fact that Kendal could not drive.

It was already 7:30 a.m. and Kendal was ready to leave home for his fourth day of work as a police officer at the Matura Police Station. By then Dorothy was awake and surprised to see that he was already dressed and ready to leave.

"Oh my goodness, Kendal, I am so sorry. I overslept."

"That's okay, Mom. I am fine."

Dorothy was proud of her son. She was beaming with joy just looking at him in his uniform and hoping that he and Henrietta would soon forget their differences and be back together again. "You look splendid this morning, son," she said.

"Is it only this morning, Mom?" he asked with a smile on his face.

"You are always magnificent to me, although I don't always say so."

"Thanks, Mom. I love you dearly."

"I love you too, son. You know that."

Dorothy and her son hugged each other and said good bye before he walked out of the door. As he approached the curb to await a taxi, she asked, "Are you going to visit Etta this evening?"

"I don't know, Mom."

"Don't you think you should?"

"No, Mom." Just then a taxi stopped. Officer O'Connor waved goodbye to his mother as he entered the vehicle and was on his way.

Sydney was already outside and started his morning chores but his thoughts were on his cousin, Joshua. As he watered the plants in the vegetable garden, he felt that something was lacking. On any other occasion he and Joshua would have been doing the same things in their neighboring backyards. Sydney did not only miss JJ, he was genuinely concerned for his health and wellbeing. That morning there was no lingering in getting the chores done. He rushed the job of irrigating the soil in the garden and moved on to his other tasks. Before seven o'clock he was finished with the chores. He showered, dressed for school and was ready for breakfast. As he sat in the kitchen attempting to review his homework, his mother, Philbertha asked, "How do you want your eggs this morning, son?"

"Hard-boiled, Mamie," he said.

"Hard-boiled eggs again?"

"Yes, Mamie. Please!"

"Okay. Hard-boiled it is."

"Thanks."

Philbertha served her son breakfast. He ate slowly as she always insisted, *take your time and chew your food properly, son*. When he was finished he brushed his teeth as she told him he must after each meal, he took his book bag which she made herself, kissed her goodbye and left. As he walked out of the door, He looked back at her and said, "Mamie, I will visit JJ this evening."

"That would be nice, Sydney."

Philbertha was happy to hear that Sydney intended to visit Joshua after school. To her it seemed that her son was coming to terms with Joshua's misfortune, so she didn't bother to mention that Joshua was expected to be released from the hospital that day. She was so happy that Sydney ate his breakfast and took the lunch she prepared for him that she also did not mention that she and Velma, Joshua's mother, planned to be at the hospital that evening to take him home in the event he was discharged.

Meanwhile, the parents of the young men who assaulted him with a deadly weapon were desperately seeking to raise money for their bail. They were not very successful in their effort. Many people in the community refused to contribute. Those who contributed did so reluctantly and offered very little to the cause. Neither parent had any assets they could have offered as surety to the bail bondsmen, so the young men continued to languish in jail.

The sort of violence that was perpetrated against Joshua Jacob had never before been witnessed in Mafeking, a quiet little enclave along the bank of the Ortoire River where most people were related or behaved as if they were. The young men involved, including Joshua were always considered wayward but no one ever thought of any of them as violent, so the sadness felt throughout the community was as much for Joshua as it was for his assailants.

Word of Joshua's impending release from the hospital spread quickly, and for the most part it was greeted with relief. Everyone in town, even the parents of his assailants, prayed for his speedy recovery. They of course knew that had he died, their sons would have faced murder charges, the consequence of which could have been the death penalty. Others prayed for him because of humanitarian concerns. Still others feared the stigma that the town would have had to bear if Joshua died and his young assailants were charged with murder.

Philbertha was dressed to go to Pierre Ville when she arrived at her cousin's to see whether Velma was ready to visit her son. To her amazement, Velma had just rolled out of bed. Her mother, Bertha's aunt, was still asleep.

"Did you forget that we planned to see Joshua this morning?" Bertha asked.

"No. I thought we were going there this evening."

"How could you? Have you seen him since you left the hospital?"

"No."

"So you don't know whether he has improved or gotten worse."

"No."

"You say that so nonchalantly. What is the matter with you, girl? JJ is your only child. Why don't you care?"

"Ah do care."

"Well, you have a strange way of showing it."

"What ah could do? He is in the hospital."

"You could do what other people generally do when a love one is sick and in the hospital."

"He eh sick. Them fellas chop 'im up."

"You are such an ass. I can't deal with that this early in the day. Bye"

Philbertha left her aunt and cousin's place and returned home. She sat for a moment, pondered the situation, and decided that she would go to the hospital without Velma, regardless of what her relatives thought about it. Having decided that, she got up, took her purse, and walked out to the curb to await a taxi. It wasn't long before she was picked up by a cab from Rio Claro. The car already had a full complement of passengers but the driver stopped for her because he considered hers to be a short ride since Pierre Ville was to be his last stop. Nevertheless, he asked, "Where to, Miss Bertha?"

"I am going to visit Joshua at the hospital."

"How is your son?"

"My nephew," said Bertha. "My son's name is Sydney." Joshua is my nephew."

"That's right! How is he?"

"He is much improved. Thank you," Bertha said with optimism. She really didn't know whether or not JJ had improved.

"That is so good to hear."

"Yes. For a while we weren't so sure that he would make it."

"That's what I heard. It is amazing that them fellas go try to kill somebody for two dollars."

"That goes to show us that we can never tell what is going on in a person's mind."

"You are right but I still can't get over it. They all seemed like such quiet fellas."

"Yes! The entire community is in shock. We had never had violence of any kind here before."

The taxi driver pulled up at the Mayaro Taxi Stand. The passengers paid their fares and went their separate ways; some left for the market place, some went to get transportation to other destinations, Philbertha walked over to the hospital. Joshua was out of bed. In fact, he was outside sitting under the almond tree with two other patients. That was something patients were encouraged to do if they were strong enough and could do so on their own.

Initially, Philbertha did not see her nephew sitting outside. She was heading to the receptionist's desk when she heard his voice. He saw her and had gotten up from where he sat.

"Aunt Bertha! Aunt Bertha," he shouted. By the time she turned around, he had reached her and asked, "How are you, Aunt Bertha?"

"I am fine," said Bertha. "I can tell that you are feeling better."

"I am better, Aunt Bertha."

"Thank God for that," she said as she embraced him.

"Where is Aunt Velma?" he asked.

"She is at home, JJ."

"Why didn't she come with you?"

"I don't know."

"Did you tell her that you were coming here?" JJ asked. His voice was low then. He looked sad.

"I did tell her that I intended to visit you this morning."

"What did she say about that?"

"She reminded me that visiting hours start at three o'clock."

"I will be going home at 3:00 o'clock today."

"Are you really? Oh Joshua! That is so nice."

"Thanks, Aunt Bertha." Joshua said. He was smiling again.

Philbertha wasn't sure what she should do next. Had Velma been there she would have asked Joshua if he received his discharge papers. She was reluctant to do so without his mother being present, so she asked him, "Could we sit under the almond tree?"

"Certainly."

As soon as they sat down, a private car pulled up in the driveway at the emergency room. A very matronly looking female stepped out and was attempting to assist another, much younger woman to get out of the vehicle. As soon as they were safely out, a third female stepped from the front passenger seat and wrapped her arms around the younger individual who was apparently ill.

"That person looks so much like Kendal's girlfriend," Philbertha said.

"That is Henrietta," said Joshua. "She must be very sick."

"You are probably right," Bertha said. She was concerned but reluctant to investigate further.

"Later today I will find out what is wrong."

"No, JJ. You do not go meddling in the affairs of any female."

"I am sorry."

"It's okay. I understand. Like me, you were only very concerned."

Yeah! Right, JJ thought but he said, "If she is seriously ill they would keep her in the hospital."

"People in these parts do not come to the hospital unless they are seriously ill, JJ. In this case, it probably means that they have tried all the home remedies they know and none worked." There was no response from JJ. Either he didn't understand what Philbertha meant, or he just didn't know what to say, so she continued, "As soon as I get back I must let Dorothy know about this." Then she quickly changed the emphasis by saying, "I am truly happy to see that you are feeling so much better." She realized her nephew's (cousin's, that is) uneasiness with the discussion about Henrietta's health.

"I am happy too, Aunt Bertha. Perhaps I can join *the river lime* on Sunday."

"Do you mean this coming Sunday?"

"Yes."

"Why?"

"Don't you think I can?"

"I haven't thought of it, JJ. Maybe you can, maybe you can't. Whether or not you should is something for your mother to decide."

"Aunt Velma doesn't care."

"Don't you say that about your mother, JJ."

"It is true, Aunt Bertha."

"You shouldn't say that, JJ. Your are just a child and your mother loves you dearly."

"So why isn't she here?" asked JJ. "You are here. If Sydney had been in this hospital, you probably would be here all day."

"I don't know why your mother couldn't be here this morning but I am confident that she would be here this afternoon."

"I doubt that, Aunt Bertha. She doesn't care about me. She doesn't care about what happens to me or what I become."

"What has happened to you recently made your mother very ill, Joshua. She needs to take care of herself so she could be around to take care of you."

Suddenly Joshua's tone changed. He became very sad. His eyes welled with tears and he sobbed loudly. Philbertha hugged him in an effort to reassure him that someone cared, that at least she cared. There was never a time when she didn't care. In fact, she had voiced her concerns about Velma's parenting skills to Dorothy many times. She was always the one individual to whom Philbertha could talk about those things with some assurances that they would never be repeated. She was overly concerned about the possibility of her falling out of favor with her aunt and her cousin, Umilta and her daughter, Velma. Based on some things Joshua had said to Sydney in the past, she was aware that they ridiculed and berated her about how she raised her son. At no time, however, did they ever openly despised her. In their own warped sort of way they loved her and were aware that she loved them.

Philbertha recognized Joshua's need for guidance. She realized long before that he yearned for some parental control in the hope that he could become like his cousin, Sydney. That yearning desire of his became quite clear when he said to her, "Sydney promised that he would teach me how to read and write and he would ask Arjune to teach me how to do math."

"That is wonderful."

"Does that mean you don't mind, Aunt Bertha?"

"I wouldn't mind at all if your mother and grandmother do not mind."

"They don't have to know about it, Aunt Bertha."

"It wouldn't be nice to keep that a secret from them, Joshua."

"It isn't anything bad."

"That is more of a reason why you should share it with them."

"No, Aunt Bertha!"

"Why not, JJ?"

"They would try to dissuade me, or they might object to it outright."

Philbertha admired the way Joshua spoke. He spoke English well. He had always spoken like that whenever he conversed with her, Sydney, Kendal, or Arjune. Nevertheless, he was able to switch quite easily to the Mayaro version of the Trinidad lilt when he was with others who paid less attention to the manner in which they spoke. That capability had convinced Bertha long ago of his potential for learning in the academics if he ever had the opportunity. His revelation about Sydney's offer did not come as a surprise. Sydney had hinted to that as a possibility in the past. She never objected before and had no intention of objecting then. Instead, she said to Joshua, "It is okay. You do not have to tell them if you do not want to."

"Thanks, Aunt Bertha."

"You are welcome."

They walked away from where they were standing and headed toward the hospital's lobby. Philbertha was accompanying Joshua back to his room when they ran into the Charge Nurse. "Joshua!" The nurse said, "You are going home today. I have you papers right here." She pointed to the left breast pocket of her apron.

"Oh! JJ, I am so glad for you," Philbertha said.

"Thank you, Aunt Bertha."

They left the lobby and were walking through the seating area of the emergency room when Bertha saw Henrietta sitting with her mother and her aunt, one on either side of her. She walked over and said, "Hello!" Henrietta barely looked up and smiled. "You must be Mrs. Riggs?" Philbertha inquired of the woman at Henrietta's right. Although they had never actually met before, they recognized each other as being clients of the same hairdresser.

In addition, Mrs. Riggs looked like an older version of her daughter when she smiled and said, "Yes. I am Claudia Riggs. This is my sister-in-law, Winnie." She glanced at the woman sitting at Henrietta's left.

"I am Philbertha Canton, a friend of Kendal's mother, Dorothy. This is my nephew, Joshua," said Bertha as she extended a hand to both women. She then patted Henrietta's shoulder and asked her mother, "How is she doing?"

"Not so good," said Mrs. Riggs. "She has been unable to eat all day. Nothing stays in her stomach and she has severe abdominal pains and is running a high fever."

"Has she been seen by a doctor yet?"

"No. She was triaged but you know this place, the wait to see a physician could be forever."

"I hope it wouldn't be as long a wait as usual."

"Thanks."

Philbertha walked with Joshua back to his room and said, "I will see you later." She wondered whether she should stick around until he was discharged at three o'clock or whether it was more feasible for her to leave and return with Velma later that day. It was quite perplexing to her. She couldn't be sure that Velma would make the effort to be with her son when he was discharged from the hospital. She knew that Sydney was expected to be out of school at the same time and he promised that he would be visiting JJ. She agonized about the situation for a while before she decided to go home and return at 2:30 p.m., whether or not Velma intended to meet her son when he was discharged.

Joshua sat on his hospital bed, looked at Philbertha and wondered, *why wasn't she my mother instead of Aunt Velma?* It wasn't the first time he had entertained such a thought. He often wished the same thing in regard to Kendal's mother, Dorothy. He loved his mother and grandmother. He appreciated the fact that they provided him with food and shelter although at times he felt that those were earned. He constantly compared his mother and grandmother to other women in the neighborhood and as he grew older, he began thinking of them as two slackers although that was a thought he knew that he didn't dare express.

"I will leave you now, JJ" said Philbertha. "Anyhow, I will let your mother know that you are being discharged and that you are looking forward to seeing her this afternoon."

"Thanks, Aunt Bertha."

As Bertha walked out of the room, she looked back and noticed that Mrs. Riggs and her sister-in-law were also leaving from a room two doors down the hallway. She stopped momentarily and waited until they reached her. "Was Henrietta admitted?" she asked.

"Yes," said Mrs. Riggs.

"Did they offer a diagnosis?"

"No. The doctor said that they would have to run a series of tests before they can say definitely what is making her sick."

"What will happen in the meantime?"

"She said they would begin treatment right away."

"How are they going to treat her if they don't know what is wrong?"

"I asked her that same question."

"What did she say?"

"She said that based on the symptoms they observed they would start treatment with a broad spectrum antibiotic, or combinations of antibiotics that work synergistically."

"Wow! You are good, Mrs. Riggs."

"I know. You are probably wondering how I remembered all of that. I didn't. I wrote it all down and have looked at it several times since."

The three women left the hospital together and walked out to the street where, before parting ways, they agreed to meet again later that day. Philbertha then took a taxi to Mafeking while Mrs. Riggs and her sister-in-law boarded one for Lagon Doux.

News of Henrietta's sudden illness and hospitalization reached Kendal while he was on duty. He and the senior officer, the sergeant from the precinct where he was stationed in Matura had just arrived in Sangre Grande after escorting two prisoners to the Golden Grove Prison (Remand Center in Arouca) . They stopped momentarily at the taxi stand in Sangre Grande where he encountered the Mayaro taxi driver with whom he traveled to the area on his first day as a rookie police officer.

"Hey! Officer O'Connor," hailed the taxi driver. "How are you?"

"I am good." The men shook hands and Officer O'Connor (Kendal) said, "Meet Sergeant Cove."

"It is a pleasure to meet you, sir."

"The pleasure is all mine," said the sergeant. Then he turned to Kendal and said, "I am going to lime (hang out) here in 'Grande for a while. You can call it a day."

"Thank you, sir," Kendal said with a sound of elation in his voice.

"Peter! You can call me Peter."

"Okay, sir. Peter!"

The sergeant left the police cruiser where it was parked on the taxi stand. "It was nice meeting you," he said and walked away.

SEVEN

Kendal sat in the front passenger seat and took a novel out of a small satchel he was carrying. He was prepared to wait until the driver got a full complement of passengers for Mayaro. *There is no better way to spend this time than by reading*, he thought. Just then the driver came in and said, "Let's go, Officer."

"What is that all about?"

"What?"

"The Officer bit. Didn't you always call me Kendal?"

"Yes."

"So what has changed?"

"You became a police officer. I have to give you that respect."

"You have never disrespected me."

"I know. But you know how it is, man." Although Kendal said nothing further, his thoughts were, *I hope you are not thinking of speeding, overloading (taking more than five passengers at any given time), or breaking the law in any other way.*

As soon as they left the taxi stand, the driver said, "Before I forget, let me tell you now that your guul (girl friend) is in the hospital."

"Which hospital is she in?" Kendal asked anxiously. He was thinking that if it were the Sangre Grande General Hospital he would have had to stay overnight at the local Police Precinct.

"Mayaro."

"Is she in the Mayaro District Hospital?"

"Yeah, man. You know there is no other hospital in Mayaro."

"Oh, my God!"

"That is what I said when I heard that she got sick after spending last night at your mother's house."

"What?"

"Yeah, man. That is what they said."

"Who are they?"

"Some people who traveled with me this afternoon." Although Kendal insisted on knowing who the passengers were, the cabby declined to give him any names.

"Just to set the record straight, let me tell you, Henrietta did not spend the night with me."

"I know."

"What do you know?"

"You were at *The Junction* drinking until about 4:00 a.m., and she wasn't there."

"I had one drink. What is so wrong with that?" Kendal asked. Then he said, "She wasn't at my mother's either."

"Ah doh know, man. Ah only telling you what everybody was saying."

"Everybody?"

"Yes."

"Mayaro! That is so very typical."

Although several people hailed the cab along the way from Sangre Grande, the driver did not stop for any of them. He had reached Cocal and was driving fast and furious under the canopy of palm trees that lined the Manzanilla/Mayaro Road.

"Watch it now. You are driving over the speed limit."

"Oh f---! I am sorry, Officer."

"Are you sorry about the obscene language, or about breaking the speed limit? Of those two offences, one can get you jail time and the other can get you a hefty monetary penalty."

"I really messed up, didn't I?" asked the cabby. He was driving much slower then. Although there wasn't any sign indicating what the speed limit was, what Officer O' Connor said instilled a measure of fear in him.

"You are off the hook for now," Kendal said laughing. Only then did the cab driver smile.

As soon as they crossed the Ortoire River Bridge and entered Ortoire, the sleepy little village at the mouth of the river it was named after, the driver stopped at the bar on the left side of the road. It was about one hundred yards from the bridge and was one of only two bars in the area.

"How about a drink?" he asked Kendal.

"No, thank you."

"Take a beer at least." Kendal looked at his watch and said, "I am still on duty."

"Okay, man. Ah go just get one for meh self."

"You go right ahead," Kendal said. He was hoping that the cabby would sit in the bar and drink his beer. That did not happen. Within ninety seconds the driver was back at the wheel with a freezing cold local beer in his hand. As he started the engine, pulled away from the curb, and sipped the beer, Kendal said, "Pull aside." The driver stepped on the brake and guided the taxi onto the grassy curb.

"What now, Officer?" he asked.

"Nothing. Just sit back and enjoy your beer. I am not in a hurry."

The taxi driver laughed and said, "You are something else, man."

"No! You are something else. This is your third infraction since you picked me up in 'Grande."

"Infraction?"

"Yes. First you broke the speed limit. Then you used obscene language in the presence of an officer of the T & T Police Force, and just a few minutes ago you were attempting to drink and drive."

"It's just a cold beer, for Christ sake!"

"It is against the law. Another officer may not have been quite as lenient with you."

"You are right," said the cabby as he finished the beer and tossed the bottle out of the window.

"No! No. You can't do that," Kendal said.

"Can't do what?"

"You should not litter the neighborhood like that," said Officer O'Connor "There you go again; Five offences in less than half an hour." Kendal was laughing when he said that. The driver was laughing too as he stepped out of the cab, picked up the empty beer bottle and tossed it in the trunk. *These are everyday occurrences. Would I have noticed them if I had not been a police officer?* Kendal wondered.

As they approached Peter Hill Road, the driver made a spur of the moment decision to turn right. The sudden turn jolted Officer O'Connor who looked sternly at the driver but before he could say anything the cab driver said, "You are not wearing your seat belt."

"Oh! That is not yet law in T & T. Very few cars have them, so I wasn't even aware that your car was equipped."

"I cannot argue with you on that one," said the taxi driver. *You are the law,* he thought but did not express it.

They arrived at the taxi stand and the driver parked. Kendal paid the fare over the driver's objection before walking across the street to the hospital to visit Henrietta. He greeted the receptionist who, without asking whom he was there to visit, directed him to Henrietta's room. She was delighted to see him. He hugged her, kissed her, pulled up a chair and sat close to her bedside. Neither apologized for the hostilities they previously exhibited toward each other. It was as if none of that ever happened. She told him that she was feeling much better than she felt hours earlier. The antibiotics she was given apparently helped, although there was no conclusive diagnosis as to what made her sick.

They spoke for about an hour; mostly about his new job and his dreams of a promising future with her. He assured her that up to that point nothing had changed. Every little step he took was still with her in mind. He was like a house plant that needed the CO_2 she exhaled in order to survive. She laughed. He always made her laugh and she liked that. Nevertheless, she was not as concerned about the future as he was. She was satisfied with her life the way it was and just wanted to enjoy it.

"I love you Etta," Kendal reiterated; something he had assured her of many times before. She, on the contrary, had never said that to him. She had never said it to anyone, just as her parents never said it to her. There was a tendency in those days among parents with many offspring not show affection openly to their spouses or to the children. The reason for that is still unclear. Perhaps it was because they never received it themselves, so they did not have it to give. Perhaps those parents with five or more children were careful and concerned about showing favoritism or bias. No one really knows for certain. It was what it was then. Kendal, like most other people knew what it was like. He never held that against her before and he had no intention of holding it against her at that time.

"When you are well enough to be discharged, we should get away for a while," he said.

"That will be nice."

"You are agreeing with me. Now, that is nice."

" Where will we go?"

"As things are right now, we will have only one weekend when I am off duty." He did not answer Henrietta's question.

"How are things right now?" she asked with genuine concern.

"Right now, as a rookie officer I am required to work all but one weekend every month."

"Are you on duty this weekend?"

"Yes."

"That's probably a good thing."

"Why?"

"Why? Just look at me. I am in a hospital bed."

"Most likely you will be out of here this weekend."

"I feel so much better. I wish they would send me home right now."

"I doubt that will happen. There is a tendency to keep people here overnight"

"I know."

There was a tap on the open door followed by the sound of the familiar voice of Mrs. Riggs,who exclaimed, "Hey! Kendal you are here. I told her that you would come. She was so concerned that you were still angry at her for hanging out with Karish."

Shouldn't I have been? Kendal thought of asking but said, "Oh! I have gotten over that."

"So you were upset?"

"Of course I was upset. I am only human."

"A very sensitive one I can tell."

"That sensitivity comes from caring too much."

"Mom, Kendal suggested that when I am discharged we should get away for a weekend," Henrietta said in an effort to change to topic of discussion that seemingly was heading for serious conflict between Kendal O'Connor and her mother. They had always gotten along quite well but she was concerned that was about to change.

Mrs. Riggs always held Kendal in high esteem but Henrietta's version of his avoidance of her after the incident with Karish, tarnished the image she had of him. She had instilled in her daughter that it was important for her to enjoy her youthful life and not be bogged down with thoughts of the future and a family. *That can come later*, she always said. Kendal, however, constantly badgered Henrietta with a different message, one his mother instilled in him.

The message from Dorothy O'Connor to her son, Kendal, was the need to aspire to achieve. Perseverance she argued was a critical tool toward that end. She encouraged educational pursuits and careful planning for the future. She did not want her only child to experience the same or similar pitfalls as she did. In a sense though, both Dorothy O'Connor and Claudia Riggs wanted their children to avoid making the same mistakes they made.

Dorothy had never gotten over the experience of being expelled from nursing school and eventually thrown out of her mother's house for being pregnant out of wedlock. On the other hand, Claudia's memory of being forced to live with Henrietta's father at the age of seventeen because she was pregnant with Henrietta, and the fact that she was pregnant every year after that for the next eight years was no less disheartening. So while the messages they conveyed were opposing ones, the reasons for those messages were the same; a mother's love that said, don't make the same mistakes I made at your age.

Sydney had arrived at the hospital at 3:10 p.m. and spent much of the time, an hour and a half after that, using phonics in teaching Joshua the pronunciation and spelling of words in an old news paper. Joshua remembered the alphabet in its proper sequence. He recognized and was able to pronounce monosyllabic words. What he lacked was confidence but he was quite at ease in the one on one setting he was in with Sydney. Learning to read was easier than he remembered from his brief stint with schooling and he was eager to master the skills just as his cousin did.

After ninety minutes of practice the lesson stopped abruptly when both their parents, Philbertha and Velma entered the room. Joshua had asked his cousin to keep his efforts to learn to read and write confidential, and although Sydney had mentioned it to his mother, no one else knew about the ambitious pursuits of Joshua Jocob. The boys were giggling when their mothers entered the room and Philbertha said, "I can see that you two are having fun,"

"We were just talking, Aunt Bertha," Joshua said.

"He is going home today," said Sydney. "Did you know that, Aunt Velma?"

"Yeah, man."

"That is so nice," Bertha commented and smiled with a look of endearment on her face.

"Thanks, Aunt Bertha," Joshua said.

"Perhaps we should walk down the hall and give you some time to get dressed, JJ."

"Okay! I will try to hurry."

"Do you need someone to help you?" asked Philbertha. "I can ask the Charge Nurse to get one of the aides to help you."

"That will not be necessary, Aunt Bertha. I can manage."

Philbertha looked at Velma as if to ask, *don't you have anything to say to your son?* She didn't ask the question and Velma said nothing. They left the room and JJ was left alone to get dressed without assistance. As they walked down the corridor toward the entrance Velma glanced to her right and asked, "Is that Kendall I saw in there?"

"It might be," said Philbertha. "That is the room Henrietta is in." She then asked, "Is the person in uniform?"

"Yes. It is a police officer."

"Then it must be him."

"She doesn't know any other policeman."

"She probably does but more likely than not, it is Kendal."

"Can we say hello to them, Mom?" Sydney asked.

"We will do that before we leave, Sydney," Philbertha said.

"Me eh know 'bout that, noh."

"What don't you know about, Velma?" Philbertha asked.

"Stopping to say hello."

"Why is that a problem?"

"Oh! He thinks he is ah big shot now."

"Whatever gave you that impression?" Philbertha asked. Velma did not answer. She could not answer because there was really no justification for what she said.

"He is an ambitious young man and that bothers you. You have to come up with something to ridicule him for, instead of being happy for him and for his mother who struggled so hard to get him this far. Isn't that it?" Still, there was no response from Velma, so Philbertha continued. "It is about time you sit back and take a good look at yourself and ask, *what have I achieved or helped anyone to achieve?* Instead, you are constantly deriding people for every progressive move they make. Get a life, woman!"

Velma pouted, her eyes bulged, her lips pursed but she said nothing. She was too angry to speak, knowing quite well that if she did, she could become vulgar. None of that mattered to Philbertha. She had become tired of the behavior of her cousin and aunt and felt that it was time for her to speak up, so she did. As far as she was concerned, that was over and done with.

"Let's sit out there and wait until Joshua is ready," she said as she pointed to the seats under the almond tree.

"Good," Sydney said. Velma, however, continued walking down the steps, out of the hospital and onto the street where she hailed a taxi and left, apparently forgetting that the reason she was there in the first place was to take her son home. Philbertha stood there bewildered as Sydney sat down under the spreading almond tree. *I can't believe what she just did*, she thought, *Joshua is her son.* She quickly dismissed it and joined Sydney. "How was school today?" she asked.

"It was very good. After the civic lesson, Ms. Gardener gave me the newspaper and I used it to begin teaching JJ how to read."

"Did Ms. Gardener hand you the class newspaper, or did you ask for it?"

"I actually asked her for it."

"So why didn't you say that?"

Before Sydney could answer his mother's question, someone called out to her. "Aunt Bertha! Aunt Bertha," the caller shouted. She looked up and saw that it was Kendal. He wasn't really her nephew, but as the son of her closest friend, Dorothy, he was taught to call her Aunt Bertha out of respect. In the same way, her son called Dorothy, *Auntie.*

"Hey! Kendal, Officer O'Connor," she corrected herself. "You are visiting your girl, I see."

"Yes, Aunt Bertha. I got the news of her illness while in a taxi on my way home this evening."

"I understand that it was sudden."

"Yes."

"How is she right now?"

"She is much improved. In fact, she might be going home tomorrow."

"That is good news. Truly, welcomed news."

"Yes. I am happy about that."

"You are an admirable young man, Kendal."

"Thanks, Aunt Bertha." he said. Then he noticed that Sydney's attention was focused on a classic literary work by Thomas Hardy and he commented, "I see that you are studying as usual, Sydney."

The young man looked up and said, "Not really. I am just trying to finish reading this novel so I can return it to the mobile library on Monday."

"Now, that's an admirable young man, Aunt Bertha." Kendal looked directly at Philbertha when he said that.

"He has been trying to follow in your footsteps. Thanks for the example."

Kendal only smiled and asked, "Did you see JJ already?"

"Yes. We are waiting to take him home."

"Oh! I take it that he has improved."

"He certainly has, both physically and psychologically."

"I will go in there and get him," Kendal said.

"Okay."

He left Bertha and her son sitting under the shade tree and walked back into the hospital. As he walked down the corridor, he looked into Henrietta's room. Her back was turned toward the door. She appeared to be resting comfortably, so he proceeded to JJ's room.

"Hey! Joshua," he called out.

"Kendal!" Joshua replied. He was surprised to see Kendal there, but delighted to see him in uniform.

"I see you are dressed to leave," Kendal said.

"Yeah, man."

"Then let's go."

"Okay!"

Kendal noticed that Joshua was clutching a newspaper. He found that to be strange because he knew that JJ was unable to read. As strange as it seemed, he did not comment. He was aware that Sydney had approached Arjune and asked him whether he would be willing to teach JJ mathematics. *No doubt he is also learning how to read,* he thought. *That could be the best thing for him. It may keep him off the streets and out of trouble.*

"You look very good in uniform," Joshua said as he and Kendal walked past the room where Henrietta was sleeping.

Kendal glanced in. JJ did not know that Henrietta was in that room and Kendal did not enlighten him. He simply said, "Thank you."

They came out of the hospital and joined Philbertha and her son. Joshua sat down next to Sydney. He was still clutching the newspaper when Kendal left to secure a taxi that would take them to Mafeking. There were several on the taxi stand waiting to get full complements of passengers to Rio Claro. However, as soon as Kendal got there, as many as four drivers offered to take him home to Mafeking and return to the taxi stand before heading to Rio Claro. Normally, a taxi driver would take, as an extra passenger, someone who was traveling for a short distance on the way to the driver's final destination, an overload, as that was called. On that occasion, however, the drivers were willing to take Officer Kendal home alone and then return to the taxi stand.

"I am not traveling alone," he said.

One driver in particular asked, "Are you ready to go, Officer?"

"Yes."

"How many people are traveling?"

"There are four of us."

"Okay."

"Let me go and get them from the hospital."

"Okay."

Kendal walked back to where he left Philbertha and the two boys to let them know that he had gotten a taxi to take them home. "Come with me," he said. They followed as he led them to the taxi driven by a well known and very popular driver on that route, Boodilal Jagdeo. Philbertha sat in the front passenger seat while Kendal and the two boys occupied the back seat. Not much was said in terms of conversation except when JJ asked Kendal whether he would be at *the river lime* on Sunday. Although he wanted very badly to be there, he responded in the negative. The driver looked at him through the rearview mirror and said, "You made the right decision, man"

Everyone else in the taxi entertained the same thought as the driver. Although no one expressed it, they firmly believed that Kendal's decision was because he almost drown due to the severe leg cramps he suffered while swimming the previous Sunday. His reason, however, was quite different. He felt that as an officer of the law he had an obligation to be discrete, to choose carefully the activities in which he participated, and the people with whom associated. He did not think of it as an aloof act on his part. He simply did not want to be in a position where he couldn't uphold the law because of some close personal relationships.

"We will miss you on Sunday," Sydney said.

"I will miss the *lime* too but I really can't be there."

"We understand," said Joshua. "I will be there."

"Thanks, JJ," said Kendal. "However, you need to be careful. In fact, you shouldn't try to swim until your arm is completely healed."

"I told him that," Sydney said.

"I know that. I plan to sit under the bridge and read." That statement from JJ struck Kendal as being funny but he did not laugh. Sydney didn't laugh either. He felt that Joshua was serious, and he in turn, was delighted to hear it.

Mr. Jagdeo stopped his taxi in front of Kendal's home and said, "You are home, Officer." Kendal paid the fare for everyone in the cab before he stepped out. He started to walk away at the same time Mr. Jagdeo was pulling his taxi away from the curb.

"Thank you so much, Kendal," Philbertha said.

"We still hope to see you on Sunday," Sydney shouted.

Kendal heard him and smiled. By then the vehicle was too far away for him to reply. One minute later it stopped in front of the home where Joshua lived with his mother and grandmother. All three of the remaining passengers, Philbertha, Sydney and Joshua alighted. Joshua headed to the door and his cousins followed. They walked into the dimly lit living room where Velma and her mother, Umilta were sitting. Joshua said good evening to them but he did not hug or kiss either one. That was not customary in the Jacob's household. Like JJ, Philbertha and Sydney also said good evening but neither made any attempt to be affectionate. They knew better than to try that. Velma was sitting in an easy chair close to the door with her legs crossed. She shook her right foot nervously but said nothing when Philbertha asked, "Why couldn't you wait to bring your son home, Velma?" Bertha then turned to her aunt and asked, "How are you today, Auntie?"

"Ah deh you know, poke ah poke (just okay)."

Philbertha should have been concerned about the situation at the Jacob's but she was not. She had grown accustomed to her relatives distancing themselves from her and from each other. Nevertheless, she didn't think that young Joshua deserved the sort of treatment he was receiving from his mother. *It is one thing for her to treat me or anyone else badly*, she thought, *it is quite another for her to treat her own son like that.*

Everyone spoke of Joshua as being a good child. He was a bit wayward but he was polite, mannerly, kind, and willing to listen and learn. He longed for the sort of guidance and discipline that his cousin, Sydney and others like him were receiving, and consequently, the progress they were making in school and in their chosen careers. Two of the young people he admired most and wanted to emulate were Arjune Bidaloo and Kendal O'Connor. Yet, those were not the people he associated with frequently.

Velma Jocob did not make schooling a priority for her son. In fact, apart from the daily chores that, in her mind, and in the eyes of her mother, were essential for their survival, nothing else mattered. Nothing else was ever given priority. Joshua was awake by 5:00 a.m. every day and most of his daily chores were completed before 8:00 a.m. Between 8:00 a.m. and 4:00 p.m. when Sydney was at school, there was nothing constructive for him to do. He spent that time, therefore, hanging out with other truants in the neighborhood. Before he was attacked with a cutlass over a gambling debt, his truancy never posed a problem, so it was allowed to continue. Neither his mother, Velma, nor his grandmother, Miss Umilta, looked beyond their immediate gratification toward Joshua's future.

Philbertha had spent the hour and a half since she arrived at the Jacob's trying to convince her cousin, Velma to change her ways. She even suggested that an apology to Joshua might be in order. Velma laughed at the suggestion. *Me, apologize to a child? You must be out of your damn mind*, she thought but said nothing.

"I get the impression that you are in no mood to have a discussion," Philbertha said.

"Why did it take you so long to figure that out?"

"I don't know, Velma."

"That's funny. You always act as if you know everything."

"I can't believe what I am hearing."

"You better believe it. I am tired of you telling me what I should and should not do."

"Okay, Velma, I have had enough. I am leaving. However, before I do, I would say one last thing......"

She paused and Velma asked, "What?"

"Take your medicine. Take it for JJ's sake." Velma did not respond, and Philbertha said goodnight.

Only Joshua responded. He said, "Good night, Aunt Bertha," as she got up to leave.

Sydney said, "Good night, Aunt Velma. Good night, Aunt Umilta." They responded together but it was a cold, "Good night."

Philbertha and her son left the Jacob's home and wasted no time getting ready for bed once they arrived at their home. At the O'Connor's meanwhile, Dorothy was glad to hear of Henrietta's improved health but she was even more enthralled at the news that she and Kendal had reconciled their differences.

"Would you see her tomorrow?" she asked.

"Yes! I would."

"Then invite her over."

"Mom, she is still in the hospital."

"She is going home tomorrow, isn't she?"

"We think so but no one knows for certain."

"Let's just be optimistic."

"Pragmatic is more like it. If she is discharged, I am sure Mrs. Riggs would want her to rest over the weekend."

"She can rest here, perhaps even better than she can at home with all of her noisy siblings running around."

"Mom?"

"What is it, son?" Dorothy asked. She didn't have to say more.

"Okay, Mom. I will try."

"Thank you."

EIGHT

Joshua and Sydney woke up early as usual on Saturday morning. They fetched water from a nearby standpipe as they had always done since early childhood. They were watering the vegetable gardens in their adjacent unfenced backyards when Joshua asked if he could get a reading lesson after they fed the pigs and tethered the goats in the field.

"You certainly can," Sydney said. He was glad to know that Joshua's enthusiasm to learn to read had not waned. He rushed inside, got one of his earlier reading books, a West Indian Reader written by a former Director of Education who was once assigned to Trinidad and Tobago by the British Government. He also took with him a copybook (notebook) and two pencils

"What are you going to do with those?" Philbertha asked her son.

"I want to show JJ something."

"Don't you get into any mischief now," said Philbertha. "You know that I have to go to Pierre Ville today."

"I know, Mom."

Philbertha, like so many others in the neighborhood, took some of the produce she harvested from her backyard to a market vendor in Pierre Ville who purchased it at a wholesale price. The funds she received were then used to acquire other essentials. On that Saturday, she was taking approximately eighty pounds of pigeon peas to market which would have earned her about twenty dollars. Her cousin next door depended pretty much on the same source of revenue except, it was Joshua who always took the produce to market. On that occasion, however, Joshua was indisposed. His grandmother was too feeble for the task and his mother's indolence, as always, got in the way of the family's progress.

In addition to his ram, three ewes and two lambs, Sydney also guided Joshua's four goats and three kids to a field nearby. JJ was there of course, but he couldn't help much. In fact, Sydney didn't want him to help for fear he might re-injure his arm. Once they reached the field, Sydney carefully tied the animals so that the length of the ropes allowed each one a circumference on the grassy knoll in such a manner that there was no overlap with that of any other animal. Once the sheep and goats were secured in the field, the boys sought a comfortable place to relax and begin the lesson.

The hillside was verdant and there was no threat of rain, so they decided to sit on the trunk of a fallen coconut tree to study. Sydney had started preparing some reading material for Joshua but it was not quite ready, so he selected passages from the West Indian Reader to begin the lesson. First he read three to four words of a sentence in a paragraph and then asked Joshua to read them. He repeated the process several times until a full paragraph was read. Each time Joshua complied. He then read the complete paragraph once more and asked Joshua to do the same. Once again Joshua did it willingly. Sydney congratulated him and Joshua smiled.

Like most boys growing up in Mayaro in the 1950's, they never had to wonder about fun things to do. Even when they were out doing their daily chores they found time for fun. It took several different forms. Sometimes they shot crabs with their slingshots which they never left home without. At other times they sought hardwoods such as guava or juniper to make tops. Spinning tops and pitching marbles were pastimes that rivaled *the river lime*. After an hour and a half of the first reading lesson, they came upon a young juniper tree with limbs that were perfect for making tops, something Joshua was good at and was glad to be able to teach Sydney.

They had the cutlass (machete) which they carried with them whenever they were out in the fields, so Joshua asked Sydney to cut what he considered a perfect limb from the juniper tree. He then instructed him to cut the branch into six pieces which he considered appropriate lengths to be shaped into tops.

"We can shape these at home," he said.

"Okay."

"The important thing for making good tops is hardwood, which we now have. We need craftsmanship, which I have and which you will soon acquire. We also need strong twine and good nails which we can get from Tang's shop."

"How are we going to pay for them?"

"The twine is a penny a yard," said JJ. "For one top we need a little less than a yard, and we can use the same length of twine with several tops."

"We still need the pennies to pay for the twine."

"I have twenty cents."

"Where did you get that much money?"

"I saved it."

"Then why would you want to spend it now?"

"How else are we going to get the twine and the nails?"

Sydney had no answer for Joshua's question. Instead he said, "I am getting hungry."

"Can you climb a coconut tree?"

"No. What that has to do with my hunger?""

Joshua started laughing, and Sydney asked, "What is so funny?"

"You can't climb a coconut tree. If you were able to, we could get some jelly (young coconut kernel)"

"I see nothing funny about that."

"It is believed that every man born in Mayaro can swim and climb a coconut tree."

"Can they do both at the same time?"

"No! Stupid."

"You didn't just call me stupid when you are the one talking foolishness."

"I have had enough of you for one day. You and Kendal always think that you are better that everyone else."

"Who or where is that coming from?"

"It is coming from me, where else?"

Sydney understood Joshua's frustration and decided not to pursue that line of discussion any further. He suggested that they take a break and get back to making the tops later that day. He genuinely wished to acquire the craftsmanship Joshua spoke about and didn't want to be at odds with his closest friend, who was also his second cousin.

Kendal meanwhile, was well on his way to work. It was his first weekend on the job as a new police officer in Matura. As the junior officer, he was required to work that weekend. Nevertheless, he hoped to be able to leave early to visit with Henrietta. He was aware that she was to be discharged from the hospital that Saturday afternoon, so he was hoping to get back to Mayaro before three o'clock, the time when most patients were allowed to leave. His goal was to spend as much time with her as possible. Several times he thought of proposing to her but every time that thought came to mind, the words of the taxi driver who took him to Sangre Grande on his first day of duty came rushing back. *She is a nice guul but take your time. Doh rush in to anything, man.*

Kendal was amazed at the impact that conversation with the cab driver had on him. Others had tried to caution him about Henrietta's behavior but none was as persuasive. Perhaps it was because no one was as direct. He recalled the words of a family friend; *that Henrietta is as pretty as a coral snake*, the man once said to his mother, Dorothy. Suddenly, several hints from other people of her unsavory behavior came rushing to his thoughts. On one occasion, in reference to her, a prominent senior citizen once warned Kendal that; *every day bucket ah go ah well, one day bucket bottom go stick down deh*. He didn't understand the proverb then, but as he reflected on it, the meaning became clear. He immediately dismissed it. *Everyone deserves a second chance,* he thought. *I love her and will give her nothing less.*

On several occasions Kendal O'Connor had mentioned to his mother some of the disparaging remarks people made to him about Henrietta. Every time he did, she dismissed them as *people's malicious intentions.* She loved Henrietta and refused to listen to or accept any of it. She had a kind of unconditional love for her. She wanted more than anything else to have her as a member of her own family one day.

As soon as he arrived at the Matura Police Station, Kendal approached the senior officer in charge of the precinct, Sergeant Peter Cove, and asked whether he could be allowed to leave early.

"How early is early, Officer O'Connor?"

"Twelve o'clock, sir."

"Huh!" The sergeant murmured. He then looked at his watch and said, "You would have been here for only five hours by then." He paused as if in deep thought.

What the hell is he thinking? Kendal wondered, *It is either I can leave or I can't. It is not rocket science.*

Such a request had never been made by any officer before, so the sergeant was concerned, and rightfully so, as to the precedent he would have been setting had he allowed the most junior officer such a privilege. He wanted to find a way out of it, so after careful consideration, he said loudly for all to hear, "I have an assignment for you, Officer O'Connor."

"Yes sir?" Kendal said in a querying tone. *Why would you want to give me an assignment when I am asking to leave?* He wondered.

"Oh! Don't worry. It will only take a couple of hours," said Sergeant Cove. "I want you to follow up on an inquiry at the Sangre Grande Police Station for me.

"I shall do my best, sir."

"I know you will O'Connor. I know you will."

"Thank you, sir."

"Give me some time to get it ready."

Well, how much time do you need? Kendal wondered. He was becoming impatient but he tried not to let it show. It was as if Sergeant Cove read his mind when he said, "I should have it for you in an hour or two. By the time you are through, it should be the end of your tour of duty for today."

You couldn't possibly be serious. I just asked you whether I can leave at twelve o'clock, and you want to send me on an assignment that could take the rest of the day. Are you nuts? Kendal's thoughts were racing but he said only, "Thank you, sir." The sergeant smiled and walked away.

"He is a wicked old man," an officer sitting at the front desk said when Sergeant Cove left the room. He looked directly at Kendal as if to solicit a response, but Kendal said nothing. Instead, he went on to check the day's schedule and saw that he, along with one of the more senior officers were to be on routine patrol from 8:00 to 11:00 a.m. For that, they were allowed to use one of two squad cars.

Police patrol in rural Matura in the 1950's was nothing short of one of life's little pleasures for those officers, five men who were fortunate enough to be stationed there. Kendal, as the junior officer was supposed to be the driver of the all terrain police vehicle. He, however, was not a licensed chauffeur. In fact, he didn't know how to drive. His partner for the day, Officer Wilfred Kanga enjoyed driving and was up to the task.

"We will make our first stop at the beach," he said.

"Did you say the beach?" Kendal questioned.

"Yes. We will go down to the shore and take a look around."

"Is there ever any sign of trouble at the beach?"

"No. We have to patrol, so we must start somewhere."

"I get it."

"This is probably the best assignment you will ever have for however long you stay in the force."

"That is an accolade I reserve for Mayaro."

"You are from Mayaro, aren't you?"

"Yes."

"It's understandable that you would think that way. After you have been here for two weeks, I am sure you will think differently."

"I doubt that."

"Believe me, man. There is never any trouble here. There is not much to do, so on weekends, Fridays and Saturdays especially, some fellas (men) get too drunk and act like fools. Occasionally, we take someone in for being drunk and disorderly. More often than not, it is the same individual. We hold him until he sobers up but he is never charged."

"That is interesting."

"It is indeed."

"Are you from Matura?" Kendal asked.

"My family was from Toco originally but my parents moved to Point Fortin where I was born. Nevertheless, I spent a lot of vacation time in Toco in my youth."

"So you are familiar with this area?"

"Yeah, man."

"I can tell you like it very much."

"You can say that. I can tell you something though, which you will soon experience yourself; people here will look up to you. They will respect you but they will expect respect in return. They may never tell you that but you would sense it."

Officer Kanga was about to give Kendal O'Connor a civic lesson on police and community interaction when they stopped at Tan Sally's house on Church Street. Hers was one of the few remaining houses made of gobar (cow dung), tapia grass, and clay. She was eighty-four and lived alone except for her dog Ruff and two cats. She had lived in that house all of her life. Over the years a few changes were made to the structure but overall, it retained the original appearance, a neat, well kept little cottage perched on a grassy knoll. Her parents lived there before her. She inherited the house but was never married and had no children. Nevertheless, she loved children, all of the children in the neighborhood, and they in turn, loved her. Everyone loved Tan Sally. Officer Kanga was especially fond of her.

When the officers first arrived at Tan Sally's, she was so glad to see them and greeted them so warmly, that Officer Kendal O'Connor thought she was perhaps a relative of his partner. The relationship became clear when she looked at him while still holding on to Officer Kanga and said, "This is my favorite policeman. You are my second best."

Laughter filled the room after Tan Sally's comment. Even Ruff joined the fun. He barked repeatedly while wagging his tail at the officers.

"So what exactly are you doing out here?" asked Tan Sally. "You know we never have any trouble in these parts."

"I know that Tan Sally. Our visit is just routine."

"Routine? I was going to ask you to stay for lunch but that was when I thought you came to visit me, but since your visit is just routine you can go about your business," Tan Sally said. She patted Officer Kanga on his back, looked at Officer O'Connor and said, "I just like to have fun with him." She turned to Kendal and asked, "By the way, what's your name?"

"Officer Kendal O'Connor, madam."

"Did your mama name you Officer, son?"

"No."

"Is your name Kendal?"

"Yes, madam."

"My name is not Madam. It is Sally Williamson. Everybody in this village calls me Tan Sally. Welcome to the Matura community, son."

Tan Sally did not ask Kendal where he was from. That didn't matter to her. Everyone was welcomed to her place. Instead, she said, "Make yourselves comfortable. Lunch will be ready in a few minutes."

"It is not yet eleven o'clock, Tan Sally."

"What is that supposed to mean?"

"It is a little early for lunch."

"Not when you have been up at five, worked in the field, and had breakfast at seven."

"You do have a point," Kendal said. He was able to relate quite well to what Tan Sally had just said. It was exactly the way he grew up.

"So that's settled. You are having lunch."

"Yes." Officer Kanga said after a quick glance at Kendal who nodded his head in agreement.

"I like that."

"What is it that you like, Tan Sally?" Officer Kanga asked.

"Neither of you asked what I was having for lunch. That would have been rude. You know that?"

"Yes, ma'am," Kendal said.

"Tan Sally is what they call me. Sally is my name. It was my niece who first started calling me Tan Tan when she was only two years old. Her older sister who was eight at the time, called me Auntie Sally. Little Katelyn couldn't say auntie, so she said Tan Tan. Today, those girls are thirty-six and forty-two. They both live in the States (USA). I hardly ever hear from them. My only sister, their mother, died about five years ago."

"So you must be very lonely here," Kendal suggested.

"No. I am alone but I am never lonely, not in this village. Someone is always here, son"

Officer Kanga glanced at Kendal as if to ask, *Isn't she feisty for her age?* Instead, it was Tan Sally who asked, "Are you ready to eat, gentlemen?" She did so while smothering the flame in the fireside (a wood-burning type of dirt stove). "Lunch will be ready in ten minutes," she said. Neither Kendal nor Officer Kanga commented so she continued with great delight, "I stewed some turtle meat to go with some cassava from the garden."

The people of Matura, like those of Mayaro, depended largely on fishing, hunting, and agriculture for their livelihood. Closer to the Atlantic shore were the coconut estates, while bananas, cocoa, coffee, and sugarcane were produced further inland as cash crops. Agriculture was the main form of employment. Tan Sally never worked in the fields of the banana or sugarcane plantations, coconut, cocoa, or coffee estates. When she was much younger she worked as a cook and sometimes as a maid in the homes of the French estate owners. In her later years she worked as a nanny for a younger generation of estate owners, the descendants of the French. She was frugal and saved enough money to purchase the land on which her house stood. It was only two acres but it was fertile. She was able, therefore, to produce enough fruits and vegetables for her own consumption and for sale. Consequently, she was self-sufficient and very proud of it.

It was 11:50 a.m. when Tan Sally set the table for three. "Come, help me with this," she said. She did not direct her call for help to anyone of the officers in particular. Kendal got up and joined her in the kitchen. "Take these to the table," she said, as she pointed to a large casserole filled with stewed meat and another serving dish which contained sliced and buttered, well cooked pieces of cassava. She in turn, carried a smaller dish with a spinach salad.

As soon as they sat down, but before anyone could bless the table, there was a knock at the door. That drew everyone's attention. A tall, imposing figure walked in. It was customary in rural villages in Trinidad for people to knock at the door and enter without waiting to be invited in. On that occasion the young man entered smiling. The smile was quickly replaced with a look of concern and he hesitated to move any closer when he saw the two police officers with Tan Sally. "It is okay Brian. These are my friends," she said.

"Bonjour," said the young man as he walked over and kissed Tan Sally on her cheek.

"Meet officer Kanga and Officer O'Connor," she said. The young man extended his hand to each of the officers and said, "It is a pleasure."

"When did you get back from France?" Tan Sally asked.

"I came in yesterday."

"Yesterday, and already you are in Matura?"

"Yes! I had to come and see you today before I get too caught up with other things."

"You have always been so sweet, Brian" said Tan Sally. She then looked at the officers and said, "I used to be his nanny."

"Tan Sally was more than a nanny to me. She was more like my mammy (mother). Mammee, like we say in France, was always at home but she paid me no attention."

Tan Sally did not comment on what the young man said. Instead she asked, "Have you eaten as yet, Brian?"

"No, Tan Sally. I left Port-of-Spain and came directly here."

"Come in, sit down and I will get you a plate."

"It is okay, Tan Sally. I can help myself"

"You are at home. Go ahead," she said.

The young man went to the kitchen to get himself a plate and some cutlery. Officer Kanga looked at Kendal. *This is what this community is like*, he thought but said instead, "Isn't that nice. Tan Sally makes everyone feel so at home."

"Well, you are all my children."

"You are one of the nicest persons I have met in a long time, Tan Sally," Kendal said.

"Thank you, Kendal."

As Brian joined them at the table, Tan Sally said a short prayer before they ate. While eating they conversed about everything; politics, sports, law and crime, the community, love, marriage and sex. Kendal was truly impressed by Tan Sally's keen acumen and her ability to remember so many things at the age of 84. Her recollections of growing up in Matura were the most fascinating to him, perhaps because of their close parallel to stories he heard from seniors while growing up in Mayaro.

When they were finished eating, Tan Sally brought in some slices of watermelon. Kendal and Brian helped themselves but Officer Kanga did not take any of it.

"What is the matter, Kanga? Isn't that strong enough for you?" Officer Kanga smiled, a smile that Tan Sally recognized and understood. She walked to a doorway, pulled back a curtain where there was no door, and entered her bedroom. Minutes later she emerged with a clear rum bottle filled with a liquid that was not the original contents. She handed it to Officer Kanga who got up and took a glass from a sideboard in the room where they had just eaten.

"Would you like some?" he asked Kendal.

"What is it?"

"Sugarcane juice," said Officer Kanga. "Only thing is that the sugar has been removed."

"That's right," said Brian. "What's left is just juice. Here we call it mountain dew. I think you call babash in Moruga."

"Moruga? I have never been there."

"That accent sounds like someone I know from Moruga."

"I am from Mayaro," Kendal said proudly.

"Mayaro, Moruga, Matura, what's the difference?'

"The spelling is different. Apart from that they are all Amerindian names," Officer Kanga said after he gulped down a glass of the clear stuff. "Are you sure you don't want some?" he asked.

"I am sure," Kendal said.

"Let me try a little," said Brian. "I haven't had that good stuff in years." Officer Kanga handed the bottle to Brian. At the same time Tan Sally asked Kendal if he would like something softer.

Water maybe, he thought but he said, "I am good, Tan Sally."

"I didn't ask you that. I know that you are good. It is so obvious." Having said that, she left the room and in two minutes she was back with another clear bottle filled with liquid. Only that time the liquid was straw-colored. She handed it to Kendal with a clean glass. He poured some of the liquid into the glass and tasted it. "This is good," he said.

"Do you like it?"

"Yes."

"It is a cashew wine, and it is well cured now."

"When did you make this, Tan Sally?"

"It was 1953. June, as I remember it, so it is well cured."

Kendal poured some more of the wine into his glass. Soon after that he glanced at his watch and realized that it was 1:00 p.m..

"Don't be too concerned about the time, son. When you are ready to leave I will give you a bottle to take with you. In the meantime, just enjoy the afternoon."

"Thank you," Kendal said but his thoughts were on Henrietta.

He realized that he and Officer Kanga were due back at the station by then but Officer Kanga was showing no eagerness to leave. He was concerned that Sergeant Peter Cove may have had the letter ready for him to take to the Sangre Grande Police Station, and he might be late getting back to the Matura Police Station. From what he was observing, Officer Kanga had no desire or intention of getting back quickly. Their entire tour of duty that morning was spent at Tan Sally's house. *No wonder she is never lonely*, Kendal thought. They never got to the beach area as they had originally planned.

Kendal was perplexed by what was taking place at Tan Sally's. He considered it a violation of the law, as it was essentially. Bush rum; mountain dew, or babash as it was known in different areas, was illegal in Trinidad and Tobago. As an officer of law enforcement, Kendal felt very uncomfortable in the situation. To all others present it seemed innocent and harmless to indulge in binge drinking of a little bootleg rum. To Kendal it tore at the very essence of his upbringing. His mother, Dorothy, always insisted that he should know right from wrong and choose accordingly. *If it is wrong, don't do it*, she said to him often.

Kendal and Officer Kanga left Church Street with Tan Sally's blessing and returned to the Matura Police Station. They signed in as they were required to do and reported that nothing unusual had occurred on their beat. Truly, nothing unusual could have happened. They were never really on the beat. That bothered

Kendal. That, however, was exactly what Officer Kanga loved about working in Matura. Kendal sat down wondering what he should do next when Sergeant Cove walked in and handed him an envelope. "You should be on your way, Officer O'Connor."

"Thank you, sir."

"Not so fast Officer. I will ask the officers going out on the beat now to drop you at the Mayaro taxi stand in Sangre Grande." Kendal was so thankful. He was at a loss for words. *Why would they drop me at the taxi stand instead of the Sangre Grande Police Station?* He wondered but said nothing.

"That's okay, son. Read that note before you get to the Sangre Grande Police Station."

"Thanks again, sir"

As soon as they left Matura, Kendal asked the other officers to drop him off at the police station in Sangre Grande. They agreed to do so. In fact, that was the instruction they received from Sergeant Cove before leaving Matura.

NINE

The note read; enjoy the rest of your weekend. Kendal had an opportunity to look at it when he had been dropped off at the Sangre Grande Police Station by his colleagues. He realized then that Sergeant Cove never intended for him to conduct an inquiry about anything. The note was written in an effort to deflect the attention of other officers from any semblance of favoritism they may have envisioned had the sergeant allowed him to leave work early.

Kendal was delighted. He did not attempt to enter the Sangre Grande Police Station. Instead, he stood at the entrance momentarily to be sure that the police cruiser that brought him there had left. He then walked back to the Mayaro taxi stand to get a cab that would take him home. He didn't have to wait long. In fact, he didn't have to wait at all. There was a Mayaro taxi at the stand with one passenger less than a full complement.

"Mayaro! Mayaro by one!" The driver was shouting to indicate that he needed one more passenger so he could leave. That was until he spotted Kendal. "Mayaro. Are you going, Officer?" he asked.

"Yes," said Kendal. "Are you leaving right away?" It was 2:00 p.m. and he was anxious to be on his way.

"Yeah, man. Let's go now,"

Kendal entered the car and sat in the right rear passenger seat behind the driver. Before he could say good afternoon, everyone in the vehicle greeted him. One person, a young woman sitting in the front seat looked back and said, "Ah didn't know you working all the way down here."

"Actually, I am not stationed in Sangre Grande. I am in Matura."

"Oui, Papa!" Another passenger exclaimed.

"It is not that good," said Kendal. "Then again, it is not bad at all."

Without asking any questions the driver turned on the car radio loudly. Calypso music came blaring over the airwaves. That ended any attempt at conversation but no one complained. It was customary for drivers to play loud music, especially when they had a full complement of passengers, all going to the same final destination. Kendal didn't mind either. He leaned back, closed his eyes and focused his thoughts on Henrietta. As the car sped along the Manzanilla/Mayaro Road with the windows rolled down, a cool, gentle breeze from over the ocean pervaded the interior of the vehicle. Kendal, like some of the other passengers was lulled to sleep. Luckily, the Atlantic sea breeze did not have the same effect on the driver. He was a dedicated professional who managed to focus his attention on the task of getting people to their destination safely.

By 2:30 p.m. the driver pulled the taxi up to the curb and parked on the taxi stand at Peter Hill Road and the Naparima Mayaro Road. Although it was a safe and relatively gentle maneuver, the sleeping passengers were jolted and awakened. Kendal opened his eyes, looked out the window and said, "Wow! We are here already." Without waiting for an answer or even expecting one he stepped out of the vehicle, stretched his arms and tucked his grey uniform shirt neatly into his trousers, paid the driver, then walked over to the hospital. He greeted the receptionist and asked whether Henrietta had already been discharged.

"Ah think so, you know, but she is still in there."

"Thanks," he said as he walked away.

He walked down the hallway to the room where Henrietta was supposed to be but she was not there. He stood at the door looking in, and noticed that the bed was unmade and some of her personal belongings were lying around the room.

"She is in the shower," said one of the aides. "She is leaving at three o'clock."

"Thank you," Kendal said as he turned to walked away.

"You are not going to leave her, are you?"

"No, not at all. I am going to sit in the waiting room."

"No! No. We can't have you do that. Come with me, wait in the office."

Kendal followed the aide who seated him in the nurses' office and left. At first he felt a bit uncomfortable but he soon settled down and waited. After he was there for about fifteen minutes, the aide returned with Henrietta at her side. They were both beaming with joy. As if it were infectious, Kendal too was smiling as he stepped forward and embraced Henrietta. I will leave you two alone," the nurses' aide said.

"Thanks," said Kendal. "We would be leaving shortly."

"Suit yourself."

Kendal and Henrietta walked out of the nurses' office and down the hallway toward the entrance. She was required to sign a release at the receptionist's desk, which she did. Just as they were contemplating what their next move should be, Mrs. Riggs and her sister-in-law showed up. They timed their arrival to coincide with Henrietta's discharge from the hospital.

"You look disappointed that we came, Kendal," Mrs. Riggs remarked.

"I didn't think it showed."

"It did, son. It certainly did." Laughter erupted in the hallway. They were like one happy family. Henrietta had one arm wrapped around Kendal's waist and the other over her mother's shoulder. Kendal leaned forward, looked over at Mrs. Riggs and said, "Mom told me to ask you if Etta could spend the weekend with us."

"Of course she can," said Mrs. Riggs. "You know that, Kendal. Henrietta knows that too. All she had to do was let me know that she would be at your mother's." After her mother spoke, Henrietta said, "I would need some extra clothes."

"Come home and get what you need." Henrietta did not respond directly to what her mother said. She looked at Kendal as if to ask, *how are we getting to Lagon Doux and back?*

"Let's go out and get transportation," he suggested.

"Where are we going first?" she asked.

"Home," he said.

"Do you mean yours or mine?"

"First we will go to Lagon Doux and get the clothes you need. Then we will travel back to Mafeking."

"Okay."

"If that is the plan, shouldn't we be out there getting a taxi?" Mrs. Riggs asked.

"I will go out and arrange a ride," Kendal said. "You can wait right here." He left them standing at the foot of the stairs. Within minutes he was back. "Ragoonath has agreed to take us to Lagon Doux and bring us back," he said.

"Are you sure you want to do that?" Henrietta asked.

"Isn't that what we agreed to?"

"Yes, but Ragoonath runs PH (a private car used illegally as a taxi) and you are now a policeman."

"I see your point but the car he is driving today is his father's. It is a legitimate taxi."

"How much is he asking for that service?"

"He wants ten dollars."

"That's a lot!"

"He is going to take us to Lagon Doux, wait for you to change, get extra clothes or whatever, then he would take us to Mafeking." said Kendal. "I think it is reasonable." *Furthermore, I am paying for it*, he thought, but he said nothing more.

"Have it your way," Henrietta said. *Rudolf would not have charged me for that*, she thought. That was the first time Rudolf Vargas' name came to her mind in at least forty-eight hours.

"That wasn't my objective," Kendal said. "I just didn't want to haggle with the man about the fare."

"That is your problem. You know that. You give in and give up too easily."

"That is your opinion."

"Not mine alone."

"What is the matter with you two? Are you having a lovers' quarrel?" Henrietta's aunt asked. It was the first time she had spoken that evening.

"I am not quarrelling. It is just that he lets people take advantage of him all the time."

"Who takes more advantage of him than you?"

Henrietta was annoyed by what her aunt asked. She clammed up immediately rather that respond and risk a really serious disturbance. Her aunt had always been frank. She had a habit of saying exactly what was on her mind without bias or concern for those who might be angered or hurt by it. She liked Kendal. She also knew of Henrietta's behavior and disapproved of it. So what she said was no slip of the tongue. That caused a temporary silence among members of the group. They walked to Ragoonath's taxi without speaking to one another. No one addressed the group as a whole either.

They entered the vehicle as they arrived; quietly. Kendal, Henrietta, and her mother sat in the rear, while her aunt occupied the bucket seat at the front. Henrietta leaned her head on Kendal's left shoulder and he held her right hand, a gesture that indicated what they may have preferred to say but didn't, *we have no quarrel with each other right now.*

It was a smooth, quiet, and otherwise uneventful ride to Lagon Doux. When the driver pulled up at the Riggs family home, Kendal elected to go in with the rest of the group. At first he thought of staying in the cab with the driver while Henrietta got whatever it was she went home to get, but he quickly ruled against that. His concern was that he might have been engaged in conversation, the nature of which may have caused him to reveal things he preferred to keep to himself, or he might have learnt of things he would have preferred not to know. He felt that there had been enough meddling in his and Henrietta's affairs.

It wasn't long before they emerged from the house. Kendal sat in the front with the driver and Henrietta occupied the back seat. That was a customary, comfortable, and accepted seating arrangement by which a couple would travel. It still is in Mayaro today. The primary reason was and still is, people's familiarity with one another. Kendal, Henrietta, and Ragoonath for example, knew one another quite well.

Once they were seated, Ragoonath made a u-turn and headed back to Pierre Ville. Henrietta was all smiles in the back seat. She was happy about the reunion with her childhood sweetheart, Kendal. He too was glad that they were back together. Athough, he was struggling with some issues of trust, primarily because he had not gotten an apology from her after his encounter with her in the dark, in a hammock, under her parents' house with Kerish. All of the gossip and rumors of her promiscuous behavior also had its impact on him. Nevertheless, he had a new perspective on their relationship. *We are putting all of the negatives behind us and making a new start*, he thought.

He assumed that Henrietta had the same view that he did of their relationship - a new beginning with a bright and promising future. He somehow neglected to ask her whether those were indeed her thinking. She really had no future plans, not for herself, not for him, nor for them as a couple. She focused only on the present. *I will enjoy the moment and let the chips fall where they may*, she thought. To some that may have seemed a regressive way of thinking. It was something she learnt from her mother who never worried about anything that didn't yet take place, and consequently, never suffered from any of the health problems that plagued many of her compatriots of the same median age. Henrietta approached life with the same, when it happens I will deal with it kind of attitude.

Three hours after Kendal arrived in Mayaro from Matura, he and Henrietta were at his mother's place in Mafeking. Dorothy

O'Connor was not expecting to see Henrietta but was overjoyed that she showed up with Kendal. She had prepared dinner as she had always done even before Kendal started working in Matura. On that day she was concerned that she might have been late but Kendal's delay in getting home was to her advantage. The meal was still on the two-burner kerosene stove where Dorothy left it to be kept warm. She had never been able to cook for just two and on that occasion she was glad there was enough for dinner for three, or more had that been necessary.

What Dorothy was experiencing was like a dream come true. She didn't really know how to explain it, and wanted very much to share the experience with someone other than the two people in her presence at the time. The first person who came to mind was Philbertha. *Bertha will understand how I feel. She is probably the only one who will understand*, she thought, and decided right then that after dinner she would go over to Philbertha's to relax and converse for a little while. Without hesitation, she moved to set the table for three and prepare a salad. She always insisted on having a leafy green vegetable with every meal other than breakfast. That occasion was no different. The only reason the salad was not ready to be served, was that she wanted it freshly made just before serving. Some people called her methodical and regimented. Whatever they thought of her, she was different from Henrietta's mother. She was quite the opposite indeed.

"Your kitchen smells so good, Ms. Dorothy."

"Well, thank you, Henrietta."

Kendal placed his arm around Dorothy and said, "My mother can cook, girl."

So can I, my mother, and many other women in Mayaro, Henrietta thought but said simply, "I know."

"Sit down you two. Let's eat," Dorothy said.

With the exception of the rice dish, the protein (fish), and a few condiments that added flavor to the food, everything else Dorothy served came from her backyard garden. Like most people in Mafeking, she owned the house in which they lived. She inherited it from her mother who inherited it from her parents. The kitchen garden as it was called, provided much of the family's staples since her grandparents cultivated it. The current cultivation was done by Dorothy herself. She grew ginger, cassava, sweet potatoes, chives, tomatoes, yams, corn, pigeon peas, and a variety of beans.

While Kendal was in high school, Dorothy did most of the work in the garden and around the house herself so as not to infringe on his study time. She requested only that he fetched water and irrigated the plots before he went to school. He was cooperative, paid close attention to the only chore he really had, and was diligent and conscientious about his studies. Consequently, he performed well in school and attained seven passes at the GCE (General certificate of education) examination, an examination for high school seniors that was set by either Cambridge or London University at the time.

Dorothy would have preferred her son to seek employment with the Department of Education as a school teacher but he elected to become a police officer. His reason was primarily economic. He wanted desperately to assist his mother financially and build a financial base for his future with Henrietta. School teachers earned considerably less than police officers with comparable qualifications, and the possibility of promotion was much greater at an earlier age with much less service for police officers. Although, it was not Kendal's intention to make a career of law enforcement, he felt it was an ideal starting point.

That Saturday evening the mood at the O'Connor's was upbeat. Henrietta was happy to be there and happier still that Kendal was no longer upset with her. Their disagreement was behind them despite the fact that she never apologized. She did not consider her relationship with Kerish to be anything more than neighborly friendship to which she felt entitled. She believed that her tryst with Rudolf Vargas was a casual encounter that she regretted but had no intention of making it known to Kendal. *What he doesn't know wouldn't hurt him*, she thought. She did not consider the fact that he was a very well liked individual and that sooner than later someone was going to let him know. The fact that the waitress who served her and Mr. Vargas at The Beach Front Hotel was a friend of Kendal escaped her temporarily. Before either she or Kendal had a chance to entertain any negative thoughts, Dorothy called out, "Come on. Let's eat."

"Good idea, Mom. I am famished."

"I am too. For the last twenty-four hours I have not been able to eat."

"Was your stomach bothering you that much?" Dorothy asked.

"No. I just couldn't stand that tasteless hospital food."

"You are such a stickler for taste," Kendal said.

"I know. I would apologize but it is really your fault."

"How did you figure that to be my fault?"

"Whenever we went out, who always complained? *The food is too salty. The food is too greasy. There is not enough salt.* I never once complained"

"I learnt that from you though."

"No, you didn't. Don't you try to pin that one on me now."

"It is so nice to see you having fun," said Dorothy. "You have always been so good together."

"Thanks, Ms. Dorothy. I must say, this food is absolutely delicious."

"Ingratiating yourself to my mother will not gain you any kudos, girl."

"What I say is the truth. You cannot say otherwise."

"Are you daring me?"

"I am," Henrietta said smiling.

"Okay, Kendal. Let's hear it."

"The food is good, Mom. Your cooking is always good."

"The way you say that is not very convincing or flattering," Dorothy said.

"It is true though. You know that, Mom."

"Anyway, perhaps I mentioned this before. Forgive me if I did. I am going over to Philbertha's in a little while."

"You didn't mention it, Mom. That's okay though. We all have those moments."

"What moments?"

"The senior ones."

"Shut your mouth!" She said, as she faked a punch, flaring her fisted right hand in the air toward Kendal. He pretended to parry the blow and laughter erupted in the kitchen. When it was quiet again, Kendal asked, on a more serious note, "When will you be back, Mom?"

"I don't know. If you have to go out, just go. Leave the door unlocked though."

"We are not going anywhere."

"Okay then. I will see you later," said Dorothy. She then turned to Henrietta and said, "If there is anything you need, just help yourself."

"Thanks, Ms. Dorothy."

"You are welcome, dear," Dorothy said and left.

Kendal got up from where he sat in the couch with Henrietta and pulled the front door in as his mother walked away. He was still in uniform and Henrietta suggested it was time for him to change. He agreed and left the room. He quickly returned wrapped in a robe with a towel on his shoulder and a toothbrush in his hand. He looked at Henrietta and smiled. She winked at him with an even broader smile on her face as he proceeded to the shower. Minutes later she heard the water pouring and was tempted to strip and join him but decided against it.

When he emerged from the shower, he looked directly at her but raced into his bedroom as if he witnessed an apparition. It was all in jest and she was pleased to see him lighten up a bit. Minutes later he came to the door with pajamas on and asked, "Are you going to join me or just sit there by your lonesome?" She did not respond verbally but got up and moved hesitantly toward him. She had never before entered his bedroom and was unsure whether she should then. On previous occasions when she visited the O'Connor's, she slept on a futon in Dorothy's room.

Kendal walked away from the bedroom door expecting that she would be right behind him. As he sat on the bed and looked around, he was surprised to see that she was still standing at the door and smiling. "Why are you still standing there?" he asked. "There is no boogeyman in here."

"I don't know that. Who are you?" she asked as she walked in and stood in front of him. He took her arm and with just a persuasive pull he was able to help her guide her graceful body onto the bed next to him. He wrapped his arm around her as she sat down uneasily and asked, "What will your mother think if she comes home and finds us in here?"

"I don't know. I never really thought about it," said Kendal. "You came to spend the weekend, or what's left of it with me. Didn't you?"

"I did. I have done so previously. Haven't I?"

"You have."

"And I always slept in your mother's room. Haven't I?"

"You have. So what exactly is your point?"

"My point is that she may not approve of me sleeping in here with you."

"Who said anything about sleeping?" Kendal asked, but before Henrietta could answer, he kissed her tenderly and she reciprocated. They kissed again as if to ascertain that it was genuine and acceptable to both. Soon they found themselves undressing each other until neither was wearing anything at all.

It was 1:00 a.m. when Dorothy arrived home. The futon in her room was still in its couch-like form as she looked around her bedroom. *Henrietta must have left*, she thought. *That couldn't be though, because I saw her purse in the living room.* Dorothy stepped back into the living room to ascertain that Henrietta's purse was there. It was right where she thought she saw it. *Perhaps they went out*, she thought. There was not a sound coming from Kendal's room. Neither he nor Henrietta snored but Dorothy stopped short of looking into the room. Instead, she changed her clothes and quietly got into bed. She lay on her back looking at the ceiling and thanking God for all the blessings she had received and enjoyed. Before long she too was fast asleep.

Sydney and Joshua awoke early to complete their morning chores in time to join *the river lime*. Sydney was very concerned about Joshua's strong desire to join the *lime*, although Joshua had repeatedly assured him that he would only go there to get some math instruction from Arjune and to practice his reading skills while the others frolicked in the warm pristine river water.

The responsibility for the chores of both boys rested squarely on Sydney because Joshua's arm was still in a sling. Although he was willing, he couldn't do much. Sydney recognized that and agreed to help only after Joshua assured him that he would not attempt to swim that morning. First, they took out their goats and sheep. Then they fetched water and watered the plants in their respective backyards. Joshua was supportive but it was Sydney who did all of the work. In spite of that, the chores were completed on time and the boys went home for breakfast.

Dorothy too was up early as usual. She went out to the chicken coop and collected some eggs for breakfast. She had some salted cod fish soaking overnight and set out to knead flour for a coconut bake (a flat bread made with grated coconut as one of the main ingredients). Bake and salted fish with scrambled eggs were on the menu for breakfast. She wanted her son, and as far as she was concerned, her future daughter-in-law to have a hearty, healthy breakfast. She wasn't out to impress Henrietta. She wasn't in a position to do so even if she wanted to.

Once the dough was kneaded to perfection (a smooth uniform mass), she covered it to allow it to rest and rise. She then prepared the codfish for the buljol (a preparation of salted and preserved cod fish with tomatoes, onions, peppers, and other condiments). When that was done, she went out, fetched water and irrigated her garden herself. After that, she returned to the kitchen, flattened the dough with a rolling pin and perforated it with a table fork to allow for easy penetration of heat. She placed the flattened dough in a pot, took it to an outdoor shed and placed it on a fireside (a wood-burning clay stove) with moderate fire under the pot and on a flat iron plate at the top of it. While the bake was cooking she set the table in the dining room for three, scrambled four eggs and waited for Kendal and Henrietta.

By 9:00 a.m. both were awake but neither attempted to get out of bed, either because they were too tired, just wanted to cuddle each other, or too afraid of how Dorothy might have reacted to them sleeping together at her place. Both knew that unlike Mrs. Riggs, Henrietta's mother, Dorothy did not encourage or tolerated the sort of behavior they exhibited.

"What shall we do?" Henrietta asked.

"Face the music, I guess."

"Are you kidding me?"

"No. We committed the crime. Now we must face the penalty," Kendal punned with a broad smile.

"This is not funny at all, Kendal."

"Hey! I never said it was funny. All I am saying is that we are guilty, so we might as well fess up."

"Do you expect your mother to ask us what we did?"

"No."

"So why do we have to confess?"

"I don't know. Perhaps our consciences are dictating that we misbehaved."

"Children misbehave. We are consenting adults."

"That's my point exactly. As such we should be independent of our parents."

"What do our parents have to do with it?"

"Nothing if it does not happen at their place."

"Why don't you just say what you want to say, Kendal?"

"I think I am making myself quite clear."

"Not to me."

"You will get it eventually. In the meantime, we do have to go out there and face her."

"You go first."

"Why?"

"It's funny you would ask that. Are you forgetting that she is your mother?"

"Oh! Yeah. You are right," he said. However, his true thoughts were, *your mother would not have cared. She didn't seem to care what you and Kerish were doing in that hammock the other night.*

After breakfast Sydney and Joshua left home for *the river lime.* They decided on the *lime* at the spring bridge that Sunday morning. Although the gathering at the saw-mill was much closer to where they lived, their preference was always the one at the spring bridge. Sydney informed his mother, Philbertha, of his desire to go there and she approved. Joshua on the contrary, simply left home. He knew that neither his mother, Velma, nor his grandmother, Umilta, would have objected or even cared. That Sunday morning the gathering was large. At least fifteen young men were there. Notably absent at the very beginning of the *lime* was Kendal. No one expressed any concern though. It was as if they expected him to be absent.

"Good morning, Mom," Kendal said timidly that morning.

"Good morning, my dear," said Dorothy. "You seem a bit under the weather this morning."

"Not really."

"Then that's good. You had me fooled there for a minute."

"Sorry about that," Kendal said on a brighter note. He was happy that his mother was not upset.

"Excuse me," she said. "I almost forget that I have a bake on the fire."

"You mean fire on a bake," said Kendal. "I will check on it for you."

"Whatever, Thank you. Before you go though, you should wake up Henrietta."

"Okay," he said and left the kitchen. He walked across the living room, stuck his head through his bedroom door and said, "The coast is clear."

"Does that mean she is not upset?"

"Not at all."

"Not at all meaning, she is not upset. Or not at all meaning, she is quite upset."

"She is not at all upset."

"Thank goodness!"

"You can come out now."

"I will. Give me a few minutes."

"You've got it." Kendal said. He returned to the kitchen, washed and dried his hands, took a plate, a kitchen towel and a table fork, and went out to the shed. The bake was ready, so he took it in, placed it on a cutting board that was on the dining table and sliced it up. His mother brought in hot beverages (tea and coffee), together with the cod fish buljol and the scrambled eggs. Shortly after that Henrietta joined them at the table.

"Good morning, Ms. Dorothy," she said.

"Good morning, my dear. Did you sleep well?"

"Very well, thank you."

They were conversing amicably as a family unit that morning while having breakfast. However, during the course of the conversation, Kendal mentioned *the river lime* and Dorothy bristled. "Any thought you may have of going there is out of the question, ah telling you one time," she said.

Kendal knew right away that his mother was angry. It was the only time she ever spoke with a typical Mayaro/Trinidadian lilt. Henrietta had never heard Dorothy speak that way. So she too was well aware of the anger and or frustration Dorothy was expressing. Kendal, however, moved quickly to alleviate his mother's fears by saying, "Mom, I have no intention of going to *the river lime* this morning. If I do go, it would be to let Etta experience what goes on there."

"Why would you want to put Henrietta in that situation when you know that there are never any females there?"

"It was only a thought, Mom. I never intended to act on it."

"Then why think of it? Put your energy into more positive thinking."

"There is nothing negative about *the river lime*, Mom."

"Are you forgetting the trauma I experienced last weekend when you almost drowned?"

"Oh, my God!" Henrietta exclaimed and immediately covered her mouth with her right hand.

"I could never forget that, Mom. Again, I am sorry," said Kendal. He then tried to reassure Henrietta by patting her on the back and saying, "It is okay, dear. I suffered a cramp while swimming last Sunday and was pulled out of the water by Arjune and Dolphin."

"So how is it that I am only hearing about it now?"

"I intended to tell you last Tuesday but you seemed so distant."

"That is just your excuse."

Joshua didn't look for an excuse to avoid doing his chores or going to the river. He didn't need one. His arm was seriously hurt, so he could simply have said, *I can't do any of it*. He didn't. Sydney helped him and together they accomplished what had to be done in reasonably good time. The cooperation of the two cousins was just wonderful.

Sydney had prepared a series of reading assignment, a sort of picture book which he called, *Reading for Fun*. He collected numerous pictures and pasted them in a copy book (note book). Under each picture was a caption explaining exactly what the picture was or what it expressed. The first twenty were of simple illustrations with one word captions. The next twenty were combinations of the first together with new ones. For those the captions were phrases. The next twenty were more complex pictures and were explained by captions of complete sentences or short paragraphs.

Sydney did not take the picture book to *the river lime* that Sunday morning. He was concerned that Joshua might be embarrassed by the simplicity of the lessons if he tried implementing them in the presence of others. While he was determined to help his cousin to achieve his goal of being able to read as well as anyone else, he did not want to cause him any emotional scars in the process. He decided, therefore, to leave the book at home so he could help Joshua when they returned from the gathering.

The young men gathered under the bridge at the base of the tower on the Pierre Ville side of the river. There was considerable yammering among them. Nothing in particular or of substance was being discussed. Then two more youngsters entered. They were well known to the group. Suddenly the noisy chatter ceased and one of the youths who was there earlier referred to the new comers as the sluggish and the tardy. One of them quickly responded. He said, "Look who is talking, Mr. bone-head himself." That served as a signal for others to join in the fatigue (friendly teasing) which was becoming somewhat of a ritual there.

Arjune knew that fatigue, or pekong as it was sometimes called, could become annoying and escalate into violence. Although it had never happened there, he decided to prevent it from ever happening. He put down his newspaper and jumped into the water. That was a signal for them to end the foolishness. Others immediately followed. Soon everyone there, with the exception of Joshua, was in the river. Some were swimming freestyle, some were doing the butterfly, others the back stroke, and there were others who did nothing in particular.

Joshua took the newspaper Arjune discarded. He leaned against the pillars of the bridge tower and practiced reading the best way he knew how, while the other boys swam. He was making progress and that made him proud. Joshua's involvement with the newspaper did not escape Sydney who frequently got out of the water to check on him and render any needed assistant and words of encouragement. "You are doing well. Keep it up," he said before jumping back into the water for the third time that morning.

As usual, Arjune came out of the water early and sat on the deck of the oil company's ferry. Two novices were swimming from the ferry to the river bank and back again. Cognizant of what happened to Kendal the previous   Sunday, Arjune was on the qui vive. He wanted more than anything else for *the river lime* to remain a safe activity for youngsters to be involved in. A few minutes after he came out of the water, Dolphin joined him on the deck of the ferry. Because of what happened to Kendal O'Connor, they became recognized as the unofficial life guards.

The ferry was moored on the Mafeking side of the river. Arjune and Dolphin sat on the deck facing the Pierre Ville bank with their legs in the water. They were observing the swimmers while conversing casually. Suddenly there was a shrill scream coming from among five swimmers to their left. They looked anxiously to see if anyone was in trouble. What they saw was all of the swimmers rushing to get out of the water. Their first thought was that a caiman or alligator may be on the prowl. They were wrong, and that became known when one of the swimmers shouted, "It's a manatee! It's a manatee!" Both Arjune and Dolphin looked in the direction of the swimmers from where the screams originated. They saw the animal and Arjune shouted, "It's harmless fellas (guys)! It's harmless!

Whenever Arjune spoke his voice had a calming effect on the other young men. On that occasion, however, his influence wasn't that great. No one attempted to get back into the water. Arjune and Dolphin jumped back in to reassure the group that it was safe to do so but there were no takers. The appearance of the manatee essentially ended *the river lime* that Sunday morning.

TEN

Dorothy was extremely happy after breakfast and it showed. She had always been able to keep her emotions in check but that was not the case on Sunday, May 13, 1956. She openly expressed her joy. The joy of knowing that her son, her only child whom, she as a single parent raised, had finally achieved something special. He completed one week as a Trinidad and Tobago police officer. Sunday marked the beginning of another week with a different turn in the rest of their lives. She could finally relax the discipline, the advice, the supervision, and take a new direction toward her own self-worth. *Oh what a happy feeling*, she thought.

"You are in a really good mood this morning, Ms. Dorothy," Henrietta said.

"I didn't think it showed but yes, I am. You are here and Kendal is here. What more can I ask for?"

Henrietta smiled sheepishly when she heard that statement from Dorothy. She was flattered but didn't know how to respond. She didn't want to say anything that might have upset the equilibrium at the O'Connor's that Sunday morning so she asked Kendal, "What is *the river lime* really?

"It is just a *lime*," he said.

"Don't be like that, Kendal. Just tell her what it truly is."

"Okay! It is an event that takes place at two venues every Sunday in the dry season."

"An event?"

"Yes."

Kendal did not want to speak of *the river lime*. He found the memory of what happened to him there to be too distressing. The mere thought that his early and untimely demise, had it occurred, could have ruined both his mother and Henrietta saddened him. She, however, didn't know that. He had never expressed how he truly felt about it so Henrietta asked, "What kind of an event is it? What are the venues?"

"It is a gathering of friends. We meet between 9:30 a.m. and 10:00 a.m. every Sunday at the saw mill or the spring bridge."

"Why would friends gather there?"

"It is a comradely act of sorts. Some of us swim or learn to swim. We joke around with one another. Some just sit under the bridge and read or practice doing math problems."

"That sounds like it is a lot of fun."

"It used to be."

"Used to be? Have the fellas (young men) stopped gathering there?"

"No, but I no longer join the *lime*."

"I thought you did not attend because I am here."

"I have no intention of going back."

Dorothy was wondering why Kendal was hedging about telling Henrietta exactly why he had chosen not to attend *the river lime* anymore. Her first thought was to intervene and tell it like it is, but after careful consideration she decided against that. She chose instead to excuse herself from their company and retreat to her bedroom. That presented the opportunity for Kendal and Henrietta to snuggle up to each other and converse.

"I feel quite at ease when I am here with you," said Henrietta. "You mother makes me feel so at home."

"She is like that with people she cares about."

"You really think she likes me?"

"Are you kidding? She adores you."

Once again Henrietta smiled that coy smile because she didn't know what else to do or say. Kendal on the contrary, had a lot to say so he continued, "Sweetheart, I sometimes wonder who loves you more."

"What do you mean?"

"My mother thinks that you can do no wrong."

"What do you think?"

"Do you really want to know?"

"Yes. I want to know the truth though."

"I don't think that my mother is right on all counts," said Kendal. "You are a wonderful person and I love you dearly but sometimes you do commit some egregious acts."

"Are you saying that I am a bad person?"

"No. You are not at all bad, although sometimes you do bad things."

"Like what?" Henrietta asked with a big grin on her face.

"Like the time you left home and no one knew where you were. Your parents came here thinking you might have been with me. You were not. Eventually, they reported you missing."

She started laughing loudly and heartily. Consequently, Dorothy smiled where she lay quietly in her bed thinking of how nice it was that they were getting along well. Henrietta leaned over and kissed Kendal on the cheek when her laughter subsided.

"What was that for?" he asked.

"That was just a reminder."

"What was it a reminder of?"

"It was a reminder of the fact that I love you, *stupid*."

"No! You didn't just call me *stupid*. You know that was no Freudian slip of your tongue. It was because of habit. I have told you repeatedly that you shouldn't call anyone *stupid*, yet you continue to do it."

As soon as Henrietta said the word *stupid*, she regretted it. She knew that Kendal would have been upset by it but she never anticipated that he would be so very angry. In fact, he really wasn't angry at all. He said what he thought was necessary for him to say, and he said it sternly. Since the incident with her and Karish in the hammock, however, Henrietta tended to become nervous and afraid around Kendal whenever he was not his meek and humble self. She had never offered an apology for her action and somehow, she believed that Kendal would seize every opportunity he got to use that against her. She was never so concerned about her tryst with Mr. Vargas. She convinced herself that Kendal knew nothing about it, and that he would never know about it. Obviously, she was naive and did not quite understand the small, close knit community in which they lived.

"I meant no harm," she said quickly. "I am sorry."

"I know that. Everybody in T & T speaks like that but it is wrong to call someone stupid even when you think that it is true."

Why? If one is stupid, one is stupid, Henrietta thought but said instead, "I understand."

"Of course you understand. You are just not making a conscious effort to stop the practice."

"Okay, Kendal. That's enough now."

"Okay, sugar. You are just so sweet!" Kendal said as he placed his arm around her waist in an effort to allay any fears she may have had. She, in turn, rested her head on his shoulder. They embraced and kissed each other as if to say, this is real. All is well again.

"Can we go down to the river?" she asked.

Kendal looked at his watch and said, "It is already ten o'clock by the time we get to the spring bridge the *lime* would have already been broken up."

"I thought that the limers there dispersed around noon."

"No. They gather early, around nine thirty and the activities continue for about an hour. However, if we hurry we might still catch the *lime* at the saw-mill."

"I heard that is not as exciting as the spring bridge *lime*."

"Does that mean you do not want to go?"

"No. I am still very curious."

"Okay then. Let's go."

Kendal was happy to take Henrietta *to the river lime* at the saw-mill. He did not want to go to the spring bridge. The memory of his near demise there was too recent and too agonizing for him to endure. Although, he did not tell Henrietta that, what he did tell her was the truth. Nevertheless, he purposely did not reveal his innermost thoughts and he had no regrets about that as he knocked on his mother's bedroom door to inform her that he was going to walk down to the saw mill with Henrietta.

"I hope you are not planning to go swimming," Dorothy said.

"No, Mom. You know that I never swim down there."

"Okay then. If I am not here when you get back, you can reach me at Bertha's."

"Would you be there long?"

"I don't know."

"That's okay, bye."

"Bye son."

With that said, Kendal and Henrietta left. As soon as they were out of the door she asked, "My God! Do you always have to seek each other's approval and inform each other of your whereabouts?"

"We don't have to. It is just something we do," said Kendal. "You must remember, it's only the two of us. All we have is each other."

"Okay! Okay! You don't have to rub it in."

Henrietta was sensitive to Kendal's veiled reference to her own family of eleven, her parents, eight siblings, and herself. In that family they were allowed to do pretty much what they liked. Both were aware of that. Henrietta of course, saw nothing wrong with it. While Kendal didn't see it as wrong in or of itself, he was concerned about how it might influence his own family should he and Henrietta ever became husband and wife. The consequences of such an approach to raising children was evident with Joshua Jacob and he did not like it.

When they arrived at the saw-mill, there was a joyous refrain of, "Kendal! Kendal! Are you coming in? Jump in! Jump in!" It seemed as if everyone in the water, all ten or so youngsters were saying the same thing at the same time. Kendal was flattered but not at all tempted to get into the river. Henrietta was impressed by the sort of reception he received. She wasn't the least concerned that the boys virtually ignored her. The way she saw it, was that Kendal was so revered that no one bothered to greet her or dared to comment, as other young men did about the way she looked.

Kendal went down to the river bank, stepped onto the raft and stooped down to shake hands with some of the young men in the water. Henrietta politely declined to do the same. She remained at a safe distance, about twenty yards away from the water's edge. Two young men sat in close proximity and stared at her. They had been in the water moments before the couple arrived but they came out to have a drink. Henrietta noticed their glances and smiled. They smiled with her but neither attempted to speak. They kept their distance, either out of respect for Kendal himself or for the police officer they knew he was.

After a brief stay on the raft, he rejoined Henrietta on the river bank. He sat on a cedar log and asked her to join him but she declined, so he got up and stood next to her. They soon realized that they had enough of that activity. Kendal's feeling was that if one is not actively participating in *the river lime*, it was essentially quite boring. Henrietta wasn't complaining but she felt that she had seen just about enough of it. The young men in the water appeared to be having fun but she wasn't.

"Let's get out of here," she said. Before Kendal could respond, one of the two young men who smiled at Henrietta earlier asked, "You go take ah drink, Officer O'Connor?"

"What are you drinking this early on a Sunday morning?"

"Babash (boot-legged rum)," the young man said gleefully.

"What the hell is wrong with you, man? He is a cop," the other whispered.

"No thank you, man," said Kendal. "We have to leave now."

"Okay," said the second of the two men. He was relieved that Kendal showed no interest in what they were doing.

Kendal and Henrietta walked back to the roadway hand in hand and headed back to the O'Connor's home. On their way several vehicles driven by friends of his stopped to offer them a ride but they declined. It was a short distance away from his home and they wanted to walk. As they approached the entrance to the family home, the driver of a speeding taxi honked his horn. It was Mr. Rudolf Vargas. Kendal recognized him and waved. Henrietta recognized him too but showed absolutely no interest. As far as she was concerned that man no longer existed.

When they entered the house Kendal shouted, "Mom! We are back." There was no answer, so he asked, "Mom, are you here?" Still there was no answer and he realized that she had not yet returned. He turned to Henrietta and asked, "Honey, can I get you something?"

"Yes," she said.

"What would you like?"

Henrietta did not respond verbally. Instead she smiled, and with the index finger of her right hand beckoned him to her. He obliged and they sat together. She wrapped her arms around him and said, "I love you, Kendal."

It was rare that Henrietta ever said that. Probably because it was never said to her as a child growing up with her parents. That was a time when parents in Mayaro felt their only obligation was to provide necessities for their children the best way they knew how. That was their indication of love. They seldom cuddled their children, or kissed them after age two. That was more apparent in large families; those with five or more siblings. Very often the older children were expected to care for the younger ones. To some that was a given and they accepted it as their lot. Others did what was required of them but they did it resentfully. Henrietta was among the former, and Kendal knew that. He was pleasantly surprised when she said she loved him.

He never doubted that but always wished he could hear it more often from her.

The words I love you rolled of his tongue with ease and sincerity. His upbringing was quite different from hers. He had been an only child and his mother, Dorothy showered him with her affection. Knowingly or not, she instilled in him many virtues that he had taken into adulthood. He was sentimental, gentle, caring, and compassionate. His love for Henrietta was obvious to all who knew them. He had no qualms about his display of affection for her. Early in their relationship, she was uncomfortable with it, and so too were the people of Mayaro. Public display of affection was taboo in those parts. However, Kendal's love prevailed.

Henrietta still had her arms around his waist when he inquired as to whether she would be spending the next day, Monday, with his mother and would still be there when he returned from duty. Before she could respond, he took her left hand and stroked it gently and said, "You still didn't tell me what you would like to have."

She smiled her own uniquely seductive smile and asked, "When is your mother coming home?"

"I have no idea. Very early this morning she did most, if not all of her cooking for today, so she might be out for a while."

Henrietta smiled again, a most seductive smile, one Kendal was quite familiar with. "What now?" he asked. She responded by unbuttoning his shirt. He didn't have to ask again. They got up and left the living room for the privacy of his bedroom.

By the time Dorothy returned home from her friend's, Kendal and Henrietta were sound asleep. It was not unusual for folks to sleep during the day, especially on a Sunday. Generally, neither Henrietta nor Kendal snored but on that occasion, Dorothy could hear them both snoring, not in unison but in alternately high and low tones. *They are asleep. That is good. It should allow me enough time to get lunch on the table*, she thought. She kicked her shoes off at the front door, walked quietly through the living room and into the kitchen. She wasted no time before heating up the meal she had prepared hours earlier.

It wasn't long before she had the table set for three with a scrumptious meal in place. The snoring stopped and she wondered whether Kendal, Henrietta, or both were awake. They were but neither attempted to leave the comfort of the bedroom right away. Eventually, Henrietta emerged.

"Did you have a good rest?" Dorothy asked. There was nothing humorous about the question but Henrietta giggled.

"Sorry," said Dorothy as she realized the chagrin associated with the giggle. "I thought you might have been tired from the walk down to the river."

'It wasn't that long a walk," Henrietta said.

"Okay."

Kendal entered the kitchen and placed his arm over his mother's shoulder. "It smells good in here, Mom," he said. "Another of your gastronomical Sunday delight I imagine." Dorothy did not respond directly to her son's statement. Instead, she asked, "How was *the river lime?*"

"Okay."

"Just okay?"

"It wasn't as good as the *lime* at the spring bridge. It is never as good."

"Does that mean you didn't enjoy it?"

"I couldn't, Mom. I wasn't a participant."

"Well, excuse me!"

"Those gatherings are in many ways like cricket or gulf. If one is not participating, they can be quite boring."

"There is no need for you to explain, Kendal. I am not really interested."

Dorothy did not say it but she was glad to hear of his spectator role. She hoped that he would never again participate in those activities but she said simply, "Come on, let's eat."

"I am famished," Kendal said as they took their seats at the table.

"It wasn't that bad," said Henrietta. "It was the first time that I had gotten so close to the river. I must say, it was a bit scary at first."

"What!" Dorothy exclaimed. "Did you take her onto the raft?" she asked her son.

"No. I went on the raft alone."

"Did you leave her on the bank among all those half naked young men?"

"Some of them were actually naked," said Kendal laughing. "They, however, were in the water."

"What is so amusing about that?" Dorothy asked.

"I was okay with it," said Henrietta. "They were quite respectful."

"Respectful naked men, eh?"

"Okay, Mom. Let's eat," Kendal said in an effort to change the conversation and the mood in the room.

Dorothy agreed that it was time for a meal. Initially, no one at the table spoke. It wasn't long though, before Kendal was his loquacious self again. He gabbed about everything, especially the people of Matura and particularly about Tan Sally. She had impressed him with her keen acumen and acrid sense of humor and he tried desperately to get his mother and girlfriend to be as interested in her as he was. They were not. That did not disappoint or deter him because while he wanted them to be interested in Tan Sally, he really didn't expect them to be.

Dorothy inquired as to when Henrietta might want to return to Lagon Doux, and started wondering what she had or could get together for her. She had assumed that Henrietta would elect to leave that day and was pleasantly surprised to hear that she was going to stay with them for yet another day. Kendal was glad to hear it also. He had attempted, in as subtle a way as he could have, to learn what size ring she wore. He intended to propose to her even though he did not discuss it with his mother. Her decision to stay on provided a window of opportunity for him.

After they had lunch, he suggested that they attend the cricket match scheduled to be convened that evening at the Mafeking recreation grounds. The match was between rivals Nuts & Bolts and Eastern Glory. Henrietta favored the idea but Dorothy declined. She wanted them to spend time together without her being there as a third wheel. Kendal understood and respected his mother's decision so they sat together and conversed for a while before he and Henrietta left for the game.

When they arrived at the cricket field, she was amazed at the reception Kendal received. Although he was best known as a football (soccer) player, he was also a member of the Eastern Glory Cricket Club. He played with them often the previous year but had taken a hiatus to pursue other interest, one of which was to become a police officer. He accomplished that and was about to make, perhaps the greatest decision of his young life. That was, to propose to Henrietta.

They arrived at the savannah hand in hand. Kendal was in the habit of holding Henrietta's right hand whenever they strolled together. On that occasion, however, he chose to hold her left hand. She hardly noticed any difference but he was intent on knowing what size ring she wore without having to ask her directly.

"Whenever I hold your hand I am always so impressed at how neat your fingers are," he said as he lifted her hand a little above their waist.

"I always had skinny fingers."

"That's what is so amazing. You are not a skinny person by any standard."

"What can I say, Kendal?"

Say what size ring you normally wear, he thought but said, "Nothing I guess." he then took off the ring he was wearing and slipped it onto her ring finger. It was much too large for her. "Wow!" You are probably a size six," said Kendal. "Two of your fingers can fit into my ring."

Henrietta laughed and said, "It's not that bad. My ring size actually is six and a half."

"That's not so bad," said Kendal. He then asked, "How do you know?"

"That is what the jeweler said when I bought this one. He measured my ring fingers on both hands and found them to be the exact size." She then took off the ring she wore on her right hand and placed it on the ring finger of her left hand, showed it to Kendal and asked, "Do you see?"

"Yes. It's really an exact fit. That's nice."

Henrietta left the ring on her left hand. She was clueless. She loved Kendal, enjoyed his company, and admired his relationship with his mother but she wasn't thinking of marriage. She never thought of it before. That day was no different. She was there to witness the cricket match and have fun with Kendal. It wasn't as if she enjoyed cricket, but on a Sunday afternoon in Mafeking in 1956 it was the best thing one could have done for recreation, relaxation, or just for fun.

Kendal looked up and saw Arjune walking into the crowd. He was with a female companion whom Kendal didn't know. They appeared to be looking for a seat. Since there were no stands, spectators sat wherever they could.

"Damn!" Kendal exclaimed.

"What is the matter?" Henrietta asked with concern and alarm.

"There is Arjune. I promised him that we would have met at *the river lime* today."

"But he wasn't there."

"He seldom joins the *lime* at the saw-mill but I am quite certain that he was at the spring bridge this morning."

"Oh! Don't worry about it. I am sure he would understand that you have company today."

"So does he, it appears."

"That is more reason why he should understand."

"I hope so."

"He will. You worry too much, Kendal."

ELEVEN

Sydney and Joshua had lunch at their respective homes before they got together at Sydney's. Joshua wanted to begin the reading lesson right away but on that day, Sydney preferred to make tops for play. He wanted desperately to learn the craft he knew Joshua could teach him. However, Joshua was having none of it. Eventually they compromised.

"If we read for one hour, we can work on the tops for as long as you want," Joshua said.

"I can teach you how to read. Let's get started right now," Sydney suggested.

"Okay!"

"Then I'll be right back."

Sydney ran inside, got the picture book he prepared and quickly returned. He walked over to a spreading caimate (star apple) tree and sat on a bench his mother kept there. Joshua followed and sat down beside him.

"I made this especially for you," Sydney said. Joshua smiled but said nothing. He took the picture book from his cousin and started reading. His technique was to look at the picture, interpret what he saw, then vocalize it according to what he thought the caption should say. He wasn't always correct but Sydney was always patient and reassuring. He would correct him without admonishing him. Joshua liked that. He repeated the lessons willingly and without any prompting from Sydney. Soon he was reading not just the one word captions, but those of full paragraphs also.

Sydney was extremely proud of his cousin's accomplishment. He had no prior experience in teaching anyone how to read. However, his efforts with Joshua proved to be fruitful. Within the very short period of time he had been working with him, the results were just amazing. There is no doubt that Joshua had been a good student, practicing on his own at every chance he got. At the end of the session, when Sydney suggested that he repeat the lesson in the picture book, Joshua grasped at the opportunity to show what he could do.

"Don't help me," he said as he started to read. He read the captions in the picture book flawlessly, either because he had a photographic memory, great comprehension, sheer determination, or all of those. He completed the assignment in less than half the time Sydney had originally suggested for them to end the lesson.

"Your performance was great," said Sydney. "In a little while you'll be reading just like Ms. Gardener."

"Who is Ms. Gardener?"

"She is my teacher. She teaches geography and civics."

"Civics, what is that?"

"That is the study of citizenship." Joshua appeared even more confused so Sydney explained, "It is the study of the rights, duties, and responsibilities of citizens."

"Okay," said Joshua. Then he asked, "Is she an old lady?"

"No. Why would you ask that?"

Joshua smiled and said, "I am just curious."

"That is your curious smile alright, but why?"

"Forget about it."

"I can't. You have made me curious now"

"Well, how old is Ms. Gardener?"

"I don't know. Maybe she is twenty-one or twenty-two?"

"That is young. She is only four years older than we are."

"So?"

"She must like you. Of all the students in her class, she gave you today's newspaper?"

"Stop it, JJ," Sydney said while laughing.

"Really, isn't it a little strange?"

"No! I asked her for the paper so I could help you with your reading."

"She could have said no."

"She could have but she didn't. What is so wrong with that?"

"Nothing, nothing at all," JJ said while laughing. He seemed unable to stop. Sydney found himself laughing too, although he didn't know or wasn't quite sure why.

"You are so silly," he said.

"Yes! I know," JJ said. He still didn't reveal what was so amusing to him.

"Clearly, you are much improved. So before you take all of this the wrong way, let me set the record straight."

Sydney paused and Joshua said, "I am listening."

"I do admire Ms. Gardener but only because she has accomplished so much at such an early age."

"What has she achieved?"

"She graduated from the University, for Christ sake, Joshua!"

Joshua couldn't quite grasp the magnitude of Ms. Gardener's achievements. She graduated from The University of the West Indies at age twenty with a major in biology and a minor in education. Sydney realized Joshua's short-sightedness but said nothing that would accentuate it. In fact, it was Joshua who spoke next.

"Is she pretty?" he asked.

"Quite frankly, she is not,"

"So what is the attraction?"

"I never said that I was attracted to her. I am simply impressed by her accomplishments."

"Hmm! Joshua murmured. The fact that his cousin could admire a young lady and not be physically attracted to her confused him. He was more like the typical teenager of his day. Sydney was ahead of his time, wise beyond his chronological age. Joshua decided not to continue that discussion, and chose instead to turn his attention to making tops as he had promised Sydney they would do.

"What did you do with the six pieces of juniper wood?" he asked.

"I have them inside."

"If you bring them out we can shape the tops then go to Tang's shop and purchase the nails and the twine."

"How will we pay for them?"

"I told you that I have twenty cents which we can use for that purpose."

"Do you still have the twenty cents?"

"Yes. In fact, I now have twenty-five cents."

Although Sydney did not ask Joshua again where he got the money, it was a matter of concern for him. He dismissed it momentarily only to remind Joshua that it was Sunday and Tang's shop was closed.

"They sell rum when they are closed. So they can sell us a few nails and a yard of twine," Joshua said.

"We can also shape the tops and wait until tomorrow to purchase those items."

"We can if that is what you want to do."

"I think so."

"Then bring the wood. Also, bring a cutlass (machete) and a file."

"I do not have a file. I always sharpen the cutlass on the concrete."

"That's okay. I have a file and a spoke-shave."

"A spoke-shave! What is that?" Sydney asked.

"It is a tool used for smoothing curved surfaces. I'll get it. You will see it."

Joshua left to get his tools while at the same time Sydney went to his room to fetch the pieces of juniper he had hidden under his bed. They got back together after five minutes. Joshua took two of the pieces of wood from Sydney and confirmed that they were still green enough for the purpose for which they had gotten them.

"They are easier to work with when they are like this," he told Sydney. "When the wood is too dry it becomes too difficult to carve unless you have extremely sharp tools or power tools."

"Power tools?"

"Oh! You wouldn't know about that, so don't even think about it. We can work very well with what we have at hand. The wood is perfect. When it is too dry, it tends to split where the nail is inserted at the tip."

Sydney was fascinated by the small two-handled tool with a blade that Joshua called a spoke-shave. "If we had a work bench and a clamp it would be very easy to use this tool," Joshua said.

"So what will we do?"

"I will show you. It may take a little longer but it works. First, you must chip away the outer portion of the wood to a tapered end."

Joshua used a pencil to trace the line along the hard wood designated for making tops. He then instructed Sydney to cut away the outer portion slowly and carefully."

"The finished product must be perfectly symmetrical so the top spins with balance," he said.

"I am impressed," said Sydney. "You really know your craft."

"Thank you," said Joshua. "Shape all six pieces while you are at it."

"What?"

"You heard me."

Sydney knew Joshua well and realized that he was serious, so he offered no resistance. Joshua, meanwhile, took the picture book and returned to the bench under the star apple tree. He sat down and started to read again. Sydney looked at him periodically but said nothing. He was simply delighted to see how determined JJ was to learn to read. He read the entire picture book without stopping once to look at Sydney or to ask a question. At the end he closed the book, walked back to where Sydney was working on the tops, took one up, scrutinized it and said, "Good job." Sydney smiled, an appreciative sort of smile, but he said nothing.

"Do you have anything else I can read?" JJ asked.

"Oh yes!"

"I am finished with the picture book. What else do you have?"

"I'll be right back," Sydney said as he ran off to get some more reading material for JJ. He went to his room where his mother kept all of his used textbooks in a box. He picked up two of them, a Third Stage (Grade three) West Indian Reader and a First Standard (Grade four) West Indian Reader. He contemplated for a moment as to which one was most suitable for JJ. He was concerned that anything too difficult just might deter his progress or discourage him altogether. He decided, therefore, that the former was the better choice. He was right.

Joshua took the reading book from Sydney and returned to the star apple tree. He didn't ask for help. Sydney, however, thought he might need it and joined him on the bench under the tree.

"Let me try this on my own," said Joshua. "If I need help I will let you know."

"Please do."

"Sure thing," said Joshua as Sydney left him.

Joshua read the first page of the textbook over and over again. At first he did it with considerable difficulty. Then he applied the phonics he learnt from Sydney and found that the task became easier and easier. He became interested not only in learning to read sentences and paragraphs, but in reading for pleasure. He found the stories written in the West Indian Reader to be quite funny, something for which some intellectuals in Trinidad and Tobago had criticized the use of those books.

Neither Sydney nor Joshua had a watch and there wasn't a clock in either of their homes. Yet they had a pretty good idea of time. On that day, they looked at the shadow the caimate tree cast and determined it was three o'clock or very close to it. Just as they woke up at 5:00 a.m. or very close to it from the sound of the roosters crowing, they knew breakfast, lunch and dinner times from the hunger pangs they felt at some particular period during the day. So too, they were able to tell the time at off periods during the day from shadows certain objects cast. On school days Sydney could have depended on the start periods, the recess intervals, and the dismissal periods to know the time of day. JJ had no such facility so how he determined time during those periods is still uncertain. On that Sunday afternoon, however, three o'clock seemed like a reasonable time for them to stop what they were doing and move on to something else.

Joshua placed the reading book on the bench and walked over to Sydney. He looked at the tops and said, "They are taking shape."

"Do you really think so?"

"Yes. You are doing well."

Joshua liked what he saw. He was excited and anxious to bring the task to completion that very day. Sydney on the contrary, wanted to move on to something else.

"Let's go up to Tang's for the twine and the nails," JJ said.

"Do you want to do that right now?"

"Yes. If not now, when?"

"We can do it tomorrow."

"Tomorrow is Monday. You have to go to school."

"Yes! You are right!" Sydney said and paused. He was concerned about leaving home to go to Tang's shop. *What am I going to tell Mom?* He wondered. *She wants to know where I am at all times. If I tell her that I am going to the shop, she would want to know why. I could always say that I am going with JJ, but in light of what happened to him recently, she might not be comfortable with that either.*

"I know. You are afraid of what Aunt Bertha would say." Sydney did not respond so Joshua continued, "I will go alone. You can continue working on the tops."

"Okay."

Sydney felt relieved at not having to explain to his mother why it was necessary for him to go to the shop with JJ. Nevertheless, he was concerned for JJ's safety. Although the perpetrators of that heinous act against him were still in jail awaiting trial, Sydney wasn't sure that they were the only ones who bore grudges against him. After all, JJ was not known to have an unblemished reputation. Sydney continued shaving and smoothing the tops. They were taking shape and he was feeling proud of himself.

Joshua returned elated. It took only ten minutes for him to go to Tang's shop, purchase the items they needed and return. The clerk at the shop opened the door immediately when JJ knocked. No doubt they had some way of seeing who was there. If they had any fear about letting someone in, it was not a fear of being robbed. That just did not happen in Mayaro in those days. Any fear they may have had would have been of the police, more specifically, plain clothes police officers from outside of Mayaro. The government had a tendency to impose severe fines on shop owners who serviced patrons during hours when the business establishment was closed.

"I got it! I got it!" Joshua shouted excitedly to Sydney.

"Did you get everything?"

"I got everything! And it didn't cost me a penny."

"What? They just gave it to you?"

"That's right. They gave them to me."

Sydney hesitated to respond. *I hope he didn't threaten them,* he thought. He knew that JJ could be tough and unreasonable at times. Before he could say anything, Joshua said, "I didn't even threaten them."

"Oh, my God! No! I hope you weren't thinking of such a thing."

"No. Stupid, I am just teasing you."

Sydney slammed down the piece of juniper wood and the spoke shave he had in his hands. Joshua was startled. He had never experienced anything quite like that from Sydney.

"What's wrong now?" he asked as Sydney was walking away.

"I have told you time and time again not to call me *stupid.*"

"I am sorry. I didn't even realize that I said it."

"Maybe you should pay more attention to the manner in which you speak."

"The manner in which I speak?"

"Yes."

"Do you mean how I speak?"

"You heard what I said and you know damn well what I mean." Joshua was laughing. Sydney had become the butt of one of his cynical jokes.

"You think it's funny. It is not. Perhaps you haven't noticed that you are the only one laughing."

"You speak funny sometimes."

"Okay, JJ. I am finished! It's over and done with."

"You can't be serious."

"Watch me," Sydney said as walked away.

Joshua wasn't perturbed by Sydney's anger. He had seen it many times before, although not as raging. He knew, nevertheless, that it would subside quickly. He tried to take over the task of smoothing the tops but experienced some difficulty using his left hand. He decided, therefore, to go home and relax for a while. He gathered the tool he brought, the supplies he bought, and the tops that Sydney had already shaped to near perfection and he left.

TWELVE

The cricket match ended with a victory for Nuts and Bolts. Arjune spotted Kendal and Henrietta as they were preparing to leave the grounds so he walked over and introduced the lady he was with. "Hey, Kendal! Henrietta! Meet Dessita, a friend of mine from Tunapuna.

"Kendal O'Connor. It is a pleasure to finally meet you," said Kendal as he stretched out his hand to greet the young lady. "I have heard so much about you."

"Thank you. I trust that you heard good things."

"Only praise," Kendal said. Dessita smiled as she reached out to Henrietta who shook her hand and said,

"Welcome to Mayaro."

"Thank you. I truly love it here. Sadly though, I am leaving this evening."

"Do you know what that means? We have to run," Arjune asked and answered his own question.

"We understand," Kendal said.

"Sorry we had to trash your Eastern Glory so badly but it's all in the game we call cricket, my friend."

"We are going to avenge that loss next month when I am back on the team."

"I am looking forward to that challenge," Arjune said laughing as he and Dessita walked away.

"Is she planning to return to Tunapuna this evening?" Henrietta asked.

"I don't know. From what she said, I will assume so."

"Isn't that risky?"

"In what sense do you think it is risky?"

"There is a possibility she may not get transportation at this time."

Kendal looked at his watch, it was 3:00 p.m. "It shouldn't be difficult for her to get a taxi at this time. The most difficult leg of the journey in terms of the accessibility to transport is from here to Sangre Grande. Once she is there, the connection to Port of Spain and points between is easy, at least until nine o'clock."

"Well, if she is having difficulty getting a cab to Sangre Grande, Arjune could drive her there."

"So she does have choices?"

"She most certainly does."

Henrietta held on to Kendal's arm just above the elbow. At the same time she rested her head on his shoulder momentarily. He in turn, placed his arm around her waist as they strolled out of the cricket grounds. They were greeted warmly by many who admired them as they walked back to Kendal's home. Others were not so generous with their accolades. Some were outright rude. One old woman's comment was, "A, a, what is this at all? You think you deh ah Hollywood."

Henrietta laughed at the comment but Kendal ignored the lady. That enraged her, and she lashed out with another jealous diatribe, "You, Kendal O'Connor! You start to not speak to people already?"

"People like you," Kendal muttered.

The old woman obviously did not hear what he said, or even knew that he said something. If she did she would have chastised him further. Had he been eight or ten, she might have spanked him. That much authority was entrusted to the elders of Mafeking. *Respect the elders or face their wrath,* was the unwritten rule that everyone knew and observed while growing up there. Sometimes, however, the elders tended to forget that some of those they once knew as children and had the freedom to discipline as they pleased, had grown up.

Henrietta was snickering but Kendal showed no emotion. Instead, he said, "Most of these folks are not at all affectionate. They never showed affection to their children, their wives, husbands, or significant others in public, or even in their bedrooms."

"How can you say that, Kendal?"

"It is the truth."

"How do you know?"

"Can't you tell? I am hugging you and whatever hormones she still has functioning are raging but she is incapable of dealing with them."

"That was not very nice of you, Kendal," said Henrietta. Her thoughts were different though. She was wondering, *Is that a veiled reference to my parents and the way I was brought up?*

"It may sound unkind and heartless but it is just the way I feel right now. Most of the people in this village are kind, good, loving, and compassionate humans. A few like her, however, are quite the opposite."

Kendal was not thinking about Henrietta or her parents when he made those derogatory statements about the old lady. Although, it might have been just as fitting if applied to the Riggs family. However, he loved Henrietta. It wasn't a conditional love. He had no intention of asking her to change her ways, thoughts, or beliefs. Nevertheless, he hoped that some of what he learnt from his mother could be emulated over time by the woman he hoped would be the mother of his children.

As they entered his home he realized that his mother was taking a nap, something she had done every Sunday afternoon for as long as he could remember. He whispered to Henrietta, "Mom might be sleeping. Let's try not to wake her up." Henrietta looked at him and smiled.

"No! Not that seductive smile again," said Kendal. "I know what you are up to but we can't take that chance."

"Why can't we?"

"You know why not."

"I do not," said Henrietta as she embraced him. "I will be quiet," she said.

"That is not the issue."

"What is it then? Are you angry at me?"

"Come on now! Why would I be angry at you? Do I seem angry?"

"No. Something is wrong though. You are perhaps bothered by what that old woman said or is it something I did or didn't do. Either way, it is my fault. Is it not?"

"Etta, please! Stop the self-blame and low self-esteem. This has nothing to do with you."

"Oh yes!" She said. She looked around. Then she said, "I don't see anyone else here."

"You are right. It's just the two of us but we are in Dorothy O'Connor's space. We need to show a little respect."

Once again Henrietta's thoughts were on her own upbringing and more recently, Kendal's encounter with her and Karish in the hammock under the house, in the dark, at her parent's place. She was filled with remorse. Not self-blame or low self-esteem as Kendal thought. Suddenly she started to cry. That surprised and confused him. He had never seen her cry before and always thought of her as being mentally tough. Somehow though, in a quirky sort of way, he loved that tender side of her which he was seeing for the first time. He held her close. She rested her head on his chest and he said, "Please Etta, don't cry."

She was sobbing softly when Dorothy walked out of her room still looking sleepy and noticed the tracts of tears flowing down her cheeks.

"What have you done to her?" she yelled at Kendal."

"I haven't done anything to her, Mom."

"Is she crying for no reason at all? Women don't cry just for the sake of it. Come with me, girl." She took Henrietta by the arm and walked with her back to her bedroom.

"What is the matter, dear?"

"It is just too much, Ms. Dorothy."

"Okay wash your face. Here is a clean towel. You can lie in bed and take a nap if you wish and we will talk later. Right now I am going out there to deal with Kendal."

"No, please don't do that Ms. Dorothy."

"Why shouldn't I?"

"He hasn't done anything."

"Like I said earlier strong women don't cry without some good reason. I am going to get to the bottom of this."

Henrietta, realizing that in order to appease Dorothy O'Connor she may have to reveal more that she wanted to. She quickly washed and dried her face, composed herself, and rejoined Kendal and his mother in the kitchen. Dorothy was still questioning her son but he revealed nothing. As far as he was concerned, nothing happened between them. Together they had a lovely afternoon. There wasn't anything he could remember that would have been so emotionally taxing to bring her to tears, and she was not about to say what was bothering her.

"I am leaving the two of you to resolve your differences. I am going back to bed," Dorothy said and left the kitchen.

Kendal walked to the kitchen window, the one at the Eastern side overlooking the garden. He leaned out and wondered, *Could it be that she suspected that I am going to propose to her and is frightened by it?* He thought briefly about what the taxi driver told him on the first day he traveled to his new assignment as a police officer in Matura. Very quickly he dismissed that thought as the words of one nosy taxi driver. He left the window, walked back to the table and sat on the bench next to Henrietta. She smiled, got up and sat in his lap. He put his arms around her and gently rubbed her tummy.

"Oh, that feels so good," she said as she leant back and stretched out her legs.

"Are you comfortable?" he asked.

"I am. Your legs are like cushions. Are you comfortable?"

"Not really."

"We can be a lot more comfortable in bed."

"That is not an unreasonable suggestion."

"So what are we waiting for?"

"I said it wasn't an unreasonable suggestion. I didn't say that I agreed."

"Are you trying to confuse me with semantics?"

"What was that sound?" Kendal asked in response to some unusual noise coming from his mother's room.

"I don't know," Henrietta said.

"It sounds to me as if Mom is snoring. She must be extremely tired. She only snores when she is exhausted." Henrietta smiled. Kendal looked at her and returned the smile.

"What's wrong?" she asked.

"Nothing is wrong, sweetheart. Can't I smile with you?"

"You certainly can, my dear." She kissed him as to confirm what she said. He reciprocated, and soon they became passionate with each other in the kitchen. Then Kendal suddenly paused and released his hold on her.

"What's wrong now? She is asleep for Christ sake!"

"We cannot be sure about that. We assume that might be the case."

"Okay! You win this one." Henrietta said. She acknowledged that when they first came in and thought that Dorothy was asleep, she wasn't. She came out to inquire as to what was wrong that caused her to be crying.

"Thank you. Now I must get my uniform ready for tomorrow."

"Can I help?"

"Do you want to?"

"I wouldn't ask, if I didn't want to."

"Okay." Kendal said. He set up an ironing board in the kitchen, went to his room and brought out his grey uniform shirt and dark blue serge pants, his black leather shoes, and tall, black and grey socks. "I can press the shirt for you but I am not touching those woolen pants," Henrietta said.

"That's okay. Thank you. Every little bit helps."

"You are welcome."

Kendal polished and shined his shoes while Henrietta pressed his shirt. When she was finished, she placed it on a hanger and sat where Kendal was sitting to watch him meticulously press his woolen uniform pants.

"Do you do this every day?" she asked."

"Yes. They are very strict about the dress code."

"Wouldn't it make more sense to press five shirts for the week?"

"Yes. It is probably wise to press five shirts and five pants every Sunday but I am just not up to it."

"Wouldn't Ms. Dorothy ever help you?"

"She has not offered to, and I wouldn't dare ask her."

"Perhaps you should ask."

"I don't think so. Mom works hard enough as it is."

He is so into his mother, Henrietta thought but said, "That was only a suggestion." She stopped short of offering to help him herself although she thought of it.

It was approaching 6:30 p.m. when Dorothy woke up and joined Kendal and Henrietta in the kitchen where they were having coffee and tea respectively.

"Would you like to have a cup of tea, Mom?" Kendal asked. He knew that she did not drink coffee.

"I would like that," she said.

He poured her a cup of tea and she added milk and sugar. Henrietta smiled. It wasn't her usual titillating, tantalizing smile with which Kendal was so familiar. It was simply a pleasant and enchanting smile. Other than that, she said nothing. Kendal, sensing that she may want to spend more time with him away from his mother, suggested that they walk over to the Jacob's to see how Joshua was doing. Henrietta wasn't particularly interested in Joshua's progress but quickly agreed. She was going to be with Dorothy all of the next day, Monday. It was only fitting, therefore, that she spent more time in Kendal's company.

"I will visit Bertha while you are gone. I don't think that I can deal with Velma right now," Dorothy said.

"That's good. You need to get out on a Sunday evening," Henrietta said. She felt that Dorothy was being too protective of her son so she was glad for the chance to be away from her even just for a little while in Kendal's company.

"On most Sundays I do get out after dinner. The only reason I am in today is that you are here."

"Oh, thank you, Ms. Dorothy. That's so nice of you," said Henrietta hypocritically. *Shit! This is when you should go away,* she thought instead.

In an effort to avert any tension that might have been building up between his mother and his girlfriend, Kendal suggested that they leave right away because he wanted to get to bed early so he could be up rested and refreshed the next day for his journey to Matura. It was going to be the beginning of his second week on the job and he did not want to be late.

"Can we go now?" he asked.

"We most certainly can. I have been ready for quite some time."

"Okay! Then let's go."

"See you later, Ms. Dorothy."

"Have fun, girl."

Henrietta did not respond to what Dorothy said. She didn't see how going to visit Joshua could be fun. To her, it was just a means to get Kendal away, even if it were just for a little while. As they walked out of the door she asked, "Are your mother and Ms. Velma related?"

"They are first cousins. In addition, they grew up together and have remained very close."

"Did you say very close?"

"Yes."

"Then how it is Ms. Dorothy said that she didn't think that she could deal with Ms. Velma right now?"

"Aunt Velma tends to be eccentric at times and Mom gets very irritated by it."

"Oh?"

"What was that all about?"

"What?"

"That *oh*?"

"I was just wondering."

"What were you wondering?"

"I was wondering whether I get on your nerves sometimes."

"Sometimes you do."

"Is it that you find me to be eccentric at times."

"Come on, Henrietta! Don't ever try to compare yourself with Aunt Velma. She can be way out field at times."

"Is it that bad?"

"When you meet her you can judge for yourself."

"I have something to look forward to, I guess."

They arrived at the Jacob's and Kendal knocked at the door. It was open but he waited for a response. There was none. He knocked again, a little louder than before. Joshua came running to the door. He looked surprised to see Kendal and Henrietta standing there.

"Hello JJ," said Kendal. "How are you today?"

"I am doing fine. Come in."

"You know Henrietta, don't you?"

"Yes. How are you, Henrietta?"

"I am fine. Thank you."

Joshua stepped back and held the drapery away from the doorway. Henrietta and Kendal entered. Velma sat in a Morris chair just beyond the doorway. She had been sitting there when Kendal knocked but she didn't budge. Since returning home from the hospital she had resumed her sedentary lifestyle. "How are you, Aunt Velma?' he asked. He leaned over and kissed her on the cheek.

"Weh you doing here?" she asked in her typical Mayaro lilt. Henrietta was surprised, unaware that Velma meant no disrespect by her question. Kendal who was quite familiar with Velma's oddities stepped back and said, "Meet Henrietta."

"Oh! I saw you at the hospital. How are you?"

"I am fine now. Thank you," Henrietta said as she and Velma shook hands.

Kendal sat down and beckoned Henrietta to sit next to him. She was waiting to be offered a seat but he knew the possibility of that happening was as remote as being struck by lightning twice in the same day.

"How is Aunt Umilta today?" he asked.

"She is not doing well today."

"What's wrong?"

"Me eh know. Old age ah guess."

"Aunt Umilta is not that old. Perhaps she needs a check-up. When last has she seen the doctor?"

"Me eh know noh."

"Then it must have been a long time ago. I will ask Mom to get the DMO (District medical officer) to visit her one evening when he does not have clinic duties, if it is okay with you."

"Ah doh care." Velma said.

Henrietta looked at Kendal as if to say, *I can't believe what I am hearing.* Kendal, sensing her disbelief said with some underlying degree of chagrin, "That's my Aunt Velma! She is like that most of the time." Henrietta made no comment. Although, she really wanted to say, *Let's get to hell out of here right now.*

Joshua had left the scene as soon as Kendal and Henrietta made themselves comfortable. He did not wait for his mother to tell him to disappear, scram, or get lost, a few of the choice words she normally used to let him know that there was no place for a child in the company of adults. However, Kendal's purpose for being there was to visit with Joshua and not Velma or Ms. Umilta.

"I will be right back," he told Henrietta as he got up to walk to the back to speak with JJ.

No! Please don't do that. You can't just leave me here with this monster, Henrietta thought as Kendal walked back to the kitchen area and out of her view.

"Is Mafeking always this quiet, Ms. Velma?" she asked.

"Quiet? It's dead. Except for *the river lime* and cricket at the savannah on Sundays, there isn't anything to do here."

"Do you participate, as a spectator, maybe?"

"Nah! Not me. I much prefer to curl up in meh bed but even that gets boring after a while."

"It gets boring in bed?"

"When you deh by yourself, yes."

"So maybe you need to go out more often. You might meet someone."

"Me? I can't be bothered with that. Them man and them eh no damn good anyway."

"You sound really bitter, Ms. Velma."

"Me eh bitter. Ah just telling it like it is."

"You truly believe that, don't you?"

"Yes. You are one of the few lucky women around. Kendal is special, a real gentleman."

"Thank you."

Just then Kendal returned to the room. "I see you two are getting acquainted," he said.

"We have been conversing," said Henrietta. "Your Aunt was just saying how lucky she thinks I am."

"I agree," Kendal said without knowing or seeking to know the details of the conversation. As far as he was concerned, Velma had no credibility whatsoever. "Joshua told me that he has to have the stitches in his arm removed this week," he continued.

"Me eh know 'bout that you know (Is that so?)"

"You mean you really don't know, Aunt Velma?"

"He eh tell me nothing."

He knows why. We all know why, Kendal thought but his comment was, "He has improved so much since I first saw him in the hospital.

"Yeah."

Is that all she could say? Henrietta wondered before Kendal said, "We have to leave you, Aunt Velma. Take care of yourself and please let Aunt Umilta know that we were here. He kissed her on her forehead and said, "good night."

"Bye, Ms. Velma," Henrietta said.

"Ah ha," Velma responded.

"What a character she is, that Aunt of yours," Henrietta said as she and Kendal left the Jacob's home.

"Yes! She is quite weird."

"She is a complicated woman."

"I think she is quite the opposite, more of a simpleton I would say."

"She does have her moments of brilliance though."

"When?"

"Like when she said that I am lucky to have you."

"It didn't take a genius to figure that out."

"What?" asked Henrietta as she tapped him gently and said, "You can be so conceited."

"Confident would be a better word choice."

"Conceited it is because that's what you are."

After that brief period of bantering, they held each other's hand as they walked back to Dorothy's. The night air was cool, fresh, and clean although there was some dampness, a threat of rain perhaps. Nevertheless, they enjoyed the walk and each other's company. Velma Jacob's comment may have had some impact on Henrietta because for the first time since she and Kendal met in elementary school, she thought of a future with him, a thought she did not express. She did, however, confirm her agreement with Velma's comment about her being among the lucky few women around, and that Kendal was special, a real gentleman. She was making a conscious comparison between Kendal O'Connor and Mr. Rudolph Vargas but felt no guilt and expressed no remorse. Kendal hugged her and reaffirmed his unconditional love as they strolled along the Naparima/Mayaro Road back to his mother's place.

"I hope Mom has something ready for us," he said.

"Something like what?"

"A snack. Already I am feeling hunger pangs."

"You eat so often. How it is you remain so slim?"

"That is an inherited trait. One can see that just by looking at my mother."

"You may have a point."

"I do have a valid point."

"Okay. You do."

When they arrived Dorothy was not at home. She knew that Kendal would have looked for a snack. He always had something light at least an hour or two before bedtime so she left him a note on the kitchen table. It read: *I am at Philbertha's. I should be home before midnight. Help yourselves.* Henrietta saw the note before Kendal did and immediately she suggested that they forgo the snack, at least temporarily. "Let's not eat right now," she said.

"Why not? I always try to have my last meal for the day about two hours before bedtime."

"Perhaps that is because I am not always here. Right now I am, and what I want is to me more important than sleep or food."

"Just what might that be?"

Henrietta smiled. She could have easily answered Kendal's question but chose instead to cross her legs. She placed her right foot on her left thigh, pulled he skirt up slightly, leaned back, looked at Kendal and smiled again. It was her usual seductive sort of smile.

"What's with the salacious act?" he asked.

"Don't you know?"

Kendal was laughing when Henrietta eased her petite frame onto his lap. She kissed him to seal his already parted lips and silence the laughter. He reciprocated. Before long they left the kitchen and headed to his room. Suddenly it started to rain.

It was a heavy downpour, the sort of torrential rainfall that is so common in the tropics. The sound of the rain drops on the corrugated galvanized roof provided a perfectly soothing rhythm to their ears. They were certain that Dorothy could not get home anytime soon. That was just the opportunity both were longing for and they did not hesitate to grasp it. Without asking they found themselves sharing something more than supper.

Kendal eventually fell asleep without his late night snack. Henrietta got up, showered, changed into her night clothes and retreated to the futon in Dorothy's room where she went to sleep. The rain stopped. Dorothy arrived home at 9:45 expecting them to be awake. They were not. She wasn't surprised to see that Henrietta was sleeping in her room. It was what she expected from her son. She raised him to be respectful but she was prepared to make an exception and accept the alternative. She didn't have to.

THIRTEEN

By the time Dorothy woke up to prepare breakfast, Kendal had already left. His mother did oversleep but that was not the reason he left earlier than usual. He was feeling somewhat guilty for the romantic interlude he had with Henrietta in the brief period that his mother was away at Philbertha's. Throughout his childhood and early adult life his mother had insisted that he should know right from wrong and act accordingly. *If you think something is wrong, don't do it,* she said often.

He arrived at the Police Station in Matura an hour earlier than he was supposed to be on duty. That gave him an opportunity to meet the night staff, all of whom were glad to meet the rookie officer. About forty-five minutes later officer Kanga arrived.

"Hey! Kendal. You are here early I see."

"Yeah, man. Transportation was easy and quick this morning."

"That's good."

"How was your weekend?"

"Not great. I spent most of yesterday at the hospital. Tan Sally wasn't doing so well."

"What was the matter with her?"

"I still don't know. The doctors didn't seem to know either. I guess it is just one of those things that older people experience."

"I am confused."

"What is confusing you, Officer O'Connor?"

"You said you didn't know what was wrong with Tan Sally and you didn't think that the doctors knew either. Then in the same breath you said it's just one of those things that older people experience."

"Yeah, I see how that can be confusing. What I meant was that as we grow older strange and unpredictable things happen to us. Sometimes those things can be responsible for our demise and in these parts our death certificate will read simply, death from natural causes."

"I understand now."

"Good!"

"How is she now?" Kendal asked as if he knew that Officer Kanga would have visited Tan Sally that morning.

"She is much better today. I visited her just before coming here."

"Could we see her later?"

"You didn't have to ask that, Kendal. If I do nothing else all day, I will be there."

"What hospital is she in?"

"Gee! I thought you would never ask. She was rushed to Sangre Grande General on Saturday evening and they kept her there."

"Can I go with you to visit her?"

"Did you check the schedule?"

"Not yet."

"You should. If we are assigned to work the same beat, you can. If we are not assigned together, you are going to have to stick with your partner who may not at all be interested in Tan Sally's well-being."

"Okay. I am going to check the schedule right away."

Kendal left officer Kanga, checked the schedule, returned and said, "We are scheduled together. We have the same beat, the same schedule as last week."

"That's good. We will be in Sangre Grande right after breakfast."

"Do you know of a good place in Matura where we can have breakfast?"

"That will depend on your diet."

"Generally, breakfast for me is very simple; bake (a type of flat bread) and eggs with coffee or tea, or bake and cheese with coffee or tea."

"Do you ever have bake and eggs and cheese?"

"Rarely do I have bake and eggs with cheese."

"Mine is even simpler than that; a buttered hops bread or two with coffee."

"Sometimes I will have pan bread or hops bread instead of bake."

"Then there are many places where we can eat."

"Good."

It was rare that anyone in Matura ate out during the 1950's. That was also true of Mayaro, Moruga and other rural districts. Even police officers took their meals with them to their respective precincts and were never seen eating in public. Kendal was cognizant of that fact and at 8:00 a.m. he asked Officer Kanga, "Shall we go now?"

"What's our beat? Did you check?"

"Yes. The schedule read Church Street and its environs."

"That's all of Matura, man"

"I figured as much."

"That's okay. I know of a place where we can eat. I must caution you though, that I have never eaten there myself."

"Oh?"

"Don't be concerned, man. The people of Matura can cook. In fact, that's all they do."

"That's all?"

"Yes. The women cook three times a day, seven days per week for fifty-two weeks each year. They are stay home wives, moms, daughters or what have you."

"Isn't that true of most rural communities?"

"It might be. I, however, can only speak for Matura and Point Fortin."

"I get it. Can we go now?"

"Sure. Sign us out and bring the cruiser around."

"I can't do that."

"Oh! I forgot. You can't drive. Please forgive me. I am not thinking straight today."

It was true that Kendal O'Connor couldn't drive but that was not the chief reason for his response to Officer Kanga's instruction. He was more concerned about the ethical aspect of his partner's request to sign him out. Kendal was an individual of moral fortitude who often struggled with behaviors that others saw as normal or routine. Eventually, they went to the front desk together, signed out, and received the keys for cruiser number two.

They left the precinct at 8:30 a.m. and drove to Church Street. Kendal was looking for a quaint little cafe where they could eat when Officer Kanga stopped at the home of Inga Sym. They parked the cruiser, entered the yard, walked up the short flight of stairs and knocked at the door. A female voice said softly, "It's open. Come in."

Kendal and Officer Kanga entered. There were two other people there who were about to finish their breakfast. Officer Kendal O'Connor did not know them. He did not know any civilians in Matura except Tan Sally. Officer Kanga knew one of the men as the clerk at the Warden's Office. The other he recognized as the forest ranger in the region, although he had never been introduced to him before.

After making acquaintances, the officers sat down as Ms. Inga, the host, requested. "What would you have for breakfast today gentlemen?" she asked.

"What do you have?" asked Officer Kanga. "We are not fussy."

"I have the usual."

"What might that be?" Officer Kanga asked since he had not eaten breakfast at Ms. Inga before.

"Today, I am serving corn bake or coconut bake with cheese, scrambled eggs, and or codfish. The beverage could be coffee, milo or ovaltine (chocolate type hot beverages) or tea.

"I will have the corn bake with cheese and a cup of ovaltine." Officer Kanga said.

"And you Officer ....?" Ms. Inga did not say the name. She perhaps did not get it quite right when introduced, or she simply forgot.

"O'Connor," said Kendal. "I will have the coconut bake with scrambled eggs and codfish."

"You've got it. Give me ten minutes or less," Ms. Inga said and disappeared into the kitchen. The Clerk followed her saying, "Ms. Inga, I have to leave now. The forest ranger was right behind him. They paid her and left. On their way out, both wished the officers a good day.

"The same to you," Officer O'Connor said. Officer Kanga said nothing. He was too focused on the delightful aroma of spicy food emanating from Ms. Inga's kitchen.

Just as she promised, Inga Sym had breakfast on the table for the officers within ten minutes. "Enjoy your meal gentlemen," she said. She did not stay to converse with them. Instead, she returned to the kitchen to prepare for her next patron or patrons. Although Kendal and Officer Kanga were served quickly without having an appointment, Ms. Inga generally required one. She always tried to space her customers so as to avoid overcrowding. In that manner there was a steady flow of patrons with only the occasional overlap.

Kendal was eager to get to Sangre Grande to visit Tan Sally at the hospital. In the short time since he had gotten to know her, he felt extremely close to her and was genuinely concerned about her health and wellbeing. He also wanted to visit the stores in Sangre Grande, specifically the jewelry stores, but they were located some distance away from the hospital. He was reluctant, however, to ask his partner to go further into town but was prepared to grasp the opportunity if presented with it.

"What are we going to do between now and lunch time?" Office Kanga asked.

"We are supposed to be on patrol, aren't we?"

"Yes."

"Then that is what we are going to do; patrol. Not before we have visited Tan Sally though."

"Okay."

"Then let's pay the lady and be on our way."

Officer Kanga called out to Ms Inga. She came right away and asked, "What else can I do for you gentlemen?"

"You can tell us how much we owe you."

"That would be three dollars," she said.

Officer Kanga took out his wallet just when Kendal was about to do the same. "No, Kendal. This one is on me. You have not yet been paid, and with the government we have, who knows when you will be paid."

He paid for the meal and Ms. Inga said, "Thank you, gentlemen. Come back for lunch. As new customers, lunch will be on me today."

"We will think about it. Thank you, Ms. Inga." said Officer Kanga. "We have to rush off to Sangre Grande. Hopefully, we will be back before lunch time."

"Well, have a safe trip, and don't forget to stop by if you are back on time."

"Thanks again. Bye." Officer Kanga said and they left.

"What does she mean by lunch is on her today?" Kendal asked.

"Certainly not what you are thinking," Officer Kanga said.

They left Ms. Inga's home and arrived at the hospital at 10:30 a.m., exactly two hours after they left the police station that morning, yet they had not performed any task that could remotely be called part of their duty. Tan Sally was up and about. She was jovial and joking with some members of the staff. When she saw the officers she was so happy and excited, she screamed joyfully and rushed to hug them. Her screams brought two security officers rushing to the area. When they got there, they stood amazed at how the old woman was hugging the police officers.

"They may be her sons," one of the security officers suggested.

"I know her well. She has no children," the other said.

"That is absolutely amazing! You are here just when I am being discharged," Tan Sally said.

"That's good. We can take you home," Officer kanga said.

"The Lord works in mysterious ways," said Tan Sally. "He delivered you here just in the nick of time."

"We are more than happy to oblige, Tan Sally," Kendal said.

"Yes. You get ready, Tan Sally," said Officer Kanga. "We'll be back to get you before twelve o'clock."

"Thank you. Thank you so much."

Both kissed Tan Sally as they were leaving. "Where are we heading?" Kendal asked.

"Sangre Grande proper," Officer Kanga said.

The Lord really works in mysterious ways, Kendal thought but he asked his partner, "Why?"

"Because we can," Officer Kanga said. He looked at Kendal as if to ask, *Do you have any objections?*"

"I am not about to argue with that," Kendal said as if he knew his partner's thoughts.

They left the hospital and arrived downtown Sangre Grande after a ten minute drive. After parking the cruiser at the intersection of Foster and the Eastern Main Road, Officer Kanga invited Kendal to join him for a drink at a dinky little bar called *Coconut Juice* on Ramdass Street, but he declined. His mind was set on finding an engagement ring for Henrietta so he continued walking down the main thoroughfare. Several street venders were bold enough to try and get his attention but he ignored them all. Soon he came upon an elegant, though small jewelry store and decided to go in. As he entered, he was approached by a polite, petite, young woman of Indian and African descent who asked, "What can we do for you today, Officer?" She spoke softly and deliberately, without the typical lilt that was so noticeable everywhere else in town.

"I am looking for a ring," Kendal said.

"Are you looking for something for yourself or as a gift?"

"It can be called a gift," said Kendal. "I am actually looking for an engagement ring."

" I can get you a good price today if you purchase a set."

"A set?" he questioned.

"Yes," said the young woman as a broad smile crossed her face. "My name is Monica," she said, and extended her right hand to Kendal.

He shook her hand and said, "It's nice to meet you."

"Come. Let me show you our selections." She walked off slowly, looking back slightly as Kendal followed.

At the end of a glass showcase furthest from the street, Monica said, "This is our wedding collection." She walked through a gap between two showcases and stood behind the counter of one. "There," she pointed to a tray of gems and said, "These are our most popular designs. She then took a key from a pocket in her skirt, unlocked a door to the glass case, took out the tray of rings and placed it on the counter in front of Kendal.

"What is her size, Officer O'Connor?" She read his name tag before she spoke.

"Size.....? Oh, she is about the same height and size as you are," Kendal said.

"She is petite but do you know her ring size?"

Kendal hesitated. For a brief moment he couldn't remember. Then he said, "Six and a half."

"That is interesting. She is petite, about the same height and size as I am, and she wears the same size ring. What a coincidence." She stretched out her left hand to show-off her diamond as she spoke. "This is it right here," she said while pointing to a similar ring on the tray.

"It is very nice, very nice indeed."

"You can get a set of three that includes this engagement ring and you can save a hundred dollars in the process."

"Is that so?" Kendal questioned.

"Don't worry about it, Officer O'Connor," said Monica. "You can get this on easy credit terms. You may choose the engagement ring, or you may select the set of three that includes the engagement ring and the two wedding bands, one for you and one for her, and save yourself some money in the process. Either way, I can have you pay the same amount every month. Of course it will take you a little longer to finish paying for the set of three."

"Let me think about it," Kendal said. Then he asked, "What time do you close?"

"Today we are closing at five. Monday to Friday we are open from 9:00 a.m. to 5:00 p.m. Saturdays it is 10:00 a.m. to 6:00 p.m.

"I will be back later today."

"Can you give me some idea of time?"

"My tour of duty ends at 4:00 p.m. today. Most likely, I will get here closer to 5:00 p.m."

"That's okay. I will wait for you. Here is my card. If you are unable to make it, give me a call."

"Thanks. I will see you later."

As Kendal turned to leave, Monica stepped from behind the counter to walk with him to the door. He realized her intention and slowed his steps. As they walked slowly toward the door she said, "My fiancé received twenty percent discount off the same set. That was because I work here. I will try to get you the same deal. I can't guarantee anything, but I will try."

"Thanks, Monica."

"I will see you later, Kendal." She did not ask the officer whether she could call him by his first name. She simply did. They smiled at each other. She tapped him on the shoulder and said again, "I'll see you later."

Kendal wasn't really deliberating much about the imminent decision. His mind was pretty much made up. He was going to purchase the set of three rings for five hundred dollars. To buy them individually would have cost him six hundred and fifty dollars altogether. For some strange reason though, Monica was on his mind. Since his first date with Henrietta he had not thought of another woman in that manner, and it bothered him.

He walked back to where he left Officer Kanga. He walked as though he was on patrol in Sangre Grande and no one knew the difference. When he arrived at the *Coconut Juice* on Ramdass Street, Officer Kanga was just walking out. He did not appear inebriated. Kendal felt relieved because the possibility of an officer of law enforcement driving drunk with a sick old lady in the squad car played heavily on his mind when they parted ways earlier.

"You are right on time, Kendal."

"That wasn't by design. We never agreed on a time to meet."

"Well, it worked out fine."

They walked back to where they parked the cruiser at Foster and the Eastern Main Road. All the while Kendal was closely observing Officer Kanga's gait. He noticed that his partner was steady on his feet and he was pleased about that. His concern was not only about the thoughts others may have harbored about them but he was concerned also about their safety.

"So what did you do in town, O'Connor?"

"I went shopping."

"You went shopping in uniform?"

"Not in the sense you are thinking," said Kendal. "I was shopping for a ring."

"You haven't gotten paid yet and already you are shopping for jewelry?"

"Not for myself."

"For whom are you shopping?"

"For my girlfriend, or rather, my fiancée."

"Are you trying to buy her an engagement ring?"

"That's right."

"Does she know that?"

"No. I plan to make it a surprise."

"Be careful with that O'Connor. You might be the one getting the surprise."

"How could that be?"

"You will be surprised if she said, *I can't marry you.*"

"Why would she say that? We have known each other since I was twelve."

"To some women that means nothing. Take it from me. I have had the experience. It is the worst thing that can happen to any man."

"What exactly did you experience?"

"I dated this girl named Laurie for about five years from the time we graduated from high school. Well, from the time she graduated from high school. I did not graduate. Anyway, I decided that I would propose to her on Easter Sunday two years ago," Officer Kanga said and paused.

"So what happened?"

"I bought an engagement ring, never told anyone about it but when I went to pick her up to go to the church bazaar, I popped the question; *Laurie, would you marry me?.* She hesitated before saying a resounding, emphatic *no.* At first I thought she was joking but she said clearly again, *I am sorry. I love you but I can't marry you.* That made no sense to me at all. To this day, it still does not make any sense to me."

"Did you ever ask what her reason was?"

"I did."

"How did she explain it?"

"She said something to the effect that she just wasn't ready to marry someone like me."

"Oh, my God! That must have been devastating."

"It was. I was crushed. We have remained friends but the experience left me suspicious about everyone I have ever dated since. As a result, I may never get married unless I am asked by someone I really care about. Right now though, there is no one I care that much about."

"I feel your pain. With time, however, your emotional wound will heal."

"Kendal, I have never disclosed this to anyone else and I didn't say it to change your mind about your girlfriend. I am sure she is a wonderful girl, nothing like Laurie. Nevertheless, even after you are engaged, take your time and get to know her well."

Damn! That's the same thing the cabby told me. They are all nuts, Kendal thought when he said, "I can't stop the waves from breaking now."

"Just try to avoid drowning. Avoid the rip tide," Officer Kanga said.

"Shit!" Kendal exclaimed.

"What was that about?"

"Nothing, nothing at all." The analogy of drowning was a bad one for Kendal. His own near death experience in the Ortoire River was too recent and surreal for thought.

"Are you in the habit of blurting out profanity for no reason at all?" Officer Kanga asked.

"No. It's just one of those things. You know, sometimes you remember things that you much prefer to forget."

"I can relate to that."

"I am sure you can."

They arrived back at the hospital. By then Tan Sally was dressed and ready to leave. Officer Kanga looked at the time and decided that they can still get back to Matura in time for lunch at Ms. Inga's. *Tan Sally may not have anything at her place for her own lunch*, he thought

"Perhaps we can take Tan Sally to Ms. Inga's with us for lunch."

"Are you forgetting something?"

"What?"

"Lunch is complimentary for us today."

"So we can pay for Tan Sally's."

"I suppose we can but shouldn't we inform Ms. Inga about that first?"

"We probably should. That would be the proper thing to do but right now we have no way of communicating with her. She does not have a telephone."

"Then that's that."

"What does that mean?"

"Tan Sally is going with us. We can share our lunch with her if Ms. Inga is already booked up."

"Good idea, O'Connor."

They walked over to where Tan Sally was sitting and Kendal asked, "Are you ready to go, Tan Sally?"

"Yes, meh dear," she said and stood up.

"Then let's go." He extended his arm and she held him just above his left elbow. Officer Kanga took the small straw bag she was carrying and together they walked slowly to the squad car. Kendal helped her into the back seat and soon they were on their way back to Matura.

When they arrived at Ms. Inga's on Church Street, officer Kanga said, "Wait here with Tan Sally, O'Connor. I am going to see if Ms. Inga could accommodate all of us. Within seconds he was back. "Let's go and eat," he said.

They helped Tan Sally out of the vehicle and assisted her up the short flight of stairs to Ms. Inga's house. Tan Sally needed no introduction. She knew Ms. Inga since she was an infant and Ms. Inga in turn, was glad to see her. They were seated together and served immediately. As it turned out, they got there later than they expected but that might have been a good thing. The civil servants in the area who had lunch at Ms. Inga's had to rush back to work so there was ample space.

After eating Officer Kanga asked, "How was the food, Tan Sally?"

"It was very good. After all, she learnt to cook from her mother who learnt from me." There was a roar of laughter but no one questioned Tan Sally any further about the historical aspect of the relationship between her and Ms. Inga.

Officer Kanga went to the kitchen to settle the check with Ms. Inga. At first she refused to take any money from him, insisting that she invited them for a complimentary meal. Eventually, he managed to convince her to accept payment for Tan Sally's lunch because it wasn't part of the deal. Although, the circumstances dictated that they had no choice other than to take her there with them.

They took Tan Sally home and made certain that she settled in comfortably before leaving. When they did leave, they cruised up and down Church Street, then North East on Toco Main Road almost to Salybia and back. They returned to the precinct, signed in, and as two other officers went out on patrol, they waited for emergency calls. None ever came in.

At 4:05 p.m. Kendal changed into his civilian clothes and waited for the evening staff assigned to street patrol to start duty. It was his hope that he would get a ride to Sangre Grande. That was a courtesy officers of one shift offered to those of the previous shift. Kendal wasn't the only officer who needed to make transit connections in Sangre Grande in order to reach his final destination. He, however, was prompt about it. While others may have chosen to *lime* (hang out with friends) in Matura, Kendal always rushed home so he can visit Henrietta. That Monday, he felt an even greater need to do so because she was with his mother at his home rather than where she lived with her parents.

While he waited he decided to read a few chapters of a novel he had recently purchased. Before his reading could progress though, Officer Kanga said, "Let's go O'Connor."

"Are you going to Sangre Grande?"

"Yes. I am taking a ride with the boys."

"Well, I guess you know that Sangre Grande grinds to a halt after eight o'clock."

"Oh yes! We are only going to be at *Coconut Juice* for about an hour."

Kendal thought of asking, *how many officers were going to the bar?* He quickly decided against it. *I am traveling with them so I will wait and see who else is making the trip*, he concluded his thought. He didn't have to wait long. While he and Officer Kanga sat in the back seat of the cruiser, the two officers who were going out on patrol arrived. The younger looking of the two moved to the driver's seat as the more senior looking officer sat in the front passenger seat. Without hesitation, they were on their way.

They arrived downtown at 4:30 p.m. and dropped Kendal off at the Mayaro taxi stand. "See you tomorrow," one of the officers shouted as they drove off. Kendal wasn't sure who it was. He was glad for the ride and said again, "Thank you."

He spoke briefly with one of the Mayaro taxi drivers who agreed to wait for him. It really wasn't much of an effort on the cab driver's part. Only one passenger was in his cab at the time he spoke with Kendal. The vehicle was licensed for five and rarely did drivers leave Sangre Grande without a full complement of passengers. Kendal assessed the situation and decided that he had enough time to set up an account with the jewelry store. He walked over there and was greeted at the door by Monica who saw him the very moment he got out of the police cruiser at the Mayaro taxi stand.

"You made it here with time to spare," she said. He looked at his watch and smiled. Then Monica said, "Come with me."

Kendal followed her to the rear of the store where the wedding collections were kept. "Here is what I managed to do for you," she said. He did not comment so she continued, "I got you an employee discount of twenty per cent, the same discount my fiancé got when he purchased my ring. So you see, there are some advantages to working here."

"I see. Thank you," he said with a smile.

"Now, instead of paying $660.00 for the set of three rings, you will pay only $528.00. That is a saving of $132.00."

"That's great. I truly appreciate it. Thank you."

"You are welcome. Don't forget though, there will be a four per cent simple interest charge added to your principal of $528.00, should you decide to purchase these on credit. If you pay cash, the total payment will be $528.00."

"I will purchase it on credit."

"Okay! It will take my manager about ten minutes to set up your account."

"Thank you."

"Give me a few minutes," Monica said. She left and walked to the back of the store with the jewelry Kendal had chosen. Shortly afterward a tall dark man came out with the rings in his hand. He shook Kendal's hand and said, "My name is Ray. I would need some personal information from you. The usual, you know; your full name, age, where you work, where you live, those sorts of things."

"No problem," Kendal said. He gave the gentleman the information he needed, and signed some papers after reading the agreement carefully. Ray then left him and shortly afterward Monica returned with the rings neatly packaged. The engagement ring was packaged separately from the wedding bands.

"Today is your lucky day," said Monica. She smiled, handed the packages to Kendal and said, "I can tell that you are a very nice man. I want to wish you all the best."

"Thank you," Kendal said and stretched out his hand. Monica did not shake his hand but instead, swiftly and without hesitation moved closer and gave him a hug. "I know your fiancée would love it. I hope she appreciates you." Monica whispered. What she did not tell Kendal was that she gave up her 20% commission on the sale just to get him the 20% discount.

"Thanks again," Kendal said before leaving.

"Stay in touch," Monica responded and quickly retreated to the back of the store.

Kendal returned to the taxi stand and found that there were four passengers in the car. "Sorry I kept you waiting," he said.

"You didn't really. John here, the fourth passenger, just arrived. If you are ready, we can go now."

Kendal sat in the rear right seat behind the driver. He was traveling in civilian garb and felt comfortable enough to lean back and close his eyes, something he never would have done had he been in uniform. He thought of Henrietta, anticipating the excitement in her voice when he presented her with the ring and ask her to marry him. He thought of her smile, not her ordinary smile with which she greeted most people. Instead, he thought of her special, gracious, seductive smile which she often shared with him. Then he thought of Monica's smile, the way she smiled at him when he was leaving the store after her bear hug. There was a striking similarity to Henrietta's seductive smile. A strange feeling came over him. He opened his eyes. *I hope I was dreaming,* he thought. He knew, however, that he wasn't sleeping so it could only have been a fleeting thought. *Why do I feel this way, and why am I thinking about Monica in this manner?* He wondered. Since he had been dating Henrietta he had never thought of another woman in a romantic light and he couldn't understand why such thoughts would occur of Monica, a complete stranger, when he was so much in love with Henrietta.

He closed his eyes again as the driver turned onto the Manzanilla/Mayaro Road from the Eastern Main Road. That time the warm, fresh Atlantic breeze blowing through the open window to his left and over the two passengers next to him, quickly lulled him to sleep. He slept soundly without snoring. So too did the other two passengers who sat to his left.

It was 5:37 p.m. when the taxi driver pulled his cab up onto the Mayaro taxi stand. The man sitting next to Kendal woke up and asked, "Are we here already?"

"Yeah, man." said the taxi driver.

The passenger shook Kendal and said, "You are home Officer."

"Not yet," said the cab driver. "He still has to make his way to Mafeking."

"Oh yes! That's right. I forgot that for a moment."

Kendal stepped out of the vehicle, paid the driver, and made certain that his prized purchase was secure and still in his possession.

"I can take you home," said the driver. "I am not going back to Sangre Grande tonight."

"That's a good idea. Thanks," Kendal said. He repositioned himself in the front passenger seat and the driver took off.

"I saw you in uniform this morning. You looked really good, man."

"Thanks for the compliment. I travel to work in uniform but I seldom wear it on my return, just in case I have things to do that are unrelated to my duties as a police officer."

"I understand, man. You are a great role model for the young children growing up here."

"I will always do what I can……." Right here! Right here," Kendal forgot to inform the driver that he was approaching his home and as a result he overshot the driveway. Kendal attempted to remove his wallet to pay the fare when the driver said, "No charge man."

"That's so nice of you. Thanks again."

"You are welcome, man."

He stepped out of the vehicle, closed the door and said, "Thanks again."

"No problem. Take care," the cab driver said and left.

FOURTEEN

Dorothy and Henrietta were playing card games when Kendal arrived home and greeted them. They were on their third game and although it was bridge, a game they both enjoyed, they ended it without discussion or discord the moment he said, "Hello! I am home." Their faces were glowing with the joy of seeing him that early in the evening. He walked toward them and kissed Henrietta. She held his arm tightly, delaying, though not deliberately, his intention to kiss his mother as he always did when he arrived home. Eventually she released her hold on him and he kissed Dorothy on her forehead and said, "Oh! It is so good to be home."

"You are here early today," Dorothy said.

"Transportation was good. The driver who brought me from Sangre Grande was kind enough to bring me all the way home."

"You see, there are advantages to being a police officer."

"Is that so? You are not a cop, Mom, but taxi drivers have done the same thing for you."

"Well, there are advantages to being a woman also."

"Are they the same advantages? That's strange."

"Please! Don't go there," Henrietta said and Dorothy immediately changed the topic.

"It is nice to see that you home safely. Now I must go," she said.

"Where are you going, Mom? I just got here."

"I promised Bertha that I would come over this evening."

"Your mother did ask me earlier to go with her but I wasn't up to it."

"Oh, Well......."

"I am sorry, son. You know how it is with us."

"Yes. I know"

"I will see you later, Etta."

"Okay! Bye Ms. Dorothy." Henrietta said with a smile, and Dorothy walked out of the door. *She is such a sweet girl*, she thought as she was leaving.

"You must be very tired from a hard day at work and all of that traveling." Henrietta suggested.

"Strangely enough, I am not tired at all."

"I always thought of police work as being very stressful and exhausting."

"That might be true for someone working in the city. In Matura, however, everyone is very laidback."

"Now that you mentioned it, I have noticed that the officers in Mayaro are also easy-going."

Kendal got up from where he was sitting and took his mother's seat on the couch next to Henrietta. He fidgeted with the deck of cards. That prompted Henrietta to say, "Oh no! I am not playing anymore card games for the rest of the day or night."

"Gee! You really made that quite clear. I guess Mom beat you up real good."

"You stop now," said Henrietta. "I won a few."

"You won a few? So I was right?" Henrietta was laughing. She did not answer but Kendal did not allow the laughter to continue. He sealed her lips with a kiss. She reciprocated as they continued kissing each other passionately for almost five minutes, pausing briefly only to breathe clearly. When they eventually relaxed their embrace, Kendal said, "Etta, I have something to ask you but only after I have showered and changed." She looked at him and smiled. He knew it was her signature smile but it seemed so much like the way Monica smiled at him earlier that day.

"It is not what you are thinking."

"Then why is the suspense necessary?"

"That wasn't intended to be suspenseful. I simply don't want to rush."

"Then can I shower with you?"

The question took Kendal by surprise. He could not give Henrietta an answer right away but she interpreted the silence as consent. He went into the shower thinking, *is she for real? Suppose mom walked in and found us naked in the shower?* He turned the water on. That was an unwitting signal for Henrietta to join him. She stripped herself naked in the living room, left her clothing on the floor, walked to the back and entered the bathroom.

Kendal did not hear her come in, so he was startled when she placed her hand on his back. She intended only to apply some soap. His unusual reaction caused her to laugh out loudly.

"That was not funny," he said. He wasn't angry though. Instead, he held her tenderly and their shower progressed slowly. Because the water wasn't pipe borne but came instead from a cistern located at the side of the house just below the level of the roof, Kendal was aware that it could be depleted if they continued to be tender with each other in the shower for too long. Henrietta, however, was oblivious to that fact and was content on enjoying Kendal's company for as long as he held her warmly in the cold shower.

They stepped out of the shower before the inevitable happened, towel-dried themselves and headed to separate rooms. Kendal went to his bedroom. Henrietta went to the living room to gather her soiled clothing before going to the room she shared temporarily with Dorothy. She put on some fresh, clean clothes, stretched out on the futon and dosed off. Kendal rapped at the door and woke her up.

"What is it now?" she asked.

"Could you come here. I need to speak with you."

"In just one minute." Henrietta looked in the mirror and attempted to fix her hair before stepping out of the room.

"Come, sit here," he said and patted the seat next to him, at his right on the couch. She sat down and leaned on him.

"There is something we need to talk about."

"Do we need to talk about it now?"

"Of course, this is as good a time as any."

"Okay."

"Do you recall when we first met?"

"Yes." Henrietta said while wondering, *where is he going with this now?*

"We have remained just as close ever since. In fact, we have been in love ever since."

Henrietta placed the weight of her entire petite frame on him. He hugged her as her breathing pattern changed from normal to rapid. He felt his pocket to be certain that he could access the engagement ring even with Henrietta leaning on him. It was accessible, a perfect scenario, he thought. He retrieved it and without any further delay, he asked, "Would you marry me, Etta?"

There was a brief period of silence before she whispered, "Yes." He took her left hand and slipped the ring onto her finger. It fitted perfectly.

"Oh Kendal, I love it. How did you know what size ring to purchase?"

"Let's just call it intuition."

"Oh! I love you so much," said Henrietta. "I wish I could make you the happiest man in the world but that would be difficult." Suddenly, she started to cry. Kendal tried to comfort her and assure her that they would do just fine together but her tears just kept flowing.

"Please don't worry," he pleaded. "I now have a good job. I wouldn't ask you to marry me if I didn't think that I can provide for a family." Henrietta shook her head indicating the affirmative and giving him the impression that she clearly understood his position but she continued to cry. He had never before seen her like that and he pleaded, "Please Etta! Darling, please don't cry." She dried her eyes, blew her nose and said, "I am sorry, Kendal."

"It's okay."

"No! No, no......," she said, and started crying again. She cried like a colicky baby. Kendal was confused. He held her close and ran his finger through her hair repeatedly in an effort to comfort her. "Would you like to go for a walk?" he asked. She shook her head to indicate no. Meanwhile, He was becoming concerned that his mother would return home soon and see her crying again.

"Is there anything at all that I can do for you right now?"

"No. I want to lie down for a few minutes."

"Okay."

She got up and so did Kendal. He held her close as they walked to the door of his mother's bedroom. He stopped short of entering the room with her. She understood without him having to explain. "Call me whenever you are up," he said.

"I will," she said as she rested her head on the pillow on the futon. Her legs were still on the floor when he turned away. He was worried, very worried. He returned to the couch in the living room, stretched out his legs and rested his feet on the coffee table; something he never would have done at any other time. He did it without thinking of the consequences if his mother came in and saw that. Or perhaps he did it thinking that he was a working adult and there wasn't much she could do about it. Whatever the reason, he leaned back, closed his eyes and thought about the situation. Eventually, he fell asleep.

Although they were in different rooms, or perhaps because of that, they both slept soundly for about an hour. Henrietta was awake first. She looked in the mirror and felt the need to wash her face. She did. She then dried her face thoroughly and applied a small amount of make-up from a compact she kept in her purse. She walked out and was surprised to find Kendal sound asleep with his feet on his mother's coffee table.

"Kendal! Kendal," she shouted. He was startled. "What are you doing sleeping with your feet on the table?"

"Uh, oh," he murmured and stretched before resting his feet firmly on the floor. "Are you okay now?" he asked.

"Yes," she said. Without waiting to hear anything else from him, she went into the bathroom, poured some rubbing alcohol on a towel and wiped down the glass top of the coffee table with it.

"What was that for?"

"If Ms. Dorothy came in and saw your feet on her table you would have known what that was all about."

"What could she have done, spanked me?"

"You know better than I do, Kendal."

"Okay! Enough of what Mom would or wouldn't do. What about you? Are you feeling any better?"

"Yes."

"That's good. You had me worried for a while."

"I am sorry. I was overwhelmed by it all."

"Overwhelmed by what? It is okay, honey. It's okay, really," Kendal said.

"That's easy for you to say."

"Alright then, is there something in particular that we need to talk about?"

"Yes. In fact, there are several things we should talk about."

"Then let's talk."

"I am afraid, Kendal."

"When were you ever afraid to speak with me?"

"Since I saw how angry you can get sometimes."

"I got angry with you once in our lifetime and you know why. Yet, here you are holding that against me."

"I am not holding it against you," said Henrietta. "Since then, however, I have been very cautious as to what I say or do."

"That is not necessarily a bad thing."

"Not in or of itself but............"

"But what?"

"Never mind...."

"Please don't do that, Etta. You said we should talk and I agreed, but it takes two to converse and there could be no conversation if one of us conceals his or her thoughts."

"This is very difficult for me, Kendal"

"Just try me."

"How can I be sure that you would stay calm and listen to me?"

"You have my word. That's my honor."

"I love you dearly, Kendal."

"Oh! Oh!"

"What? Didn't you know that?"

"I do know that, but the manner in which you said it gave me the impression that something more serious was to follow."

"You are right. This is difficult for me but I have to let you know that I am in the family way."

"You are pregnant?" Kendal used the word that was taboo in the Mayaro community. It was considered to be rude and disrespectful to use the word *pregnant*, although no one ever said so outright.

Henrietta shook her head. Then she said very softly, "Ah ha." She did not normally speak to Kendal like that, so he asked, "Is that a yes?"

"Yes," she said.

"How is that possible? We have always been so careful. You know how I feel about having children out of wedlock. Mom had to struggle to raise me all by herself"

We will already be married by the time the baby arrives, she thought but said, "It is not for you, Kendal."

"What do you mean?"

"The baby is not yours."

Kendal was shocked into silence. Neither of them spoke for at least two minutes, which seemed to each as an eternity. Finally he asked, "Karish?" Henrietta shook her head indicating no. "Oh! my God, no!" He exclaimed. He was trying desperately to be even-tempered.

"Contrary to what you thought that evening you saw us together, Karish and I were never intimate."

"You are forgetting something, Henrietta. I didn't just see you together walking to the shop or something like that"

"I know, and I am sorry." That was actually the first time that she apologized for her action that so infuriated him.

He sighed. It was not a sigh of relief but one of burden. *What are we going to do?* He wondered. Then he asked, "Who is the father of this unborn child, Etta?" With tears in her eyes she said, "Rudolf."

"Who the hell is Rudolf?" Kendal questioned.

"You promised not be angry."

"Yeah, right!" I just proposed to you. Now you are telling me that you are pregnant with another man's child and I am not supposed to be damn mad, he thought but maintained his composure and asked again, "Who is Rudolf?"

"Mr. Vargas."

"Dumb ass Vargas?" he questioned angrily.

Henrietta shook her head and said softly, "Yes."

"Lord! Lord, Lord."

"I cannot explain this, Kendal."

"You don't have to. I know how it happened," he said. He bent over and supported his head with the palms of his hands while resting his elbows on his thighs. He was silent but breathing hard. Henrietta knew how angry he was. Yet, she stroked the back of his head. He did not respond, so she said again, "I am so sorry, Kendal. I really am." For someone who never before apologized for her actions, she had apologized to Kendal O'Connor twice in one evening. She was sobbing softly by then and the tears were pouring down her cheeks.

Kendal sat up, put his arms around her and asked, "Who else knows that you are pregnant?"

"No one else knows."

"Are you sure?" Henrietta hesitated so he asked, "Did you tell Vargas that you are pregnant?"

"No."

"Does your mother know that you are pregnant?"

"No."

"Then who knows?"

"I suspect the nurses at the hospital may know. They took several blood and urine samples from me while I was there."

"That's not a problem. Even if they know that you are pregnant, they do not know for whom. Knowing Mayaro and its people as well as I do, I can guarantee you that everyone would be saying that I am the father of your unborn child."

"Wouldn't you be bothered by all the gossip?"

"No. We are engaged to be married, so what could people gossip about?"

"So what if........?"

"What if Vargas claims it is his baby?" Kendal asked as if he knew exactly what concerned Henrietta although she did not complete the question.

She shook her head and Kendal responded by saying, "He wouldn't dare."

He certainly wasn't pleased that his fiancée was pregnant for someone else but he was confident that their love for each other would endure any storm of controversy. He felt certain that after the baby's birth there could be no clear cut phynotypical evidence that he was not the biological father. That would not have been the case had Henrietta named Karish as the biological father. Although the structure of DNA was only recently deduced, Kendal understood the concept fully and had some concerns. Nevertheless, he was determined to take that chance on love; his love for Henrietta and their child. Their future looked bright and he wasn't going to let something like an unplanned pregnancy get in the way.

"Here is what we will do," he said. "From this day on, Etta, it's you and me and our child or children. We will not allow anyone else to get between us."

Henrietta smiled and said "Yes. I made an egregious error in judgment. I am truly sorry." That marked the third time that evening that she actually expressed regret to Kendal.

"We can work through this if we work together."

"I know we can," she said.

"All we have to do is try hard."

They were smiling again. They had made a pact to continue to love each other in spite of Etta's little gaffe. *Could this have been the reason why I was having those strange thoughts of Monica?* Kendal wondered, but he quickly dismissed it. He hugged his bride-to-be and kissed her. She parted his lips with her tongue, closed her eyes and drifted away.

Suddenly, the front door opened. It was never locked but apparently they expected that someone coming in would knock before entering. Dorothy, however, expected them to be asleep and simply pushed the door in gently in an effort not to awaken them.

"I am sorry." she said. She wasn't sure whether she was sorry for not knocking before entering, or sorry that the door wasn't locked, or that her son and his girlfriend were making love in her living room right before her very eyes. Either way, it didn't seem to bother either Kendal or Henrietta. Neither one responded. Although, they eventually detached themselves from each other long enough for Kendal to say, "We didn't expect you back so soon, Mom."

"I have been gone for quite a while. It was 10:45 when I left Philbertha's. I am sure it is even closer to eleven o'clock now."

"We wanted you to be the first to know."

"What did you want me to be the first to know?"

"That we are engaged."

"Engaged? As in engaged to be married?"

"Yes."

"Oh! My goodness! That is the best surprise I have had in my entire life. Congratulations!"

"Thank you," Henrietta said.

"Come here, girl. Let me give you a hug." Henrietta stood up and she and Dorothy hugged each other tightly.

Kendal sat feeling very pleased. He knew how much his mother liked Henrietta and was never in doubt of the acceptance. The big question on his mind was whether or when should they inform her of the pregnancy, how much information should they divulge, and when was it most appropriate to let her in on their most private issues yet. There were no easy answers so Kendal decided that unless Henrietta slipped up, they would just give it time.

Henrietta showed the ring to Dorothy who examined it and said, "Oh, girl. I love it. Did you choose it yourself?"

"No. Kendal did. I didn't even know of the plan."

"The boy has good taste."

"The man has good taste, Mom." Kendal corrected his mother. He had been trying for a long time to get her to stop referring to him and other grown men as boy; an old, bad habit among Trinidadians.

"You stop now." Dorothy was laughing when she said that.

This is not a joke, Mom, he thought. At the same time Henrietta said, "It's in the blood, I guess."

"It's in the genes," Kendal corrected her.

"Whatever! I am going to bed," said Dorothy. "It is almost mid-night. You two could stay up until dawn if you wish. Good night."

"Good night, Ms. Dorothy."

"Good night, Mom."

Dorothy O'Connor left the room and left her son and future daughter-in-law in somewhat of a quandary. They too realized that they should retire to bed because Kendal had to travel to Matura to his job the next day. What they couldn't decide upon was their sleeping arrangement.

"Now that we are engaged to be married and have reconciled our differences, do we share the same bed?" Henrietta asked.

"I am tempted but I don't know how that would go over with Mom."

"So you have doubts."

"You could say that. Yes!"

"Then that answers the question. We will maintain the status quo, for tonight at least."

FIFTEEN

Breakfast was on the table by the time Kendal was ready to leave the house that Tuesday morning. Dorothy was up early as usual and she did not miss a beat when it came to the chores she routinely performed. Henrietta too managed to wake up earlier than usual to see her fiancé off to work. She was amazed at how much Dorothy had accomplished before 6:00 a.m. At first she was inclined to think that it was just a display of efficiency on Dorothy's part, designed to demonstrate to her how household chores are to be done or how her son should be treated when she, Henrietta, became Mrs. O'Connor. She soon realized though, that Dorothy's performance was no act. She had done the same thing the day before, and 363 days before that, for the past twenty or so years.

Dorothy tried to persuade Kendal to sit down and have breakfast but he politely decline, insisting that 6:30 a.m. was much too early for any human to eat.

"I will have only the coffee," he said.

"Okay," Dorothy said. She poured freshly brewed coffee into his cup and he added cream and sugar.

"How about you, Etta? Would you like some coffee?"

"I would but not right now. It's much too early. Thank you."

"This coffee would be no good by the time you are ready for it."

"Why not?"

"Brewed coffee is best when served within twenty minutes of brewing."

" I wasn't aware of that," said Henrietta. "What goes wrong with it after twenty minutes?"

"It tastes like hell."

"A taste of hell? That must be awful."

"Awful, is putting it mildly." They laughed and had fun about coffee from hell until Kendal said, "I must go now."

Dorothy and Henrietta got up and walked him to the door where he kissed them both, said good bye, stepped out to the curb and hailed a taxi. He was gone in a flash.

"That's a routine you would become accustomed to, my dear," Dorothy said.

"I hope so," said Henrietta. "I am usually up early but my early is somewhere between six and seven o'clock."

"Well, I don't have to tell you, it is not yet seven o'clock and already he is gone."

"I don't know how you do it, Ms. Dorothy."

"I don't know either. I have only been doing it for a week now. Making him an early breakfast, that is"

"I know. It probably helped that you have been accustomed to getting up very early."

"You are right. That does help. Anyway, there is no need for you to stay up now. You are going to have plenty of time for that."

"You are right again. I am going back to bed."

"You do that. Before you do though, what would you like for lunch?"

"I have no preference, Ms. Dorothy. Anything you prepare I will eat."

"Good."

"Oh! Would you mind if I stayed another day and leave tomorrow morning?"

"Why would I mind? I love your company," said Dorothy. "Wouldn't your parents be concerned though?"

"I doubt it. They know where I am."

"Okay."

"Besides, I want to surprise Kendal this evening."

"Hmm," Dorothy murmured. *I wonder what she is planning to give him this evening that is so different.*

Sydney and Joshua meanwhile, were in their respective backyard vegetable gardens. They had already watered the plants that morning and were removing weeds when Joshua suggested that they try out the finished tops for accuracy and design.

"When did you finish the tops?" Sydney asked.

"I completed them a few days ago. In fact, it was the same day you got angry and walked off."

"Well, my guess is that your arm is completely healed. I notice that you are no longer using the sling."

"It is better but by no means completely healed."

"Did they remove the stitches as yet?"

"I am going to get that done today."

"What time are you going to the hospital?"

"I was told to be there at 11:00 a.m., so that's when I'll be there. Why?"

"I was hoping that it could have been at 3:00 p.m."

"Why?"

"That's when school is dismissed, stupid."

"Now, when I speak to you like that you get all testy with me."

"When you speak to me like what?"

"Whenever I call you, *stupid.*"

"I find that to be annoying, yes."

"So it annoys you to be called *stupid* but it is okay for you call others *stupid*?"

"It's only a manner of speaking."

"Only when you are the speaker, right?"

"You know something, JJ, It is after seven o'clock. I have to get ready for school."

"I know. You run away every time you are proven wrong."

"Say whatever you want to say, JJ. I am out of here."

"It's Ms. Gardener. Isn't it?"

"You could say that. She is a good teacher and I am in her class."

"Yeah, right!"

"What crap!" Sydney exclaimed and walked away.

In Joshua's mind either Sydney was attracted to his teacher, Ms. Gardener, or Ms. Gardener was providing him with more than an education and an occasional newspaper. Joshua himself had stopped attending school at age six or seven and started liming (hanging out) with older boys whose focus was on all things other than education.

Joshua was never allowed to participate in conversations between his mother and grandmother, but he was, more often than not, within hearing distance of some rude, crude, suggestive, and sometimes erotic comments they made. Much of what he heard at home was reinforced by behaviors he observed among the other wayward boys in the neighborhood.

The constant ridicule of others, particularly women, in the Jacob's household, fostered in him, a level of disrespect for women in general and younger women in particular. He, unfortunately, was unable to separate the caring and interest that Sydney's teacher showed toward him as an excellent student from what he, Joshua, perceived as a romantic interest. He also did not quite understand Sydney's desire to aspire and achieve. As far as he was concerned, life was good. He was never hungry, and he had someplace to sleep at nights.

Joshua did have a desire to learn to read, primarily to be able to glean information from sports magazines, fliers and rosters. There was no clear explanation why he wanted to learn to do mathematics. Perhaps he had an underlying desire to be like Sydney, Arjune, or Kendal. In spite of how he acted sometimes, he was proud of his cousin, Sydney.

When he was alone and reflected on his latest feud with Sydney, Joshua felt remorseful. He understood that sometimes his anger was uncontrolled but in their latest disagreement, he was convinced that Sydney was being disrespectful toward him.

Kendal arrived at the Matura Police Station early and ready to work. He checked the schedule and found that it was identical to the previous day's schedule. He and Officer Kanga were assigned to patrol duty from 8:00 a.m. to 1:00 p.m. with one hour for lunch which was allowed anytime between 11:00 a. m. and 1:00 p.m. Shortly after Kendal's arrival, Officer Kanga walked in, greeted everyone there before he turned to Kendal and asked, "Whom are you patrolling with today?"

"I am with you."

"What's the schedule?"

"It is the same as yesterday."

"Then I will get the cruiser. It's breakfast time, man."

Officer Kanga walked to the back of the station to get the vehicle while Kendal exited the building at the front. There, he waited briefly and was picked up by his senior partner. They drove down the hill without saying much to each other. Soon they entered Church Street and headed directly to Inga Sym's house. Officer Kanga knocked on the open front door and Ms. Inga said, "It's open. Come in."

The officers took off their caps and walked through Inga's neatly furnished living room. They walked past the dining area and stood at the door to the kitchen.

"Good morning," they said together as if they rehearsed it. Inga turned around, smiled, and said, "Good morning officers. It's so good to see you again."

"We couldn't stay away. The aroma from your kitchen literally dragged us out of the station."

"You are Mr. Mamaguy (flattery) himself," said Inga. She laughed. Then she said, "I am flattered though. I like that."

"You should. We are for real."

"Thanks."

Officer Kanga was doing all the talking but he noticed that Ms. Inga was directing her responses to Kendal. He looked at him and winked. Then he whispered something which Kendal didn't hear but nevertheless, he responded by saying, "I think I will have the same thing I had yesterday."

"That would be the coconut bake with scrambled eggs and codfish, isn't it?" Ms. Inga asked.

"That's correct."

Officer Kanga winked at Kendal again. Then he said, "Ms. Inga doesn't miss a beat, man."

"She has a really good memory," Kendal said.

Ms. Inga smiled and asked, "What are you having Officer Kanga?"

"For me it will be the same as yesterday except for the ovaltine. I would prefer local coffee today."

"Okay. That would be.............." Ms. Inga hesitated and Officer Kanga completed her trend of thought. .. "............. corn bake with cheese," he said.

"Coming up,"

"Do you see it now, Kendal?" Officer Kanga whispered.

"See what?"

"What I told you earlier."

"You whispered something but I didn't hear what it was you were saying. I am unable to read lips."

"These are skills you are going to have to develop as a police officer. Some day your life may depend on them. Anyway, she is on to you."

"Why do you think so?"

"She forgot your name but she remembered what you ate yesterday."

"What one thing has to do with the other?"

"You will learn, lad. You will learn."

"I imagine I will learn something new every day I am on patrol with you."

"I can promise you that much."

Ms. Inga brought their breakfast to the dining table and asked if there was anything else they may want. Neither of the officers made any request, so she excused herself and turned to return to the kitchen to prepare for her other patrons. She did not make them an offer of a free lunch again but it was her hope that her promotion of the previous day was effective and that they would return for lunch. As she walked away, Officer Kanga looked at her and commented to his partner, "Lord! Is she well stacked?" There was no response from Kendal.

As they ate they conversed. The topics varied but strangely enough, police work was not discussed. That could have been because of the peaceful nature of the inhabitants of Matura. The precinct was there and it was staffed but the officers had very little to do. Nevertheless, the government had no choice but to ensure that security, as perceived by the presence of law enforcement, was in place. Office Kanga loved it there and said to Kendal, "If I am ever transferred to the city, Nelson Street perhaps, I would resign."

"Why?" Office O'Connor asked.

"I do not want to work anywhere else."

"Did you ask to be sent to Matura?"

"No."

"So when you learnt that you were coming here didn't you think that it was too remote and country for you?"

"No. I think I told you before that I grew up in Toco, so I was quite familiar with this area before coming to work here. As you can see, it can hardly get any better than this."

"You say that with such authority."

"Of course, just look at us. It is 8:30 in the morning and we are being served breakfast in the dining room of a house owned by one of the prettiest women in town. In fact, we are served by the prettiest woman herself, and she does it with such charm and grace."

"You can probably get the same or similar service elsewhere."

"Where else can we get that service?"

"I can't think of any place in particular right now."

"There is none."

"You don't know that."

"Okay! Does this happen in Mayaro?"

"I don't think so."

"Does it happen in Guayaguayare, Rio Claro, or Moruga?"

"I don't know."

"Then I am right. Unless you can prove me wrong, you are lucky to be working in paradise, man."

They were finished eating and Officer Kanga called out to Ms. Inga for the check. "It's the same as yesterday," she responded.

"Does that mean lunch is included?"

Ms. Inga laughed and said, "You are something else, Officer Kanga."

"Something else, how does that differ from a piece of something?"

"I don't know. You are funny too." Ms. Inga was laughing again. So too was Kendal.

"Okay. We will be back for lunch but this time it is our treat."

"Whatever you say, officer."

"Then we will see you around noon."

"That's fine."

"Okay then. Bye."

"Just how do you plan to treat her to lunch?" Kendal asked as they walked out to the squad car.

"I have no plan. That was just sweet talk (flattery). She knows that and she enjoyed hearing it."

"Don't you think it is dishonest to say to someone something you do not mean?"

"No! Everybody does it. When you said good morning to me earlier, did you mean it?"

"Yes."

"Crap!"

"I really wished that your morning would be good."

"So far, it has turned out fine. Thanks."

"You are welcome."

"The issue is unresolved though."

"Why was that an issue in the first place?"

"It is a source of conflict and misgivings. How many times have you said I love you to someone only because the three little words rolled off your tongue easily without meaning?"

"I have never done that."

"You may have picked the wrong vocation, O'Connor."

"Why do you say that?"

"You are so honest, so trusting, and so delicate. In this business one should never be any of those things." Kendal pondered what his partner had to say but did not respond to it. Instead, he asked, "Can we check on Tan Sally before going back to the station?"

"We certainly can. In fact, we should. I intended to suggest that myself."

"Shouldn't we have gotten breakfast for her?"

Officer Kanga looked at his watch. It was 8:45 a.m. so he said, "No. She wakes up at 5:00 a.m. every day. She would have had breakfast a long time ago."

They drove directly to Tan Sally's. The front door was open so they walked in. As they entered, Officer Kanga called out, Tan Sally! Good morning."

Does he mean that? Kendal wondered as he himself said, "Good morning, Tan Sally." There was no immediate answer and both police officers became worried. Just when they contemplated investigating further, Tan Sally walked up the kitchen steps and asked, "Who deh?"

"It's O'Connor and Kanga," said Officer Kanga. "We were becoming concerned when we got no answer."

"Oh! My sons, my dear sons. What happened, you thought I died?"

"We were not thinking anything so drastic. We only hoped that you were not sick again."

"I am fine. I am not yet ready to kick the bucket (to die)" Tan Sally said. She was laughing. Officer Kanga was laughing with her. Kendal, however, didn't think any of it was funny and although he tried, he couldn't laugh.

"Why you came so late?" asked Tan Sally when she composed herself. "I already had breakfast."

"Oh? We were hoping to take you out to breakfast this morning."

"What a liar you are," said Tan Sally. "You know that I wake up early and have breakfast early." That caused Kendal to laugh. *Someone else thinks that he is being dishonest*, he thought, but he asked, "Would you care to join us for lunch then, Tan Sally?"

"I can fix you lunch. I told you Inga learned to cook from her mother who learned from me."

"We know that your cooking is as good, if not better than hers but we want to save you the trouble," Kendal said.

"My cooking is better and to me it is no trouble at all."

"We have already made the reservation, Tan Sally."

"Why do you need a reservation to eat some home cooked food, son?"

Kendal was unable to answer Tan Sally's question and Officer Kanga offered no suggestions or assistance. They were in a quandary. Obviously, Tan Sally didn't want to go to Ms. Inga's for lunch. She was exhibiting a measure of jealousy they had never before seen in a person of her age. Both wanted to know something of the family histories that may have engendered those feelings or qualities but neither could bring himself to ask Tan Sally that. Eventually, Officer Kanga came up with a compromise. "Tan Sally," he said. "We are coming back to have lunch with you but we just had breakfast so keep it very light. Will you?"

"How does a Matura woman fix her sons a light lunch?" she asked. Then she offered some suggestions of her own. "Stewed corned fish and crushed plantains with stewed pigeon peas? Or Creole rice with stewed chicken and callaloo? Or would you prefer just a chip-chip pie?"

"The chip-chip pie would be nice."

"Chip-chip pie it is."

"What time?" Officer O'Connor asked.

"You tell me, son."

"Eleven thirty," he suggested.

"That's good," said Tan Sally. "I will be ready."

"Okay. We will be back at eleven thirty."

"Don't be late. Those pies have to be eaten hot."

"We know."

"Good. See you then.

"Bye, Tan Sally." The officers left feeling satisfied that they could return for a light lunch with Tan Sally and still keep their appointment with Ms. Inga.

They cruised around the village, made a quick run to the beach and returned to Tan Sally's. She had the pies ready and had prepared a spinach and tomato salad to complement the meal. The fact that the officers were on duty did not stop her from offering them some of her home made wine. It was not against the law to make or consume wine. She did, however, clearly breach the law by having a bottle of babash (bootleg rum) on the table. Officer O'Connor was uncomfortable with that, but Officer Kanga was delighted. Both officers knew that producing or possessing bootleg rum was against the law. They disagreed as to who should abide by the law. In spite of those differences in opinion, they enjoyed Tan Sally's chip-chip pie and salad. Before leaving they promised that if they are assigned together the next day they would make a visit with her their first stop.

The officers left Tan Sally's and headed over to Ms. Inga's. They were still famished. The meal Tan Sally provided sufficed only as an appetizer. That was exactly what they hoped would happen so they could keep their luncheon appointment with Ms. Inga without upsetting Tan Sally.

Ms. Inga Sym was at the front door saying farewell to another patron when the officers arrived. She was very glad to see them. The mere fact that they returned, indicated to her that there was something good about her cooking. She had gained two new customers. She was delighted. However, she hoped for more and conveyed that in her greeting although it went unnoticed by the officers.

"Come in gentlemen. Your lunch is ready. I hope you would become regulars."

Officer Kanga stepped inside first. As Officer O'Connor walked in, Ms. Inga followed and gave him a nudge about his shoulder. "Don't be shy, Kendal," she said as they walked through the door.

"He is not shy at all," said Officer Kanga. "He is mild mannered but not shy."

"Whatever! If it works for him, that's fine."

"It works for him alright."

"I can believe that."

"You can believe it, but do you?"

"Of course I do," said Ms. Inga. She was looking directly at Kendal and smiling. Although, the smile was not the same he received from Henrietta or Monica.

"Why do you keep speaking of me in the third person?" asked Kendal. "Are you forgetting that I am here?"

"Oh! No. How could we," Ms. Inga said and leaned on him. That caused Officer Kanga to wink at him again, and Ms. Inga promptly resumed her business persona.

"Sit anywhere gentlemen. Your lunch is coming right up," she said, although there were only two place settings at the table. She left the officers there and hurried to the kitchen. As quickly as she left, she returned and placed the meal on the table.

"This looks so good," Officer O'Connor said.

So do you, Ms. Inga thought, but she said, "I think it would taste as good as it looks."

"It certainly does," said Officer Kanga. He had already tasted the food.

"Enjoy your meal," Ms. Inga said and left the room.

"I told you she was into you," said Officer Kanga. "I guess you are not interested."

"Actually, I was waiting to give you an invitation to the wedding before telling you that my girlfriend and I got engaged yesterday."

"What? "

"You heard me. I am engaged to be married. I asked her last night and she said, yes."

"I am happy for you. Perhaps I was a bit pessimistic when you mentioned your intention to propose to her."

"That's okay. There was nothing wrong with you sharing a valuable life experience with me. I appreciated it."

"My God, O'Connor! Are you always that gracious?"

"If you see me as gracious, that is your perception of me. It is not how I see myself."

"You are an amazing man."

"You are too, in your own way."

In spite of their differences in age and experience in the police service, there seemed to be a considerable degree of compatibility between them. Kendal was twenty-two and new to the service. Officer Kanga was ten years his senior with as many years of police service and he was a good mentor. Kendal's tolerance for some of Kanga's idiosyncrasies made him the perfect partner.

On that very day at 1:15 p.m. Joshua had the stitches removed from his arm, even though he had been asked to be at the hospital for 11:00 a.m. He had no complaint about the delay, only praise for the staff. The doctor said that he should regain full use of his arm within a month, and recommended some simple exercises for him to engage in daily because there was no facility for physical therapy in Mayaro at the time. He suffered no severe nerve damage in that vicious attack on him at the Mafeking Community Center. The best news of all to Joshua was when he heard the doctor say that he would be able to return to swimming and with time, he should be able to return to competitive athletics.

After the reading assignment at school that morning, Sydney asked for and received from Ms. Gardener, the news paper used in the classroom. The class newspaper was never acquired as a cooperative effort as was customary in other classes. Ms. Gardener purchased the paper herself and was free to give it to whoever she had chosen. Since no other student showed any interest in taking the paper home, Sydney became the logical recipient.

Joshua meanwhile, was contemplating whether he should wait around to meet Sydney after school was dismissed. After careful and considerable deliberation, he decided to walk down to the beach. *Perhaps I may get a fish or two*, he thought. It wasn't unsual for the captain of a fishing boat to give part of the seine's catch to people who were not employees but who volunteered in helping to bring the net ashore. Joshua was aware of that and thought that since he had no money to purchase anything, it might be one way of acquiring some fish protein for his family. He knew also that work with a seine was difficult and particularly strenuous on one's arms. He did not want to cause any further damage to his healing arm. Nevertheless, he went.

When he arrived at Plaisance, there were several fishing boats ashore and teams of fishermen were pulling their nets in. Joshua could tell that the net closest to shore had a large catch. He, like everyone else, could see the fish stirring up the surf. He decided there and then to lend a hand. He did so cautiously. His hands were on the ropes and he displayed a pulling motion but exerted no force. He faked it.

As the seine was getting closer and closer to the shore, people gathered around; locals, bathers, tourists and fishmongers were there, all vying either to purchase fish or just cadge some. People realized that it was a larger than normal catch, and suddenly the area around that seine became crowded as many hangers-on abandoned the other seines. Joshua was among the fortunate. For his efforts, genuine or faked, he was rewarded with two medium sized King fish.

He was very pleased with his reward, ill gotten or not. He decided that he was taking one fish home and the other he was going to give to his aunt Bertha, Sydney's mother. It made no difference to him that he and Sydney disagreed early that morning.

They had disagreements in the past but always reconciled their differences. He saw no reason why that day should have been any different.

With his two King fish in hand he walked back to Pierre Ville to await Sydney's school dismissal. He didn't have to wait long. Within ten minutes Sydney was at the entrance to the hospital looking for Joshua, although he knew that JJ had an eleven o'clock appointment. He also knew that no one in Mayaro was a stickler for time, and was hoping that either Joshua would be late or the hospital service would be slow as usual. He was fortunate. The latter was true, though not to the extent that Joshua would still be around. The fact that he was in the vicinity was because he too was making an effort to wait around for Sydney.

They spotted each other as Joshua started walking away from the taxi stand when he saw school children approaching. Sydney looked up from where he was standing at the entrance of the hospital and their eyes met.

"Why are you still here?" Sydney asked.

"Because I knew you would be looking for me."

"You are so full of yourself."

"Perhaps that is why you are standing at the entrance to the clinic."

"Yeah, rght! Fool yourself."

"Cut the bull, Sydney. Take this." Joshua said as he handed one of the fish to him.

"Is this a bribe?"

"No, stupid, it is for Aunt Bertha."

"You really can't help yourself, can you?"

"What do you mean?"

"You cannot speak without calling the person you are speaking to, *stupid*."

"Did I do that again? I didn't mean to. I am sorry."

"Your apology is accepted. However, you need to make a concerted effort to speak differently."

"Why? I think I speak as well as you."

"Of course you do. You learnt from the best, me."

"You are just so full of it, Sydney. You probably learnt from Ms. Gardener."

"In part, yes," said Sydney. "Good teachers do have that kind of influence on their students."

"Enough of that crap. How are we getting home anyway?"

"The way we always do. Correction! The way I always do, by walking."

The boys set out on their journey to Mafeking. They walked up and over the old Naparima/Mayaro Road which, for some reason, they believed was a shorter leg of the journey. It was the path Sydney took every day to and from school. Even so, he was concerned that in the time it would take them to get home in the tropical heat the fish may have spoiled. When he expressed that concern, Joshua responded by saying, "The fish venders we left back there would still be there selling their fish by the time we get home."

"What does that have to do with us?"

"Can't you see *stu...*?" Joshua attempted to say something. He stopped short of saying the word, *stupid*. "If their fish aren't spoiled, ours wouldn't either."

As the boys came down the hill and entered Spring Flat, a small black car, a Prefect, pulled over to the curb and stopped just ahead of them.

"That looks like Ms. Gardener's car." Sydney said. The driver blew the horn, put her hand out of the window and motioned for them to come. They sprinted toward the car. Joshua got there first, just a second before Sydney but once there he hesitated. As soon as Sydney was there, the boys climbed into the back seat of Ms. Gardener's car.

"One of you must sit in the front," she said. The boys looked at each other and Joshua poked his right index finger into Sydney's rib as if to indicate, *you go*. Sydney responded. By saying, "You sit in the front JJ." That left Joshua no choice. He stepped out of the back seat and moved to the front. Once he was seated and closed the door, Ms. Gardener drove off slowly. There were very few cars on the road and fewer if any were driven by women. Joshua was impressed although he did not speak or look in the direction of the teacher until she asked, "Do you live here, JJ?"

"Yes," he said. He glanced at Ms. Gardener as he spoke. *She is young, very pretty too, and with some really drop dead (nice) legs,* he thought, having caught a glimpse of her left thigh where her skirt rose slightly above her knee. Female teachers could not wear slacks or jeans to work in those days.

"How is it I have not seen you in school, JJ?"

"I no longer go to school."

"Is it that you graduated early?"

Before Ms. Gardener could ask anything else, Sydney pointed to their home and said, "This is where we live, Miss."

"That was quick. Somehow I thought you were going further."

You wish, JJ thought when Ms. Gardener pulled her vehicle up to the curb and stopped.

"Thank you, Ms. Gardener," Sydney said.

"You are most welcome."

"Thank you, Miss."

"You are welcome, JJ."

The boys alighted, and Ms. Gardener drove off. Joshua was giggling. It was an incessant, annoying sort of giggle which prompted Sydney to ask, "What's wrong with you, man?"

"Nothing, nothing at all."

"Then stop the foolishness, would you?"

"I just think it is so funny."

"You are so doltish. That's what is funny."

The only reason Joshua was still laughing was that he didn't fully comprehend what Sydney said. As a result, they parted ways on a much better note than they did during the morning hours. Joshua went happily to his home knowing quite well that the responsibility to clean, season, and possibly cook the fish was his. Sydney on the contrary, was neither happy, excited, nor impressed. Joshua gave him a fish to take to his mother and that's what he did. Philbertha, however, was delighted to receive the fish and set out immediately to clean, slice, and season it. She said that she would go over to her aunt's later that evening to personally thank her little cousin. Sydney heard his mother's comment but did not respond. He was indifferent.

He opened his backpack and realized that he still had the newspaper he received from Ms. Gardener at the end of the reading period that morning. His intention was to have given it to JJ but he forgot. *Perhaps he would be better served if I use it to prepare some new reading material for him,* he thought, and went on to do just that.

At the same time Sydney and Joshua arrived at their respective homes, Officer Kendal O'Connor arrived at his. He was greeted warmly by his fiancée who informed him that his mother went to visit a friend who was a little under the weather.

"Was it Aunt Bertha?" he asked.

"I am not sure. She did mention the name but I forgot."

"It doesn't matter. Mom visits every sick person in this village and she attends every funeral in Mayaro. That's just the way she is."

"You mother has a good heart."

"She has too much of a good heart and that is of no benefit to her."

"Don't say that"

"I know. I shouldn't but I already did. It's the truth though," said Kendal. "Because of her kindhearted nature people are constantly taking advantage of her."

"Perhaps that will change now."

"Why? It has been happening since my birth." Kendal was thinking of his father's neglect when he said that. The man he knew as his father had never contributed to his support.

"You are grown up now and you are highly respected throughout Mayaro."

"What does that have to do with the kind of things people do to my mother?"

"You may not realize it but the respect people have for you translates into respect for Ms. Dorothy. Everyone admires the way she raised you. Initially, some said that she was too tough and too much of a disciplinarian, but the day your name appeared the newspapers as having passed GCE (General Certificate of Education) with distinction in three of seven subjects, you became the pride and joy of the entire community and your mother was highly praised."

"Yeah! Right." Kendal said with skepticism.

"I am serious, Kendal. Every day I hear the things that people say about your family. You, and your mother, that is. Some speak directly to me. Others speak so that I can hear. All speak highly of you. The only negative remark I have ever heard came about two weeks ago." Henrietta paused without saying what that negative comment was. She expected Kendal to ask but he did not, so she continued, "A man I know only as *Dust Off* said in a taxi the other day that you never should have joined the police force."

"Why shouldn't I?"

"That is exactly what another passenger asked him," said Henrietta. "Do you know what he said?"

"How will I know that? I wasn't in that taxi and you haven't told me."

"He said that you are too much of a gentleman and much too qualified for the job."

"That does not sound as a negative comment to me."

"There you have it. That's how well respected you are."

"That's how nosy some people are. Why what I do with my life should become a conversational piece for strangers? I am not a politician."

"These are not strangers, Kendal. These are people who watched you grow up before their very eyes."

"Does that give them the right to get into my affairs?"

"In this town people will do that with or without your permission. For the most part they do so without malice."

"That does give me some solace," Kendal said sarcastically.

"If I were you, I know that I would find comfort in that thought."

"Whatever! That's enough about Mayaro people. Let's focus on what we plan to do."

"As you wish, my dear."

"Okay then. What time are you leaving here this evening?"

"Why? Is it that you are in a hurry to get rid of me?"

"Not at all, sweetheart."

"Then I am leaving with you tomorrow morning when you are going to work."

"You are aware of the time that I leave, aren't you?"

"Yes, of course. That is not a problem for me. I am accustomed to rising early."

"Good! Then we have some time to talk."

"Just talk?"

"I did not say that but it is important that we talk. I want to be sure that you understand what we agreed to."

"Did we agree on something?"

Kendal laughed, although he didn't think that there was anything funny about Henrietta's question. He understood fully that she had always been a fun loving person and he thought that was fine to a point. There was no doubt in his mind that her gregarious nature was in part the reason he was so attached to her. He firmly believed though, that life was not all fun and games and he wanted Henrietta to at least acknowledge that fact.

"It is nice to be friendly and sociable but sometimes we have to set limits. If we do not, sooner or later people would start to disrespect us."

"Where is that coming from?" she asked.

"Nowhere in particular."

"So why all of a sudden you are giving me a lecture?"

"It is not my intention to lecture to you. However, we have taken an important step in our relationship and with that comes certain responsibilities."

"Responsibilities that are yours or mine?"

"They are our responsibilities."

"Then why it is you are the one doing the lecturing?"

"I am not lecturing, Etta. There is no semblance of a lecture in what I am saying. I am simply trying to get you to understand the serious nature of what we are about to do."

"Just what is that?"

Kendal was losing patience with Henrietta's subtle resistance to what he wanted to say. He decided, therefore, to get directly to the point. He realized that such an approach could trigger an outburst of anger from her but he concluded that she left him no choice.

"You made me the happiest man on earth yesterday when you agreed to become my wife," he said. He thought about Officer Kanga's experience of two years prior then he continued, "I would like ours to be a happy and prosperous marriage."

"Why would it be anything but....?" asked Henrietta. "You are still beating about the bush. Why don't you say what's on your mind?"

"I want us to live our lives without interference from others."

"Are there specific others that you may have in mind?"

"As a matter of fact, I do."

"I thought so because if we continue to live in Mayaro people would get into our business whether or not we like it."

"I am aware of that."

"Whom are you thinking about?" Henrietta asked. *Is it you mother?* She wondered.

Although Kendal decided earlier to get directly to the point, he was unable to do so. He couldn't bring himself to mention Rudolf Vargas' name as a person who might pose a possible threat to their relationship and or impending marriage if Henrietta continued to have any interactions with him, however simple or innocent.

"I want a solemn promise from you, Etta."

"You want what?"

"You heard me."

"Okay! I heard you. Now what?"

"Mr. and Mrs. Riggs would be very excited when you tell them that we are engaged."

"I think they would be. They love you very much," said Henrietta. "I must let you know though, my parents were never married." Kendal's jaw dropped. *How could that be when Mr. Riggs has always been such a faithful and dedicated husband and father?* He wondered.

"That comes as a shock to you. I know."

"Shocking is putting it mildly. I never would have imagined that."

"I only recently became aware of it myself," said Henrietta. "I am not bothered by it though. I really couldn't desire any better parents."

"They were both always there for you and your siblings. That is a lot more than I can say for my father."

"Well, your mother has done an excellent job. I am sure your father, like the rest of Mayaro is very proud."

"He has no pride and nothing to be proud about as far as I am concerned."

"Don't be so tough on him, Kendal," said Henrietta. "I am willing to bet that he is bragging about your successes to anyone who would listen."

"That means nothing to me. When I needed him most, he wasn't there. He was out there enjoying his life."

"Does that mean you are not going to invite him to our wedding."

"I will not invite him but it's not for the reason you are thinking."

"What other reason could there be?"

"I do not know the man. He is a stranger to me. Our wedding is a private, personal matter. It is not the kind of affair to which the public would be invited."

"Wow!"

"What is the *wow* about? Those are my true feelings, honey."

Henrietta was thinking seriously of her unborn child. *Would the baby's father have any desire to be involved in the child's life?* She wondered. Then she reasoned, *not if he doesn't know that the child is his.*

"I hope this baby never feels like that when he or she grows up," she said.

"There is no chance. I promise that I will always be the best dad any child can hope for, unless..........."

"Unless what?"

"Unless you or the good Lord decides differently."

"Huh!"

"Yes. I expect you to keep your promise. I certainly will keep mine."

"What was my promise again?"

"Etta! We made a pact that no one, no one at all should ever know that this baby, *he touched her abdomen,* is not ours together."

That would be denying Rudolf of fatherhood, she thought.

"Fatherhood could not be denied if it is not sought," Kendal said, as if he read Henrietta's thoughts.

"That is an eerie thought."

"What is so eerie about it?"

"Never mind what I just said."

"Okay! We have been together since high school. Now we are engaged to be married. There is no chance that anyone would question the paternity of this child." He touched her abdomen again.

Henrietta sighed. She wasn't quite at ease with what Kendal said. In fact, she was thinking of the waitress, the concierge, the clerk at the Beach Front Hotel, and Rudolf Vargas himself as people who may have reasons to question her child's paternity.

"Why did you sigh? Don't you feel the same way?"

"I do," she said. She lied.

"Then we are in agreement. Are we not?"

"Yes. We are."

"Good! Soon we will be Mr. and Mrs. O'Connor and Kendra or Kendal, Jr."

"It will be months before this baby arrives, Kendal."

"Months are not years. It wouldn't be long."

Philbertha arrived at Dorothy's that evening only to be told that her friend was not at home. She had taken five slices of fried fish for her and proudly left them with Kendal. He thanked her and informed her that his mother was visiting someone whom he understood was seriously ill.

Who could that be? She wondered but quickly dismissed the thought, said goodbye, and turned to leave. She was about to walk down the short flight of stairs when Kendal said, "Mom should be home soon, Aunt Bertha. Perhaps you can wait for her."

Before she had a chance to reply, she spotted Dorothy approaching the entrance and said, "Here she is now."

"Girl, I just had you in thoughts. I was wondering whether I should walk down to your place," Dorothy said.

"Why do you have to wonder about that?"

"It's just one of those things. That's how the mind works, I guess."

"Well, it is still early. Come on down," said Philbertha as she and Dorothy met at the curb.

"That would give the soon to be wed couple a little more time alone."

"What! Did you say soon to be wed?"

"Yes. My son proposed to Henrietta yesterday and she accepted."

"Congratulations! Girl, you must be so proud."

"Thank you. I am truly blessed and extremely proud."

"All of your hard work has paid off," Philbertha said with tears in her eyes.

"Things were tough at times but I never gave up hope. I always knew that the Lord wouldn't give me more than I can bear."

"You are a remarkable woman, Dorothy."

"You are no less noteworthy, my dear," said Dorothy. "I hope the critics are taking note."

"I do not pay attention to those who do nothing but sit around and criticize others."

They arrived at Bertha's place and walked to the kitchen. It was Philbertha's hope for them to have coffee or tea while they sat and converse well into the evening. However, her son, Sydney had other things in mind. He had occupied the kitchen table where he always did his homework.

"You must have an awful lot of homework today," Philbertha said.

"Not really. I have already completed my homework."

"So what is all this?" She pointed to the papers on the table.

"I am putting together a picture book for JJ."

"Are you preparing another one?"

"Yes."

"How many of those he needs?"

"He needs quite a lot. His reading skills are progressing faster than I can prepare the texts."

"So why don't you just have him read from the newspaper?"

"Good idea! Why didn't I think of that?"

"I don't know. It would save you a lot of time."

"Thank you."

"You are welcome," said Philbertha. She turned to Dorothy and said, "Let's sit in the living room."

Once Dorothy was seated, Philbertha returned to the kitchen and placed a kettle of water on the fire. She then rejoined her friend in the living room.

"It is so admirable how you get along with you son."

"Sometimes he tries to be stubborn but overall, he is a good child. I have had no trouble with him."

"You are amazing, girl."

"I learnt a lot from you, Dorothy."

"You are so unlike Velma. Sometimes it is difficult to believe that you are so closely related."

"Our behaviors were learnt in different settings."

"Vastly different settings, I can tell."

"Yes. Well, you know Aunt Umilta, and Velma is no different."

"Huh!" Dorothy murmured.

"It's okay. You can say what you think."

"You know that I do not hesitate to speak my mind. Right now, I just don't know what to say about them."

"Just tell it like it is. Or tell it the way you see it."

SIXTEEN

By the time Dorothy arrived home from Philbertha's the newly engaged couple was already asleep. Once again Henrietta had chosen to spend the night on the futon in Dorothy's room rather than in her fiancé's bed. Dorothy tiptoed barefooted around the room to avoid disturbing her while getting ready for bed herself. Soon she too retired and fell asleep.

She woke up very early as usual on Wednesday morning and had breakfast prepared by the time Kendal and Henrietta were awake and dressed to leave.

"Come," she said. "Breakfast is on the table."

"Mom, I can't believe you did that again."

"Just what have I done again?" asked Dorothy. "I have done the same thing since you were five."

"I am no longer a child. I prefer to have breakfast a little later."

Dorothy paused. She was dismayed. Henrietta saw the look of frustration and disappointment on her face and said, "I will have some, Ms. Dorothy."

"Yes girl. You go right ahead. He is a man now."

Why it took you so long to realize that I am grown up now? Kendal wondered but said nothing. He had never been rude to his mother and had no intention to be then. So he kept his thoughts private and sat with Henrietta at the kitchen table. Dorothy left the kitchen. She retreated to her bedroom where she would spend the day in solitude.

"I think you hurt your mother's feeling, Kendal."

"That was not my intention."

"That is not the point. Whether or not you did it intentionally, you did it. You should apologize."

"Are you joking?"

"No. You need to apologize to your mother now."

"What am I to apologize for?"

"What you have done. Please don't ask me what that is because we just spoke about it."

"I am not apologizing for anything."

"What is wrong with you Caribbean men that you can't fess up and apologize for your wrong doing?"

"Since when did you become an authority on the behavior of Caribbean men?"

"What I say is based on my observation. I am not claiming to be an expert."

"How many Caribbean men have you had the opportunity to observe outside of Trinidad and Tobago?"

"Where are you going with that?" asked Henrietta. However, before Kendal could respond she said, "Wherever it is you are heading, I am not going there with you."

That essentially ended what could have escalated into a nasty quarrel. Kendal's thoughts were on Rudolf Vargas who was not born in Trinidad and Tobago. He came to Mayaro at age eight when his mother and stepfather migrated from Grenada. There was no doubt in Kendal's mind that Vargas had, at some time or another, done Henrietta wrong and refused to apologize. Neither Kendal nor Henrietta considered that Mr. Vargas and others like him had experienced much of their social development in Trinidad and Tobago, so the behavior they exhibited may not have been indicative of the manner in which men behaved in their native lands.

"Okay! You can stay here," said Kendal. "I have to go to work." That caused Henrietta to laugh, which is exactly what Kendal intended to lighten the tension that was building between them.

I have to let go, get over Vargas and whatever existed between them if our relationship and eventual marriage are to be successful, Kendal thought. Then he said, "After work I would pay your parents a visit."

"What time might that be?"

"Sometime between five and five-thirty this evening."

"Would you be going home first?"

"No."

"Would you come to Lagon Doux in uniform?"

"I do not normally come home in uniform. Why do you ask?"

"I am curious," Henrietta said.

She was thinking that Karish would be terrified if he saw Kendal as a uniformed police officer. She knew that he was intimidated by Kendal's presence even before he became a cop, and although she had vowed no intimacy with Karish, the fact that they were neighbors and close friends ruled out any possibility that they would have no contact whatsoever. In addition, she had hoped to organize an impromptu party to announce her engagement to her family and a few close friends, not including Karish of course. She was faced with the task of convincing Kendal that he should first go home and change before coming to Lagon Doux.

"Your folks have not seen me in uniform,"

"So?"

"Don't you think that they may be excited or at least curious to see how I look?"

"They know that you have joined the force and they are quite familiar with the uniform of an officer of the Trinidad and Tobago Police Force."

"Sometimes you are just too pragmatic for me, girl."

"There is no pragmatism about what I am saying. It just makes sense; common sense."

"From that standpoint, it will make more sense for me to stop off at your parent's place in Lagon Doux before going home to Mafeking."

"For once Kendal, Just do what I ask of you, please," Henrietta said with a hint of frustration in her voice.

"Okay! Okay," he conceded. Then he added, "If we do not get out there and hail a taxi, I might get to work late today."

"You are right," agreed Henrietta. "Give me a minute to say goodbye to Ms. Dorothy."

She left him and went to Dorothy's room. After she was there for ten minutes, Kendal became impatient. Just then she came out, looked at him and smiled. He did not smile with her. "What happened to you in the short time I left?" asked Henrietta. "Get in there and say goodbye to your mother. She is disappointed in you and is quite upset."

"Come on now!"

"Come on, nothing. Just do it."

Reluctantly, he followed Henrietta's suggestion and knocked at his mother's bedroom door. "Come in," she said.

He entered the room and stood just beyond the doorway. Dorothy did not stir. She sensed his presence but said nothing. Kendal stood there briefly before saying, "Bye, Mom."

"Have a blessed day, son," she said in a detached sort of way. She did not turn to look at him.

He moved forward and sat at the edge of the bed. He gently placed his left hand on her right shoulder as she lay with her face toward the wall. She rolled over and looked at him. She was distraught. He hugged her. She hugged him, and their eyes became filled with tears. Neither sobbed and not a tear drop fell.

"I love you, Mom."

"I know that. I love you dearly, and I am sure you know that."

"I do, Mom. I do"

I do? She wondered. *Soon he would be saying that to someone else. She is most deserving though*, she thought but said, "If you do not leave now you may be late for work." At that point, she got up and they walked arm in arm toward the door. They were smiling. Henrietta was pleased and she also smiled. Kendal kissed his mother as he had always done since childhood whenever he was leaving the house. "I have to run, Mom. Have a good day," he said.

"I will try. You do the same."

"Thanks."

"Bye, Ms. Dorothy," Henrietta said.

"Bye Etta, my dear."

Dorothy stood in the doorway as her son and future daughter-in-law walked to the curb to await a taxi. It wasn't long before one arrived and the young couple left. Dorothy went to her room and laid back down. That was a rather unusual move for a woman who had become accustomed to getting up early and engaging herself in the many chores which directly or indirectly, contributed to the livelihood of her son and herself.

When they reached Pierre Ville, Kendal and Henrietta parted ways but not before they hugged each other and promised to get together that evening when he returned from work. She caught a taxi to Lagon Doux immediately. He was forced to wait a few minutes before the driver who approached him had a full complement of passengers for Sangre Grande. Soon he too was on his way.

Sydney and Joshua tended their livestock and completed their other chores. They then assumed relaxing positions on the bench under the star apple tree. Sydney wanted simply to talk but Joshua was having none of it. He wanted to read.

"Oh man! I have never met anyone with such an obsession for reading," Sydney told him.

"You haven't met anyone at all."

"What is that supposed to mean?"

"Just forget about it. Can we read?"

"You can. I have no need to."

"You what?"

"You heard me. I have no need to read." What Sydney wanted to say was, *I can read but you need to learn.*

"Everyone needs to read in order to glean important written information independently."

"In order to *glean*........?" Sydney was amazed at Joshua's correct usage of the word.

"Yes. It means to obtain information over a period of time."

"I know what the word means."

"Oh! I got it. You know what the word means but you are wondering how is it I know when to use it."

"Never mind my thinking."

"No. I will tell you."

"Okay!"

"I was reading a magazine article when I came upon this strange word. I looked it up in the dictionary, learnt the spelling, and practiced the pronunciation. This is the first opportunity I have had to use the word."

Sydney literally choked on his saliva when he attempted to swallow and speak at the same time. He suffered a brief spell of coughing but quickly regained his composure.

"Are you okay?" JJ asked.

"Yes."

"So can we read?"

"You are relentless, man. I will get you some reading material," said Sydney. "Let's see how much you have progressed."

Sydney left Joshua under the star apple tree and hurried inside to get the new picture book he had prepared. He quickly returned and handed the book to him.

"Thanks," said Joshua. "I hope I can make you proud."

Sydney did not respond so Joshua started reading. He read flawlessly and completed the twenty-page picture book in record time. Then he asked, "Do you have anything else for me?"

"Oh, yes!"

"What do you have?"

"I will get it," Sydney said. He left and quickly returned with an old issue of a sports magazine that showcased a popular boxer on the cover. Joshua was elated. He had been quietly improving his reading and comprehension skills by regular and extended practice. He was diligent and by then confident of his ability and eager to demonstrate it to Sydney. He took the magazine from his cousin, turned to the page related to the boxing championship and read flawlessly. Sydney was impressed. "I have never seen anything like this," he said.

"What is it you haven't seen, Sydney?"

"I have never seen anyone go from not being able to read a word of English to reading fluently and flawlessly in two weeks."

"Thanks to you, man. You have an effective method of teaching reading that should be publicized," said JJ. "Have you given any thought to becoming a teacher?"

"No."

"Why not? It is obvious that you would be very good at it"

"JJ, perhaps you are forgetting something; I am just a kid. I have not given any serious consideration to anything, or to what I may become. I am enjoying my live just the way it is."

"You are already a good teacher, why wouldn't you pursue that as a career?"

"I know nothing about good teaching. As I told you, I have not given serious consideration to any vocation."

"Don't you want to be like Ms. Gardener?"

"No."

"Why not?"

"Listen JJ, Ms. Gardener is a nice person and a good teacher. I like her but I have no desire to be like her."

"Ah ha! So you do like her?"

"Yes. Who wouldn't? Just look at her."

"Yeah! She is nice. Does she teach extramural classes?"

"I don't think so. She lives in Rio Claro and does not like staying in Mayaro for more than an hour or so after school."

"Oh! That's too bad."

"What is so bad about that?"

"I was thinking of registering for evening classes and hoped that I would have her as my teacher."

"Why?"

"Why do I want to register for extramural classes, or why do I wish to have Ms. Gardener as my teacher?"

"Why do you want to have Ms. Gardener as your teacher?"

"You have made the case for her as being a good teacher."

"Is that really your reason?"

Joshua thought briefly about Sydney's question. Then he said, "Yes."

"Let me assure you, JJ. The other teachers are just as good."

"Is that so?"

Joshua wrongfully believed that all Sydney had learnt and was able to teach him, he learnt from Ms. Gardener. While he learnt to read quickly, he still had a very narrow view of the educational process. He was feeling overly confident that he could achieve the same success in other subject areas in just as short a time. He possessed a drive, a desire to persevere and achieve that Sydney had not seen in any of his classmates. Still, he cautioned Joshua that it takes time for anyone to achieve his or her educational goals.

"I want to be able to write the School Leaving Certificate Examination in one year from now, if not sooner."

"It cannot be sooner. The examination is given once a year, and this year's exam is already scheduled for next month, June that is."

"Okay! So is it given every June?"

"I believe so."

"Did you take that exam?"

"No."

"Why didn't you?"

"That is a post primary exam and I went to high school at age twelve."

"Isn't high school post primary?"

"In a sense it is. True post primary though, are standards six and seven (Grades nine and ten)."

"So?"

"So what?"

"So why didn't you take that exam?"

"Joshua! That is not an exam that high school students take."

Joshua felt dejected. He wanted so much to be like his cousin, Sydney. Suddenly, he felt that he was different, and that no matter how hard he tried, he could never be like Sydney. What he didn't realize right away was that extramural classes were an alternate path, and if he stayed on track, ultimately he could have achieved similar or even greater success than his cousin.

"Did you ever ask Arjune if he would be willing to teach me mathematics?"

"I believe Kendal did?"

"Kendal? Why?"

"I don't know."

"How did he know about that?"

"I am not sure."

"You told him. I asked you not to let anyone know about that and you deceived me."

"I did not."

"I thought you were my friend but you are not," Joshua said and stormed off.

At about the same time, Kendal arrived at the Matura Police Station to assume his duties. He was early as usual and greeted the officer at the desk who said to him, "You just missed a call. Anyway, I took a message. What a sweet voice she has!" He handed Kendal the piece of paper on which he wrote the message.

He took it and said, "Thank you."

"You are a lucky man, O'Connor."

"Thanks again," Kendal said. He looked at the note. It read: Please call me before you leave Sangre Grande this evening. Thanks, Monica.

Kendal's only access to a telephone was in the precinct and the only available one was on the sentry's desk. Although he didn't see the need for privacy when making a call to Monica, his very nature as an extremely private individual precluded any thought of him using that telephone for a personal matter. He decided, therefore, that he would call on her in person while in transit in Sangre Grande that evening.

Fifteen minutes after he had gotten to the station, officer Kanga arrived. "What assignment do you have today, O'Connor?" he asked.

"I did not check the schedule."

"Oh man!" Officer Kanga remarked as he walked off to see who was assigned with him for that day. He quickly returned and said, "We are patrolling together again today, O'Connor."

Liming together is more like it, Kendal thought but he responded by asking, "Is it the same beat?"

"Yeah, man! What other is there?" The question was not unreasonable because rarely were there more than two officers on patrol anywhere in Matura except on a festive occasion.

"It is time to go," Kendal said after looking up at the clock on the wall.

"I will get the cruiser."

"I shall meet you up front."

When Officer Kanga received the keys from the desk clerk and walked to the back of the station to get the squad car, Officer O'Connor went to the front and waited for him. It wasn't long before the senior officer drove up and said, "Let's go." It was another joyous morning for Officer Kanga. He genuinely loved working in Matura and expounded on the virtues of the place. Kendal heard it all before so he decided to listen and make no comments. Officer Kanga continued with what Kendal considered trite until he pulled up in front of Tan Sally's place.

"We have arrived," he said.

"At our favorite work place," Kendal said sarcastically.

"If you know of a better place to be please tell me."

They stepped out of the vehicle and walked into Tan Sally's yard. As they approached the open front door, they saw her legs moving back and forth behind a sheer curtain but her feet were not leaving the floor. She sat there reclining in an old Bentwood rocking chair as if she was expecting them and was becoming impatient that they were taking so long to arrive. Officer Kanga knocked at the door. It wasn't necessary because Tan Sally had already seen them.

"What took you so long?" she asked. Then she said, "Good morning, come in."

"Good morning, Tan Sally," Kendal said.

"The mornings are always good in Matura," said Officer Kanga. "The breakfasts are often better."

"We know that. My son, however, is just very mannerly. Don't pay him any mind, Kendal." She patted his back as she spoke.

Once again Kendal said nothing. He was at a loss for words and didn't want to make any comments that might be wrongly construed by either his partner or Tan Sally.

"Your breakfast is ready. You should eat before it gets cold," Tan Sally said. The officers exchanged glances that caught her eyes, so she asked, "What's the matter? Didn't you think I would feed you?"

"No, Tan Sally. That's not it."

"Then what is it, son?"

"We didn't know that you were preparing breakfast for us."

"Did you know that you were coming here this morning?"

"Yes."

"So did you expect to come here this early in the morning and not get breakfast?"

"Well.....," Kendal paused. *We were thinking of breakfast at Ms. Inga's*, he thought. In the mean time, Officer Kanga was already enjoying the hot chocolate and cassava bread with corned fish and scrambled eggs that Tan Sally had prepared. She made the chocolate from beans she grew and prepared herself. It was sweetened with sugar made from sugarcane grown in her backyard. The eggs came from hens she raised herself. Even the milk the chocolate contained came from one of her own cows.

"Come on, son. Eat and enjoy yourself like your partner here," Tan Sally pointed to Officer Kanga when she said that. He responded by saying, "I love it. Thank you."

By then Officer O'Connor started eating. That was the first time he had ever tasted cassava bread. He loved it. "Everything is so delicious, Tan Sally," he said.

"I am glad you like it even though nothing you are eating this morning came from the grocery."

After breakfast the officers spent another two hours with Tan Sally. They spent the time listening mostly to her discussions about her youth as she reminisced about growing up in Matura. It was an oral history lesson of sorts but neither officer ever thought of verifying the facts.

When they left Tan Sally's they perused the village in an attempt to exercise their patrol duties. That turned out to be nothing more than a joyride for Officer Kanga. First, he stopped at the home of a friend who offered them stewed turtle meat. Both officers declined. They explained that it wasn't long before their arrival there that they had breakfast.

"At least you can taste it," the host insisted.

"Okay! Just a little," Officer Kanga said. He then looked at his partner and winked as if to say, *taste it. That would make her very happy.*

"What about you, Officer..........?" She paused as if she needed some assistance with the name.

"O'Connor, Officer Kendal O'Connor."

"Would you like some Officer O'Connor?"

"Yes," said Kendal. "Just a little, please."

Kendal was skeptical. He had always been choosy about food but on that occasion he didn't want to appear as being disrespectful to a gracious host. It was rare that he ever tried anything new as it pertained to food. He had never eaten so-called wild meat and he considered turtle meat to be in that category. He was also ahead of his time in other ways. Conservation was one of those things he held dearly. He sincerely believed that it was wrong for people to capture and kill the leatherback turtle that came to the Matura shores to lay their eggs. At that time, however, Kendal knew of no law against such acts. He realized, therefore, that the poachers could not be stopped. Even if the law favored protecting the leatherback turtles, Kendal's partner, the senior officer, was so self-indulgent that nothing would have been done to uphold the law.

Before the host could return with the cooked turtle meat, her husband came out with three very cold beers of the finest quality that could have been obtained anywhere. "Have a beer fellas (men or guys)," he said.

"Certainly, local beer that is freezing cold, it doesn't get any better under this tropical mid-day sun," Officer Kanga said as he took one of the bottles off the tray. His friend then offered one of the other two bottles of beer to Kendal. He took it reluctantly and said, "Thank you."

Kendal was feeling terrible. It seemed as though he was being forced to do things against his will and in violation of the law on every tour of duty he had with Officer Kanga so far, and for the first time he questioned his suitability for the job of a police officer. He quickly dismissed that thought and sipped the beer. Officer Kanga's friend's wife returned with two plates of steamed Creole rice and stewed turtle meat. She handed one to Officer Kanga and the other to Officer O'Connor.

"Thank you," said Kendal. "This, however, is much too much for me. Could you take some of it back, please?"

"As you wish, sir," she said and fetched a clean plate from the kitchen. She then transferred half of the food from Kendal's plate onto it.

"Thank you," he said. He tasted the rice that was left on his plate. *This is good, very well done*, he thought. He tasted the stewed meat and exclaimed, "Wow!"

"It is good. Isn't it?" asked Officer Kanga. "Once you eat this stuff you could never become a vegetarian."

"It is good. In fact, it tastes a lot better than I expected."

"What did you expect, O'Connor?" Officer Kanga asked.

"Nothing I would like."

After another hour and a half, the officers left Matura beach but instead of returning to the precinct, Officer Kanga made a stop, his second that was, at one of the local bars. It was close to the beach and one of only two in the village. The establishment known as *The Shop* was run by an Asian family and had been there for three generations. It was an unusual business by today's standards. The rear of the building served as the family's residence and part storage area. Two-thirds of the front served as the grocery store, while the other third, separated by a flimsy partition, served as a bar or rum shop as it was called then.

Officers Wilfred Kanga and Kendal O'Connor entered and were greeted by *Pitch Oil*, a local young man of African descent who worked there as a bartender. Pitch Oil, was of course a sobriquet. Very few people knew his real name.

"Officer Kanga!" exclaimed Pitch Oil. "What a surprise to see you here so early."

"I hope you are not doing anything illegal," said the officer. "As you can see, I have a new partner and he is all business."

"It is Thursday afternoon at 1:00 p.m.," said Pitch Oil as he looked at the clock on the wall. "All we do is sell liquor."

"No groceries I hope"

"No,sir."

Officer Kanga was being facetious. *The law is an ass*, he thought. *It would be illegal for one to buy milk for a baby at this time but any amount of alcohol could be sold after the shop is closed on a Thursday afternoon, or on a Sunday for that matter.* In spite of what he thought, Officer Kanga said to Pitch Oil, "That's good."

"We operate within the limits of the law here. You know that, Officer Kanga."

"Our concern is not with what you are doing right. We are here primarily to prevent you from doing wrong."

Is he for real? Kendal wondered. *He has broken the law everyday that I have been on petrol with him.* Beyond those thoughts, he said nothing.

"We do the best we can, sir."

"Let your best be the right thing always," Officer Kanga said.

"Yes, sir."

Just then a hunched-back, aged Asian man, with jet black hair walked into the bar area and said, "Give the officers what they want, Pitch Oil." He apparently was the current owner and was becoming uneasy with the tone and trend of the conversation Pitch Oil was having with Officer Kanga.

"What is it?" asked Officer Kanga. "Are you in a hurry to get rid of us?"

"No, not at all, we like serve you better," said the old man in somewhat broken English.

"You'd better watch your mouth or we would shut you down," Officer Kanga said.

Is he nuts? Kendal wondered. He looked at the clock. It was 1:47 p.m. "We should be on our way back to the station by now," he said.

"Why?"

"The officers who are going on patrol next would need the vehicle."

"There is another cruiser at the station. Don't you know that?"

"I do."

"So what is the problem?"

"There is no problem, none whatsoever."

"Good. Then let me have a puncheon, Pitch Oil."

The bar tender quickly poured a shot of puncheon rum in a small glass and handed it to Officer Kanga with another glass filled with tap water. Then he asked, "What will you have Officer......? He did not know the other officer's name. They were never introduced, so Kendal assisted him by saying, "Officer O'Connor, Kendal O'Connor, sir."

"What will it be, Officer O'Connor?"

"Nothing, thank you."

"We are not familiar with that drink," said Pitch Oil. The other patrons laughed.

The hunched-back Asian man with the black hair returned from the grocery area and said, "No charge for the officers, Pitch Oil."

"Yeah, Boss. Ah know that." Pitch Oil then said to Officer O'Connor, "It is hot everywhere, man. At least take a cold beer."

"Okay. I'll try a Carib."

"Good choice," Pitch Oil said as he opened a freezing cold beer and handed it to Officer O'Connor."

"Thank you," Officer O'Connor said.

"For a while there I thought you were playing the pious one today." Officer Kanga said.

"Why?"

"You seemed to be refusing any food or drink while in uniform."

"I think that you are reading too much into my actions."

"Maybe I am."

Officer Kanga asked for another shot of puncheon rum which Pitch Oil quickly served him. He gulped it down. He then said to Kendal, "Pour some of that here as he presented him with the empty glass. Kendal poured some beer in his partner's glass. He drank it as a chaser to the enzyme denaturing, cell-destroying, Puncheon rum. Then he said, "Let's go."

Kendal was about to leave without his beer when Officer Kanga said, "Take your drink, man." Although he was uneasy about having alcohol in the squad car, he took the beer and they left. Officer Kanga drove slowly to avoid swerving all over the road like a drunken sailor. It was obvious that the over-proofed puncheon rum had taken a toll on his nervous system. Kendal meanwhile, consumed a half dozen dinner mints in an effort to mask the smell of alcohol on his breath. He had a terrible feeling of guilt as his mother's words, *you know right from wrong. If you think it is wrong, don't do it*, reverberated in his ears.

It was 2:55 p.m. when they arrived at the precinct. The sergeant in charge was at the front desk. He looked at them and said, "Fellas, you are two hours late. There must have been trouble in the village today."

"No real trouble, sir. There were a number of disorderly drunkards. That's all," Officer Kanga said. He lied.

Kendal cringed but said nothing to confirm or deny his partner's claim. He was concerned that sooner or later their adventures while they were supposed to be on patrol will become known and disciplinary action may be taken against them. That thought frightened him. *Should I ask to be reassigned with a different partner?* He wondered. *That may seem ungrateful to Officer Kanga, a man who otherwise had been very kind to me,* he thought. He was in a quandary.

Officer Kanga took the chart in an attempt to complete the day's report but was unable to begin. His hands were unsteady and his thoughts irrational. He began staring around the room and into space. That prompted the sergeant to ask, "Wilfred, are you okay? Your eyes are red. Did you get a full night's sleep?"

"Yeah, man."

He is drunk, Kendal thought. No one else knew that he had a problem with alcohol and although cannabis grew as an indigenous plant in the area, no one in the country had a problem with it or any other drug for that matter. So neither drug nor alcohol abuse was suspected.

"Go home and get some rest, both of you" the sergeant said.

"We will leave as soon as this report is completed," Kendal said.

"Good."

SEVENTEEN

They arrived at the Mayaro taxi stand in Sangre Grande at 3:47 p.m. That was a little earlier than usual for Kendal but only because they had been dropped off there by the evening crew from the Matura Police Station. Officer Kanga headed directly to *Coconut Juice*, the dinky little bar on Ramdass Street. Kendal declined an offer to join him. Instead, he stood at the taxi stand, ignored the hustle of the many drivers, and focused his attention on the front door of the jewelry store with the hope of seeing Monica there. The driver with whom he traveled on the first day of his assignment told him, "You shouldn't have to wait long, Officer." Kendal smiled. That was his only response. *I never said why I was waiting. So what is he talking about?* He wondered.

Just then someone tapped him gently on his right shoulder. He turned around and saw Monica standing there smiling. She hugged him and whispered in his ear, "I am glad you are here early." Anyone who saw that may have thought they knew each other for a very long time. They did not.

"Why aren't you in the store?" Kendal asked.

"I worked through my lunch hour so I could be off an hour earlier."

"It seems as if you have a plan."

"I do have a plan."

"Oh! Yeah. What might that be?"

"To drive with you to Mayaro this evening."

"Why?"

"Do you know that I asked myself that very question?"

239

"Since you did, my question is still, why?"

"I am not sure. Perhaps it is because I would like to get to know you better."

"Why me?"

"Walk with me to my car. We can talk on the way."

"Where is your car parked?"

"I am parked on Ramdass Street, opposite to *Coconut Juice.* Are you familiar with that bar?"

"I can't say that I am familiar with it. I have heard of it."

"Some people think it is dinky but it is very popular. I understand that the drinks are cut-rate."

When they arrived at the spot where Monica's car was parked Kendal became concerned. He had declined the offer to join Officer Kanga for drinks because he had to get home in a hurry. Yet, there he was in front of the very bar. He was frantic, uneasy, or both, and hoping that his partner will not see him. He was lucky. They entered the vehicle and headed toward Manzanilla. There was a brief period of silence when neither spoke. Then Monica asked, "Have you ever felt drawn to someone the very first time you met?"

'No."

"I suppose men are not emotional like that."

"I do not know much about men. I speak only for myself."

"I can understand that. Nevertheless, you knew I was attracted to you the first day you walked into the store. Didn't you?"

"No. I thought you were courteous and helpful, which as you know are rare qualities in this town."

"What you are saying is that I acted differently from other sales associates you have encountered."

"That's it, more or less."

"Did you then, or do you now have any thoughts as to why that was so?"

"Yes. I thought you either worked on commission or you were the niece or daughter of the owner and was intent on increasing the profit margin."

"Shit!"

"What was that about?" Kendal asked as he looked back to see whether Monica saw something that he missed. She did not respond to the question. On the contrary, her mood suddenly changed and for several minutes neither spoke. Kendal broke the silence when he said, "Monica, you need to slow your speed. Around that corner a landslide has occurred that damaged the roadway." She acceded to the request and soon realized that there was only one lane at the point of the landslide. She was apprehensive when an oncoming driver yielded to her.

"Just take it slowly. You can do it," Kendal assured her. She took her foot off the accelerator completely and allowed the car to crawl past the broken piece of roadway.

"You see. I knew you could do it."

"Thanks," she said and tapped his right thigh with her left hand. She was slow in removing her hand and he was tempted to hold it there but managed to resist that temptation.

As they approached the cemetery, Monica was again forced to slow her speed because of the uneven road surface. That time she did it without any prompting from Kendal. As she turned right onto the Manzanilla/Mayaro Road, she asked, "Are you in an awful hurry, Kendal?"

"Not really," he said. Either he forgot for a moment that he had to be at Henrietta's, or he didn't feel a need to be there in a hurry.

"Then you wouldn't mind if we stop at this picnic area for a little while."

"No."

"I take that to mean we can stop."

"What else could it mean?"

"Never mind," said Monica as she made a sharp left turn into the picnic area. They both stepped out of the vehicle and without asking any questions, they headed toward the beach. The tide was low, very low, and neither suggested what they should do. They simply started to stroll up the beach. They walked close to each other but made no contact. Kendal had been curious as to why Monica was going to Mayaro and the reason she made the effort to have him travel with her. He resisted asking her before but decided that the time was as good as any to do that so he asked, "What's taking you to Mayaro this evening?"

"The chance to be in your company," she said. She was laughing but Kendal did not seem amused so she quickly tried to allay his fears. "My fiancé went to visit his aunt yesterday and asked me to join him there for the weekend.

"Today is only Thursday. Don't you have to work tomorrow and Saturday?"

"No. I am off those days."

"It is just as I thought."

"What have you been thinking?"

"That your father or uncle owns the place."

"Don't say things like that, Kendal."

"Why not? You haven't said it isn't true."

"I know that."

"Is there some truth to it?"

"I don't know."

"You don't know!" Kendal exclaimed and snickered.

"It is not funny, Kendal," said Monica as she held him close. "I may have to confide in you if we are to be friends."

"I am sorry."

"Don't be. If you were from Guaico you would know my story."

"Okay," Kendal said in an apologetic tone.

"As you can see, I am a person of mixed race. My mother is of African descent and so is my father. Well, that is the man I have always known as my father. And believe me, he is the best dad I could ever have hoped for. He has never, and I repeat, never one day made reference to my appearance or the possibility he may not be my biological father. However, rumor has it that Mr. Ramloogan, the jewelry store owner is my biological father. I had a difficult time with it in elementary school but by the time I got to high school the teasing stopped. Some people say that my mother was pregnant when my parents got married and that my father, the man who raised me, was aware of it."

"Did you ever ask your parents?"

"No."

"I can relate to that."

"How?"

"Simply because I know that it happens," Kendal said but did not elaborate. He of course, was thinking of his own situation, with Henrietta being pregnant for Rudolf Vargas while engaged to be married to him.

"Does this happen a lot in your community?" Monica asked.

"It happens. I don't know if it happens a lot."

"Strange, huh."

"Are you bothered by it?"

"As a child I was. Now I am comfortable in my skin."

"So why did you exude profanity when I suggested that you were either the niece or daughter of the jewelry store owner and was intent on increasing profits?"

"It was just so weird to me to hear you say that."

Kendal looked around and said, "It is a bit desolate up here. Perhaps we should walk back."

"No one would dare bother us. I feel safe in the company of a police officer."

"An unarmed officer as I am may not be able to defend and or protect you."

"That thought never crossed my mind but you may be right."

"Then we should walk back to the car."

They stopped, faced and hugged each other, then turned and started walking back down the beach. Without asking they held hands instinctively. As they strolled along the beach and conversed they became more and more comfortable together. Monica started revealing pleasant and unpleasant situations that have arisen since her engagement. They were mostly things of which she had been unaware before. They included her fiancé's problem with alcohol, his continued close relationship with former girlfriends, and his tendency to be a spendthrift. Kendal listened attentively and sympathetically but offered very little about himself in return.

When they reached the car, Monica leaned back on the front door at the driver's side. She stretched a hand out to Kendal. He held her hand and she drew him toward her. Not much effort was required. She really only had to indicate what she needed him to do and he complied. They hugged each other again and for the first time they kissed. At first it was a spurious sort of kiss. It wasn't long, however, before they were kissing each other passionately as if it would never end. Then they stopped abruptly. Monica unlocked the car and entered through the right rear door. Kendal followed her and she locked the doors. Suddenly it started to rain, heavy torrential rain as is typical for that tropical paradise. There were severe thunder and lightning but neither Kendal nor Monica noticed.

When the deluge subsided, they stepped out of the vehicle, smoothed their clothing, and resumed their original positions in the driver and front passenger seats. Monica turned the key in the ignition to start the engine and they left the picnic area on Manzanilla Beach and followed the coastal road under the canopy of tall palm trees that lined the roadway. Kendal opened the window slightly to enjoy the warm, refreshing ocean breeze. Monica clutched his right hand and told him how glad she was that they met when they did. "Although," she said, "It is a pity we didn't meet before we became engaged to other people." Neither expressed a willingness to dissolve their engagement, and neither pressured the other to do so.

"I do hope that we could continue to be friends," Monica said.

"I see no reason why we can't or shouldn't."

"It is rare that I meet someone with whom I can converse amicably and in whose arms I am so comfortable."

"I will take that as a compliment."

"It is," said Monica. Then she asked, "How do you feel?"

"Okay."

"Is that it?"

"No. I am only teasing. I am very comfortable with you." She pulled the car onto the curbside at the Nariva River Bridge, leaned over, kissed him and said, "Thank you."

"You are welcome."

As they traversed the bridge, the cracked hardwood planks from which the metal spikes had become loose began to rattle. Monica found it difficult to control the vehicle. She was petrified so she reduced her speed to a crawl. I think you should drive when we get across," she said.

"If we get across," said Kendal adding to her fears. "That murky water is teeming with anacondas and alligators." He was exaggerating. "It is also the home of the manatee in Trinidad but those are harmless," he said.

"Oh, my God!" Monica cried out.

"Why are you calling on God? He has already gotten you across the bridge."

Monica was breathing hard. She pulled off the roadway and said, "You drive, please."

"Not me. No thank you." Kendal did not tell her that he couldn't drive. She assumed that he, like all police officers she knew, was a licensed chauffeur but on that day, he just preferred to be driven. She had no choice but to continue.

"There are a couple more bridges ahead" he said.

"Not like the one we just crossed I hope."

"Not quite as bad."

"How much further is it to Mayaro?"

"Oh! I don't know. It could be four miles, maybe five."

By then they had reached Cocal. Monica pulled up to a make-shift market stand and asked the vendor, "How much for the blue crabs?"

"A dollar per dozen."

"How much are the water melons?"

"Those are three dollars for one or fifty cents per slice."

"Let me have a dozen crabs and this water melon." She tapped the largest and greenest of the melons while she listened for that hollow sound that she believed indicated it was properly matured.

The young man handed Kendal the crabs. He then took up the melon and walked to the car trunk. Monica opened the trunk and her purchases were placed in it. "Thank you," she said as she and Kendal re-entered the vehicle. She drove off quietly but with the thought of the other couple of bridges Kendal mentioned riveted in her mind. She was scared but determined to stay calm.

Seven minutes later they arrived at the Ortoire River Bridge, a brick red, steel monstrosity with a rickety wooden platform. Monica approached cautiously but not as intimidated as before. She drove slowly in an effort to keep all four tires on the parallel planks that were laid down for that purpose and was relieved when she emerged on the other side of the river. "I will not be driving back, that's for sure."

"How will you get back?"

"Flynn will drive."

"Flynn? Is that a first name?"

"No. His full name is River Boat Flynn. He is my fiancé."

"I can understand why you call him by his surname?"

" He doesn't like his first name."

"It is an unusual name but it is his given name."

"I thought so too when I first met him. At first I thought River was a nickname."

"Oh well, what's in a name? It is the personality of the individual that counts."

At the intersection of Manzanilla/Mayaro Road and the Naparima/Mayaro Road Monica asked, where do I turn?"

"To your left is Plaisance and Mayaro beach. I live in Mafeking which requires you to turn right. Where does your fiancé's aunt live?"

"He said Guayaguayare."

"Oh! Lord, that's another half an hour from here. It is about twelve or thirteen miles away. Well, I do have to be in that vicinity this evening although not quite as far as Guayaguayare. I can ride with you and take a taxi back to my destination."

"Will you really do that for me, Kendal?"

"As long as it does not create some unnecessary problems for you."

"What problems could arise from such an act of kindness?"

"Oh! You would be surprised, my dear, very surprised."

Monica had turned right and was driving along the Naparima/Mayaro Road when Kendal told her, "You are heading in the direction of my home."

"You are making me nervous, Kendal."

"Why?"

"Your fiancée might be irate. That's why."

"I don't think so. In any case, she doesn't live where I do."

"Where in Mafeking does she live?"

"She doesn't live in Mafeking at all. She lives in Lagon Doux which is about half way between Mayaro and Guayaguayare.

"What will your parents think?"

"My parents? The only parent I know is my mother."

"How would she feel about us *liming* together?"`

"She is a woman with a strong sense of morality, so she might not be appreciative. However, she doesn't have to know."

"How could she not know?"

"Hey! You are giving me a ride home. I will go in, shower, get dressed and be out again in a flash."

"Wouldn't she be concerned about that?"

"She might. I can handle it though."

"Okay, whatever you say, my friend."

They reached Spring Flat. Monica spotted the spring bridge that spanned the Ortoire River where it flowed between Pierre Ville and Mafeking. "Oh, my God!" She blurted out.

"What is it?"

"It is another bridge."

"Oh yeah, it is another rickety one at that."

"What are we going to do?"

"Cross it. If you had a full complement of passengers we would have had to get out and walk across, but since it's only the two of us, we may be allowed to stay in the vehicle."

"Is it that bad?"

"Yes. That bridge is crumbling, breaking down. Nevertheless, it is where *the river lime* is held every Sunday morning in the dry season.

"*The river lime!* What is that?"

"It is a gathering of friends."

"Why would friends gather at an old dinky, breaking down bridge?"

"It is not the bridge *per se* that draws them together. It is the ambiance."

"The ambiance, what ambiance is there?"

"There is a typical atmosphere or mood to the venue that one must experience in order to appreciate it."

As they crossed the bridge Monica glanced around and said, "There is nothing here."

"There is nothing that you can see from up here."

"Do I have to go into the river in order to see it?"

"That's correct," Kendal said. He was laughing at Monica's question.

"Very funny, Officer O'Connor."

"I am not trying to be funny. It is a fact. We gather under the bridge every Sunday morning in the dry season to swim or learn to swim in the river."

"What's the fun in that?"

"The fun is in the experience of it all; the athletics, the comradeship, the jokes, the intellectual exchanges, and the mere nonsense that is sometimes exuded out of the mouths of some of the participants."

"It sounds as if you really enjoy *the river lime*."

"I do. Or rather, used to."

"I take it that you no longer participate."

"I haven't for several Sundays since I suffered a cramp and had to be pulled out of the water."

"Do you mean that you almost drowned?"

"Yes."

"Oh! I am so sorry. On the other hand, I can consider myself lucky and thank God for the intervention."

"I am sorry. You lost me somewhere."

"Don't you see? You were saved so we can meet."

Kendal laughed and said, "You mean that of all the ways God can use me, he chose for me to become your paramour?"

"Well, I didn't mean it quite like that."

"Okay! Okay. Stop right here. This is where I live." Monica pulled up to the curb and Kendal asked, "Why don't you come in and meet my mother?"

"I prefer not to. Thank you."

"Okay then. I wouldn't be long."

"I will go up the street, turn around, come back, and wait for you here."

"That's fine."

She drove off and Kendal ran inside. He greeted his mother, who as usual, was glad to see him home safely. She had been anticipating his arrival for more than an hour after she had prepared dinner. She was getting ready to visit with Philbertha when he rushed in and gave her a quick smack on the cheek.

"My goodness, you are in an awful hurry."

"Yes. I am, Mom. Someone is giving me a ride to Lagon Doux."

"Oh yeah, I forgot that you were going to visit Etta this evening. Had I remembered I would not have spent my time cooking ."

"That's okay, Mom. You know that I wouldn't mind eating the food tonight or tomorrow."

"You'd better. It is woefully wrong to willfully waste food."

"I know, Mom. We have struggled too hard for me to do that now."

"Well, at least you haven't lost your senses yet."

"Did you expect me to?"

"I kept hoping that you wouldn't but I am very well aware of what can happen sometimes when people become progressive."

"What can happen, Mom?"

"They can become swellheaded."

"Swellheaded?"

"Yes."

"What's that?"

"That is when a successful person becomes arrogant and conceited."

"That's not your son. I would never get to that point." Kendal kissed his mother again and said, "Sorry, Mom. I have to rush. I can't keep my ride waiting too long."

"You take care. I am going up to Bertha's so we will talk when you get back."

"See you then," Kendal said as he rushed off into the shower.

Ten minutes later he was dressed and out the door. He rushed across the street to where Monica's car was parked but she wasn't in it. *What the hell?* He wondered. He looked up and down. She was nowhere to be seen. *There is no place around here for her to visit*, he thought. *Except, the shop up the street perhaps.* He started walking toward Tang's shop when he heard the rustle of bushes a little off the roadway, just beyond where Monica's car was parked. He turned around quickly. There she was smiling broadly with her left hand on her hip. "Are you looking for me?" she asked.

"Yes. What are you doing standing kimbow (with your hand on your hip) in the bushes?"

"Catching a little of the shade. It is too hot out and the car isn't air-conditioned." She did not tell him the truth. She went to relieve her bladder.

"I am ready to go."

They got into the car and Monica drove off cautiously. Since they left Sangre Grande Kendal noticed that she was always cautious when driving. Whether or not she was timid, he couldn't tell and didn't ask. As they drove along the Naparima/Mayaro Road, Monica commented that the area was sparsely populated and Kendal asked, "How did you determine that?"

"By the number of houses I see. Those that are present are all on the left side of the road. The entire right side is forested except for two shacks and something of a parlor I noticed further back."

"So that is what you based you determination on. You haven't considered the size of the houses you saw. You have no idea how many people live in them. You do not know how many more homes are at the back of those and beyond, but you have concluded that the population is sparse."

"It is just my observation, honey. I didn't say it for the sake of argument."

"I am not arguing with you. I am just so surprised."

"Why?"

"I always thought that only our people spoke like that."

"Only our people spoke like that? She repeated part of what Kendal said in the form of a question. Then she asked, "Who are our people?"

"By that I mean people of this district."

"What is it about their speech that is so much like mine?"

"It is not the speech *per se*, not the intonation."

"Then what is it?"

"It is the fact that they often speak authoritatively about things they know nothing about."

Monica was silent for several minutes. She felt insulted by Kendal's remark so she kept her eyes focused on the roadway but not too far ahead of her, so much so that she didn't even realize when she crossed the spring bridge, in spite of its wave-like motion as she drove across. Kendal sensed her displeasure and said, "I didn't mean any harm by what I said."

They were leaving Spring Flat by then. She took her eyes off the road momentarily, glanced at Kendal and asked, "Do you mean that?"

"Yes."

As soon as he answered, she spotted a stand pipe and pulled up next to it. That was the first one she saw with running water since she stepped out of the bushes near where Kendal lived, although, there were several along the way. She opened the door and was stepping out of the car.

"What are you doing?" Kendal asked.

She did not respond but proceeded to wash her hands at the pipe. She then pulled a handkerchief from her bosom and moistened it with tap water. She got back into the vehicle and used the dampened handkerchief to wipe the steering wheel.

What the hell? He wondered but said nothing.

"Were you being honest when you said that?"

"What did I say again?"

"That you didn't mean any harm by what you said."

"Yes."

"Then kiss me," Monica said, and before Kendal could react or respond one way or the other, her lips were next to his. He embraced her. She closed her eyes and parted his lips with her tongue. His cooperation made it so much easier. They remained conjoined for several minutes before slipping back into their individual bucket seats.

Monica drove off but at the fork in the road, where the new road diverged from the old, she was a little uncertain as to whether she should stay to the right or the left. She chose the latter. Kendal knew that either section of the road would have taken them back to Pierre Ville but he said nothing to reassure her. He was too bothered by his own conscience. He closed his eyes and reflected on his first date with Henrietta. He had never kissed another woman passionately until he kissed Monica earlier that day. At the time he thought to himself that it was just a flirting fancy but

to his amazement, he had done it again. *"Where is all this leading to?"* He wondered. *We are both engaged to other people.*
There were no answers to Kendal's self-searching questions. To make matters worse, he was also bothered by his daily duties, or lack thereof, as a police officer. That was even more troubling to his conscience than his chance encounter with Monica. At least he did not have to see her every day, and he hoped that whatever the attraction was, it would soon wane.

EIGHTEEN

Claudia Riggs was so delighted in the thought that her oldest child, Henrietta was engaged to be married to Kendal that she was determined to make what was intended to be a gathering of a few close relatives, a truly grand affair. When she mentioned it to her brother, Clifford, who was so well known in the village as a miser, that his nickname was *poor gut*, he did not hesitate to ask, "How much money do you need?"

"I came to invite you over. I did not come here to ask you for money, although I could always use a few dollars."

"It's Henrietta's engagement. I would have been there whether or not you invited me, so how much do you need?"

"How much can you spare? You know ah eh working nowhere to pay you back."

"Did I ask if you needed a loan? No! I ask how much do you need."

Claudia Riggs had no clue as to what it would cost to have an engagement party for her daughter, even a small party. So her brother said, "I will give you three hundred dollars. If you have anything left over save it for the wedding."

"Thank you so much, Cliff."

"Doh mention it, guul (girl). What is family for?"

Mrs. Riggs, as everyone knew her, left her brother's place feeling extremely pleased. They always got along well and she had never before asked him for financial assistance. Even on that occasion, when she needed it most, she did not ask. Her brother, Clifford, somehow understood the need and stepped up to the plate. He had one other surprise for his sister and her family; he planned to speak with the management at the Beach Front Hotel to see if the ballroom was vacant for the evening and whether he could rent it on such short notice. "I am going to the Village (as Pierre Ville was sometimes referred to) soon. On my way back I will stop in to see you."

"Okay. I will see you then. Thanks again."

"Don't you ever mention it again," he said sternly.

As soon as his sister left, Clifford came out and hailed a taxi. When the car stopped he said to the driver, "I want to go to The Beach Front Hotel. Can you take me there?"

There was a brief moment of silence when the driver hesitated, then he said, "Yes. Come on, let's go."

All employees, past and present, of The Beach Front Hotel knew that it stood on rented land owned by Clifford Riggs. So whenever he entered the hotel, as rare as that was, he commanded respect. On that occasion, he was met at the door by the concierge who asked, "What can we do for you today, Mr. Riggs?"

"Is your ballroom booked for the evening?"

"No, sir."

"Then I would like to rent it."

"Certainly. What type of function are you having, sir?"

Mr. Riggs found the question to be intrusive and did not respond immediately. The Concierge, therefore, felt a need to explain why he asked it in the first place.

"I only asked so that we would have some idea of how to prepare the room, sir."

"Ah!" Mr. Riggs blurted out. He smoothed his moustache and said, "An engagement party."

"What time period are you considering, sir?"

"I am not sure. Perhaps from 6:00 p.m. to 10:00 p.m."

"That is simply a formality type question. It really doesn't matter since no one else would be using the room this evening," said the concierge. "Would you be interested in having music, sir?"

"Yes, of course. What kind of engagement party will it be without music?"

"Would you prefer live music or a recorded session?"

"Live music is always preferred."

"We can have a steel band quartet here by 5:45 p.m."

"That's great."

"Would you require food and refreshments?"

"We do need your refreshments but no food. We will provide our own food." *I am sure Claudia has already prepared food*, he thought.

"We can have people to serve your guest if you wish."

"How much will all of that cost?"

"There would be no charge for the actual ballroom, sir. However, the musicians and the servers would expect to be paid."

"At what rate?"

"That would be fifty dollars an hour for both groups. That is, the musicians and the four servers including the bartender. There is also a flat fee of one hundred and fifty dollars for the refreshments, irrespective of how much is consumed."

"Five hundred and fifty dollars, eh?" Mr. Riggs had calculated the amount long before the concierge was able to do so with pencil and a legal pad.

"That's about it," said the concierge. "If you decide to take the room, we will have everything in place by 5:45 this evening."

"That's in forty-five minutes."

"That's our guaranty, sir."

"I hope you are right," Mr. Riggs said as he put his hand in his pocket and pulled out a wad of notes. He counted $550.00 and handed it to the concierge. "That is a lot of money to spend in such a short time. Do you know that?"

The concierge did not concur. He said simply, "Thank you, sir." Mr. Riggs put whatever was left of the cash back into his pocket.

"Can I get a taxi to take me to Lagon Doux from here?" he asked.

"Yes. They come in every ten or fifteen minutes. Oh! Here is one now." the concierge raised his hand and beckoned the cab driver to come over. He did. "Can you take Mr. Riggs home?"

"Sure. Let's go Mr. Riggs."

He hopped into the cab and sat back. Along the way the driver took up three more people. To the rest of the world that may seem strange but that's the way it was in T & T then and it has remained that way ever since.

As soon as Mr. Riggs was dropped off he entered his home and wasted no time in getting himself dressed for the occasion. At the same time he asked his son to run over to his aunt Claudia's and tell her that he had reserved the ballroom at The Beach Front Hotel for four hours from 6:00 to 10:00 p.m. that evening.

"Your father is strange," Mrs. Riggs told her nephew when he gave her the news. Nevertheless, she was glad to hear it, although surprised that her brother didn't drop in himself as he had promised.

Mrs. Riggs sent a note by one of the well known and perhaps the most liked taxi driver in town, to Dorothy. It was brief and to the point. It read, *we had originally planned on having only a small gathering to announce the engagement of Kendal and Henrietta. However, that has changed. We are now having a party at The Beach Front Hotel starting at six o'clock this evening. Please try and come. Thanks, Claudia.*

Dorothy O'Connor read the note and did not hesitate to get dressed. She then walked up to Philbertha's with the note and asked for her company to the event.

"I have nothing new to wear, girl."

"Please don't be so vain, Bertha. Just look at me. You have seen me in this dress a dozen times at least but it is the best thing I have on such short notice."

But Kendal is your son, Philbertha thought

"Yes. I know. He is my son so I must do whatever it takes," Dorothy said as if she read Philbertha's thoughts. "Now don't you forget, he knows you as his aunt. He looks up to you, girl."

"Don't make me feel guilty now. I'll go."

"Yes!"

"I guess I could wear the dress I wore to church last Sunday."

At about the same time Kendal and Monica reached New Lands where he decided to leave her and return to Lagon Doux. He told her that Guayaguayare Village wasn't far and that she should be on the alert for the sign that read, *Entering Guayaguayare.* She had no problem with that so as soon as she entered the village she inquired about her future aunt-in-law's residence and was directed to a grey brick house a short distance away from where she made the inquiry.

Kendal had no trouble getting a taxi to take him back. When he arrived at the Riggs family (the children carried their mother's last name) home everyone was dressed and ready to leave. Henrietta's father, who was known as Mr. Riggs but whose family name was Pedrosa, had already left. Apparently he had to help in getting the food to the venue.

Henrietta was quite upset that she had not been informed of the change of venue until the last minute. Her mother tried desperately to get her to understand that the entire plan was put together haphazardly. Claudia Riggs found it difficult to reason with her daughter. In fact, no one really knew about Henrietta's concerns. No one asked about them because no one could ever have imagined what those concerns were. She wasn't willing or ready to volunteer that information either. *There are some things one must be ready to take to one's grave,* she thought.

After trying unsuccessfully for several minutes to get Henrietta to at least say what was bothering her, Claudia Riggs said to Kendal who had just arrived there, "You deal with her. I am out of here."

She walked out to the curb with several of the other children to await a taxi that will take them to The Beach Front Hotel. As it turned out, Kendal had no more influence on Henrietta than her mother did. Perhaps he didn't try hard enough because he too was guilt ridden after his philandering with Monica. Nevertheless, he did manage to get her to leave the house and try to get a taxi to take them to the venue.

Kendal was not comfortable with the way he was dressed. He never wore jeans or sneakers, so to everyone else he looked fine. A taxi approached, he raised his hand and the driver pulled over toward them. He opened the back door and Henrietta stepped in. Kendal followed her and asked, "Could you drop us off at *The Beach Front Hotel*?"

"Sure, man. That's right! You two are getting engaged today. Congratulations!"

"Thank you," Henrietta said and smiled for the first time since Kendal arrived at her parents' home that evening.

"That is so nice," said a woman in the front passenger seat. "Young people today don't bother to get married before they take on adult responsibilities."

"You are right," said the driver, a man about Mr. Pedrosa's age. "They have the baby first. Then they expect their parents to take care of the child so they can enjoy their youthful life."

That was not pleasing to Henrietta's ears but she quickly dismissed it. Her thoughts were on the waitress who served her and Mr. Vargas when they spent a night at the hotel. *Suppose she is one of the servers tonight, what will I do?* She wondered. *Is that very pleasant night clerk the one on duty tonight? Who is the concierge on duty tonight?* She questioned herself but there were no answers.

Although she did reveal that she was pregnant and for whom, and they determined how they would deal with it privately, Kendal never asked about the details that led to her pregnancy and that was still a matter of concern for her. She did not volunteer the information to him but she was afraid that someone else might.

When they arrived at the ballroom, she looked around quickly. She was relieved that none of the people she remembered seeing the night she and Mr. Vargas were there was present. She smiled softly. At the same time Dorothy's eyes met hers. Dorothy was smiling too. She thought Henrietta was smiling with her so she started walking across the floor. They met halfway and hugged each other tightly for several seconds. The crowd cheered.

"It's quite a nice gathering you have here, girl."

"Yes. It was supposed to be held at home with just a few family members and close friends."

"He never told me that."

"He didn't know. I asked him to visit me after work today. I insisted that he did not come in uniform."

"You are lucky. What if he came in sneakers and jeans?"

"I knew that would not happen."

"You probably know him as well as I do."

"I probably know him a little better." They both laughed.

"I wouldn't doubt that," Dorothy said as both women walked back to the side of the room from which they came. The steel band started playing *Stardust* so Henrietta and Kendal had the first dance. Other couples joined in and the party essentially began. There was no ceremony except for a mock presentation of the ring which Kendal had already given to Henrietta.

Tables seating four to six people were placed all around the periphery of the ballroom leaving the central area free for dancing. Nothing was scripted. The band played continuously and people were free to dance if they so desired. They could also have chosen to sit and be served. Drinks of every kind were constantly being passed around. The avaricious Mr. Riggs truly exceeded expectations. He loved his niece who was also his godchild and he was beaming with joy as he witnessed her engagement to Kendal O'Connor, one of the bright prospects who would later become a Mayaro success story. Where he sat smoking his pipe, Mr. Riggs had a paramount view of the proceedings and he loved it.

"I like to see the young people enjoying themselves," said the man sitting next to him, a cousin whose name was *Prosper*. That of course, was not his real name. It was, however, the only name by which most people in Lagon Doux knew him.

"It's money well spent," Mr. Riggs said.

"Yeah, it is about time you spend some of that money."

"You know what, life is funny. You obviously had a better start than I did. You had better and greater opportunities. You chose to squander them. You never saved a penny. Forty years later today, you are talking nonsense about my money. When I was struggling, catching meh ass, eating cane top and grass, you never said heh, take ah dollar ,boy. Now you talking fart. Just shut up, man. Stop the crap."

Prosper got up and left the room but no one noticed. He swore that he would never speak with his cousin again. That did not bother Mr. Riggs. His contention was that when He needed him most he was of no help. *Why should I worry about his fragile ego now? I made sacrifices to achieve what I wanted to achieve. He elected to have fun with his money. He squandered it on many women, music, and liquor. Why is he trying now to play the victim and act as if I robbed him or others of something?* He questioned himself but there were no answers.

Henrietta was having a ball. All thoughts of Vargas and who might have seen her with him were forgotten, temporarily or not, they were out of her mind. She danced with her father. She danced with her mother. She danced with her uncle, Philbertha, and Dorothy. Most of the evening, however, she felt safe in the arms of her fiancé.

Kendal too seemed focused on Henrietta only. From the time they arrived at *The Beach Front Hotel,* he had no thought of Monica whatsoever. He did not think of Vargas and the possibility of him becoming a distraction in the lives of his young family members. He was determined to enjoy the evening and he looked forward to a bright future with his beautiful bride-to-be. They danced together, ate, drank, and enjoyed a few good laughs. Kendal also danced with his mother. He danced with his aunt Bertha and Henrietta's Mom, Claudia.

The band played for four hours straight. There was no intermission and at no time was the dance floor empty. In fact, everyone was on the floor when an old calypso; *Guul, you goin' home with me tonight*, was played.

At 10:00 p.m. very few taxis were arriving at *The Beach Front Hotel.* Very few people had private cars. Those who had them, took as many passengers as they could and promised to return for others. The few taxis that came in also took more than a full complement each. Many people grew impatient of waiting and some started walking out toward the Guayaguayare/ Mayaro Road where they knew the possibility of catching a cab was much greater. Henrietta, Kendal, Dorothy, and Philbertha stayed together. They walked out to the Guayaguayare/Mayaro Road but sought transportation in the opposite direction from which most other folks were traveling. Henrietta had informed her parents that she was going home with Kendal that night.

"Don't forget the young man has to go to work tomorrow," Claudia Riggs told her daughter.

"How could I forget that, Mom?"

"I know you. Sometimes you just don't think."

"Okay, Mom. That's enough."

It wasn't long before a taxi arrived. The driver pulled up to the where the four people were standing.

"Where are you heading?" he asked.

"Mafeking," someone in the group replied. With his left hand, he motioned them to get in and they did.

"This is my last run for the night."

"I suppose we are in luck," Kendal said.

"You can say that. These days fewer and fewer drivers are working at nights." No one asked why. They all knew why.

Henrietta rested her head on Kendal's shoulder and both of them leaned back in the seat. Kendal closed his eyes. *Only a few hours earlier I was traveling this route with Monica,* he thought. *Now, here I am again with Henrietta.* They reached the spring bridge. There was no one there to regulate the crossing and the driver expressed no concern. He simply drove across with all the passengers in the vehicle. None of them expressed any concern either.

Henrietta fell asleep, as did Philbertha. Kendal and his mother stayed awake for the duration of the trip. Dorothy was in the front passenger seat and that may have accounted for her alertness. The driver never stopped talking and she was the only one responding. When they drove past Tang's shop she said to him, "Stop at the next house on the left." It was where Philbertha lived.

"Aunt Bertha, you are home," Kendal informed her as he shook her by the shoulder.

"My goodness, are we here already?"

"Yes."

"I must have fallen asleep."

"You certainly did," said Kendal. *Alcohol can do that to you*, he thought.

Philbertha stepped out of the vehicle, said good night, and staggered into her yard. Kendal smiled. There was no reaction from Henrietta. She too had fallen asleep.

"Stop at the third house on the right," Dorothy said.

The houses were far apart so she expressed no urgency but minutes later Kendal shouted, "Right here! The taxi had overshot the entrance to their home by the time it came to a screeching halt.

"I am sorry about that," the driver said.

"That's okay, man," Kendal said as he leaned forward to access his wallet in his left rear pocket. That motion awakened Henrietta. They stepped out of the car and Kendal paid the driver who then reversed into the old Rio Claro/Mayaro Road, otherwise known as the Old Road. He turned around and headed back to Pierre Ville.

As soon as they entered the house, Henrietta threw herself onto the couch. She was groggy although she drank no alcohol at the party.

"You must be very tired," said Dorothy. "Why don't you go to bed right away?"

"I am not really tired."

"Then you must be pregnant." There was complete silence in the room. Dorothy realized her transgression and corrected herself by saying, "You are probably in the family way." Still, no one spoke. "Go and lie in the bed," she said, but Henrietta was hesitant. *Which bed?* She wondered but didn't have to wonder very long.

"Help her to bed, Kendal," Dorothy told her son. He did not ask which bed. He held Henrietta around her waist and led her to his room. There was no objection from his mother so he said excuse us and closed the door as they entered.

Dorothy retreated to her room smiling. She changed into her night clothes and laid across her bed. *I am becoming a grandmother. How wonderful?* She was beaming with joy and her smile seemed as if it were painted on. She eventually fell asleep smiling. She slept soundly until 5:00 a.m. Friday morning.

She woke up smiling, said a short prayer and headed for the kitchen to prepare something for Kendal. She was becoming accustomed to his objections to having breakfast that early in the morning and resigned herself to making just fresh delicious coffer for him and tea for herself. On that occasion, she made enough coffee so that Etta could enjoy the morning brew with her fiancé.

By 5:30 Kendal was awake. He showered, dressed, and joined his mother in the kitchen. "What are we having this morning, Mom," he asked right after he said good morning and kissed her on the forehead. "The usual," she said.

"Not breakfast again, Mom?"

"No. Coffee has replaced breakfast as the usual. You know that."

"That's good."

"I don't know, son," said Dorothy. "Who has been fixing you breakfast in Matura?"

"On occasions it has been Tan Sally. At other times it has been Ms. Inga."

"Who are these women? Does Etta know about them?"

"I told you about Tan Sally. Didn't I?"

"Yes. You did mention an old spinster who cooks and tells you fables about her youth but you have never said anything about Ms. Inga. Who is she?"

"Ms. Inga is a young bi-racial woman, part Amerindian and part African predominantly. She may have some East Indian genes also. She is extremely beautiful, and can she cook! Tan Sally claims she learnt from her. I don't know about that. To me, she cooks better than Tan Sally. Anyway, do you realize that your description of Tan Sally is offensive, Mom?"

"I am sorry if I offended you. I was simply telling it as I envisioned it."

"I am not personally offended. The term spinster is an offensive description of women like Tan Sally."

Suddenly Dorothy grasped the significance of what she said. *That description could be applied to me and a number of other women in this community,* she thought. She didn't quite understand what she was feeling. *Is it jealousy, suspicion, or fear that has taken a hold of me?* She wondered.

Her son had grown up and was receiving the attention of other women, old and young alike. She should have credited herself for a job well done in raising him to be so likable but she did not. Instead, she was becoming grumpy at the thought of not having his undivided attention.

"Now, I understand your fondness for Tan Sally. However, I am still concerned about this Ms. Inga."

"Mom? You are forgetting something."

"What could that be?"

"I do not question you about the people you associate with."

"You shouldn't. I am your mother. Those are my rights and privileges."

"Why am I not accorded the same rights and privileges?" Kendal spoke in legal terms he heard during his attendance at the Police Academy.

"You are the child. That is why."

"You are wrong, Mom. I am the man. I am grown up now. It is about time you acknowledge that."

"You may be big and tall and in a police uniform but you are still my child."

"I am you son but I am a man. I am no longer a child. Can't you get it?"

Dorothy grabbed a large wooden spoon hanging from a rack in the kitchen and raised it above her head. She was angry when she said, "You are not too big for me to burst your ass!" She had never before spoken to Kendal in that manner and never before had she threatened him with violence. For the first time since he started working in Matura, he got up and left home without kissing his mother goodbye. He was overwhelmed by emotions and felt like crying but he did not. Dorothy was not as strong emotionally. As she watched him leave, the tear drops came rolling down her cheeks. She tossed away the wooden spoon and tried to dry the tears with her hands but by then they had become flowing tracks of fluid on both of her cheeks. She retreated to her bedroom, closed the door, grabbed a towel and buried her face in it and into the pillow. She was sobbing but the sound was muffled by the pillow. Henrietta could not hear her as she literally cried herself to sleep.

By ten o'clock Henrietta was awake and bewildered. She knew that Dorothy always got up early to prepare something for Kendal. She walked into the kitchen to see if that was done. As far as she could have seen, coffee was freshly made, although whatever was left of it was no longer fresh. She spotted the wooden spoon on the floor and picked it up assuming simply that Dorothy may have dropped it inadvertently. Since she was unaware that anything was wrong she decided to go ahead and prepare breakfast for herself and her mother-in-law to be. She walked down the kitchen steps to the fowl coop and collected three eggs. From the vegetable garden she gathered fresh thyme and two ripe tomatoes and headed back up the stairs to the kitchen.

NINETEEN

Sydney brought the daily paper home from school every day and gave it to Joshua. He was pleased at how well his cousin's reading skills had progressed. Joshua didn't only read the news paper. He read labels on food items. He read flyers, posters, magazines, political manifestos, and even his mother's personal letters. He was proud of himself and would read aloud to anyone who would listen. He was either becoming overly confident or he was becoming a showoff.

Sydney mastered the art of top making and spinning, and he was preparing to engage in the sport competitively although he had not yet gotten his mother's approval. The competition was loosely organized and no prizes were ever awarded, just bragging rights. Those who participated were known to be the neighborhood's tough guys and more of them were Joshua's friends than Sydney's. They were all well known to Sydney, however, and he didn't mind being in their company as long as Joshua was there also. What Sydney didn't know was that Joshua had no plans to participate in what was billed as Top Fest 1956. One reason was that it was planned for Sunday morning, the same time as *the river lime*. The venue was to be in front of Tang's shop. Incidentally, that area had been a favorite place for many other events. Political rallies were held there. Prayer meetings of at least three different denominations were held there every month.

Sydney was unaware of Joshua's plans not to participate in Top Fest 1956. What Joshua wanted more than anything else was to rejoin *the river lime*. His arm was well healed. He felt strong, and the doctor said it was okay for him to swim again.

Arjune never seemed to have the time to tutor Joshua in mathematics. He had been approached by Kendal and Sydney's mother, Philbertha, and although he never objected to helping JJ, the biggest problem was always one of time constraint. Joshua understood that and registered for extra-mural classes in mathematics at Mayaro Elementary School. He actually wanted to register at Mayaro High so he could have had Ms. Gardener as a tutor but a counselor advised against it until such time that he mastered the basics.

That Friday morning Sydney was very excited. While he and Joshua were doing their chores he asked, "What time are we going to leave for the Top Fest on Sunday morning, JJ?"

"There are no we, Sydney."

"What is that suppose to mean?"

"I will not be there. You are on your own."

"You can't do that to me, JJ. You know that I will not be allowed to go if you will not be there."

"I am sorry, Sydney. I have decided to be at *the river lime* instead."

"Damn! I was so confident one of us could win. You won last year. You could have won again."

"Once again, I am sorry, man. When you make these plans, you must inform me ahead of time."

"That is so unfair."

"Why?"

"You know."

"I don't know why. We do not go everywhere together."

"That is true but............"

"But what?"

"Forget about it." Sydney could not tell Joshua the reason he felt that his mother would not have allowed him to attend the Top Fest if Joshua was not going to be there.

"Have it your way, man," said Joshua. "Anyway, I heard that they are going to have a party at the river bank this weekend."

"Who told you that?"

"Arjune. He also asked me to contribute something."

"That's no place to have a party."

"That's what I said when I heard of it."

"So?"

"I was told if there is a *lime* (a gathering of friends) there will be a party."

"Why is there need for a party?"

"I think they want to celebrate Kendal's achievements."

"Really, what has he achieved?"

"Come on now. Don't play dumb and blind. He passed his GCE and did the A levels. He graduated from the Police Academy and is now a rookie officer, and last night he became engaged to his childhood sweetheart."

"Big deal! "

"You are jealous and I don't understand why. You are not Kendal's age. You have not yet done any of the things he has. In addition, you are a minor. You couldn't get engaged to your sweetheart, Ms. Gardener."

"You are just so stupid. It is not funny anymore."

"There you go again. When you have no response to the truth, you call me *stupid*. Who is acting stupid now?"

"JJ, I am done, finished. I am going home," Sydney said and left.

Joshua was smiling at Sydney's inability to cope. He sat on a fallen coconut tree on a hill near the statue of St. Andrew and looked over at the seemingly endless rows of palm trees interspersed with flowering immortelles and poui trees. "Magnificent! What a beautiful landscape?" he whispered softly, but no one heard. There was no one there to hear him and that was fine. He was enjoying the solitude. *It is so peaceful up here*, he thought. *Why do I ever need the company of others? I do wish I had a dog though.*

Joshua had been wayward but he had never gotten into trouble with the law. He was expected to testify as a witness for the prosecution against the young men who attacked him with cutlasses (machetes) at the Mafeking Community Center because of a gambling debt he owed to someone else. They remained in jail. Their families were unable to raise bail, and the trial was set to begin in September. In the meantime, he had committed himself to turning his life around. He learnt to read and was improving that skill daily. He was being tutored in math and he was taking that seriously. The counselor told him, "If you can read and do mathematics, you can learn anything else." Joshua took those words very seriously.

After an hour of solitude, of meditating, of being one with nature; the flora and the fauna, the sun and the clouds, Joshua decided to go home. He strolled down the hill nonchalantly and arrived home in about ten minutes. No one asked him where he was, whether he had eaten, or how he felt. That was really no surprise to him. He grew up that way. On that occasion, however, it was more noticeable to him than ever before. He didn't know why. *Perhaps it was because I sat alone with St. Andrew for so long,* he thought, but he quickly dismissed it. He did not grow up religious. Although he was christened Roman Catholic, he was never confirmed and was never required to attend church on a regular basis, or even occasionally for that matter.

His mother, Velma sat in a Morris chair near the door listening to a Grundig radio but did not look up when he walked in. Just about everyone in the village had a Grundig radio but no one sat around all day listening to it like Velma Jacob. Her sedentary life style was nothing new and it did not bother Joshua before. For some reason, which he himself could not understand, on that day he was disgusted by it. *I can't stay here all day and look at her wasting her life away like that,* he thought. *Where can I go? What can I do?* He wondered?

Suddenly, as if by divine inspiration, he decided that he was dexterous and neat and might do well at woodwork such as cabinet making, joinery, or carpentry. He got up immediately, left the house, and ran down to the furniture shop operated by one Mr. Drexel.

"Good morning, sir," he said to the man in charge. "My name is Joshua Jacob and I am looking for a job."

"First of all, it is afternoon, son. Secondly, I know who you are. Thirdly, these jobs require highly skilled individuals."

"I am good with my hands, sir."

'How old are you, son?"

"I am sixteen, sir."

"Would you consider taking an apprenticeship?"

Joshua was silent. He didn't know what it was like to be an apprentice but he was reluctant to ask. Mr. Drexel sensed his uneasiness and asked, "What do you do when you are not in school?"

"Do you mean all day, sir?"

"Are you attending school?"

"No."

"So what do you do all day?"

"Nothing at all."

"Does your mother give you an allowance at the end of the week?"

"No. She needs an allowance herself."

Mr. Drexel laughed. "You are quite funny too," he said. Joshua said nothing so he continued, "Here is what I want you to do. Go home and ask your mother if it is okay for you to become an apprentice with Drexel Furniture and Cabinet Manufacturers. If she agrees, then you come back on Monday and we will get you started. Now, as I said before, this job requires skill. It takes a long time to acquire the skills needed to be good at the job. If you are willing to make the sacrifice I will assign you to work with someone here who is the best in the business. As an apprentice, there is no salary. You will receive $2.00 per week for personal expenses. Everyone else here gets paid for the jobs they complete. In other words, they are paid by the piece. If you learn fast and you do good work, you can do very well financially. Do you understand?"

"Yes sir."

"Now, go home and discuss it with your mother and get back to me on Monday."

"Thank you, sir."

"You are welcome. Run along now."

Joshua left there the happiest he had been since birth. He rushed home, ran inside and stood in front of his mother who was still listening to the radio and rocking back and forth in the Morris chair. "What the hell you standing there looking at me for?" she asked.

"Nothing," he said. Then he mumbled, "I am not telling you shit."

"Woh you just say deh?"

"Nothing."

"It better be nothing, otherwise ah go beat you little ass."

You can't even get up off your backside all day, how are you going beat mine? Joshua thought but he said nothing.

He had always wondered why Philbertha or Dorothy could not have been his mother. More than ever before he wished that could have been the case. It was not and he accepted that. He was determined, however, not to be daunted by his mother's sedentary life style and ineptitude, and made the decision to tell Mr. Drexel on Monday that she had no objection to him becoming an apprentice with the firm.

Sydney, meanwhile, had gotten the newspaper from Ms. Gardener. She had also given him two reading books she purchased at a book store in San Fernando the week end before but kept forgetting them at home. "Those are for JJ. I think that he would appreciate them," she said.

"Thank you, Ms. Gardener. He would be delighted to know that they are from you." Ms. Gardener wondered why but she did not ask. Instead, she told Sydney that she was leaving early and that he could get a ride home if he wished.

"How early are we talking about, Ms. Gardener?"

"I am leaving immediately after school is dismissed."

"Is that at three o'clock?"

"3:30 p.m. is my usual time, isn't it?"

"Yes, but that is really early for me."

"I wouldn't come looking for you. If you want a ride, you must show up when I am ready to leave."

"I will be there, Miss."

Sydney was still thinking about Top Fest 1956 and ways in which he could prepare for it. He felt that if he got a ride home he would have an extra two hours at least to practice. He refused to consider the possibility that his mother might object to his participation because Joshua wasn't going to be there. *I can win the whole thing with or without JJ being present*, he thought. He gave absolutely no consideration to attending the festival at the bridge that Sunday.

When school was dismissed he waited in the parking lot. It was an open, unpaved plot of land adjacent to the school but it was not government property. Very few people knew that and very few of those who knew cared. Sydney rested his book bag on the bonnet (hood) of Ms. Gardener's car and started going through the motions of spinning his top with the intention of connecting with and eventually destroying his opponent's. The rules of the game were simple: A coin would be tossed to determine which top of two competitors would be targeted. The loser's top would be placed on a hard surface. The winner's objective was to aim for the target when he released his top with speed and skill to punch and ultimately split open his opponent's top. If he missed on three consecutive attempts, his top then became the target. At the end, a winner was determined based on the number of direct hits the target sustained. One may also have been declared the winner as soon as the other's top was split open and destroyed.

For the benefit of young readers; a top is a toy. The type Joshua and Sydney made and used were wooden tops with wound cords and metal tips or fingers. They were spun on an axis and balanced on the metal tip which was a sharpened nail.

Ms. Gardener arrived at the parking lot and saw Sydney standing next to her car shadowing the moves he anticipated making during the contest. He was also talking to himself. *What is he doing?* She wondered. When she reached her car she asked Sydney, "What was all that?"

"All of what, Ms. Gardener?"

"All of your gesticulating and talking to the wind."

"Oh that! I am practicing for the Top Fest on Sunday."

"Shouldn't you be using a top to practice?"

"Yes."

"So why aren't you?"

"I am not allowed to bring my toys to school."

"Why not? Other students do."

"I know, but Mom will have a fit if I do."

"I don't quite get it. She will be upset if you bring a top to school, yet she will allow you to participate in the Top Festival."

"I do not get it either, Ms. Gardener, but that's my Mom. She contends that I cannot mix school and play."

"Quite frankly, that is what recess is all about, play and physical activity."

"Try telling that to my mother. She believes that we play and party too much hence we achieve so little."

"Oh! Does she realize that you are always at the top of your class? No pun intended."

"She is aware that I do my school work and do it well. Her reference is not to me in particular but to children of African descent in general."

"I have to speak with your mother about that. She shouldn't make such blanket (general) statements to you."

"No, Ms. Gardener! Please don't."

"Why shouldn't I?"

"She will know that I have been talking to you about these things and she would not like it."

"What will she do, spank you?"

"No. She never does, but she will be very upset with me."

"Well somebody needs to let her know that some of the best performers in my class, in the entire school for that matter, are children of African descent. The problem is not with the children. It is with the parents who are not willing to make any sacrifice to help their children further their education. While the ramifications of that are not yet evident, I guarantee you that in thirty to forty years from now it would become quite obvious."

"Wow! Ms. Gardener! You sound angry."

"I am teed-off."

"I am sorry, Ms. Gardener. I did not intend to annoy you."

"You are not at fault, Sydney. Quite frankly, you are one of the best students any parent or teacher could hope for."

"Then why are you annoyed?"

"It irks me when I see parents, especially fathers in this town, spending hundreds of dollars every month on whisky and cigarettes and would not sacrifice one penny for the advancement of their children's education."

Sydney was puzzled. He wasn't sure what his teacher was talking about. *Was she alluding to the lack of a father figure in his life? Was she herself deprived of the type of assistance she thinks her father could have given her if he sacrificed just a little? Or was she castigating all fathers of African descent?* He wondered.

"Let's get going," said Ms. Gardener. "I am running late already."

Sydney didn't know why or for what Ms. Gardener was late and he wasn't interested enough to ask. When they got into the vehicle and left the school's parking lot, she drove cautiously until the throngs of school children were out of view because there were no school crossing guards to regulate traffic. She then accelerated and the little prefect (a British made compact car) sped off. There was not much conversation between them after that.

As they approached the old, rickety Spring Bridge, Sydney expected Ms. Gardener to slow down, stop, and receive instructions from the guard on duty as the red sign indicated. She did not, and the guard didn't take notice. He was either drunk, asleep, or both.

As they crossed the bridge into Mafeking, Ms. Gardener spoke for the first time since leaving Pierre Ville. "I hope you enjoy your weekend and that you are victorious at the Top Festival."

Sydney smiled and said, "Thank you, Ms. Gardener. I hope you have a nice weekend too."

"I will try, Sydney. I will try."

Shortly after that brief exchange, she pulled up at the entrance to the house where Sydney lived with his mother, Philbertha. She was in the yard speaking with Joshua who came to ask if Sydney could be allowed to go *to* the riverside party on Sunday. Philbertha, however, was reluctant to give her approval in light of Kendal's near mishap two weekends earlier. Joshua of course, needed no parental approval. His mother simply did not care that much.

"Is that your mother standing there with Joshua?" Ms. Gardener asked.

Sydney looked out the window and said, "Yes."

"I wish I wasn't rushing. I would take the opportunity to speak with her right now."

"Thank God you are rushing," Sydney said.

"You are too funny. Do you know that?"

"I never thought of myself as being funny."

"You are sometimes," said Ms Gardener. She shook Sydney's hand gently and said, "You take care of yourself and your lovely mom."

As Sydney left the vehicle, Ms. Gardener waved to Philbertha and Joshua. Philbertha waved back but Joshua did not. Philbertha made no notice of it but Sydney did. *That JJ*, he thought. *He is so jealous.* As Sydney walked into the yard, his mother greeted him with a great big hug. "How was your day, son?" she asked.

"Very nice, Mom," he said. Then he turned to Joshua and asked, "What's up, JJ?"

"Nothing," JJ replied. He was glum and Sydney sensed his displeasure. He wasn't sure whether it was because Joshua saw that Ms. Gardener brought him home, or that his mother greeted him so warmly upon his arrival. He knew that JJ's mother never did such things. If anyone attempted to hug her she would always pull away. Sydney had become accustomed to Joshua's moodiness and wasn't bothered by it. His mother never noticed.

"JJ told me that you are good with the top and wanted to participate in Top Fest 1956."

"I would like to participate but it is JJ who is very good. Have you forgotten that he won last year?"

There was a brief moment of silence before Joshua said, "I am going to *the river lime.*"

"Does that mean I cannot join Top Fest 1956, Mom?"

"You never asked to be allowed to participate, son."

"I intended to ask you as soon as I knew what JJ's decision was."

"Now you know," Philbertha said hoping that her son would still want to be a participant in the Top Festival.

Sydney was silent. He was looking at JJ as if to say, *say something.* Joshua did. He said, "Don't look to me for answers."

"What will it be?" Philbertha asked.

"Top Fest if you would allow me, Mom."

"Then Top Fest it is." Philbertha was relieved to say that. Although she had reservations, she was a lot more comfortable with the Top Festival than with *the river lime,* and she planned to be there as a spectator to cheer her son on.

TWENTY

She had been waiting at the Mayaro taxi stand in Sangre Grande for more than an hour when Kendal arrived there. She didn't mind the wait or the scathing comments she heard from men whose advances she rebuffed. All she wanted was to see Kendal, to touch him, to hold him, and to be held close to him. She was irrational and did not consider the ramifications of her actions. As soon as he was dropped off by his colleagues in the patrol car, Kendal was approached by a taxi driver who asked, "Mayaro, Officer?"

"Yeah, man."

"Come on. Leh we go, man. Ah ha four already." The driver needed one more passenger to have a full complement of five for the trip.

As Kendal was attempting to enter the vehicle, Monica called out, "Kendal!" He turned around and there she was, standing right before him. He was baffled. She hugged him and whispered in his ear, "I am parked at the same place. You do not need a taxi."

"Go ahead, man," said Kendal. "I am going to speak with the lady for a while." He was smiling but it was more out of chagrin than pleasure. "What are you doing here?" he asked.

"I was waiting for you."

"Waiting for me? How could that be? I got the impression that you were spending the weekend in Guayaguayare."

"I am. However, I had to work today."

"Correct me if I am wrong. Didn't you tell me yesterday that you had today off?"

278

"No. I have tomorrow off. I spent last night in Guayaguayare and I am spending the weekend, Saturday and Sunday there."

"I know what days constitute the weekend but I also know what you said and what I heard."

"You know what you thought you heard me say, honey."

"Monica, please! Don't play games with me."

"This is no game, sweetheart."

Monica lied and Kendal was beginning to doubt himself. *This is not how a police officer is supposed to operate*, he thought. *I have to be more alert when speaking with her. In future I will question what she says so that she repeats herself. This way, there shall be no doubt as to what was said or what I heard.*

She was smiling broadly when Kendal asked, "Are you making fun of me?"

"No. I am only smiling with you."

"I am not smiling."

"Never mind that," said Monica. She held his hand and said, "Walk with me." He offered no resistant. He did not ask, where to? It was as if he already knew.

They walked slowly toward Monica's car. She had parked it in front of *Coconut Juice* again. When they got there she asked, "Would you like to go in and have a drink?"

"No."

"That was flat and dry," she said.

"What are you talking about?"

"How you answered me."

"Oh!"

"Are you angry?"

"No."

"It certainly seems that way."

"Well, I am not."

"I am happy to hear that. It wouldn't be nice for us to be angry at each other so early in our relationship."

"What do you mean by our relationship? We just met. There is no relationship."

"Well, to me it is a budding relationship but a relationship none-the-less."

"I do not see it that way."

"Why don't you?"

"Because.............." He did not complete the statement and she did not pursue it.

Instead, she asked, "Are you rushing home this evening?"

"It is funny that you would ask me that."

"What is so funny about the question?"

"What is funny is not the question itself. It is the fact that this is the one evening that I am in no hurry to get home." Kendal was thinking of his disagreement with his mother earlier that day.

"Good!" Monica said, and for a brief moment both of her hands were off the steering wheel. She was trying to unpin her hair with her right hand while reaching over and touching Kendal with her left.

"Please don't try that."

"What! Don't you want me to touch you?"

"That is not the point."

"What exactly is the point, Officer O'Connor?"

"You need to keep both hands on the wheel," he said smiling. Monica was not amused. She felt that she was risking everything just to be with him and he wasn't taking her seriously. Quite the contrary though. Kendal was very serious. He was a safety conscious individual and although he didn't drive, he realized the danger of not holding on to the steering wheel on the winding, undulating, Manzanilla Road with its uneven surface and many landslides.

"Do you want to drive?"

"I never said that I wanted to. However, I do want to arrive home safely."

"Don't you think that I can get you there safely?"

"I think you are capable and I trust that you will."

"I think we had enough bickering for one evening."

"Yes. I think so too."

"That's good then. What time do you have to get home?"

"What kind of a question is that?"

"I asked a simple and straight-forward question. Let me repeat; What time do you have to get home?"

"I do not have a curfew if that is what you are implying. I do, however, try to be home in time for dinner."

"What time is dinner?"

"We usually have dinner between six and seven o'clock."

"What happens if you are there later that seven?"

"I cannot recall ever getting there later than seven."

"What will happen if you do?"

"The dinner might be cold and Mom may be upset that I kept her waiting. I don't know, for Christ sake!"

"Did you always sit down to dinner with your mother?"

"As far as I can remember, yes." said Kendal. "Why are you asking all of these questions?"

"Hey! I am not a cop. I just want to know how much time you can spend with me this evening."

"Huh!"

"What is the *huh* about?"

"I am just thinking."

"I want to leave you with something to think about. The funny thing is, there is not a guest house or hotel anywhere along this route."

"What does that have to do with anything?"

No! He can't be that naive, she thought. In fact, he was. His naiveté was real. The only woman he had ever been romantically involved with before was the one to whom he was engaged to be married, and they had limited sexual encounters before their engagement. His experience was woefully lacking.

"I will soon show you," she said. That statement aroused Kendal's curiosity, and although he didn't say it, he was eager to find out. As the car descended the hill at the Manzanilla cemetery and entered the Manzanilla/Mayaro Road, she slammed on the brakes. The car came to a screeching halt.

"What the hell was that?" he asked.

"Just a taste of the excitement you are about to experience."

"As I said before, I would like to get home safely."

"I promise I will get you there. That has more to do with me than with my driving skills."

Suddenly some thick, grey clouds blocked the sun's rays from reaching the earth's surface in that area. The ocean also took on the color of the clouds as huge waves slammed against the shoreline.

"It looks as if it is going to rain," Kendal said.

"That's not unusual. We have these torrential down-pours throughout the country."

"I know but this looks really bad. It is more like a storm coming up over the Atlantic."

"Then I am going to pull off the road. I wouldn't want to be caught driving in that." Kendal nodded his head in agreement. It would not have mattered to Monica if he didn't. She had decided long before, that was what she wanted to do. The impending rain was an added bonus.

At a clearing under the canopy of palm trees she turned left sharply onto what appeared to be a regularly used, though unpaved path. She stopped at an embankment which was formed by sand deposited by waves of previous high tides. Before she had time to pull up the emergency brakes, the patter of rain drops were heard on the roof of the car. At first they were few but large. Then the rain started pouring. There were flashes of lightning and rumbles of thunder. It was raining heavily when Monica sudden reclined the driver's seat, held Kendal's arm with her left hand and pulled him closer to her. "I enjoy making love when it is raining," she whispered. Those were the last words spoken in that car for the next half hour. By the time the rain ceased, they both looked as if they slept in the same clothes for several days. There were wrinkles all over their clothing.

"It is a good thing I didn't travel in uniform," Kendal said.

"That would have added a new dimension to the tryst."

"This was no tryst. We did not plan to meet."

"Call it what you will," said Monica. *I had it figured out*, she thought. Then she added, "It would have been different had you been in uniform." They stepped out of the car to try and smooth the wrinkles away.

Kendal sighed loudly as Monica drove off after their failed attempt at smoothing their clothing. She looked at the clock on the dash board. It was nearly two hours before that they turned off the main road.

"We are running on time," she said.

"Running on time for what?"

"We are running on time for Mama's boy here to have his dinner. I told you that I would get you there."

"We are not there yet," Kendal said.

You are so naive, she thought. Then she said, "You arrived and didn't realize it."

"Arrive where? I live in Mafeking."

"Okay, Kendal. You can view it anyway you like. The truth is I got you there."

"That is the reason I do not like reading the bible."

"Now, what the bible has to do with what just transpired?"

"It is written in the same manner that you are speaking, in parables."

Monica started laughing hysterically. "You are a lot of fun to be with. Do you know that?"

"What is so funny?"

"It is just plain, clean fun."

Kendal was laughing too, although he wasn't quite sure why. As they approached the rickety Nariva River Bridge, Monica stretched out her left hand to him. He held her hand and she squeezed his as if to gain support and confidence to drive across the structure which terrified her. They got across safely and Kendal made no mention of the anacondas and alligators he spoke of when they crossed the bridge a day earlier.

"I feel safe and comfortable with you," she said. Kendal did not answer, so she continued, "I hope we can spend a lot more quality time together in the future."

"Not after you are married."

"Why not?"

"Why would you even ask that? It would be very wrong."

"Isn't it wrong for us to have done what we did?"

"We acknowledge our transgressions, so why should we repeat them?"

"We acknowledge? Maybe you have transgressed but I haven't." Kendal did not respond so Monica continued, "I would never have been so relaxed with you if I felt it was wrong. Somehow I get the impression that either you have been squeaky clean all your life or your fiancée is an angel."

"She is in many ways."

"Yeah, right!"

"What is that supposed to mean?"

"You figure it out, Officer."

They were traveling on the Naparima/Mayaro Road when Kendal noticed two young men, boys really, engaged in a fist fight. A small crowd was gathering around them in the vestibule of Hong's shop. Monica saw the fight also.

"Stop! Stop," Kendal shouted. Instead of stopping, she accelerated. There was a brief period of silence, then, he asked, "Why didn't you stop?"

"My man isn't going to get hurt in a silly dispute between two wayward teenagers."

"Your man?"

"My man is what I said."

"What gave you that impression?"

"The way you made love to me. Initially, I thought you were really a rookie but with time you relaxed and performed exceptionally well."

"I am afraid you are taking this too far, Monica."

"I am taking it too far?"

"I think so."

"Suddenly it is my fault."

"I never said that."

"You implied as much."

"That is your interpretation of the facts," said Kendal. "This is getting us nowhere."

"You are so wrong, mister. We have already gone the distance. We can end the trip here or we can return to the starting point and do it all over again. It is your call, Officer O'Connor."

Kendal was silent. His thoughts were racing. Monica seemed to be the domineering type so he was curious to know what her fiancé was like. He didn't want to ask her directly for fear that in turn, he may be asked to divulge personal information about Henrietta, some of which he knew was not flattering.

They reached the dilapidated Spring Bridge and crossed it without any concern. It was 6:50p.m. by then and darkness had already set in. There were no street lights in Mayaro or Guayaguayare so Kendal was concerned as to how Monica would travel another thirty minutes to Guayaguayare by herself. It was obvious that he had mixed feelings about her. He thought she was too demanding, too bossy, and promiscuous. *Wasn't I being promiscuous also?* He wondered. Then he sought to justify his actions by saying to himself, *I never cheated before and never will again. Am I the only man she has gotten involved with since her engagement?* He wondered. He wanted an answer to the question but was afraid to ask her.

"Are you angry with me?" Monica asked suddenly.

"No."

"So why aren't you talking to me?"

"It takes two to converse and you seemed so detached."

"I am sorry. My thoughts do drift at times."

"Whose doesn't?"

"I don't know. Somehow, I thought that was something very few people experienced."

"Everyone does," Kendal said authoritatively. Then he asked, "Are you comfortable with driving to Guaya' tonight?"

"If I said no, will you go with me?"

"Do you ever give a straight forward answer to a question?"

"Do you?"

"Yes."

"Tonight you cannot. Don't ask me why not because I already know. I will tell you. It's the dinner thing, isn't it?"

"Yes."

"Suddenly you have become monosyllabic?"

"You could say that." *Or you can just leave*, he thought. Monica had pulled up in front of the house where Kendal lived with his mother. That night his fiancée, Henrietta Riggs was also there, and although he wanted to let Monica know that, he somehow couldn't.

"It is a clear night," he said.

"Yes. A far cry from what we experienced earlier."

"The rain suited us then."

"Just as the moonlight suits me now."

"Are you sure you would be okay?"

"I am not sure. No one is ever sure about anything, but I think I'll be fine. My car is practically new. It is a dependable vehicle, and I have a full tank of gas."

"Then have a safe trip," Kendal said as he leaned over and kissed her.

"Not so fast, buddy," said Monica. "Will I see you tomorrow or Sunday?"

"Tomorrow is out of the question but you can on Sunday."

"Is that so?"

"Yes. I will be at *the river lime*. The fellas (guys) are throwing a party for my fiancée and me. Come and bring you man along."

"Where is *the river lime* held?" Monica asked again.

"It is held under the Spring Bridge."

"That broken down, old bridge?"

"Yes. One lime is held there and another is held further down the road near the saw-mill."

"Which one do you normally participate in?"

"I prefer the one at the Spring Bridge."

"Is that where the party will be held?"

"Yes. You should come."

"I don't know."

"What don't you know?"

"Under the bridge, on the bank of a murky river does not seem like the ideal place to have a party."

"No one ever said it was ideal. It most likely would take the form of a picnic."

"Why didn't they just call it a picnic?"

"Monica, I don't know. I did not organize the thing."

"I don't know, Kendal. I really don't know."

"Well, think about it."

"I will."

"Will you come or will you think about it?"

"I will think about it."

"That's cool." They kissed good night before Kendal stepped out of the car. Monica then made a u-turn in the narrow street, waved to him, and sped off.

He walked the short distance along the narrow path to the front door of his mother's house and opened it. There was a kerosene light burning in the living room and one in the kitchen but no one was at home. In the kitchen he found his dinner on the table. It was still warm, an indication that it wasn't long before he arrived that his Mother and fiancée left the house. There was a note on the table. It read; *Son, we are going over to Philbertha's. Enjoy your dinner. Love you, Mom.* Kendal had his dinner. He then brushed his teeth, took a shower, and went to bed.

TWENTY-ONE

Saturday morning Dorothy woke up early as usual. The night before she had gathered everything she needed to take to the market and arranged to be picked up by taxi. Philbertha was also taking produce to be sold at the open market and she intended to use the same taxi service. Although they had essentially the same produce, there was little or no competition between them because they sold at wholesale to different vendors.

Kendal slept later than usual that morning. Perhaps he was tired from traveling to and from Sangre Grande all week. Or he was overly exhausted from his exploits with Monica. Whatever the reason, he was still asleep when Henrietta got up. She was happy and eager to tell him how joyously his mother accepted the news of her pregnancy but she did not disturb him. Instead, she went to the kitchen to prepare breakfast just as Dorothy would have done. She knew the kitchen well because she had spent so much time there in the past. Without hesitation, therefore, she set out to do what Dorothy would normally have done. A Saturday morning breakfast at the O'Connor's was never as elaborate as Sunday's and Henrietta knew that.

She made some fried bake (flattened bread dough that is fried rather than baked), sliced up an avocado, scrambled some eggs, sprinkled grated cheese over it, and brewed some coffee. She was setting the table for two when Kendal walked in. He had gotten up, brushed his teeth, and showered but Henrietta didn't notice. She was so engrossed in trying to prepare the perfect breakfast for him.

"Good morning," he said.

"Good morning," said Henrietta. She pulled off the flower-patterned apron she was wearing to protect her clothing, ran over to the kitchen door where he had just entered and gave him a big hug. He hugged her but with less enthusiasm than he normally would have. She, however, never noticed the difference. She was just so happy to be fixing him breakfast on a Saturday morning.

"Come, sit down," she said as they walked toward the kitchen table. The kitchen was not just an area to prepare food. It was used more frequently for dining than the dining room itself.

Kendal and Henrietta walked hand in hand toward the kitchen table and sat down. "When did you do all of this?" he asked.

"A few minutes ago," she said. She was smiling and looking directly at him as if to ask, *are you pleased?* He offered no comment or compliment so she continued, "I hope you are hungry. I prepared the eggs just the way you like it, scrambled soft."

"I can see that. Thanks," he said.

"Are you okay, honey?"

"Yes. Why do you ask?"

"You seem so lethargic."

"I am tired and there are so many things on my mind."

"Just what is bothering you, sweetheart?"

Is it my pregnancy? Henrietta wondered but did not ask. She was concerned that in spite of Kendal's suggestion and what they had agreed upon, that her being pregnant for someone else may become an issue. Her indiscretions, she was afraid may come back to haunt her. Kendal's concern on the other hand, was for Monica. *What if she became pregnant for me? Would she be upfront, and honest with her fiancé? How will he accept it?* All of those things were bothering him. He felt worse because he could not talk about them with Henrietta. There was no one he could trust sufficiently to confide in. His closest confidant was his mother and she adored Henrietta. He knew that he didn't dare mention anything like that to her. He was alone in his dilemma, and he felt lonely in the company of others, particularly Henrietta's.

Kendal did not respond to Henrietta's question so she asked again, "Why are you so pensive, dear?"

"I believe that is one reason my brain and yours too, are encased in bony structures called skulls."

"In other words, what you are saying is, don't you bother me."

"Please!"

Henrietta felt dejected at what she considered an insult. She was hurt, although not emotionally scarred. She immediately lost her appetite, got up from the table where she had been seated opposite to Kendal and said, "Enjoy your breakfast, sir." She left the kitchen crying and went to Dorothy's room where she threw herself down onto the futon. There she sobbed and sobbed until she fell asleep. She had never cried that much in her entire life. Kendal had never seen her cry that much either but he showed little concern.

Two hours later she woke up, rolled over, looked around hoping that he would be lying or sitting next to her. He was not. On the contrary, he walked out of the house when she left the table. He walked up the Old Rio Claro/Mayaro Road. Just after the statue of Saint Andrew, he left the beaten path and trekked down to the bank of a pristine brook. Although unnamed, the little stream by which he sat in solitude on a tree stump served as a quiet retreat. "I need to clear my head," he whispered to himself as he gazed into the crystal clear water that flowed slowly down stream.

Suddenly, he was captivated by the variety of flora and fauna all around him. The vegetation was particularly a rich green. It was not a forested area. It was more like an abandoned agricultural estate that had become a verdant thicket from which numerous coconut trees grew tall above everything else to form a canopy that shaded the stream and surrounding area. Kendal sat there at peace with himself. It was a hot day but he felt rather cool in that environment. He tried not to think of his job and the lassitude he was experiencing on the daily beat with Sergeant Kanga. He tried not think of his fiancée or of Monica but none could be kept entirely out of his mind. Eventually, he decided to return home.

When he arrived, his mother was there. She returned from the market-place and was at work in the kitchen marinating the beef she bought with some of her earnings from the produce she sold. She was smiling and happy to see him. She expected to be hugged and kissed but he was hesitant. He never had a falling out with his mother before so he wasn't sure what might be an appropriate response.

"Listen, son!" said Dorothy, "Whatever it was that we were angry about, and God knows I don't remember now. It is behind us. So come over here and give your mother a hug." She washed her hands and dried them in her apron.

Kendal smiled sheepishly. He walked over to the kitchen counter where she stood with outstretched arms and they embraced each other. Neither spoke for at least a minute. They simply held each other closely, an indication of the unyielding love between a mother and her son. When they eventually released their grasp, Kendal said, "Whatever it was, Mom, I am sorry." He too could not remember what their disagreement was about.

"We should try not to let it happen again," said Dorothy. "If either of us is displeased about something, we should find the time to discuss it. The same is true if you and Etta should disagree. You should talk about it." Kendal was silent. His thoughts were on Monica, not Henrietta.

"Do you understand me, son?" Dorothy asked. Kendal jumped as if taken by surprise.

"Why are you so jittery?"

"Am I jittery?"

"Yes. For a moment there I thought you would jump out of your skin."

"I am sorry, Mom?"

"Is something bothering you, son? Anything other than whatever it was we disagreed about?"

"No."

"I am so sorry that it has taken such a toll on you."

"There is nothing bothering me, Mom."

Henrietta woke up and came out to the kitchen. "Good morning Ms. Dorothy," she said.

"Good morning, my dear," Dorothy replied. She glanced at Kendal and looked at Henrietta and asked, "Are you two seeing each other for the first time this morning?"

"No, Mom."

"Oh ho! I was beginning to think that something was very wrong."

"Nothing is wrong with me, Ms. Dorothy."

When will she stop this Ms. Dorothy, crap? She wondered. She was hoping that by then Henrietta would have called her mom but she asked, "If nothing is wrong with you, Etta, what is wrong with Kendal?

"I don't know. He has been acting strangely of late."

"What do you have to say for yourself, Kendal?"

"Nothing," he said with a coy smile on his face.

"Then there is no problem."

"No problem at all," he said. He was very cocky.

Henrietta was not satisfied with his responses but she chose not to continue the discussion. Much to his delight, Dorothy asked nothing further of either of them. Instead, she hinted about a certain buzz in the village that suggests there will be a river lime of a different sort the next day. "People around here gossip too much," Henrietta said.

"I don't think that we are especially malicious. All over Mayaro people talk. Let's face it, what else is there to do?"

Have sex, Kendal thought but he didn't dare say that in his mother's presence so he said, "To every word of gossip, there is a glimmer of truth."

Henrietta cringed. She was aware of all the unflattering things that were said about her in and around the district. Dorothy never believed them or she simply chose to ignore them. Kendal never confronted her about them until he encountered her in the hammock with Karish and of course, by her own revelation, she was pregnant for Rudolf Vargas. She couldn't help but wonder whether Kendal was alluding to any of those situations, or to all of them.

"What is that supposed to mean?" she asked.

"Exactly what I said," he retorted.

"Come on now!" Dorothy quibbled. "Stop acting like children and start thinking about tomorrow." She meant that literally and figuratively.

"There isn't much to think about. We are going to *the river lime* tomorrow," Kendal said.

"Have you made that decision without consulting me?"

"Yes. It is planned to celebrate our engagement. We are the guests of honor. We must be there."

"Well, suppose I had other plans?" Henrietta asked.

"What other plans could you have? You are spending the weekend with me and that is what I want to do."

"It is always about you or what you want"

"No. Shall I remind you?"

"Excuse me!" Dorothy said and retreated to her room. There was a brief period of silence. Then Henrietta said, "Okay, Kendal."

"Okay about what?"

"I will attend *the river lime* on Sunday."

"Is that it?"

"Isn't that what you want? Isn't it what you expected of me, your fiancée the dutiful *yes woman?*"

Kendal was at a loss for words. *Mom has always been there to support me, like a plinth upon which I was placed. Now, she simply walked away and left me in a lurch,* he thought. *What am I suppose to do?*

"Yes. I wanted you to go with me but it was not my intention for you to feel cajoled, or coerced." Kendal said.

"Well, you managed to accomplish that without any effort."

"If that's the way you feel, then don't go. I am sure I can give a plausible explanation for your absence." Henrietta was expecting Kendal to plead with her to join the gathering and was disappointed when he didn't. Nevertheless, she agreed to go with him.

"I will go," she said.

"I do not expect you to do anything against your will.

"I said I will go, and I said so on my own volition," said Henrietta. "Will Ms. Dorothy be going?"

"I seriously doubt that."

"Why?"

"There is never anyone there over the age of twenty-eight."

"That's too bad."

"Why? I am certain there are other things she would prefer to do."

Neither of them noticed that Dorothy was standing at the kitchen door smiling. She was happy to see that there was some sort of harmony between them again.

"It is always so nice to see you getting along. And yes, there are other things I would like to do. For example, I would prefer to attend Top Fest '56 tomorrow. As a matter of fact, I promised Bertha that I will be there to see Sydney compete."

"Were you eavesdropping on our conversation, Mom?"

"Kendal! How dare you?" Henrietta asked.

"It's okay, Etta. He knows better but he wants to be mannish. It wasn't enough for him to tell me yesterday that he is the man, he feels he has to prove it."

"It's nothing like that, Mom."

"Anyway Henrietta, you make sure he doesn't enter that river tomorrow."

"There will be no swimming, Ms. Dorothy. I assure you of that."

"Good."

"Who will want to swim when there are lovely people to converse with and nice food and drinks all around?" Kendal asked.

He was thinking more of the people who might be there rather than the food and drinks. His hope was that Monica would show up with her fiancé as she promised. He wanted to introduce Henrietta to her in a manner that said; *here are some of the people I associate with. They are certainly not the likes of Karish and or Vargas.*

"Alright mister man, you seem to have forgotten that it is not a good idea to eat just before swimming and that it is even worse to drink alcohol and go swimming."

"I have heard the saying, the legend, if I may call it that."

"You may call it what you wish but let me tell you, it is no myth," said Dorothy. "It is a bad idea." That wasn't quite what she wanted to say and Kendal realized it. Although he understood what she meant, he asked, "Is it a bad idea to call it what it is; a legend? Or is it a bad idea to actually carry it out?"

"I am finished, oui. Ah done with that," Dorothy said.

Kendal started laughing which amazed Henrietta. *Why is he making fun of his mother?* She wondered but said nothing as Dorothy asked, "What is so funny?"

"The way you spoke."

"What is so funny about the way I speak?"

"The way you use English and French in the same sentence."

Dorothy hissed her teeth and said, "You better stop being fresh with me. Whom do you think taught you to speak?"

"You are right, Ms Dorothy. There is really nothing funny about it. At home we generally speak like that. In fact, there are days when little or no English is spoken in our house," Henrietta said.

"What then? Do you mutate?" Kendal asked, He had a fit of laughter again. No one else was laughing at what he thought of as a joke.

"It is not a joke, Kendal. It is a carry-over from the French Colonial days, a time when French was the official language of the land. Most people spoke broken French. It was commonly known as French Creole or Patois. In many parts of this country, Mayaro included, some of us continue to speak the language, generation after generation. The same is true in other Caribbean countries such as Haiti, Martinique, and St. Lucia, to name a few. I am sure you hear it spoken up there in Matura where you are stationed."

"I cannot remember anyone speaking like that."

"You are an officer of the law so you need to pay attention, Kendal."

Although Henrietta was speaking in defense of Dorothy, she wasn't too thrilled at the idea of someone else reprimanding her son, especially in her presence. *What she does when she is his wife and they are in their house is their business, but right now it has gone too far,* she thought, and she quickly moved to change the topic of the conversation.

"Why don't we start fixing something for lunch?" she asked, directing the question to Henrietta.

"We can do that. How can I help?"

As his mother and fiancée moved to prepare lunch, Kendal informed them that he was going to the soccer field. He intended to stay no more than ninety minutes, the duration for which one of the regular practice games normally lasted. When he arrived, however, a game was already in progress. In those days, young men from the district gathered at the playing field on Saturdays and on evenings during the week to lime (hang out with friends) or play cricket or football (soccer). Some cricketers did not like the footballers using the field. They contended that the cricket pitch got damaged in the process. Most of the youngsters, however, played both games. So the dissenters were few and ineffective.

Cricket was played in the dry season; January to May. Soccer was played in the rainy season; June to December. It is imperative to note, however, that the seasons were never quite clearly defined. There were torrential rain-falls at times during the dry season and the rainy season presented hot and humid weather with parching dry days at times.

Kendal arrived too late to be selected to play. There were two other young men there who shared the same experience, and quite a number of teen-aged boys who found other activities that held their interest while the game was in progress. Very few people, if any, ever stayed long enough to witness one of those practice games through to the end. Kendal was no exception. He felt that if he wasn't participating, the games were always too boring to watch. Suddenly it occurred to him that the fellas (guys) must be practicing for the Top Festival on Sunday. *The logical place for them to practice would be in front of Tang's shop*, he thought and rushed over there. He was wrong.

The youngsters did assemble in front of Tang's for practice but Mr. Tang objected because it was during regular business hours. He was concerned for the safety of his customers. Undaunted, the boys moved about two hundred yards down the Mafeking Branch Road. That portion of the roadway was paved with asphalt and although it wasn't ideal, everyone thought that it should suffice.

Sydney was there, and so was Joshua who seemed to have acted as Sydney's coach. They were both happy to see Kendal who asked JJ, "Didn't you win this thing last year?"

"Yes, but this is Sydney's first time at competing," said JJ. "Do you know that before last week, he had never even spun a top?"

"I didn't know but I do believe that."

"Now he is a master at it. That's not all though."

"What else is there, JJ?"

"He made the tops himself."

"That's great. Who would have thought so? They look as if they were commercially produced."

"Thanks, Kendal. However, the credit should go to JJ. He taught me how to make good tops."

"That's good. One hand washes the other. Rumor has it that you taught him how to read."

"It is no rumor, Kendal. It is true. He helped me immensely. Now I can read anything that is written in English," Joshua said proudly.

"Fantastic! Now here you are, both of you, looking like champions. May the better man win tomorrow."

"I do hope Sydney wins tomorrow because I am not competing."

"Why wouldn't you compete? Is it because your arm is still not completely healed?'

"No. My arm is fine now."

"So what is the problem?"

"There is no problem. I have chosen to go to *the river lime* instead."

"Joshua! *The river lime* is great but shouldn't you, the top spinning champion, be at the Top Fest '56 to defend your title?"

Joshua laughed and said, "It's nothing that sophisticated, Kendal. If I am absent, which I will be, I will lose by default. That's all."

"You are telling me that you intend to leave your cousin out on a limb like that."

"He will survive. He is like a squirrel, very agile on limbs."

Not only has he learnt to read, his vocabulary has also improved considerably, Kendal thought but he said, "Enjoy whatever you do tomorrow, JJ. I wish you good luck at the festival, Sydney."

"Thank you," Sydney said.

"Kendal, you sound as if you didn't know that *the river lime* will be held in your honor this Sunday. What's up with that?" JJ asked.

"I have heard the rumor. As I understand it, a surprise party is planned for Henrietta and me."

"It is not just a rumor, man. The party is on and it is going to be big."

"Is that so?"

`Yes! Another thing, there will be very few swimmers in the water. You in particular, will not be allowed to swim. Only six of Mayaro's best are selected to compete against the best of what Rio Claro has to offer."

"What Rio Claro has to offer?"

"I don't know, man. There is no large body of water there so I don't know where the fellas (guys) learned to swim."

"Well, in a few hours we will find out," said Kendal. "By the way, who are the six people selected to compete?"

"As I understand it, they are Arjune, Dolphin, Submarine, Mullet, Boodlall and...." JJ stopped short of mentioning the sixth swimmer selected.

"You only mentioned five people, Joshua. Who is the sixth person?"

"He is," Sydney said before Joshua could overcome his modesty and answer the question.

"You were better than all of the others before your injury. I am confident that you will perform well in spite of it."

"Thanks, Kendal."

Sydney was the only Top Festival competitor who hadn't practiced that morning. From the time Kendal arrived there Sydney's attention was diverted but no one seemed to notice or if they did, it didn't seem to matter to them. He was not concerned either.

At the home of the O'Connor's meanwhile, Dorothy and Henrietta had the lunch menu near completion. It was Henrietta, however, who did most of the actual cocking. She baked some fish which Dorothy had seasoned earlier and would have preferred to stew after flying, but she had no complaint. Henrietta also steamed some Creole rice and prepared a salad. The only thing that Dorothy actually accomplished apart from marinating the fish, was to prepare an iced cold star apple drink, and of course, she gave her seal of approval to Henrietta's cooking.

"You did well, girl," she said.

"Thank you, Ms. Dorothy."

"You are most welcome," she said while thinking, *at least I wouldn't have to worry about what my child (the man as he has been insisting) is eating on a daily basis. He knows that whenever he longs for a good home cooked meal, Mom is always here.*

"Shall I set the table?" Henrietta asked.

"Yes, of course," said Dorothy. "I do hope the man has the presence of mind to be here before this food that you have so diligently prepared, gets cold."

"He'll be here, Ms. Dorothy."

"He'd better be because I am hungry and I am sure you are too."

"I hardly ever eat when I cook."

"You cook so well, how could you not like your own cooking?"

"It is not that I do not like it. I think that the constant smell of the food during its preparation takes away my appetite."

"I have not heard that before but I guess everybody is different. I believe, however, when one enjoys what one cooks, there is always that desire to strive to do even better."

"You may have a point there, Ms. Dorothy. That is certainly something for me to consider."

My goodness! She is receptive and open to suggestions too. Those certainly are good characteristics, Dorothy thought but she said nothing, so Henrietta continued, "I think I will start sampling my cooking as of today and hope that I do not gain a whole lot of weight in the process."

"Don't you worry about that, girl."

"That's easy for you to say, Ms. Dorothy. You have been lucky so far."

"It is probably more because of genetics than luck, my dear."

"Perhaps."

"My mother died in her early fifties but she weighed the same at age fifty as she did at age fifteen."

"It hasn't been that way in my family. I don't have to explain. You already know."

"I know, girl. Your mother, Aunt, and uncles have that predisposition but you shouldn't worry."

"I am concerned, being in the family way and all, but I am not really worried as such."

"That's good. You can enjoy your meal if that young man gets here before it is cold."

"If he doesn't we can warm it up. Can't we?"

"We can. Personally, I hate reheating food. That's how I grew up. When the meal was ready everyone was there and ready to eat. Yeah! That was my mother and I, for the most part."

"That is amazing."

"What is so amazing, girl?"

"The fact that you have stayed so slim is truly amazing."

"Well, thank you," Dorothy said with a smile.

Kendal walked in. He was smiling too, although, his smile was for different reasons. What Joshua told him about the elaborate preparation for the upcoming river lime to honor him and Henrietta, and the thought of Monica and her fiancé in attendance seemed to have invigorated him. In addition, he was very pleased to see that his future bride and his mother were having an amicable discussion. To see them talking and smiling happily was a particularly joyous moment for him.

"There must be something very pleasing in this kitchen," he said.

"Your wife's cooking," his mother responded.

"I always knew she could cook, Mom."

"Well, what more can I say?"

"Nothing, I suppose," said Kendal. "Anyway, I heard the party in our honor will be an elaborate affair."

"Oh! really? When will it be?"

"Tomorrow."

"Where?"

"At the Spring Bridge."

"Who told you that?"

"JJ did."

"Are you telling me that a party is organized in your honor and you had to hear about it from JJ?"

"Well, he told me in confidence because Arjune and them wanted it to be a surprise."

"Arjune and them?"

"Arjune and they. You know what I mean, Mom."

"I know what you said. That is not necessarily what you meant."

Dorothy O'Connor taught her son to speak English properly and expected nothing less from him even though she slipped up at times and spoke broken English with a typical Mayaro/T & T lilt. Kendal, however, was beginning to feel that the manner in which he spoke was boring to some people with whom he came into contact on a daily basis. He was gradually changing that, although it was not a conscious effort.

When will she stop treating him as if he is a two-year old? Henrietta wondered but said, "Most people admire the way he speaks but there are a few who are always critical about it."

That statement infuriated Dorothy. She wasn't angry at Henrietta and was quick to point out that her displeasure was with those few whom she believed had done nothing to improve their lot in life but found pleasure in criticizing a progressive young man, her son.

"To hell with them. Some of them left school in fourth standard (seventh grade) and have done nothing with their lives since. So who are they to mouth off about my son?" She was thinking also about the same type of criticism leveled at her by Velma weeks earlier.

"Please forget about it, Mom."

"Kendal is right, Ms. Dorothy," said Henrietta. "Those people are not hurting by what they said but you are. You are putting your health at risk when you react so angrily about it."

Although her pregnancy, out of wedlock years ago, prevented her from completing her nursing training, she learnt enough to be aware of the dangers of hypertension as a risk factor for strokes and heart attacks. Velma Jacobs' experience was also a testament to what could happen.

"You are right," Dorothy said and calmed down immediately when she heard someone knocking at the front door. She walked over to see who it was. It was Arjune standing there with a broad smile across his face.

"Good afternoon, Ms. Dorothy," he said.

"Arjune! Good afternoon. Please come in. He stepped into the living room and said, "I am sorry, Ms. Dorothy. I can't stay long. I just wanted Kendal to know that we have planned a little gathering for tomorrow on behalf of the adoring couple."

"Kendal and Etta?"

"Yes."

"You can tell them yourself, Arjune. They are in the kitchen."

Arjune walked through the living room and into the kitchen where Kendal and Henrietta sat.

"Hey, Bro!" He greeted his friend..

"Hey, Bro! What about me? Am I the empty calabash in the bucket?"

"Oh, Etta, I am so sorry. That is a bad habit we have."

"Who are we?" she asked.

"Men in general, I suppose."

"You mean Mayaro men in general, don't you?"

"Those are the only men with whom I am quite familiar." Having said that, Arjune stepped over to Etta and gave her a hug. Then he partially repeated what he said earlier, "I am so sorry." She seemed pleased with that and said nothing further so he continued to state his purpose for being there. "I came to let you know that we have organized a little something for you tomorrow. I hope you do not have other plans."

"We do not have any plans. Do we, Kendal?"

"No."

"What could that little something be anyway?"

"It is nothing grand so I am hesitating to call it a party."

"So what is it?" Henrietta insisted.

"Let's just say it is a more elaborate *river lime*."

"What's the venue?"

"The Spring Bridge, said Arjune. "As compared to the others, we find that to be readily accessible and acceptable to all."

"What were the other possible venues?"

"The saw-mill area and Grande Basé were two possibilities."

"I have been to the saw-mill *river lime* with Kendal, but I am not familiar with this Grande Basé."

"It is off the Mafeking Branch Road, an area where there is a bight in the course of the Ortoire River."

It was only then that Kendal spoke. He of course, already knew of the planned affair because Joshua couldn't keep anything confidential. Nevertheless, he thought it was fitting to say something about the choice of venue. "The bridge seems like the logical choice," he said.

"Why? The saw-mill is closer to us."

"True! However, the platform of the bridge offers shelter in the event of rain and it shades us from the sun during the hot dry periods."

"Am I to interpret that as a concession?"

"Well, I don't know that I am giving up anything. I think we will be there, if it's okay with Etta."

"How about it, Etta?" Arjune asked.

"It's okay." She glanced at Kendal when she said that.

"Then that's it. I will see you tomorrow. Say goodbye to Ms. Dorothy for me."

"We will," Kendal and Henrietta said together as Kendal got up to walk Arjune to the door.

Dorothy had retreated to her room. It wasn't just a place for sleeping and solitude. It was where she found sanctuary from some of life's cruel and tumultuous moments, from some of her distresses and some of the excessive pleasures. On that occasion, however, she retreated so that she would not be tempted to interject her thoughts and feeling into the young people's plans.

Henrietta had a concern and sought Kendal's advice in the matter. "How does one dress for an occasion like the one Arjune described for tomorrow?"

"Girl, I don't know. Why didn't you ask him while he was here?"

"Kendal, I couldn't ask your friend that"

"Why not?"

"If you don't know, then forget about it."

"Okay."

TWENTY-TWO

The practice session ended and both boys returned to their respective homes feeling confident about Sydney's prospect of winning the Top Fest 1956 competition the next day. However, Sydney still wasn't able to sway Joshua into foregoing his plan to attend *the river lime* and join the Top Fest as the defending champion.

"I am going to relax and read this evening," he said when Sydney tried to persuade him to compete.

"You have become an avid reader now I see."

"Thanks to you, I enjoy reading now."

"Is it that you enjoy reading so much that you are willing to give up everything else?"

"Not everything. I will abstain from the things I do not like and those that I consider dangerous."

"What! How is the 1956 Top Festival dangerous? Please tell me because I know that you have always enjoyed spinning tops."

"Spinning tops and the Top Festivals are not in or of themselves dangerous. However, some of the participants are scary."

"That is just too bad."

"What is so bad?"

"The way you have changed in such a short time."

"Are you sorry now that you taught me how to read?"

"No."

"Do you realize that if I did not have that choice I most likely would be practicing right now for the competition tomorrow?"

"I am conscious of that."

"And you still have no regrets?"

"I have none whatsoever."

"You are just so amazing."

"I guess I should say, thank you."

"Say whatever you want to say, cousin."

Sydney knew that Joshua was always an obstinate character so he concluded that there was no joy or justification in trying to convince him to join in the 1956 Top Festival. Since there was no cost to the participants, he decided that he would attend alone and give it his best shot. He was unaware that his mother and Kendal's mother would be there to cheer him on. He was seeded fifteenth in a field of twenty competitors, a clear indication that the organizers didn't think much of his chances of winning. He, however, felt that such a late start would allow him sufficient time to prepare himself psychologically. He was physically fit and had mastered the art of spinning the top and the skill to destroy those of his competitors. That was the objective of the sport.

At the O'Connor's Dorothy suggested to Kendal and Henrietta that if they were serious about attending the function that had been planned to honor their engagement, they should have a date set for the wedding. Kendal responded by saying, "Mom, we have not accumulated any funds that we can designate for that purpose"

"The date you set can be tentative. The date that matters is the one printed on the invitations you would mail out."

"Really? What is the purpose for that, Mom?"

"It is simply to show your friends that you are serious. In addition, people will ask about the date. If you set a tentative date, you can answer those questions with confidence."

Dorothy was being conniving. She wanted to make it as difficult as possible for her son, so he would not be able to renege on his promise to marry Henrietta, a woman she would have chosen herself if the culture of Africans in Trinidad and Tobago was in anyway similar to that of the Indian population. Neither Kendal nor Henrietta realized her devious intent when she took a five year calendar from off the wall and handed it to them. "I will be back in a few minutes," she said and left the kitchen.

Kendal circled the date June 17, 1959 and looked at Henrietta for her approval. "That is a Saturday," she said.

"So?"

"You know that weddings are never held on a Saturday in these parts."

"Everywhere else in the world it is the preferred day for nuptials."

"This is T & T. We are a unique people, hon."

"What do you prefer?"

"It doesn't matter to me. Any day of the week is fine if we are together and are the main focus."

"We are the main focus."

"The main focus, I hope that does not exclude our relatives and friends, many of whom we will be dependent on for quite some time to come."

Just then Dorothy returned to the kitchen and asked, "Have you chosen a date?" She directed her question to both of them but Henrietta looked at Kendal as if to say, *ask him, not me.*

"Kendal?" Dorothy called out in a questioning tone.

"Yes, Mom."

"What date have you chosen?"

"June 17th"

"Let me see that." She reached out for the calendar and Kendal gave it to her. She looked at it with amazement and said, "June 17th is a Saturday."

"It is the day we chose, Mom."

"We?" Henrietta asked alarmingly.

"Okay. It is the day I chose."

"Do you realize that you selected a Saturday in 1959? That is three years away."

"That will give us a chance to save some money, Mom."

"Money! Is that all you can think of? Don't you know that Etta is in the family way?"

So? She is pregnant. The baby is not even mine. I could have walked away, Kendal thought but he said, "Yes, Mom.

"And this is the best you can do?"

There was no answer from him. Dorothy was furious. It marked the second time in a week that she became so very angry at her son. In that instance she was thinking of her own youthful pregnancy which derailed her plans of becoming a nurse and she was determined not to let that happen to Etta, forgetting for the moment that Henrietta was not professionally inclined. She adjusted her trend of thought quickly and decided that no woman should be put in a position where she was forced to have a baby out of wedlock. Since Kendal seemed reluctant to speak, she continued, "Try that again, son," she said calmly. "This time select a date within the next eleven months, preferably no more than six months from today."

"What?"

"You heard me."

"Mom, we have no money."

"I have enough." She had been saving for what she termed a rainy day, an occasion just like the one they were dealing with. She left him no choice so he sat down with Henrietta again and together they decided on Boxing Day; December 26, 1956, a mere six months from the time of their discussion. When they suggested it to Dorothy she was elated.

"That's good, very good," she said. "With your diminutive stature you shouldn't be showing that much." *Is that all she could think of?* Kendal wondered but he did not speak.

"Thank you, Ms. Dorothy," Henrietta said.

"You are welcome, dear. May the Lord bless you and your baby. Those words brought tears to Etta's eyes but she tried to compose herself. There was no sobbing or wailing.

Her baby? Kendal questioned himself.

"What do you have to say for yourself, son?"

"I have nothing to add, Mom. You have made all the decisions for us."

Henrietta wasn't sobbing but her tears kept flowing. She was concerned that if Dorothy ever found out that the baby she was carrying was not Kendal's it would arouse suspicion about everything she purported to be. She was happy in the thought that she was always welcome at the O'Connor's and was afraid that knowledge of her wrong doing may change that. She pondered the situation for a while then decided that she must stop crying otherwise Dorothy would soon be bombarding her with questions about the reasons for her depressed state.

Since a date was set for the wedding, Henrietta decided to approach the future on a positive note. *I must find a legitimate means of earning a living other than cooking, washing, cleaning, and depending on Kendal,* she thought. *What can I do?* she wondered. She was always very good at baking and had earned some kudos for it. *Why don't I bake cakes and cookies at home and sell to shops and schools?* she asked herself. As the thought lingered with her, she decided that she would try it if Kendal does not object. *He tends to be funny about things like that,* she thought. *I never understood why because his mother sells her produce to the market vendors.*

Henrietta considered several other options before coming to firm decisions about two; baking at home was the first. She was already good at it and could start with very little money and no overhead cost. Also, she didn't need a business plan and never really considered one. Her second option, one of her greatest passions, was to become a seamstress. That, however, required extensive training either as an apprentice or at the Trade and Career Institute in the capital city, Port of Spain.

It was impossible for her to travel to and from Port of Spain, a round trip of 104 miles every day. Although several taxis made the trip routinely, the cost was definitely out of her reach. In addition, she viewed the cost of tuition at the institute and her pregnancy as other obstacles. There were no mitigating factors, so she decided on an apprenticeship. The question then was which seamstress would be willing to take her on? There were several good and well known seamstresses in the district but she had no preference and was willing to be under the tutelage of whoever was willing to have her. She decided, therefore, to seek Dorothy's advice.

She was aware that Dorothy sewed for herself, her son, and a few other people in the village but she was by no means a recognized seamstress. The limited volume of work she received and the unconventional manner in which she operated was not conducive to learning in the discipline. So timorously she asked, "Who taught you to sew, Ms. Dorothy?"

"No one," said Dorothy. "I learnt from my mother but she never really taught me. I learnt by watching what she did, in the same way that I learnt to cook, wash, and iron."

"So you have never done any of that professionally."

"No."

"Suppose you wanted to become a professional seamstress, with whom would you do an apprenticeship?"

"In Mayaro?" asked Dorothy but without waiting for an answer, she said, "Ms. Pattie of course."

"Ms. Patricia Orr?"

"She is the best," said Dorothy. "She makes all of my formal wear. I sew only everyday things, skirts and tops, things like that."

"Do you know Ms. Pattie very well?"

"Yes, of course. Why all of these questions, Etta?"

"I want to learn how to sew but I want to learn from the best seamstress in town."

"How are you going to do that with the baby on the way and you making preparations for your wedding?"

"The baby isn't due for another seven and a half months. If I start now, I can have at least six months of training before I deliver."

"You are putting a lot of pressure on yourself, girl."

"I don't think so, Ms. Dorothy. If I do nothing at all, there will be more pressure on Kendal financially."

"You are so right," said Dorothy. "That is very constructive thinking."

"Thank you."

"On Monday I will pay Ms. Pattie a visit and discuss your situation with her."

"Thank you so much, Ms. Dorothy."

"You are most welcome."

"I am going to say a prayer and hope that she agrees to take me on."

"You do that. There is something else though."

"What, Ms. Dorothy?"

"That right there." Henrietta looked puzzled so Dorothy continued, "It is time you stop calling me Ms. Dorothy. Just call me *Dorothy*."

"That wouldn't be right, Ms. Dorothy."

"Then call me, Mom."

"Okay."

At that point, Kendal felt he heard enough. He excused himself and left the kitchen where the family had gathered for a late lunch to discuss the wedding. As he walked out of the door, Dorothy seemed confused and asked Henrietta, "What's the matter with him?"

"I don't know," she said shrugging her shoulders. Kendal heard the question and responded, "I am just too tired for any more of that."

"What are you too tired to have any more of?" Dorothy asked.

Anymore of your crap, he thought of saying but did not respond. He continued to walk away. He went to his room, laid across his bed, and fell asleep.

Henrietta washed the dishes while Dorothy cleaned up the kitchen. There was no food left over so there was nothing to put away. Dorothy didn't have a refrigerator. In fact, no one in the village had a refrigerator. Some homes had an ice box. It was an insulated box in which large blocks of ice were kept for household use. Dorothy didn't have one. She didn't need one because she had developed a knack for cooking just enough for a day's serving, irrespective of how many people were to be served.

When they were finished in the kitchen, she informed Henrietta that she was going over to Philbertha's and invited her along but she declined, claiming she wasn't feeling very well. Actually, she was fine. She simply wanted to spend some time alone with Kendal.

As soon as Dorothy left, Henrietta entered Kendal's room. At any other time she would have knocked at the door before entering. On that occasion she was attempting to surprise him pleasantly by taking off all of her clothing and leaving them on the floor outside of his bedroom door before entering. She wasn't expecting him to be asleep and was herself surprised at how soundly he slept. Disappointed and unwilling to awaken him, she walked out, picked up her clothes, went to Dorothy's room, dropped the clothes on the floor and tossed herself on the futon. As she lay their looking at the ceiling and wondering what exactly the future held for her and her unborn child. She too fell asleep.

It was 12:10 a.m. when Dorothy returned. Kendal was still sleeping but Dorothy had no way of knowing that. She assumed that the engaged couple were together in his room so she locked the front door behind her. There was an unwritten and perhaps never discussed policy at the O'Connor's household that the last person to come in at nights would lock the door. At all other times the door remained unlocked even when they were out at the same time.

Dorothy entered her room and was surprised to see Henrietta lying there on her back naked. Mosquitoes were having a blood meal of her but she seemed numbed to the penetrating proboscises of the little blood sucking invertebrates. Dorothy turned a fan on in the room to blow away the pestiferous insects. Then she covered Henrietta from neck to toe with a sheet before she got ready for bed herself. When she eventually laid her head down, she couldn't help but wonder as to what went on in that futon. She thought of some of the many proposals she has had, all of which she declined. The thought of what might have been had she accepted one in particular started to arouse feelings in her that were not altogether strange, but they were feelings she had not experienced for a very long time. Soon she too fell asleep.

TWENTY-THREE

They woke up a little later than usual that Sunday morning. Dorothy was up first and started to prepare breakfast. Henrietta joined her in the kitchen shortly thereafter and together they had a scrumptious meal ready by the time Kendal was awake. He walked into the kitchen smiling and immediately hugged his mother and his fiancée. They stood at the center of the kitchen floor for at least two minutes. Nothing was said during that period. They just hugged one another tightly as if to suggest some special bond among them.

Kendal broke the silence when he mentioned the anticipated crowd at *the river lime* that morning. "I understand that people are expected from all the surrounding towns and as far away as Erin and Chaguaramas."

"Where will they accommodate all those people?" Henrietta asked

"Under the bridge I guess?"

"What?"

"I know. That was my reaction exactly when I heard it, but then I was told that they cleared two areas on either side of the East anchorage and under the deck itself. There, I understand that they intend to set up tables with food and drinks but no chairs."

"Why wouldn't they have chairs?" Henrietta asked.

"I don't know," said Kendal. "Perhaps the organizers do not want people to get too comfortable."

"Why wouldn't they?"

"I don't know. Generally, *the river lime* is of an hour and a half to two hours in duration. Perhaps they do not want to extend it beyond that."

"I don't see why not, it is Sunday and no one has much of anything else to do."

"I never said that was their reason. I suggested it might be. I really don't know and I am not going to pretend that I do. Who knows? Maybe there would not be that many people after all."

After that exchange between Kendal and Henrietta, Dorothy, in an effort to change the topic of discussion, suggested that breakfast was getting cold so they should sit down to eat.

"Nice idea," said Kendal. "I smell something good and I am famished."

"Come on, sit down both of you," Dorothy said as she also took a seat at the table.

They served themselves as they chatted at the breakfast table. Somehow though, the topic of *the river lime* never came up again until the end of the meal when Dorothy suggested meeting Philbertha early enough so that they would not miss any part of the 1956 Top Festival's opening ceremony which was scheduled to begin at 10:00 o'clock that morning. It was no coincidence that *the river lime* was scheduled for the same time. The organizers of Top Fest `56 were well aware that the popular river lime started at about 10:00 a.m. every Sunday morning in the dry season. Their intention was to draw participants and spectators away from *the river lime*. Their reason was simply for bragging rights. There was nothing else to be gained; no commercial sponsorship, no financial reward, just pure, clean fun.

Those activities, in addition to cricket, soccer, schooling, and routine daily chores, provided the youngsters with a sense of discipline, responsibility, dedication, and hope. Those activities and strict parental control kept most youngsters off the streets and out of trouble with the law. That is not to say there weren't a few rogue parents like Velma who neglected their parental and civic duties, but for the most part, the community involvement in the welfare of all children made Mayaro a safe and model society.

By 9:30 that morning, Dorothy left the house to join Philbertha so they could walk together to the 1956 Top Festival which was being held in front of Tang's shop. When they arrived, there were many other parents already in attendance. Based on previous experience, everyone was prepared for a long drawn out event. There were no seating accommodations and no one brought their own. Perhaps it was because they knew that the event was not conducive to sitting. One really had to stand, above the crowd where possible, to get a very good view of the proceedings. For that reason some people brought peeras (small benches) to stand upon. That was particularly true of the shorter folks in the village. Very few of the elderly came out to witness the event. That perhaps, was due to their frailty and lack of stamina to stand for the duration of the festival.

Kendal and Henrietta left the house shortly after Dorothy did. They, however, took a taxi to the Spring Bridge where *the river lime* was being held in their honor. Upon their arrival, they were greeted warmly by Arjune and his girlfriend, Dessita. Arjune had asked her to attend the very moment it was decided that the young men would sponsor an even in honor of Henrietta and Kendal. She agreed without question and spared no effort to be there on time.

"It is so nice to meet you again," she said.

"The pleasure is ours," Kendal said. He spoke for Etta and for himself.

Henrietta was in awe at how much was done and the manner in which it was presented. Several tables covered with oil cloths (plastic tablecloths lined with sheets of cotton) were set up against the East anchorage of the bridge and on both sides of it. Each table was adorned with a bouquet of freshly cut, local flowers. The tables that were under the bridge also contained local foods that reflected the ethnic and cultural diversity of the community. Some of the presentations included roti, curried goat, curried chip-chip (a mollusk harvested from the shores of the Atlantic Ocean in Mayaro), cascadura (an indigenous river fish with an exoskeleton), rice and peas, callaloo, crab and dumplings, fruit cakes and sponge cakes (pound cakes), and much more.

The outer tables to the left of the anchorage contained the drinks. Those were non-alcoholic for the most part, except for some local beer. The drinks consisted primarily of sorrel, mauby, ginger beer, sour sop (guanabana), barbadine (granadilla or parcha), and a variety of pineapple/citrus combinations.

On the outer tables to the right of the anchorage were nuts and fresh fruits, some of which were on ice. There, one could have indulged one's taste buds to the delightful flavors of sugar apples, star apples, watermelons, sea grapes, sapodillas, mamisiporte (mammy apple), golden apple (June plum), mangoes, pawpaw (papaya), chennette (guinep), coconut water which was a preferred thirst quencher, cocorite, and jackfruit or bread nut.

"Very nicely done," Henrietta said after she viewed all of the preparations.

"I agree," said Dessita. "I was astonished to see how much was done and how tastefully it was all put together."

"I doubt whether the people involved in the organization would have worked as hard had this been for anyone other than Kendal and Henrietta," Arjune said to Dessita.

"I can tell that you are highly regarded here."

"I don't know about that, but thank you," Kendal said.

"Let's mingle," said Arjune. "I want you to meet everyone here." His statement was directed to Dessita, Henrietta and Kendal.

They walked away from the tables and into the crowd. They were shaking hands, wishing people well, and receiving good wishes from those they met when Dolphin introduced himself to the crowd, stated the purpose of the gathering, and some of the swimming events that were scheduled that morning. That caused

Arjune and his party to stop abruptly. Henrietta was standing at Kendal's left. With her right hand, she was holding him just above his left elbow when someone tapped him on his right shoulder. He looked around and saw Monica standing there smiling. There was a young man with her.

"Hello, Officer O'Connor!" She said.

"Hi, Monica, I see you made it here on time."

"Yes. I would not have done it any other way. Meet my husband," she said as she glanced at the man standing there with her, and before Kendal could extend his hand, she continued, "We got married yesterday." *What the hell!* Kendal thought as he shook the gentleman's hand. "This is my fiancée," he pointed to Henrietta. "These are my good friends, Dessita and Arjune," he said in introducing them.

All parties shook hands and in the process of getting acquainted, they all missed what Dolphin had to say. Arjune realized what happened and said, "I will fill you in on the activities that are scheduled." All the while Monica was captivated by Kendal's presence. So much so that she didn't hear anything Arjune said. That did not go unnoticed. Her obsession was obvious to everyone in the party, except, perhaps, her newly wedded husband. It didn't seem to bother him, or was he really her husband as she claimed?

On Friday she told me that she was going to meet her fiancé who was visiting his ailing aunt in Guayaguayare. Today she tells us that she got married yesterday. If that is not puzzling enough, she and I made love during that torrential downpour of tropical rain on Friday evening, Kendal thought. *Obviously, she lied to me.* What he didn't realize was that Monica had been telling him lies from the very moment they first met when he walked into the jewelry store in Sangre Grande. The price of the rings he purchased for Henrietta and himself was fabricated. She inflated the price and took twenty per cent off to give him the impression she had gotten him a discount. Her assertion that she got him a sales associate discount, the same as her fiancé received on their rings was a lie. The account of her father not being her biological father was true but the tale that neither she nor he knew about it for years was a lie. *Can I ever trust her again?* Kendal wondered. Strangely enough, he never questioned whether Henrietta should ever trust him.

Dolphin announced that everything was being served buffet style and that the food tables were open. There were sanitary plates, knives, forks, spoons, cups and glasses, and no one hesitated to partake in the feast. At the same time Arjune told those in his company that the first event of the morning was a fifty yard swimming race. "If you look up river, you will see a red ribbon strung across from bank to bank. That indicates the starting point. If you look down river, the finish is where the blue ribbon hangs across."

At that point in its meandering, the river ran from West to East. East being toward the ocean, a direction with which everyone there was familiar. That presented a little bit of confusion. People were looking to the East as being up and the starting point.

"No," said Arjune. "That is down-stream. The red ribbon is to your left." There was some chuckling as they quickly turned their attention in the proper direction just when the whistle blew to start the race. The swimmers were at the finish in a flash. A teen-aged boy from Rio Claro won.

"Where did he learn to swim?" shouted one of the spectators. Everyone in attendance expected a representative swimmer from Pierre Ville or Mafeking to win. Very few realized then that Mayaro's best were not in the race. Arjune, and Dolphin were among the organizers and they had too many other responsibilities that early in the morning. Joshua, who before his injury was known to be faster than either Arjune or Dolphin, did not participate. He preferred the longer distances. Nevertheless, Mayaro still managed to place second and third with very good performances from Mullet and Boodlall.

As people ate and mingled, Monica was trying desperately to get Kendal's attention and although she wasn't aware of it,

Henrietta was on to her. Her other impediment was that her husband never left her side. Poor fellow; he knew no one else there. Although the same could have been said for her, somehow it was different. She was sociable, and to her, it seemed as if she had known Kendal and his friends forever.

Everyone present seemed at ease in the environment so Arjune and Dolphin felt comfortable enough to relinquish their responsibilities temporarily to participate in the one hundred yards race. The country had not yet converted to the metric system, so the distance was fitting and it was what the swimmers were accustomed to. Mayaro's best; Arjune, Dolphin, Mullet, and JJ were among ten contestants swimming around at the starting line.

The whistle blue and they were off to a fair start. Joshua was in the lead immediately and never relinquished it. Following closely behind him were Arjune, Dolphin, Boodlall and Mullet. At the end Mullet overtook Boodlall and while there were several changes in positions among the other contestants, the Mayaro contingent, with the exception of Mullet and Boodlall, maintained their positions from start to finish and dominated the race.

"That is how Mayaro man does swim," shouted the same spectator who earlier questioned where the Rio Claro teenager learned to swim.

The next event was the dive of endurance. It was free style diving. There were no rules except that each contestant had to dive from the same position on the suspension cable of the spring bridge, though not at the same time. Submarine asked to be allowed to dive last and the request was granted. There were only five other divers, and only one of them was from Mayaro. He was nicknamed Brick because he couldn't swim very well or very fast. There were three persons designated as judges for the diving contest. All that was required of them was that they timed the dives from the moment the divers hit the water to the time they emerged. Each diver was allowed three dives but could elect to dive only once or to stop diving at any time during the contest.

At the end of the diving competition the results were as many had predicted; Submarine won. That was his longest dive ever. He remained submerged without any diving equipment for four minutes. Some in the audience content that he was not human. Brick was second, and the teenager from Rio Claro placed third.

Someone cranked up an old gramophone and calypso music by The Roaring Lion started. Later when the lyrics of Jean and Dinah by the young calypsonian, The Mighty Sparrow was played, the crowd went wild. There was dancing and prancing on the river bank, and that reached a crescendo when news came that young Sydney Canton was crowned champion of Top Fest 1956. No one was happier than Joshua. He jumped, pranced, and yelled as if he had won.

Monica's husband was a calypso enthusiast and he struck up a conversation about the art form with a stranger in the crowd of spectators. That gave Monica the opportunity she was waiting for to seek Kendal's attention. Sadly though, she was disappointed because Arjune had solicited Kendal's help with the final stages of the contest, so she was forced to converse with Henrietta and Dessita, neither of whom seemed to have cared very much for her. Nevertheless, they were polite and spoke with her respectfully. She wanted to know when Henrietta and Kendal planned to be married, and although Henrietta felt that the question from a stranger was intrusive, she answered.

"We have set Boxing Day as a tentative date,'" she said as she thought, *Ms. Dorothy was right when she said someone will ask.*

"Is that this year or next year?"

"This year, December 26, 1956," Henrietta said.

"I would imagine that you would be in attendance, Dessita?"

"I would be delighted, but that is seven months away. Who knows what can happen by then?"

"Well, we cannot predict the future but for Henrietta and Kendal's sake, we can hope for the very best."

Monica was trying her very best to be liked by the two women who by then had become friends, but her efforts were futile. Both of them found that her initial pushiness was distasteful and wanted little to do with her. She spoke and they responded because they were polite. However, they were terse at times and she soon got the message.

"Enjoy the rest of your day, ladies," she said while thinking, *I have had just about enough of you fools.*

When she returned to her husband, he virtually ignored her. He was so rapt in the discussion about calypso as an art form, he didn't see when she came and stood next to him, or he pretended he didn't. To get his attention, Monica said, "It is approaching twelve o'clock. I think that is when *the river lime* comes to a close. We should try and make our way out of here now."

"Aren't you going to say goodbye to your friend?"

"Who?"

"What's his name again? Ken?"

"Oh! Kendal? I already did." She lied again.

"Okay. Then let's go."

They shook hands with the calypso enthusiast and Monica's husband said, "If you are ever in Sangre Grande, look me up."

"How will I do that?" the stranger asked.

"I am always at *Coconut Juice* on a Friday evening between six and ten o'clock."

"Oh! Is it that little bar on Ramdass Street? That's difficult for us though…"

"For us? What do you mean?"

"What he means is that....." Monica started to say something but her husband interrupted. "He can speak for himself," he said.

"I am sorry," said Monica. "I am out of here." She walked away without saying anything further.

The stranger seemed stunned but explained that after 6:00 p.m. on any given day, it is difficult to get transportation from Sangre Grande to Mayaro.

"Is that the problem?"

"That is a major problem for those of us who do not have relatives or friends in the Sangre Grande area."

"Don't worry about it, man. Like I said, if you happen to be there on a Friday evening, stranded or not, look me up at *Coconut Juice.*"

"Okay. I will do that." They shook hands and Monica's husband left to join her. She was seated in the front passenger seat of her compact car. He opened the car door and sat at the wheel. Neither spoke as he turned the key in the ignition and drove off.

By 1:00 p.m. that Sunday afternoon, May 20, 1956, spectators started to disperse. *The river lime* came to a dramatic conclusion. No trophies were handed out. There was no monetary gain for any of the athletes, only a claim to fame, locally or in a regional sense. As expected, Mayaro had triumphed over Rio Claro.

One mile away, in front of Tang's shop, the 1956 Top Festival ended with Sydney Canton crowned champion. Dorothy and Philbertha smothered him with kisses and he basked in the adulation. He felt really good that afternoon because news reached the Junction, the site of Top Fest '56 that Joshua won the hundred yard free style swimming race. He heard about it but neither his mother nor Dorothy knew.

"We are both winners, Mom," he said.

"Who are we?" Dorothy asked, thinking that perhaps he meant his mother and himself.

"JJ and I," Sydney replied.

"News certainly travels fast in this town," Dorothy said.

"That is true for good and bad news. You know that, don't you?" Bertha asked.

"You are right about that," Dorothy replied.

After that exchange, there was a brief pause. Neither of the two women spoke for a while. Their attention was on the behavior of the crowd, very controlled, orderly, but purposeful. Tang had only one half of one of the five double doors open. That portion of doorway was open to the bar or rum shop as it was called. People waited their turn patiently to be able to enter the bar and make a purchase of their favorite liquor. Strangely enough, one could not legally buy groceries, including milk or bread on that day if one's life depended on it.

There at the bar, unlike at *the river lime*, the spectators were not in a hurry to leave. The Sergeant in charge of the Mayaro Police Station and one of his patrol officers were in a private room at the back of the shop. That fact was well known to all present because he arrived there just when the festival began, and when it ended the squad car was still parked in the same spot, on the side of the Mafeking Branch Road closer to the shop.

The sergeant always expected Tang to entertain him and his officers whenever they were in Mafeking. He was corrupt but no one ever said that. Corruption among government officials was becoming a way of life even then, but as long as no one was hurt physically or financially, nothing was said or done about the situation. In return, Tang earned the privilege, unofficially that is, to sell groceries and liquor when the shop was supposed to be closed on a Thursday afternoon after 1:00 p.m. and all day on Sunday.

The regulars at *the river lime* assisted in cleaning up the area and packing up everything that was brought there for the occasion. Arjune made certain that all tables and utensils were returned to their rightful owners. Participants and spectators alike were allowed to take away the excess fruits, vegetables, nuts, and prepared foods.

Kendal and Henrietta thanked Arjune, Dolphin, and all of the other *limers* (friends who gather at a specific venue) for their kindness and appreciation.

"We were happy to be able to do it," Arjune said.

"It was truly nice," said Dessita. "You guys should do this every year."

"An annual event like Top Fest would be nice," said Henrietta. Then she asked, "Who is getting engaged next year?" Everyone present looked at Dessita and Arjune and smiled but neither one of them gave any hint about their intentions.

Kendal and Henrietta were gracious and delightful. After they said goodbye and shook hands with everyone who was still there, they seemed inseparable. They wrapped their arms around each other's waist as they walked to the roadway to begin their journey home and anticipate a life of love and happiness together as husband and wife.